The Betrayer

Sunday Times #1 bestselling author Kimberley Chambers lives in Romford and has been, at various times, a disc jockey, cab driver and a street trader. She is now a full-time writer.

Join Kimberley's legion of legendary fans on Facebook/kimberleychambersofficial and @kimbochambers on Twitter.

D0676548

Also by Kimberley Chambers

Kimberley CHAMBERS

The Betrayer

HarperCollins*Publishers*

This novel is entirely a work of fiction.
The names, characters and incidents portrayed in it are
the work of the author's imagination. Any resemblance to
actual persons, living or dead, events or localities is
entirely coincidental.

HarperCollins*Publishers* Ltd
1 London Bridge Street
London SE1 9GF

www.harpercollins.co.uk

This paperback edition 2017
5

First published in Great Britain by
Preface Publishing 2009
Published by Arrow Books 2010

Copyright © Kimberley Chambers 2009

Kimberley Chambers asserts the moral right to be identified as the author of this work

A catalogue record for this book is available from the British Library

ISBN: 978-0-00-822862-0

Set in Times New Roman by Palimpsest Book Production Limited, Falkirk, Stirlingshire

Printed and bound by CPI Group (UK) Ltd, Croydon, CR0 4YY

All rights reserved. No part of this publication may be reproduced,
stored in a retrieval system, or transmitted, in any form or by any
means, electronic, mechanical, photocopying, recording or otherwise,
without the prior permission of the publishers.

This book is sold subject to the condition that it shall not,
by way of trade or otherwise, be lent, re-sold, hired out or otherwise
circulated without the publisher's prior consent in any form of binding
or cover other than that in which it is published and without a similar condition
including this condition being imposed on the subsequent purchaser

MIX
Paper from
responsible sources
FSC™ C007454

FSC™ is a non-profit international organisation established to promote
the responsible management of the world's forests. Products carrying the
FSC label are independently certified to assure consumers that they come
from forests that are managed to meet the social, economic and
ecological needs of present and future generations,
and other controlled sources.

Find out more about HarperCollins and the environment at
www.harpercollins.co.uk/green

In memory of
Mathew Hoxby
1973–2008

ACKNOWLEDGEMENTS

First and foremost, I would like to thank Rosie de Courcy. Rosie is an absolute star, not only as an editor, but also as a person and a friend.

I would also like to thank my agent Tim Bates, my typist Sue Cox and everybody at Preface and Random House for the belief and backing that I have been given.

A special mention to Toby Clarke for the wonderful covers, Kevin Redmond for his fantastic support, Garry Perry who has worked tirelessly to promote me, and Julie for ferrying me around to signings.

Last but not least, I would like to thank you, the reader. Without your support I would be working back on the markets or driving a cab . . .!

God bless each and every one of you.

Goodnight you moonlight ladies,
Rock-a-bye sweet baby James.
Deep greens and blues are the colours I
    choose.
Won't you let me go down in my dreams
And rock-a-bye Sweet Baby James.

James Taylor
1970

PROLOGUE

July 2006

'I'm very sorry, Mrs Hutton, but we are talking weeks here, rather than months.'

Walking away from the hospital, I feel calmness within. My cancer has returned and being told I'm riddled with it was exactly what I'd expected. Unless you've had the dreaded disease, you wouldn't know where I was coming from. Tiredness, lack of appetite, an inability to do the simple things that you once found so easy. The signs are plentiful. To put it bluntly, you just know when you're dying.

As I sit on the bus, I gaze out of the window. Deep in thought, I watch the world go by. As strange as it may seem, I notice silly things. Mothers doing school runs in their luxury four-wheel drives, children as young as ten chatting away happily on mobile phones. Smiley, happy people, who wouldn't know hardship if it smacked them in the face.

Not wanting to become bitter, I turn away from the window and think about my own life. I take my pad and pen out of my bag and begin to make notes. Unlike most sufferers of cancer, I'm not that bothered about dying. Part of me would even go as far as saying that in some ways leaving this life will be a relief.

Happy people don't want to die. They are the lucky ones who are blessed with good times. I was happy once, but not now. For people like me, death spells an end to all of the suffering. I don't mean to sound like a manic depressive, but I've had years full of stress and turmoil and I can't take any more. I've had enough with a capital E.

I had a terrible upbringing. I'm an only child, and my father left home when I was three years old. I don't remember him and have never set eyes on him since. My mother was a dear soul, but died when I was ten, a victim of the same bastard disease that has now got hold of me.

My aunt kindly offered me a home and then gave me a dog's life. Living with a violent alcoholic, I was regularly beaten senseless. She treated me as her slave and I had to beg for my dinner, like a dog on all fours. At sixteen, desperate to escape her, I married the first bloke I laid eyes on. Tommy Hutton was his name. He was twenty-one, and in my eyes cool, brash and handsome. I thought he was my saviour; how bloody wrong was I?

Approaching my stop, I gingerly get off the bus and start the short walk home. I unlock my front door and put the kettle on. I'm tired, but determined not to sleep. There are questions I need answering, things I need to plan, stuff I need to tell. So many secrets and so many lies. To rest in peace, I need to tell and know the truth. Picking up my pen and paper, I talk out loud as I try to remember the past.

I don't know how to start. Will I read this to anyone? Or even show them? I choose my first line with care.

My name is Maureen Hutton and this is my story . . .

ONE

1975

'Fuckin' hell, Tommo, he ain't moving.'

White as a sheet, Tommy Hutton bent down to try and wake his victim. 'Wake up Smiffy, please wake up,' he said, as he frantically prodded and shook him.

Tibbsy, Benno and Dave Taylor stood rooted to the spot. Along with Tommy they were members of a notorious local gang known as the Stepney Crew.

Tonight they had organised a big off with a rival firm from Bethnal Green. Top four versus top four. Both gangs were determined to be crowned Kings of the East End; both thought they were the business. Tommy Hutton, AKA Tommo, had formed the gang: therefore he was their undisputed leader. Terry Smith, AKA Smiffy, had started the other firm and he was their top boy.

Tonight, however, things had gone very wrong. Determined not to be outdone by Smiffy, who had recently threatened him with an air gun, Tommy had decided to steal his old man's fishing knife. He'd been keen to frighten Smiffy, cut him, scar him, show him who was boss. He certainly hadn't meant to stick the knife straight through him.

Taking charge of matters, Tibbsy picked up the weapon. 'We'd better get out of 'ere lads. The cunt's dead, I'm telling yer. You take the knife, Tommo, get rid of it.'

Tommy shook from head to toe. He couldn't move, his legs weren't doing as they were told. 'What am I gonna do? I didn't mean to kill him,' he sobbed.

Tibbsy grabbed his arm. 'We've gotta go, Tommo, before anybody sees us. Don't fuck about or we'll all be going down.'

Tommy tucked his flared trousers into his socks and urged the others to do the same, fashion was a no-go at times like these. Ashen faced and panic stricken, the four lads ran for their lives.

Less than a mile away, Maureen was totally unaware of her son's dilemma.

'See yer on Saturday then, if I don't see yer before, Sarn. It starts at seven, so don't be bloody late.'

Maureen Hutton smiled as she shut the front door. It was her thirty-second birthday on Saturday and she was having a party to celebrate.

House parties were a regular occurrence on the Ocean Estate in Stepney. All skint as arseholes, she and her neighbours got together every Saturday night for some cheap booze and a knees-up. Maureen had numerous good mates who lived near by. Some were single mums who had it hard like herself, but her best friends Sandra and Brenda, they both had husbands. Neither she nor her friends dwelled on their poverty. Like most cockneys, they made the best out of what little they had. Every now and then they'd take it in turns to watch one another's kids so they could have a night at the bingo. Apart from their Saturday night parties, bingo was their only other source of entertainment.

Maureen put the kettle on and made herself a brew. Her life had always been hard, but lately she'd been content. Her husband Tommy had left her years ago.

4

A gambler and a piss-head, she was far better off without him. Sometimes he'd turn up like a bad penny, but he never hung about for long. A quick pop in to say hello to the kids or the occasional visit to his mother was about all he was good for. Alcohol was far more important to him than his family.

His mother, Ethel, was a legend in her own manor. At fifty-six she was a coarse, boisterous woman and as famous in the East End as Ronnie and Reggie. She swore like a navvy, drank like a fish, regularly went out on the thieve, and could tell a story to match the best of them. Hard as nails, she was. In the war she would wash down the dead bodies and help patch up the casualties. When the war ended, she set herself up in business with her friend, Gladys, and together they would perform illegal abortions. A tin bucket, a syringe and a bar of washing soap was the method they used. They were no experts, but were always careful to keep the end of the syringe in the bucket. One slip of the hand and the air bubbles could be fatal. Ethel had come up with the idea herself. She'd used the same method on the kids to wash out their worms. Many a time she'd shove a syringe of lukewarm water up their harrises and smile as their screams echoed from Stepney to Soho.

Maureen glanced at the clock. Her son, Tommy, was well late tonight and she'd skin the little bastard when he got home. Thankfully, her other two were safely tucked up in bed. Tommy was her eldest child – she was seventeen when she had him and he'd been a little bastard from the moment he'd let out his first cry. He was fourteen now, a cocky, streetwise little bleeder who was forever getting himself into trouble. Tall, dark and cheeky, he was popular with the girls, but even they found him a handful. He rarely went to school, was always fighting and she knew full well that he went out thieving with his pals and his gran.

Susan, her twelve-year-old daughter, was another worry. Sullen and obnoxious, she had a plain face, a plump body and a spiteful streak in her. She was unpopular at school, with very few friends, and even the kids on the street steered well clear of her.

Thankfully, her youngest son, James, was no trouble at all. Sweet, kind and funny, he was everything that Maureen had ever wanted in a child. She hadn't known what to call him when she was carrying him. She had plenty of girls' names, but no boys'. Her friend, Brenda, had chosen his name. A massive fan of the singer James Taylor, Bren had played his album till the grooves wore white. Maureen herself had fallen in love with the track 'Sweet Baby James' and, at Brenda's insistence, agreed that if her unborn was a boy, she'd name him James.

The title of the song suited her son perfectly and Maureen was over the moon when her mother-in-law thieved her a record player along with the album. For hours she'd play that record to James when he was a baby. She'd sing the words as she rocked him to sleep, her special boy with his own special song. Trouble was, as the years went by, he became known as Jimmy Boy. Tommy had started the trend by insisting that James made him sound like a poof. Maureen had been pissed off at first by his change of identity, but as time went by she'd accepted it. A name's just a name and he'd always be James to her.

All her neighbours had been shocked by her last pregnancy – she had been split up from her Tommy for years when she'd fallen. A drunken night of passion for old time's sake had been her excuse. Little did they know what had really happened!

Maureen's reminiscing was ended by the sound of the front door opening and the arrival of her eldest son. 'Tommy, I'm gonna marmalise you, get your arse in 'ere, yer little bastard,' she shouted at the top of her voice.

Ignoring her, Tommy Hutton ran up the stairs as fast as his legs would take him. His clothes were covered in blood and he had to get changed before his mother spotted him.

Just about to chase the cowson up the stairs and drag him back down by his hair, Maureen had a change of heart. He shared his bedroom with James and if she ran upstairs like a raging bull, she'd be bound to wake him up. Maureen lit the gas and put the kettle on to boil. She needed to calm down and a cup of Rosy was usually the answer. Tomorrow she'd have the little bastard's guts for garters. Yawning, she made her brew and took it into the living room. Just lately she'd taken to sleeping downstairs on the old sofa. The house only had two bedrooms. The boys shared one and her and Susan the other. Ethel lived slap-bang opposite in a nice little one-bedroom flat.

Over the last few months, her daughter had become a nightmare to share a bed with. She'd nick the blanket then wriggle like an eel all night, and Maureen had a feeling that the little cow was doing it on purpose. Worn out by her lack of shut-eye, she had no alternative other than to move out of her own bedroom.

Tommy lay in bed wide awake. Now he'd pulled himself together, he felt a right prick for crying in front of his pals. He was meant to be the leader of the gang, not some fucking mug. After they'd legged it, him and the lads had headed to the park to sort out an alibi, and a plan, and as luck would have it, they'd bumped into Lenny Simpson.

Seeing the blood on Tommy's clothes, and the state of the four of them, Lenny guessed that some major shit had hit the fan and had fired awkward questions at them. Stuck for answers, they'd had no choice other than to spill their guts to him. He was sound, Lenny, and if he couldn't help them, no one could.

'I'll be your alibi. I'll say you were round at mine all night. We had a few beers and were playing David Bowie records. I've got all his stuff, every album, so if anyone asks, we were boozing while listening to Bowie, right? If you stick to the same story as me, you'll be all right, boys.'

Tommy hugged Lenny and repeatedly thanked him. Lenny had his own reasons to want to help out. Smiffy, the piece of shit in question, had terrorised his younger brother for the past three years. Lenny had been planning on disposing of the scumbag himself, but didn't quite have the bottle to go through with it. Tommo had done him and his family a massive favour.

The other thing they'd discussed were the other lads in Smiffy's gang. They'd all scarpered in separate directions when it had got a bit naughty. Tommy had chased Smiffy for at least five minutes before he'd caught him and, apart from his own crew, there'd been no one else about.

'There's no way the Bethnal Green boys'll grass,' Tibbsy said confidently.

'All they'll do, if anything, is come after us for revenge. They definitely won't involve the pigs,' Benno insisted.

Tommy looked at Dave Taylor. 'What do you think?'

Taylor shrugged. 'Dunno. Our top four boys have done their top four, case closed. You can never say never, but I'll doubt they'll grass.'

Tibbsy called an end to the meeting. 'Look we can't stay out 'ere all night, it's too suspicious. Let's all go our separate ways and when we get home, we must act normal.'

Tommy stood up. 'I can hardly act normal, can I? I'm covered in Smiffy's blood. What am I meant to say to me mum?'

Tibbsy put an arm around his pal. 'Just leg it up the stairs before your mother sees yer. You need to wash the knife so none of our fingerprints are on it. Bag up all your stuff, wait till your mother's asleep, creep out and dump it.'

As he lay awake in bed, Tommy thought over his pal's advice. He'd bagged the gear up, washed the knife, but was far too scared to leave the house. Say someone saw him? Say his mother caught him or the pigs were lurking near by?

Seeing his brother stir gave Tommy his solution. He'd lifted James out of the window a couple of months back to run a couple of errands for him. The boy had shit himself and he didn't really want to get him involved again, but what choice did he have? He couldn't go himself, it was far too dodgy.

Tommy was an expert at climbing out of his bedroom window. There was an old coal bunker below and as long as you positioned yourself right, the drop was a piece of cake. What he'd have to do was climb down first with the gear, then climb back up and lift James down. Umming and aahing with his conscience, he made his choice.

'Jimmy boy, wake up.'

James sat up and rubbed his little eyes. 'Whatta matter Tommy?'

Tommy put his finger to his lips. 'Get dressed, Jimmy, I need yer to do summink for me.'

James obediently did as he was told. He loved his big brother very much. Tommy was his hero and he'd do anything he could to make him happy.

TWO

James was petrified as he stood in the back garden and lifted up the bag. Gladys, his gran's friend, lived in nearby Whitehorse Lane and his brother had given him strict instructions to creep around her back alley and hide it in the bushes at the rear of her garden. He hated going out alone in the dark – he was frightened of the bogeyman that his mum had always told him about. Even at the tender age of five, he knew not to ask Tommy too many questions. He wasn't silly, he knew the bag must have something very important inside, but he knew better than to be nosy. Taking a peek was totally out of the question. As he reached his destination, he began to cry. He wanted his mum and his nice warm bed. Realising that the bag was far too heavy to shove into the big bushes, he hid it at the bottom of them and quickly ran away.

Tommy must have smoked ten fags as he nervously waited for his little brother to return. Smiffy wouldn't be the only cunt dead if James was caught outside, his mother would make sure that Tommy was buried in the grave next to him.

Hearing a noise from behind, Tommy felt relief flood through his veins as he spotted James. 'You OK, Jimmy boy?' he whispered. 'Did you do exactly what I told yer to?'

James nodded. 'I did what yer said, Tommy.'

Tommy smiled as he helped the frozen child onto the coal bunker. Trying to get him back in the window was a damn sight harder than trying to get him out. After a bit of a struggle, he shut the bedroom window and hugged James tightly. Kneeling down, he took a couple of five-pence coins out from under the mattress and handed them to him.

'You, Jimmy boy, are the best bruvver in the world. Take this money and buy yourself loads of sweeties. But remember, this is our little secret and you must never tell anyone about tonight, not ever.'

James nodded. He perfectly understood what his brother was saying. Living in Stepney, you learned the dos and don'ts from a very early age. James hid the two shiny coins in his sock drawer, crawled into bed and fell straight to sleep. His nightmare began almost immediately. The bogeyman had kidnapped him and had hidden him in the alleyway behind Gladys's house.

Still hyped up, Tommy lay awake for hours. He wondered if Smiffy had been found yet, or maybe he wasn't even dead and had woken up and gone home. The incident had happened around the back of the old garages, just off the Mile End Road. It was a pretty remote area of a night, and chances were, if he was brown bread, he wouldn't be found till morning.

Tommy sighed. He'd have to move the bag that James had hidden at some point, although it should be OK for now. It was well away from the scene of the crime, and there was no reason on earth why the pigs should search old Gladys's street. Even if Smiffy was dead, with no suspects, the case would die down within weeks and then he and the lads could retrieve the bag of evidence and burn the bastard to cinders. Satisfied he'd be in the clear, especially with Lenny's alibi, Tommy finally got some much-needed shut-eye.

Maureen was up at six the next morning. By eight o'clock she'd done all the washing and ironing and everything was put away neatly in the airing cupboard. Just about to start vaccing, she heard the door open.

'You got that fuckin' kettle on yet, birthday girl?'

Maureen smiled as Ethel let herself in and sat down. Her mother-in-law had her own key and came and went as she pleased. Rooting through her shopping bag, Ethel pulled out two tins of Spam, a tin of corned beef, a box of chocolates and a leg of lamb.

Maureen smiled. Ethel's little gifts came in more than handy. In fact, without her help, she sometimes wondered how she'd manage to feed the kids.

Ethel stood up. 'I'm off down the waste now to meet up with Glad. Do yer need anything off the market?'

'You can get us some pickles, Mum,' Maureen said. She always called Ethel 'Mum'. It was the done thing in the East End to refer to the in-laws as you would your own parents.

Tommy opened his eyes and leaped out of bed. Yesterday seemed like a bad dream and he wished that it was. He usually loved Saturdays – he and the rest of the gang normally hung about down Roman Road market. The Roman was a buzzy old place on a Saturday and there were always a few bob to be earned. On a good day, they would treat themselves to pie and mash from Kelly's. On a bad one, they'd share a bag of chips or two. Today he couldn't face going to the market; neither did he feel hungry. Nervously, he slung on his clothes and ran down the stairs.

'Oi, yer liberty-takin' little fucker,' Maureen shouted. Chasing him up the path, she grabbed his arm. 'Where were you last night? Yer didn't get home till half past one. How many times have I told yer, midnight at the latest.'

Tommy looked at her sheepishly. 'Sorry, Mum. I was round at Lenny Simpson's. We were listening to David Bowie records and having a few beers.'

Maureen looked at him in amazement. She could always tell when he was lying. 'Since when have you been into David fucking Bowie? Listen, I don't care if David turns up round Lenny Simpson's to sing to yer in person, you get your arse back 'ere by midnight in future, do you hear me?'

Tommy nodded. 'I'm sorry, Mum.'

Maureen tutted as she watched him sprint down the road. He'd be the death of her, that boy. He drank like a fish and the way he was going he'd have no liver left by the time he was twenty-one. The selfish little bastard hadn't even wished her happy birthday.

James woke up, got dressed and fished in his drawer for his new-found wealth. It was his mum's birthday today and he wanted to creep out and buy her the best present ever.

Maureen was busy preparing for her party that evening. She had dozens of eggs, plenty of cheese and, with Ethel's leg of lamb, Spam and corned beef, she could really push the boat out for once.

James quietly let himself back in. 'Happy birthday, Mummy.'

Maureen had tears in her eyes as her youngest handed her a card, a small cake and a beautiful potted plant. 'Oh James, you little darling, you've made mummy cry now.

Where did you get these from? Where did yer get the money, love?'

James had already prepared himself for this particular question. 'I saved all my pennies that Nanny gave me for ages and ages,' he said confidently.

Maureen picked him up and smothered him in kisses. 'You are a very special boy, James, and your mummy loves you very much.'

James wriggled out of her arms. 'I'm going to play on my space hopper now.'

Susan stood at the kitchen door with a sullen expression firmly intact. 'I'm starvin'. Can I 'ave some breakfast?'

James turned to his sister. 'It's Mummy's birthday today.'

Susan scowled at him. 'So what?'

James squeezed past his nasty sister and ran into the garden. He'd had just enough money left to buy himself a gobstopper and he wanted to suck it in peace and savour every moment.

Tommy sprinted to his pal's house in record time. Tibbsy shot straight out the door and the two of them ran round to Benno's. Dave Taylor was already there, but no one said a word about the previous evening until they had reached the serenity of the park. Searching through the bushes, Tibbsy pulled out a bottle of sherry. His nan, bless her soul, was senile and he'd chored it from her house and stashed it a couple of days ago.

'Don't think bad of me,' he said, as he unscrewed the lid. 'Me nan don't even drink, someone must 'ave bought it for her.'

All four lads took it in turns to swig from the bottle. None of them had slept well, and their nerves were shot to pieces.

Tibbsy stood up. 'Right, what we gonna do? Has anyone heard anything yet?'

The other three shook their heads. 'Me muvver had the telly on – there was nothing on the local news,' Benno said.

Tommo took another large gulp from the sherry bottle. 'What we should do is send someone down that way. Maybe Smiffy was just unconscious. He might not be dead.'

Dave Taylor shrugged his shoulders. 'We've never seen a dead person before, so none of us would know what one looked like.'

Tibbsy shook his head. 'I'm telling yer now, the cunt was dead. Someone must 'ave found him by now, and I bet yer it's swarming with police down there.'

'Who can we send down there to 'ave a nose?' Tommy asked. 'We don't wanna involve any of the other lads that weren't with us last night. It's a good job we kept the meet a secret, and never told any of 'em.'

Tibbsy agreed. Sometimes their gang consisted of about twelve but last night's pre-arranged encounter was top boys only.

'If we're not gonna tell anyone else, the only one we can ask to go down there is Lenny Simpson.'

Tibbsy slapped Benno on the back. 'Good thinking, Batman. We'll finish this booze, then we'll go and find him.'

Lenny Simpson was at home looking after his younger brother when the lads knocked. 'I'll go and check it out for yer, lads. I'm gonna have to take Matty with me though, there's no one else to look after him.'

Lenny Simpson was one of the put-upon people of this world. His mother sold her body to fund her drug habit, and his two sisters were selfish and a complete waste of space. Lenny's younger brother, Matthew, was fifteen and mentally retarded. It had been him that Smiffy had taunted and terrorised for years. Lenny looked after Matty almost twenty-four seven, and if it wasn't for him, the poor little sod would have been stuck in care years ago.

'Right, what's the plan then?' Tibbsy asked, as Lenny appeared with his little bro.

Lenny grabbed Matty's hand. He had a terrible habit of running into the road. 'I'll go down there with Matty. You and the lads go to the park and I'll meet yer back at the shelter.'

Tommo searched through his pockets and ordered his gang to do the same. Counting up the money, he handed it to Lenny. 'Get us some cider, Old Man Tatler won't serve us. Whatever's left over, you can spend on sweets for Matty.'

Lenny went into the shop, handed the lads their booze and said goodbye. He couldn't wait to find out what had happened to his brother's tormentor. With a bit of luck Smiffy was brown bread and would rot in hell.

Tommy and the boys sat anxiously in the shelter, drinking and chain-smoking. The hour they waited for Lenny to come back seemed more like an eternity, and as they spotted him and Matty in the distance, they sprinted towards them. Tibbsy was the fastest runner and reached them first.

'Well?' he asked expectantly.

Lenny Simpson loved a bit of excitement. If it hadn't been for having to take care of Matty, he would have been a gang member himself. Plonking himself on the grass, he relayed the full story.

'Smiffy was found at 'alf six this morning, apparently.

Old Mother Kelly said he was as stiff as a board. It's swarming with Old Bill down there and they've even shut off part of the Mile End Road. I saw Graham Roberts, he said the Old Bill had been round his asking lots of questions. He reckons they're doing loads of house-to-house enquiries. There's tons of people hanging about, but the police 'ave put tape round. Everyone down there reckons that Smiffy had so many enemies, they'll never find the killer.'

'Wee wee, Lenny. Wee wee.'

Lenny glanced at his brother. He'd already got his cock out and was pissing on the grass.

'Don't piss 'ere Matty. Be a good boy and go over there by that tree.'

Cock in hand, Matty shuffled away.

Overcome by shock that he was actually a murderer, Tommy sank to his knees.

'Move over Tommo, you're kneeling in piss,' Tibbsy said, laughing.

Tommy ignored his pal and put his head in his hands. Fuck the piss, that was the least of his problems. He was a killer, he'd wiped out someone's life and he didn't have a clue what to do about it.

Lenny put an arm around him. 'You'll be OK, Tommo, just stick to the story. Mine, records, beer, Bowie. Me mum and sisters weren't about and I've clued Matty up on what to say.'

Tommy looked at Matty who was waddling towards him with his cock in his hand. That imbecile's gonna be a lot of fucking use, he thought inwardly.

Dave Taylor downed the last of the cider and chucked the empty bottle. 'I'm starving, who's up for some chips?'

Tommy shot him a look of hatred. 'I don't believe you,

Taylor. I'm looking at life and all you can think about is your gut.'

Taylor shrugged. 'It was just a suggestion.'

Tommy stood up. These pricks were doing his head in and he needed to be alone. He forced himself to be polite. 'I'm off now, lads. It's me mum's birthday and she's having a party, she needs me to give her a hand with some stuff.'

The crew nodded.

'See yer, Tommo. If we hear anything we'll let yer know,' Tibbsy said.

Tommy dug his hands deep into his pockets and trudged away. He couldn't believe what had happened. He wasn't that bothered about Smiffy – he hated the cunt, always had. It was himself he was worried about. Say the police found some evidence? Or the Bethnal Green wankers grassed him up?

Tommy's instincts told him he was in shit street. Filled with worry, he took a slow walk home.

THREE

'Susan, what yer doing? Three times I've asked yer to help me with these sandwiches. Now move your fucking arse.'

Susan lolloped into the kitchen, picked up the knife and lunged at the bread as though she'd had an argument with it. She hated doing favours for anyone and on the odd occasion she was forced to, she made her feelings known.

Seeing the mess that her daughter was making, Maureen grabbed the knife and ordered her to go and get changed. 'And make sure you 'ave a wash, yer dirty little cow.'

Tommy sat on the back step and lit up a fag. It was only recently that his mum had allowed him to smoke indoors. She wasn't happy about it, but had told him he was old enough to make his own choices. 'If you're gonna do it behind me back, you may as well do it in front of me,' she said.

Tommy's ears pricked up as he heard his gran arrive. Her voice was like a foghorn and you couldn't miss it. 'There's been another bloody murder down the road, Maur,' she exclaimed. 'You know Mary Smith, dontcha? Her lad, Terry, was found this morning. Apparently, the poor little bastard had been laying there, brown bread for hours.'

Maureen was preparing the pickles and nearly dropped the Tupperware dish in shock. She knew Mary Smith very well. She was a regular at the bingo hall and they'd often sit together and have a chinwag.

'Gordon Bennett! I can't believe it, Mum. It's terrible, she's such a nice woman, is Mary. She idolised her Terry, was forever talking about him. What must the poor woman be going through?'

Ethel shook her head. 'Poor fucker. I dunno what this bleedin' world's coming to. There was none of this in my day – yer could leave your fuckin' door open then, yer know. If yer left it open now, some bastard would rob yer and murder yer in your bed.'

Maureen agreed with her. 'I feel so sorry for Mary. I'll have to pop round to her house in the next couple of days and offer my condolences.'

Unable to listen to any more, Tommy felt physically sick as he jumped next door's fence and clambered into their back alleyway. Crouching down by the bushes, he held his head in his hands. He never had a clue that his mum and Smiffy's mum knew one another. Learning they were friends was like a smack in the face to him. What the fuck was he meant to do now? If he was rumbled, his mother would skin him alive. Wishing more than anything he could turn back the clock, he sat deep in thought. He had to force himself to go back home, get changed, and join in with the birthday party. If he didn't, it would look odd and he didn't want anything to look suspicious.

DC Perryman and PC Rogers had been sent to investigate a black bag that had been found by a dog walker. The bag had been spotted amongst some bushes in an alleyway that backed onto the Ocean Estate. DC Perryman had been desperate for promotion for a very long time and couldn't hide his delight at the contents.

'Look at this, Rogers. Bingo!' he said, as he looked at the blood-stained windfall.

The party was in full swing by the time Tommy arrived back home.

'Where yer been, yer crafty little bastard?' Maureen wanted to know.

'I'm sorry, Mum. I popped round me mate's and . . .'

Cutting him dead, Maureen shoved him towards the stairs. 'You look like a tramp and I will not have you showing me up on my birthday. There's hot water in the immersion, get upstairs and get washed and changed.'

Maureen's anger at her eldest diminished as James flung himself at her. 'Uncle Kenny's here, Mum. He's over there with Nanny.'

Feeling flustered, Maureen dashed into the kitchen to pour herself a drink. She was having one of her funny turns again.

Kenny was her husband Tommy's younger brother, Ethel's other son. He and his wife, Wendy, had done well for themselves. A scrap-metal dealer, Kenny had recently brought a posh house in Essex, much to Ethel's annoyance. 'What's a matter with bleedin' Stepney? Not good enough for him any more? That's her doing, Lady fuckin' Penelope,' she moaned. Wendy came from Upminster and her parents were quite well-to-do. Ethel had disliked her from day one.

'Look what Uncle Kenny brought me,' James said, as he ran into the kitchen and thrust a toy police car at her.

Maureen looked at his happy face. The poor little sod didn't get many toys; they couldn't afford them, as a rule. 'Go and put it in your bedroom and you can play with it tomorrow. It'll get broken if yer leave it laying around tonight.'

James did as he was told. On reaching the bedroom, he was surprised to see Tommy there. 'Why are you lying down?'

Tommy sat up. 'I'm fine, just tired, that's all.'

'Do you like my present? Uncle Kenny brought it for me. He's brought you summink, and Susan.'

Tommy smiled. Ruffling his brother's hair, he stood up. 'I'll race yer downstairs, Jimmy boy.'

The Old Bill shop was brimming with excitement. Bloodstained clothes, a murder weapon and a dead body found. Even Benny out of *Crossroads* could have put two and two together and come up with four for this one. The icing on the cake came five minutes later when a letter from the school was discovered in the back pocket of the trousers. Addressed to a Mrs Hutton, it was a letter asking why her son, Tommy, had not been attending school. DC Perryman picked up the envelope and danced around the station. Like a cat that had got the cream, he eagerly awaited his promotion.

Back at the party, Ethel encouraged James to stand in the middle of the circle. He was dancing to 'Simple Simon' and knew all the actions and words, bless him.

Ethel nudged Maureen. Normally she loved nothing more than to watch James perform his party piece, but tonight she seemed uninterested.

'I'm sorry, Mum. I'm just keeping me eye on the other two. Tommy's been acting strange all night. I'm sure he's pissed and I've just seen Susan clump Sylvie's little girl.'

'Who the fuck is Sylvie?'

Maureen pointed her out. 'She's new round 'ere. Comes

from Hackney, she does, and has just moved into the flats round by Old Man Tatler's. I caught Susan picking on her little 'un the other day as well. Pushed her off the swing in the park, she did.'

Ethel tutted. 'Vindictive little fucker, that daughter of yours. I'd brainwash her if she was mine. 'Ere, get us another drink, Maur, I'm empty again.'

Maureen stood up. She was desperate for a top-up herself.

Clocking Wendy studying her, Ethel put her hand up her skirt and adjusted herself. 'Cutting me ha'penny in half, these bleedin' knickers,' she shouted.

'Do you have to do that, Mum?'

Ethel stared at Kenny with a devilish look in her eye. 'It's my crotch, I'll do what I fuckin' well like with it.'

'Time to go,' Wendy said, nudging him. She'd only come in the first place because he'd promised her a new fur coat.

Kenny sighed. 'We're gonna make a move now, Mum. Wendy's not feeling too well, she's got a touch of flu.'

'Flu! Fuckin' flu! More like miserableitis or stuck-up-cunt disease, yer mean,' Ethel cackled.

Kissing her on the cheek, Kenny ignored his mother's nasty comments and headed off to find Maureen. 'Happy birthday,' he said, handing her two tenners. 'I've gotta go now, Maur. Wendy's not well. Treat yourself to something nice, eh?'

Maureen angrily chucked the money back at him. She wasn't a bloody charity case. 'Look Kenny, you don't have to make up for yer brother being an arsehole. Please don't insult me, I don't want yer money.'

Looking sheepish, Kenny pocketed the money, said goodbye and grabbed Wendy's hand. The quicker he made an exit, the better.

* * *

24

As the police van drove towards the Ocean Estate, various orders were given out. All the officers present were more than aware of the Hutton clan. They'd had many run-ins with them over the years. The old man was a waster, a two-bit thief and a drunk, the eldest two of the three kids were shoplifters and bullies, even the gran was a well-known fence and on their wanted list. All the Old Bill were excited about the outcome of this particular arrest. To nick a Hutton for something big was fantastic news, kind of payback for all the years they'd run riot.

Back at Maureen's, the celebration was in full swing and everyone was doing the Hokey Cokey.

With the help of a few alcoholic beverages, Maureen was now the life and soul of the party. Standing in a circle with Sandra and Brenda either side of her, she was enjoying herself immensely. James and a couple of the other kids were in the middle of the circle and Maureen's heart was filled with emotion as she watched her youngest having a ball. Her other two were nowhere to be seen, but that was nothing unusual. Susan had never joined in with anything family-oriented in her life and Tommy felt he was far too old and too cool to be dancing with his mum.

Maureen bent down and tickled James's waist. 'Bend your knees, James, and shout, "Ra, ra, ra!"'

James giggled. He loved the party songs and knew most of the actions off by heart.

As the Hokey Cokey came to an end, a drunken Sandra decided it was time for a speech. 'You see this woman 'ere,' she said loudly. 'This woman 'ere is the bestest friend I could ever wish for. I love 'er to death, we all love 'er to death and I think we should sing to her.'

*   *   *

25

Realising there was a party going on, the police decided to park away from the house. The last thing they wanted was to be seen and give young Tommy time to do a runner. Creeping towards the front door, they awaited their orders from their superior.

'Right, lads. Go, go, go.'

Sandra was standing on a chair, waving her arms about as if she was conducting an orchestra. All eyes were focused on Maureen.

> Happy birthday to you,
> Happy birthday to you,
> Happy birthday, dear Maureen,
> Happy—

They never got to chant the last line. The police entering the house spelled the end of the singalong. Maureen Hutton's birthday party was well and truly over.

FOUR

'Thomas Arthur Hutton, I am arresting you on suspicion of the murder of Terence John Smith. You do not have to say anything, but anything you do say may be put into writing and given in evidence...'

The party fell into a shocked silence as a screaming Tommy was dragged from the room.

Ethel was the first to find her voice. She hated the filth with a passion. As she leaped off the armchair, she laid into the coppers with her fists.

Maureen, who had initially felt her legs buckle underneath her, pulled herself together and followed suit. 'Leave my boy alone, you no-good bastards,' she screamed as she chased them into the hallway.

'He's only a kid, get your dirty hands off him,' Sandra yelled, desperate to stick up for her pal.

One of the coppers pushed Sandra out of the way and sent her flying. A free-for-all followed as Sandra's husband, Pete, went apeshit. Like true cockneys, most of the other guests quickly joined in. The fracas went on for a good ten minutes or so and there were four other arrests made, which included Ethel. The spirited old gran

27

had smacked one officer in the teeth and kicked another in the bollocks.

Finally, some kind of order resumed and an extremely pissed-off DC Perryman re-entered the living room. 'Tommy needs an adult to accompany him down to the station. The four in the van are no use to him – any other offers?' he asked sarcastically.

Cuddling a hysterical James, Maureen immediately stood up. 'I'm his mother. I'll go with him.'

'Let me come too, Mum, I wanna see Tommy. Please, Mummy, please,' James sobbed.

With the police waiting impatiently, Maureen had very little time to soothe her youngest. Assuring him that everything was gonna be OK, she handed him to Sandra. 'Look after him and keep an eye on Susan for me, mate.'

Sandra nodded. None of the women would leave the house until Maureen returned. They were her friends and would tidy the place up and be there for her when she got home. 'Good luck, Maur. There's bound to be some cock-up. Your Tommy might be a little sod, but he's no fucking killer.'

Maureen wasn't allowed to travel with her son on the journey. The police had called in reinforcements and she was shoved into a car on her own. She didn't know where Ethel or the others were, so maybe they were with Tommy. Everything had happened so quickly, she'd had little time to think about the actual accusation. It couldn't be true. The Old Bill must have been desperate to pull someone in and, knowing her Tommy was a local tearaway, had picked on him. Maybe they thought her son was in the know. Being so streetwise, they probably thought that he'd heard a whisper and would grass up the real killer.

*　　*　　*

Sandra ordered Susan to put James to bed and then go to bed herself. She needed to discuss the situation with the others and didn't want to say too much in front of the kids. James was too young to really take in what they were talking about, but Susan had ears like a bat.

Most of the neighbours had gone now. The men had been sent home with the older kids and the other little 'uns were up in the bedroom with Susan and James. There were now just four of them left and they all considered themselves to be Maureen's best friends. Sandra had been insistent that they didn't discuss stuff with anyone they didn't know that well, or trust. Chatting amongst themselves, all the girls were positive that there had been some kind of mix-up. They all knew Mary Smith. Like themselves, she'd had it tough and was one of the old school. None of their kids, including Terry or Tommy, were angels, but none of them were cold-blooded killers. There had to be some mistake.

Tommy sat in the interview room next to his mum, feeling confident. 'I've already told yer, I was round at Lenny Simpson's all night. I was with Michael Tibbs, Ben Thompson and Dave Taylor. We had a few beers and were listening to David Bowie records. If yer don't believe me, go and ask 'em,' he said cockily.

Sitting next to her son, Maureen squeezed his clammy hand. Her Tommy might be a fucker, but he certainly wasn't capable of what he was being accused of. The pigs had a bloody liberty, trying to put the blame on her son.

Maureen stood up; she'd had enough of this shit for one night. If it wasn't bad enough that the bastards had ruined her birthday party, they now seemed content on keeping them there till the cows came home. 'Look, you ain't got nothing on him, so why the fuck won't you let us go home?'

DC Perryman smiled at his colleague. He'd given Hutton twenty minutes to stew, wonder and make up stories. Now it was time to show him the real evidence and watch the little bastard crumble.

As the bag of evidence was shown, Maureen's heart sank, and she let go of Tommy's hand. Her son's clothes she recognised immediately. He didn't have that many and the ones he did have, she'd had to scrimp and save for. For months he'd driven her mad for a pair of flares and here they were, ripped and covered in blood. She stared at the knife – she didn't recognise that, but he could have got it from anywhere.

'The clothes aren't mine. Tell 'em Mum. Tell 'em they ain't mine,' Tommy said frantically.

Maureen couldn't speak. Her voice had disappeared and her mouth wouldn't open.

As DC Perryman put the school letter on the table, Tommy broke down in tears. 'I didn't do it. It wasn't me, I swear I didn't do it,' he sobbed.

DS Arnold tried a different tactic from his colleague. He was always a big believer in the nice and soft approach. 'Look, son, we know the blood is Terry's and we know the clothes are yours. All we need to know now is what really happened. Was it a fight that went wrong? An argument that got out of hand? You aren't doing yourself any favours, Tommy, by not telling us. We've got you bang to rights and if you help yourself, the judge will be much more lenient with you.'

Maureen thumped him on the arm. She'd always brought her kids up to tell the truth. 'Cat got your tongue, has it? Answer the fucking man,' she screamed.

Ignoring the duty solicitor's advice, a petrified Tommy

30

spilled his guts. He told them about both of the gangs and his long-term feud with Terry. He said that he'd stolen the fishing knife from his dad, but had acted in self-defence. The police were keen to know if any of the other lads were present. Tommy was no grass and had no intention of dobbing in his mates. 'I was on me own when I chased Smiffy. The other lads had all gone off in different directions to chase the others,' he stated.

DS Arnold smiled. At least they were getting somewhere now. Perryman was a prick and a bully, that's why he'd never been promoted.

'Just one more question, Tommy. Did the other lads know that you'd committed murder? Did you tell them what had happened?'

Tommy wiped his tears on the cuff of his shirt. 'I didn't know he was dead meself. I thought he was just injured and would get up and go home. I told the other lads what had happened and they just thought he was hurt, the same as me. I never meant to kill him, it was an accident. I swear on me life, I didn't mean it.'

DS Arnold stood up. He could tell the kid was telling the truth. The likes of the Huttons were not his kind of people, but that didn't stop him feeling sorry for them. He'd only been working in the East End for the past year and the poverty-stricken area had been a real eye-opener for him. He'd spent most of his working years in much nicer places and the way the people acted in this neck of the woods had been a pleasant shock to him. They were rough and ready, all right, and would lie through their teeth to avoid prosecution. But once they had them bang to rights, they never grassed their mates but took the rap themselves.

'We'll leave you to it for a few minutes. I'll get you both a cup of tea.'

31

Leaving the room, Arnold dragged Perryman with him. He could sense the mother was deeply stunned and guessed she'd appreciate a few quiet minutes alone with her child.

As the door closed on them, Maureen burst into tears. 'Why, son, why? How could you do such a thing? Mary's my friend. How can I ever face her again?'

'I'm sorry, Mum,' Tommy sobbed. 'I swear it was an accident. Smiffy tried to shoot me with an air gun a couple of weeks ago. I didn't mean to hurt him, I just wanted to frighten him.'

Maureen stood up. Wiping away her tears, her mood quickly changed to anger. 'You stupid little fucker. Years you'll get for this, fucking years. And as for stealing the knife off your father, I bet yer didn't. I bet the silly bastard gave it to you. Don't lie to me, Tommy, I want the fucking truth.'

'I swear, Mum, he never gave it to me. I nicked it when I went round to see him a couple of weeks ago.'

Lifting her hand, Maureen clumped him around the head. 'You're a fucking idiot, Tommy. All my life I've tried my best for you and this is how you repay me. It's not only your life you've fucked up, but mine too. And what about Susan and James? They'll suffer for this as well. You're just like your father, a fucking arsehole. I've done my utmost to keep you on the straight and narrow and all you do is kick me in the teeth. Maybe it's my fault, perhaps I've been too lenient with yer, but I'll tell you summink, you've broken my heart and I'll never forgive yer for this. This time, you've gone one step too far, son.'

As the two Old Bill returned, Maureen walked towards the door. 'I take it you're keeping him here tonight?'

The DS put the teas on the table and nodded.

'Well, I'm off home. You can lock him up and throw away the key for all I care. I have another son indoors, a decent one that needs me. My priorities lie with him now, not this fucking waster.'

Head held high, Maureen marched out of the interview room.

'Please don't leave me, I'm scared, Mum. Come back, please come back.'

As Maureen heard Tommy screaming for her, part of her wanted to hug him and assure him everything was gonna be all right. Wiping away her tears, she carried on walking. Sometimes in life you had to be cruel to be kind. Tommy had made his own choices and now he had to face the consequences. She couldn't be there for him while he was banged up, so best she cut the apron strings now.

Pete, Sandra's old man, was charged with assaulting a police officer. The other three, including Ethel, had been let go with a caution. The police had originally planned to charge Ethel with assault as well, but due to her big mouth spouting non-stop and lack of cell space, they chose to let her go. After all, they had bigger fish to fry.

Ethel gave the Old Bill a barrage of abuse as she walked out of the station. She'd wanted to stay and wait for Tommy and Maureen, but wasn't allowed. The police told her she'd have too long a wait. They also said that if she wasn't off their premises in five minutes flat, they'd have no alternative other than to rearrest her. 'Fucking arseholes,' Ethel muttered, as she trudged down the road.

Sandra, Brenda and the other girls had made the house look as clean as a whistle. They had taken down the cards and banners, put the food away and cleared up any traces of the party. 'It's best she's not reminded of it,' Brenda insisted.

When Ethel arrived she had no update on Tommy's arrest, and no idea where Maureen was. Sandra made her a cup of tea and told her the little they knew. Ethel, being Ethel, was still furious about her own arrest. 'Fucking load of cunts. What a fucking liberty,' she kept repeating.

Maureen's heart was beating nineteen to the dozen as she neared her house. What the hell was she meant to tell everyone? It was such a close-knit community; everybody knew everybody. Mary Smith might live in Bethnal Green, but it was only down the road and she was still part of their community. The East End wasn't perfect, it was littered with thieves, wide boys and scoundrels, but there was one unwritten rule: 'You don't shit on your own doorstep.'

Taking a deep breath, Maureen put her key in the lock. It was time to face the music.

Sandra was the first to greet her. 'Well? Where's Tommy?' she asked expectantly, as Ethel and the others stood behind her.

Maureen could barely look at them. 'Get me a drink, summink strong. I need to sit down.'

James had lain awake for hours. He was so worried about his big brother. Why had the police taken him away? And when was he coming back? Hearing his mum return, he crept onto the landing. He needed to earwig and find out what was going on.

Maureen gulped the whole glass of brandy and put her head in her hands. Ethel guessed what had happened and decided to help her daughter-in-law out. 'Don't bother trying to explain, we can guess. The little bastard's guilty? He killed Terry Smith?'

Between sobs, Maureen somehow managed to speak. 'Yes, Mum. Our Tommy's a murderer, he's admitted to it.'

Sandra, Brenda and the other girls all glanced at one another. No one said a word.

James frantically ran back to his room. His brother was the best, he couldn't be a murderer. The policemen must have made a mistake. Remembering the new toy his uncle Kenny had brought him, he pulled it out from under the bed. He'd always had a thing about police cars. 'I'm gonna be a policeman one day when I'm a big boy,' he'd told everyone. Well, not any more – he hated them now. They'd taken away his beloved brother.

James opened the bedroom window, 'I hate you, you pig bastards,' he shouted, as the car smashed on the coal bunker below.

Shivering, James climbed into bed and sobbed himself to sleep.

FIVE

The next six months were probably the worst in Maureen's life. She'd fully expected her Tommy to be charged with manslaughter and receive a lesser sentence, but it wasn't to be. The authorities had decided to make an example of him. The jury had found him guilty of murder and he'd received fifteen years for his crime. As the judge announced the sentence, Maureen felt her legs go from under her.

'Noooo! It was an accident. Tell 'em, Mum, tell 'em,' were the words she heard her son scream as her friends helped carry her out of the court.

Once a respected pillar of the community, Maureen felt this was no longer the case. Everywhere she went she heard the whispers, noticed the stares, and even the rag-and-bone man now gave her a wide berth. No one had actually blamed her face to face and even Mary Smith had squeezed her hand outside the court and offered her words of comfort. Maureen had felt terrible about this. She had expected the murdered lad's mum to come at her like a rabid dog, but Mary hadn't blamed her at all. Mary's friends and family most certainly did. Maureen could see the hatred in their eyes. It was as though they were silently trying to tell her that if she had been a better parent, none of this would have happened.

Her mother-in-law and her own friends had been fantastic. They were always popping round to check she was all right and she was never left alone for long. Maureen's social life had flown right out of the window from the day that Tommy was arrested. She could never face going to the bingo hall again. Mary and her friends had used it for years and Maureen couldn't face the gossip and the shame. She'd even stopped joining in with the regular Saturday-night parties. How could she dance, drink and be happy, when her son had wiped out a young boy's life? The odd cup of tea with a friend or a quick pop up the shops was all she could manage these days. She seemed to have lost her sparkle, her sense of humour, and the lack of activity suited her down to the ground. Maureen's thoughts were disturbed by her daughter's whining voice.

'Mum, I'm bored sitting upstairs. Can I go outside and play? I'm sorry for what I said the other day, and I promise I'll never say it again.'

Maureen shot her daughter a disdainful look. Susan had been grounded for the last two days and had been sent to her room in disgrace. The headmistress of her daughter's school had contacted Maureen and asked her to pop in. Apparently, Susan had been threatening some of the kids there. She'd been demanding their dinner money, while bragging about Tommy.

'You either pay up, or when my bruvver gets out, I'll make sure you're next on his hit list,' she'd boasted cockily.

One of the teachers had witnessed Susan demanding money from fellow pupils on numerous occasions. When questioned, two of the kids had broken down. This was why the headmistress was now involved and Maureen was bloody well furious.

'You can go out, Susan, for two hours. But, I swear, girl,

if I ever hear that you've been bragging about your bruvver again, I will personally fucking doughboy yer. Do you understand me?'

Susan nodded and walked away.

Maureen made herself a brew and went upstairs to see James. Her poor baby was a shadow of his former self and she was so worried about him. James had idolised Tommy and had followed him about like a lost puppy. Now his brother was no longer about, James spent most of his time alone in his room. Maureen's heart went out to him as she opened the bedroom door. He was kneeling on the carpet playing with a toy truck, his face a picture of sadness.

'Are you all right, darling?' she asked.

'Yes, Mummy,' James said quietly.

Maureen sat on the bed and handed him a white paper bag. 'I bought you a present from the baker's. It's a gingerbread man, your favourite.'

James took the bag and sat on the bed next to her. He wasn't hungry, but nibbled his present out of politeness. 'Mummy, when you go and see Tommy again, please let me come with you. I'll be a good boy, I promise.'

Maureen held him close to her. Tommy was in Feltham Borstal and it was miles away, a poxy journey. With money being tight, she'd only been there the once herself. 'Where Tommy's staying is not a very nice place, James. I'll take you there when you're a bit older.'

James threw himself against her chest and sobbed. Lifting his head, he looked her in the eyes and pleaded with her. 'Please take me to see him, Mummy. I don't care if it's not nice. Please, Mum, can I go?'

Maureen looked into his angelic little eyes and didn't have the heart to say no. She didn't want James to visit a bloody borstal, but what could she do? 'OK, I'll arrange a visit and take you, but first you must eat all that ginger-bread man and promise me that you're not gonna sit in your bedroom all the time from now on. *Mr Benn*'s on telly in a minute, let's watch it together, eh?'

James smothered her with kisses. 'When can we go, Mum? Can we go tomorrow?' he asked excitedly.

Maureen cupped his precious face. He looked happier now than she'd seen him in months. 'You musn't be impatient, James. Mummy has to organise some money and book the visit. I'll try and sort something out tomorrow, see if I can scrape together the train fare for this weekend.'

James picked up his gingerbread man and tucked into it. He was so excited, he couldn't wait to see his big brother. Surely once Tommy saw him, he'd want to come back home. And then they'd be happy again, like they were before.

Susan was filled with excitement as she watched Jeanette Dickenson walk into the sweet shop. Grinning, she urged her friend Tracey to follow her and hide behind the furniture shop. Susan couldn't stand Jeanette Dickenson. Jeanette had everything in life that she didn't. Her mum was slim and modern, her dad had a good job. She had a brand new Chopper bike, a cute little puppy called Simba, and she always had loads of money for sweets and stuff.

Peeping around the wall, Susan saw Jeanette coming towards her with her usual bag of goodies. Nudging Tracey to follow her lead, she leaped out from behind the wall and grabbed Jeanette by her stupid ponytail. 'Give us your sweets and your money,' she demanded.

Jeanette's eyes filled with tears. She'd had run-ins with Susan Hutton in the past and was petrified of her. 'I can't, the sweets are for my little brothers and the money is my mum's change.'

Tracey was desperate to impress her new friend. Spotting the puppy, she aimed a kick at its head.

The dog's yelp was enough to make Jeanette change her mind.

'Just take it,' she said, handing over the bag and her mother's change.

Susan released her grip on Jeanette's hair and pointed a finger in her face.

'If you say one word to yer mum or dad, I'm gonna do the same to your dog as what my bruvver did to Terry Smith.'

Jeanette shook with fear as she picked up poor Simba. 'I promise I won't say a word. I'll pretend to mum that I lost the pound note she gave me.'

'Best yer get yourself home then,' Tracey said, giving her a sly kick in the ankle as a farewell present.

Arm in arm, Susan and Tracey ran down the road laughing their heads off. Satisfied with their five minutes' work, they sat on a wall and counted their earnings. Fifty-two pence, two Curly Wurlys, a Mars bar, two Sherbet Fountains and a big bag of penny sweets.

Susan smiled at her friend. 'Go back to the shop, buy some bubble gum and get some change so we can split the money.'

Susan stuffed her face with penny sweets as she watched Tracey run off up the road. Up until a couple of months ago, she hadn't a friend in the world.

Tracey Davis and her family had recently been moved from Canning Town to Stepney. Tracey's brother, Andrew, had apparently mugged an old pensioner in Newham and the old dear had later died of head injuries. There had been a lot of ill-feeling in the area about the incident and Tracey and her family were rehoused by the council on the Ocean Estate in Stepney. Her brother, Andrew, was now in prison paying for his crime. On sharing secrets about their brothers, Tracey and Susan had an immediate bond. Both shared vindictive personalities and, having palled up, were a match made in heaven.

Tracey was out of breath as she ran back to her mate. 'That's your half and that's mine,' she rasped, as she counted out the money.

Susan giggled. 'Let's have a bet. First one to eat a Curly Wurly gets the packet of bubble gum.'

Tracey laughed as she counted down. 'Three, two, one – go.'

Mouths full, the race was on.

Unaware that his sister was making money out of his name, Tommy Hutton trudged out onto the playing fields with the other lads. He smiled at his pal, Freddie, as Finchy gave them their orders.

'Right lads. No kicking, spitting, biting, punching or slide tackling from behind. Got it?'

Twenty-two heads nodded and the whistle was blown. Today's game of footie was a proper match for once. Usually they just trained or had a game amongst themselves, but this was different, it was one wing against another.

Tommy already had his orders. He was to scythe down the Paki kid, Ranjit Patel. Apparently, Patel had set fire to his family home, killing his kid sister and grandmother. Tommy got his chance within minutes, seeing his prey lying on the ground, he pretended to go for the ball, but instead kicked the sicko full in the mouth, loosening two of his front teeth. Tommy was immediately shown the red card.

'It was an accident, sir. I went for the ball.'

Finchy was having none of it. 'You're off, Hutton. Go and sit down on the grass and I'll deal with you later.'

Tommy smiled to himself as he sat alone watching the game. He'd hated Feltham when he'd first arrived. In fact, he'd made a right prick of himself, crying himself to sleep night after night. Things had changed after about six weeks. He'd got his head together, found his inner strength, and hit it off with Freddie Adams.

In the early days of being caged, Tommy had kept himself to himself. He'd spoken to some of the lads, but not at length. A couple of them were all right, but a lot of them were thickos. Bored with his own company, he searched his wing for someone on his wavelength. He couldn't find anyone but, as luck would have it, Freddie then turned up.

For the first couple of days, Tommy eyed the new boy suspiciously. Freddie was a typical jack the lad. He had a way with people, knew how to work them, had them eating out of his hand. Tommy found himself alone with Freddie for the first time about a week later. They clicked immediately and were best buddies within the hour.

Freddie was in for murder as well, but had gone one better than Tommy. He'd nicked his brother's gun and shot his victim straight through the head. Obviously, he lied in court. He said he was just threatening the lad and the gun had gone off accidently. The judge had fallen for Freddie's baby face and boyish charm, and had given him a rather lenient twelve years.

'I was lucky really, I sort of acted simple. I think the jury thought I was a bit backward and by the time the case ended, even the judge felt sorry for me,' Freddie boasted.

Tommy was fascinated by his new-found friend. Freddie was a year younger than himself, but acted far older and wiser. He came from Manor Park and his older brother and uncle were armed robbers, so maybe that's where he got it from.

Tommy's attentions were turned back to the present as he noticed the commotion on the football pitch. Seeing Freddie had gotten his marching orders, Tommy smiled as he walked towards him. Freddie's intended target had been Kevin Wallis, who was a complete weirdo and by all accounts a nonce-case. Rumour had it, he was locked up for fiddling with a six year old.

'I was daydreaming. I didn't see yer do him,' Tommy said, as his pal flopped on the grass next to him.

'I elbowed the cunt as I went up for a corner. I did that good a job, I think I nearly took his eye out.'

Tommy laughed. 'Whaddya think our punishment will be this time?'

Freddie shrugged. 'Don't know, don't care. We'll be all right, Finchy knows we only do the wrong 'uns.'

At the end of the game, both Tommy and Freddie were summoned into Finchy's office.

'Look lads, I won't go to the guv'nor, but that's the second week in a row two lads have received medical treatment on your behalf. I have to punish you, so it's no TV for either of you for a week, starting from tonight. Now go and get showered, then back to your cells, both of you.'

Tommy and Freddie were in high spirits as they got showered and changed. Their punishment was a piece of piss. Freddie's cell was right next door to Tommy's, and they'd learnt how to communicate by tapping on the wall. They had their own code and were able to have some basic conversations.

'Right, I'll see yer at dinner,' Freddie said, as they reached their cells.

'What we gonna do if we can't watch telly?' Tommy asked.

43

'We can have a nice little chat. We need to talk and plan our future.'

Tommy shook his head. 'We're gonna be locked up for years. What's the fuckin' point?'

Freddie grabbed Tommy by the shoulders. 'Look at me, Tom. We might be boys now, but when we get out we'll be men. We have to be ready for it.'

Tommy smiled. As usual, his pal was right.

SIX

Ethel Hutton stood outside the hardware store in Dagenham Heathway and eyed the contents suspiciously. A stout woman, Ethel had an old-fashioned dress sense, grey curly hair, and due to her bloody hard life, looked far older than her fifty-six years.

Ethel had been thieving for years – case of bloody having to. She never chored locally. A, she'd never take from her own, and B, she was far too well known in the East End even to attempt it.

Dragging her shopping trolley behind her, Ethel entered the store. Tools always sold well and she needed to have a good day today. Her Maureen was taking James to visit Tommy and she'd promised to give them the train fare.

There were a few people standing at the counter and the man who was serving was far too busy to be noticing her. Filling her trolley with anything expensive and saleable, Ethel was just about to exit the store when she heard shouting.

'Oi, stop, thief!'

Unaware that a second member of staff, posing as a customer, had been watching her, Ethel had no other choice than to leave her trolley and leg it. Running up Heathway Hill, she didn't see the dodgy paving stone.

Seconds later, Ethel was lying face down on the ground, writhing with pain.

'Gertcha, cowson,' she said to the shop worker, as she clutched her ankle.

The police arrived within minutes.

James pushed the pouffe towards the window. It was heavy, but he could just about manage to move it without any help. Standing on top of it, he pressed his face against the glass. The old woman who used to live next door had recently died and now there were new neighbours moving in. James was hoping there'd be a boy his age for him to play with.

'Your sore throat seems miraculously better. Don't be so bleeding nosy, come away from that window,' Maureen ordered, as she handed him a tray with his egg and chips.

He'd jibbed off school earlier, saying he was ill, and she was sure he was playing a fast one.

James smiled as he dipped his bread in the yolk. 'Do you think there'll be some boys I can play with, Mummy?'

Maureen shook her head. 'Afraid not son. I spoke to 'em earlier. They've got a little girl, same age as you.'

'Aw, I wanted a boy to play with. I don't like girls.'

Maureen ruffled his head. 'You will do when you're older. At least I hope you will.'

Hearing his favourite programme about to start, James forgot about the neighbours and concentrated on *Mr Benn*. The man in the bowler hat was a legend and today he was a cowboy.

Leaving him to watch his hero, Maureen smiled and left the room.

Ethel avoided arrest by lying and pretending to have a broken ankle. She seemed truthful and in so much agony that the police called an ambulance and decided not to prosecute her. She'd told them it was a one-off. 'I swear, I've never nicked anything in me life,' she insisted. 'I only did it 'cause me poor daughter-in-law needed the money for train tickets to visit me grandson.'

'Where's your grandson living, then?' one of the officers asked.

'Norfolk. He's retarded and they've put him in one of them homes – you know, a funny farm.'

The two officers had a quick chat among themselves. They'd retrieved the shopping trolley, the store had its goods back, so there was no harm done.

'Poor old cow,' the young copper said to the older one.

After hearing that she was being let off, Ethel waved at the two Old Bill from the back of the ambulance. As soon as the doors were shut, she cackled with laughter and did a wanker sign at them.

Arriving at the hospital, Ethel gave the doctors a false name. She refused to go into a cubicle, saying that her leg now felt better and she'd rather sit in the waiting room in a wheelchair.

'I'm claustrophobic. I'll wait 'ere for me x-ray,' she lied.

As soon as the coast was clear, Ethel half ran and half hobbled out the door. She didn't have a clue where she was or how to get home. Asking a passer-by, she learned that she was in Romford.

'Romford. Fucking Romford,' she muttered as she trudged towards a bus stop.

After a lot of wrong directions, Ethel finally got a 103 back to Dagenham East station. She knew her way home from there. The district line took her straight through to Stepney Green.

As she sat on the train, Ethel wondered how she was

going to tell Maureen that she didn't have the money for the train tickets. The poor cow had booked the visit and was going up there in less than forty-eight hours. With her shopping trolley confiscated, there was no way that Ethel could get the cash before then. Not only that, having a near escape and falling arse over tit had slightly unnerved her. She'd have to give it at least a week before she felt confident enough to go out on the rob again.

Maureen was sitting on the carpet, playing dominoes with James, when Ethel let herself in.

'What a bleedin' day I've had. Nearly got arrested, and I've been stuck at a fuckin' hospital in the middle of nowhere.'

James listened to his nan's antics with interest. He had never forgiven the police force for arresting Tommy.

'You should have hit them, Nanny, and kicked them.'

'Stay here and watch telly, James,' Maureen ordered, as she shoved Ethel towards the kitchen. She'd had one son go off the rails and was now determined to keep the other wrapped in cotton wool.

Hearing her trip to Feltham was now in serious jeopardy, Maureen put her head in her hands.

'What am I gonna tell the boys? I spoke to Tommy yesterday, he sounds so much brighter. As for James, his heart's gonna be broken.'

Ethel stood up. 'I'll tell yer what we're gonna do. Get yer coat, and we'll go and find that no-good bastard son of mine. He never gives you a fuckin' penny, yet he's always got money to spend in the pub.'

Maureen hated her husband and despised asking him for anything. Tonight was different though. She was that desperate, she'd have gladly asked Jack the Ripper to fund her journey, if it meant she could get to see her son.

'Put your parka on over your jamas, James. Quickly put your shoes on, we're going to see Daddy.'

Usually, Maureen would rather go without food for a week than have herself or her family walking the streets looking like tramps, but this was an emergency. Anywhere else in the world they might have looked a funny sight traipsing down the road. Ethel's back and ankle were playing up and she was walking like Quasimodo. Maureen had her curlers in and James looked like an orphan in his pyjamas, navy anorak and scuffed black shoes, but no one took a blind bit of notice of them as they headed towards the pub. The East End had a culture of its own.

Tommy senior was an easy chap to find. If he was skint, he was at his bedsit in Whitechapel. If he had money, he was either in the Horn of Plenty, or the nearest betting shop. Today, Tommy had had one of his better days. He'd won a score this morning on traps one and six. Now he had his arm around Shaking Sheila, and was in the process of worming his way back to hers for a quick leg-over.

Sheila had been a real beauty in her heyday. That was before the alcohol had ravaged her face and body. She now woke up like she had St Vitus's dance every morning and it took her at least six drinks to stop the shakes, hence the nickname.

Tommy wasn't in the habit of being fussy. She had big tits, and he wasn't exactly Warren Beatty himself. Buying another round, he decided to go in for the kill. Grabbing her arse, he stuck his tongue straight down the back of her throat. Paralytic and virtually unable to stand, Sheila grabbed him and responded as if her life depended on it.

Ethel spotted her son immediately. 'There he is with some dirty stinking whore,' she said, as she dragged his family towards him.

49

Maureen didn't give a shit that he was mauling some rough old bird. He repelled her and as long as he never laid another finger on her, he could maul whoever he wanted.

Seeing his mum approach, Tommy withdrew his tongue from Shaking Sheila's throat.

'Whassa matter?' he slurred.

Ethel held open the palm of one hand and pointed at Maureen and James with the other. 'Your wife and son need money to go and visit your Tommy in Feltham. I've tried to help 'em, but I can't this time.'

Tommy shrugged his slouched shoulders. 'Whaddya want me to do? I ain't got no money.'

Squinting through one eye, Sheila suddenly realised that the cute little boy must be Tommy's son.

'Is that your daddy?' she slurred.

Frightened of the woman with the big boobies, James nodded and quickly moved away from her.

When sober, Sheila hated children. They were a bloody nuisance. When drunk, she loved every hair on their little heads.

Ethel made Tommy empty the pockets of his dirty trousers. 'One pound, ten pence. Is that all you've got? You might be my son, but you make me fucking sick, Tommy Hutton. Pissed up in 'ere, day in, day out, and not a penny towards your family's upkeep.'

'Issall gone,' Tommy slurred.

Sick of the mad woman who kept pestering him, James moved to the other side of the pub and sat at a table. Sheila, who was desperate to get away from the family argument, decided to play chase with him.

'Where you gone, little boy?' she shouted, as she staggered his way.

Seeing her lunge towards him, James leaped off the

chair and ran back towards his mum. Hearing a commotion, he looked behind him just in time to see Sheila fall into the table and land flat on her back.

'Can we go now, Mummy?' he said, tugging Maureen's arm. His dad hadn't even spoken to him and he didn't want the mad woman to chase him again.

Having kept her trap shut until now, Maureen looked at the one pound ten pence in her hand and felt her blood boil. Slipping James the coin, she ripped the pound note up in shreds, dropped it in Tommy's pint and then promptly poured the contents over his drunken head.

'You fucking arsehole,' she said viciously. 'Come on, we're going.'

Grabbing Ethel with one hand and dragging James by the other, she marched out of the pub, head held high.

An hour later, back home with a brandy in her hand, it was Ethel who started laughing first.

'Did you see his face when you poured the beer over his head? I didn't know if he was gonna cry or lick it up off the bar.'

Maureen knocked back the contents of her glass and forced a smile. She was still worried about the visit, but had an idea. It was the last resort, really. Maureen didn't have a phone indoors, but Ethel had one and allowed her to use it if she needed to.

'Mum, do you think Kenny would lend us the money for the train fare? I can pay him back within a month.'

'Course he would,' Ethel said immediately.

Unlike Tommy, her youngest boy was extremely wealthy and a credit to her. He and his wife Wendy had no children, but Kenny loved kids, and Ethel was positive he'd be only too pleased to help his family out. He wouldn't see Tommy have no visitors, that was for sure.

51

'I'm surprised I never thought of Kenny. Run over to mine and ring him,' Ethel insisted.

'No. I don't like to,' Maureen said sharply. 'You do it, Mum. Ask him for me.'

'You're a funny girl, Maureen. He don't bleedin' bite, yer know,' Ethel said, as she picked up her bag.

Five minutes later, Ethel was back with good news. 'You ain't even gotta get a train, Maur. He's driving yer down there in his new car. He said he'll probably bring Wendy for the ride. He also said that he's gonna get you a phone installed, he said you should have one now so that Tommy can ring yer.'

Maureen was horrified. She always felt inadequate around Kenny and Wendy. Their lives were so different from hers and she felt extremely uncomfortable in their company.

'I don't wanna go in the car. I'd much rather go by train.'

Ethel poured them both another brandy. 'Don't be so bleedin' stupid. You'll enjoy going by car, and James'll love it.'

Hearing his name mentioned, James wandered into the kitchen. Ethel grabbed him and sat him on her lap. 'Uncle Kenny's gonna take you to see your bruvver in his brand new car.'

James bounced up and down excitedly. He loved cars, they were his obsession. 'What car has uncle Kenny got?'

Ethel lifted him off her knee. Her bloody ankle was playing up again. 'He's got a Jaguar.'

James's eyes lit up. 'Really? And he's gonna take me to see Tommy in it?'

Maureen looked at her son's happy face. He deserved a treat, her baby, and if it meant suffering Wendy and Kenny for the day, then so be it. At least they would get to see Tommy and the visit would still go ahead. Maureen downed her drink in one and topped her glass up again. She rarely drank in the week, but today had been stressful, to say the least.

She smiled at Ethel. 'Come with us on Saturday to see Tommy. Even if we can't get you in on the visit, just come for the ride.'

'Whaddya want me there for?'

Maureen squeezed her hand. The drink had made her go all sentimental. ''Cause I bloody well love yer, and sometimes I don't know what I'd do without yer.'

Normally Ethel was as tough as old boots, but Maureen's words struck a nerve. Unusually for her, her eyes welled up. 'Of course I'll come, yer silly cow.'

Hearing Susan come in, Maureen shouted for her to come into the kitchen.

'Tired. Going to bed,' came the reply.

'That is one horrible little fucker, needs a good fawpenny one, she does,' Ethel said bluntly.

By ten o'clock, both Ethel and Maureen felt tipsy. After a long, tough day, James had provided them with some light entertainment and had been singing, dancing and telling jokes.

Feeling worn out, James plonked himself on his mum's lap. 'Mum, you know that mad lady in the pub? Did you see her fall over?'

'I didn't see anything. Who you talking about?' Maureen asked him.

'The mad lady who was with Daddy. When you weren't looking she chased me and fell on the floor.'

Maureen looked at Ethel and they both burst out laughing. Holding her sides, Ethel had trouble getting her words out.

'Did the mad woman get back up, James?' she chortled.

James shook his head. 'No, she was still lying on the floor when we came home.'

James stood up. He'd never seen his mum and nan laugh so much. Joining in the fun, he leaped up and down excitedly. Apart from Tommy, his mum and his nan were his world, and making them happy filled him with glee.

SEVEN

Wendy Hutton sat in the front of her husband's car with a face like a slapped arse. She couldn't stand her Kenny's family, and was unable to think of a worse way to spend her weekend than being stuck in a confined space with them. In Wendy's mind, the Huttons were the ultimate dregs of society. She hated sharing their surname and couldn't believe that Kenny had come from such a repulsive family. At first, she'd flatly refused to go on the journey.

'If you think I'm giving up my Saturday to visit a murderer and be stuck with your uncouth family, you can think again,' she told Kenny.

Kenny had bargained with her. 'Please come, Wendy. I know they're common, but they are my flesh and blood. We'll drop them off, then me and you will go for lunch. Go on, come with us, and then on Sunday I'll take you out to look for that sports car you so badly want.'

Reluctantly, Wendy had agreed to accompany him. Kenny liked a quiet life. He adored his wife, loved his family, and wished that everyone would just get along for his sake. He knew his wife could be above herself at times. She'd come from a well-to-do family and was unable to help the way she was. He was sure that she loved him, though, because he hadn't had money when she married him. He'd always be indebted to Wendy and her family, as it was her dad who had set him up in the scrap-metal game and lent him the money to start his first business.

Kenny knew the reason for Wendy's bad moods. They'd had a lot of problems in the past, which had left his wife feeling bitter and blaming him. For ages they'd unsuccessfully tried for a baby. Finally, they'd gone for tests and were told the problem lay with him. The doctors said that they were unlikely to conceive naturally, because of his low sperm count, but not to give up trying.

Wendy had never seemed the same towards him since that day. Feeling a failure, Kenny had thrown himself into work. His business had thrived and he tried to compensate his wife in other ways. A big house, foreign holidays, cars, clothes and jewellery. Wendy wanted for nothing, but still she wasn't happy. The one thing she really wanted was the one thing he couldn't give her.

'Pull over by them bushes, son. I'm bursting for a slash.'

Ethel annoyed Kenny. She knew that Wendy hated that kind of talk and he was sure his mother purposely tried to wind her up.

'Can't you wait a minute, Mum? I'll find a garage or something. They'll have a proper toilet there.'

Ethel nudged Maureen. She loved winding Wendy up. The stuck-up cow gave her son a dog's life.

'No, I can't bleedin' wait. You know I've got a weak bladder. Pull over quick, before I piss meself on the seat.'

Kenny quickly pulled over. Maybe it was a mistake to bring Wendy with him. He hadn't realised his mum was coming. If he'd known, he wouldn't have brought his wife.

James screamed with laughter. 'Quick, look at Nanny. Look, quick!'

Wendy glanced out of the window and was disgusted at the sight of Ethel's fat arse. Stony faced, she glared at her husband. 'Never again. I mean it, Kenny.'

Maureen and James couldn't stop laughing. 'We saw your bum, Nanny,' James informed Ethel as she returned to the car.

'Ain't you got no decorum, mother?' Kenny said, awkwardly.

'No, I ain't. Now shut up and fuckin' drive.'

Ethel winked at Maureen. She hadn't even wanted a wee and she'd flashed her arse on purpose, just for Wendy's benefit.

Freddie and Tommy were in high spirits as they waited for their visitors to arrive. Tommy couldn't wait to see his little brother. Freddie was just as excited, because his mum was coming with his auntie Pauline. Tommy was positive that James hadn't said anything about sneaking out in the night and hiding the black bag for him. If he had blabbed, his mother would have gone apeshit and disowned him for good. His mum idolised James, and she certainly wouldn't be visiting him if she thought he'd involved his kid brother in a murder charge.

Kenny pulled the Jag into the car park. Jumping out, he opened the back door for his family.

'Me and Wendy are gonna grab a bite to eat, so I'll meet you back here in a couple of hours. You'll probably be hungry yourselves by then. Shall I bring back some sandwiches?'

'We're fine, Kenny. Thanks ever so much for bringing us,' Maureen said, gratefully.

'You might be fine, I'm bleedin' starving,' Ethel said.

57

'I'll have summink and none of that fancy shit. James'll be hungry as well, so get us both a bit of grub.'

Kenny nodded, sent his regards to Tommy and quickly got back in the car. Wendy had a face on her like a bulldog chewing a wasp and he knew he was in for an earful.

Maureen was surprised to see how happy and well her son looked. On her previous visit, he'd been tearful and had looked depressed and ill. Today, he looked like a different boy. James wouldn't leave his brother alone. He clambered onto his lap, refused to budge, and wouldn't let anyone else get a word in edgeways. Maureen had tried to explain on the journey down there that Tommy wouldn't be coming home with them, but James was having none of it.

'You must come home, Tommy. You can't stay here, I won't let you,' he told his brother.

Tommy laughed and ruffled James's hair. He didn't have the heart to tell him that he wouldn't be allowed home for Christ knows how long.

Ethel made Tommy roar with laughter at the story of her near arrest.

Maureen tutted. 'Watch what you say in front of James, Mum.'

Ethel didn't take a blind bit of notice. 'The two Old Bill were soppy cunts, wet behind the ears,' she continued.

Maureen stood up and grabbed her by the arm. 'Come on, let's go and get a cup of tea. It'll give James some time on his own with Tommy. Explain that you're not coming home to him,' Maureen mouthed, as she dragged Ethel away.

Tommy lifted James off his lap and sat him on the seat next to him. 'I take it you never said anything about that night when you hid the bag for me?'

James shook his head. 'You said it was our secret, Tommy.'

Tommy lifted his brother's chin towards him. 'It is. You must never tell anyone about that, not ever, Jimmy boy.'

James nodded. He understood perfectly. 'Are yer gonna come home with us, Tommy?'

Tommy shook his head. 'I can't, Jimmy, I've been a naughty boy. I had a fight with someone and now I've gotta be punished. That's why I've gotta stay here.'

'Can yer come home soon, though?'

Tommy sighed. He wished his mother had done the explaining. He wasn't much good at this type of thing.

'It won't be soon, mate. I'd love to come home with yer today, but I'm not allowed.'

James sat silently for a minute or so. He wanted to ask something, but wasn't sure how to. 'Did yer kill someone, Tommy? Everyone at school said yer did.'

Tommy shrugged. 'I did, but I didn't mean to. I swear to yer, Jimmy boy, it was an accident.'

Seeing tears in his older brother's eyes, James grabbed his hand. 'Don't be upset. I believe yer and I won't tell anyone. I don't think uncle Kenny knows, so it'll be another one of our secrets.'

Tommy nodded. He was relieved that his mum and nan were walking towards him. He felt all soppy and emotional explaining things to his brother. Freddie was only two tables away and he didn't want to make a prat of himself in front of him.

'Thanks, Mum,' he said, as she handed him the plastic cup and a Kit-Kat.

Maureen smiled when Tommy pointed out his best mate, Freddie, and spoke fondly about their antics. The day he'd been arrested and admitted to murder, she'd sworn that she was going to wash her hands of him for good, but her decision hadn't lasted long, and two days later, she'd been begging to see him again. She knew he was a fucker, but he was her son and she loved him. She'd never be able to totally forgive him for what he'd done, but deep down, she knew he wasn't a bad lad. If anyone, it was her Susan that was rotten to the core, not Tommy.

As the bell signalled the end of visiting time, James began to cry. He clung to his brother like a jellyfish and refused to let him go. 'If Tommy can't come home with us, can't I stay 'ere with him?' he sobbed as he was finally prised away.

Tommy tried his utmost to not get upset himself and somehow managed it.

'Bye Mum, see yer, Nan. Love yer, Jimmy boy,' he shouted as his family left the building.

Kenny was waiting in the car park as promised. Wendy had been a complete bitch to him over lunch. 'Your family are absolutely disgusting. I look at them and sometimes I'm glad that all you could fire was blanks,' she'd said, nastily.

Kenny had nibbled his ploughman's and said nothing. It was his own fault – he should never have brought her in the first place. He tried so hard to make the family thing work, but it was never going to. Taking Wendy out with his mob was like taking the Queen Mother out with Alf Garnett for the day.

'How did it go?' he asked, handing out the sandwiches.

'Good as gold. Doing his bird like a man,' Ethel said proudly.

Overcome by tiredness, James cried himself to sleep within ten minutes of the journey home. Wendy sat silently while her husband and dysfunctional family discussed the visit.

'He got a bit emotional when James got upset. Other than that, he was OK. He's met a mate in there, Freddie. We saw the kid and he looked a nice lad. His mum and aunt were visiting him, they seemed decent people as well,' Maureen said.

Wendy nearly burst out laughing at her sister-in-law's description of the other boy's family. How did she have the front to say that they seemed decent? Neither Maureen nor Ethel would be able to recognise the word decent if it fell out the sky and smacked them on the head. She could hardly believe her ears when Maureen said, 'I know our Tommy's been done for murder, but he ain't a bad lad, yer know.'

Getting the family back to Stepney seemed to take for ever. As they drove off the shit-hole estate, Wendy poked her husband nastily in the ribs.

'I know I've said it before, Kenny, but don't you ever expect me to suffer your family again. Your mother is a disgusting old woman, your sister-in-law is pathetic and your nephew happens to be a cold-blooded killer.'

Kenny tried to smooth things over. 'Look, I know all their faults. They're hard work, I admit that, but they mean well. And what about James? He's a fantastic kid. Who wouldn't be proud of a son like him?'

Wendy shot him a look and pursed her lips. The youngest wasn't a bad little boy, but stood no chance. Kenny might have broken the mould, but there was no hope for the rest of them, James included. 'Believe me, Kenny. That child's future is already mapped out. He'll either live in poverty or choose a life of crime. He'll end up like the rest of them, you mark my words.'

EIGHT

Instead of cheering James up, the trip to see Tommy seemed to have the opposite effect on him and he spent the next few days moping about the house. Maureen was worried and annoyed with herself. He wasn't even eating properly and she wondered if taking him to the borstal had been a stupid thing to do. Maybe he was too young for such visits, and in future she should wait until he was old enough to fully understand what was going on.

'I'm going out now, Mum,' Susan said, nicking a biscuit out of the tin.

'Don't you want any dinner?' Maureen asked.

'Nah. I'm having some round Tracey's house.'

Susan smiled as she left the house. She'd bullied some money out of the kids at school earlier and Tracey and her had gorged themselves on pie and chips. Susan skipped happily down the road. She was becoming an expert at lying and her dopey mother believed every whopper she told.

Tommy lay stretched out on his bunk. Hearing the four knocks on the wall, he gave two knocks back. Tuesday was games night, and he and Freddie couldn't wait

Whether it was pool, table tennis, board or card games, they relished the challenge and were determined to be the best at everything.

Tonight they were more excited than usual. There was a new face on the block and they were desperate to meet him. Leroy Wright was notorious in the borstal system. A Jamaican from Brixton, the kid was a legend with a reputation to die for. He'd been locked up since he was twelve for mutilating an Indian shopkeeper. Since then he'd been shunted around the country and been slung out of five different borstals. Apparently, he had taken over each one, given the screws hell and run the places as though he owned them. Tommy and Freddie had heard he was due at Feltham over a week ago.

'We run this place, and we ain't letting no new boy take over. We've gotta put a stop to him,' Freddie said.

Tommy reluctantly agreed. He didn't like the sound of the newcomer one little bit, but he wasn't about to voice his doubts. Freddie was brighter than him and what he said went. After all, he was lucky to have been chosen as his best pal in the first place.

James grabbed his pogo-stick and bounced up and down along the garden path. His nan had gotten him his new toy a few weeks ago and he'd spent hours amusing himself on it.

'Hello, I'm Maria. What's your name?'

Shocked that he had a spectator, James swung around to see where the voice was coming from. Unfortunately, he lost his balance, the stick flew out from under him and he landed flat on his face.

'Are you OK?' asked the friendly voice.

Picking himself up, James felt a right wally as he spotted the new girl from next door looking at him.

'Course I'm all right,' he said, as gruffly as he could. He wasn't really. His knee was pouring with blood and he'd smacked his head on the path, but he wasn't letting on. As James hobbled towards her, he felt himself go all funny inside. She was beautiful, like a princess. He looked at her enchanting face, took in her long dark ringlets, and was kind of lost for words.

'Whaddya want?'

Maria smiled. She had the sort of smile that lit up the garden. 'Do you wanna be friends? What's your name?'

Momentarily, James felt short of breath. 'Me name's James, but me bruvver calls me Jimmy boy and yes, I'd love to be your friend.'

'Wait there,' Maria said. 'I'm gonna ask my mum if I can come in your garden and play with you.'

James nodded dumbly. He was thunderstruck.

Tommy potted his ball without even properly looking at it. He couldn't concentrate, as he knew very shortly things were about to go off. He'd noticed Leroy when he'd first walked in earlier. A tall boy, he was quite good looking, had dreadlocks and, as you moved closer, an evil look in his eye. Word had it that in the past, within days of his arrival at a borstal, he would trample on the top boys and take over as the daddy.

Tommy glanced at his friend. Freddie didn't seem to have a care in the world but, personally, he was crapping himself. They were the top boys here and by the look on Leroy's face, the ones he'd shortly be gunning for. Freddie was an extremely perceptive lad. Noticing the two screws leaving the room to sort out a small fracas outside, he pulled a sock out of his pocket and slid it to Tommy.

'Stick some balls in there, shove it down yer bollocks and we're leaving.'

Tommy nodded and did as he was told.

Susan and Tracey stood outside the run-down, filthy old house, awaiting their latest victim. Silly Billy Barnard went to band practice on a Tuesday. His family was skint, so they knew he'd have no money. They just wanted to torment him, terrorise him, like they usually did. Seeing his fat figure waddling their way, they ran towards him. Tracey was the first to reach him. Desperate to impress her friend, she grabbed his thick rimmed glasses and threw them in a nearby bush.

'Please can I have my glasses back? I can't see properly. Please don't hurt me.' Billy was a softie and couldn't help his tears.

Susan smiled at Billy's anguish. She scared the absolute living daylights out of him and she knew it. Each time she confronted him she'd force him to do a little task. These had included pulling his trousers down and showing his willy, crawling along the pavement while meowing like a cat, and digging up his neighbour's plants and eating them. Today, she wanted to teach him the art of movement.

'Dance,' she said, laughing at him.

'I can't dance. I don't know how to,' Billy stammered.

Tracey aimed a kick at his ankle. 'Do as you're told. Now, fucking dance.'

Billy tried to jig up and down to the best of his ability. Both girls were now in hysterics and their uncontrollable laughter made him cry all the more.

'Can I go home now?' he sobbed.

Susan could barely speak for laughing. 'You can't go home until you've done the teapot.'

'What's that?' Billy whimpered.

Susan put her left hand on her hip and positioned her right in the shape of a spout.

Billy understood now. Desperate to get home, he copied his tormentor and stood for five minutes rocking side to side. The girls were enjoying themselves so much that they didn't notice Old Mother Kelly and her sister walking towards them.

'Leave him alone, yer wicked little cows,' screamed the sisters.

As Susan and Tracey legged it into the distance, they could hear Old Mother Kelly cursing them. 'God's watching down on you, you know. What goes around comes around and he's bound to have a plan for evil little girls like you.'

On reaching the corner shop, Susan and Tracey stopped for a breather. Seeing Old Mother Kelly waving her fist at them, both girls lifted their skirts and flashed their bums. Giggling, they continued their journey.

Maureen and Ethel were amused as they sat watching James devour his fish fingers and chips. All of a sudden he had the appetite of a horse and between every mouthful was telling them something else about Maria.

'She's not like other girls, yer know. She can run as fast as me and she can climb trees.'

Maureen smiled. 'Why don't you invite her in for her tea tomorrow, James? We'd love to meet her and I'll check it's OK with her mum.'

James put his empty plate on the table and jumped up and down excitedly. 'Can I, Mum? Can I ask her now?'

Ethel grabbed both his hands. 'Don't ask her yet. You've gotta play it cool, yer don't wanna act too keen.'

James was bemused. 'What do yer mean, Nanny?'

Ethel winked at him. 'You'll know exactly what I mean in a few years' time, won't he, Maur? You tell him.'

Maureen decided to carry on with the wind-up. 'Yer sure will, James. Anyway, it was only last week that you told me you didn't like girls.'

James giggled. 'I don't, but I do like Maria.'

Ethel ruffled his hair. 'Is she your girlfriend, James? Go on, you can tell yer old Nan.'

James put both hands over his face. His mum and nan were so embarrassing sometimes.

Maureen nudged Ethel as she goaded him. 'Come on, James, you can tell us. Girls don't like shy boys, so you've gotta be honest.'

James took his hands away from his eyes. He stood up and put his hands on his little hips. 'OK, I'll tell yer, but you musn't tell anyone. I love Maria and one day I'm gonna marry her!'

'Marriage, eh? Shall I go and buy me outfit now?' Ethel laughed, ruffling his hair.

About to torment James even further, Maureen was stopped by the furious knocking on the front door.

'Who the bleedin' hell's that? The noisy bastards sound like the Old Bill,' Ethel joked.

Making her way into the hallway, Maureen was relieved to hear the voices of Old Mother Kelly and her younger sister, Flo.

'Are you OK? Is something wrong?' she asked as she clocked their serious expressions.

Old Mother Kelly did all the talking. 'I'm sorry Maur, but it's your Susan. She's been pickin' on poor Billy Barnard again. There was her and another girl this time, treating him like a performing monkey, they were. The poor little sod was hysterical by the time we chased 'em away. It's not on Maur, it's bloody wicked. I mean he can't help bein' backward, can he? And he certainly doesn't deserve to be bullied, bless him.'

Maureen's heart sank. The Barnards were a simple bunch, but they wouldn't hurt a fly. 'What exactly was Susan doing to him?' she asked, dreading the answer.

Placing her hands on her oversized waist, Old Mother Kelly pursed her lips. 'Makin' him dance in the middle of the street, she was. She had him rockin' to and fro like a friggin' teapot. Christ knows what would 'ave happened if me and Flo hadn't come along when we did.'

Maureen felt terrible. The Kelly sisters had served their country in the Second World War. Nurses they'd been, and apparently were two of the East End's finest. To try and make excuses for her Susan's behaviour would be an insult to their intelligence.

Unable to look them in the eye, Maureen shook her head. 'Thanks for tellin' me, ladies. It won't happen again, I promise yer that. I'll give that daughter of mine such a fawpenny one when she gets home, she won't sit down for a week. And tomorrow I'll go and see the Barnards. Susan can apologise in person, tell 'em how sorry she is. I'll drag her round there by the hair if I have to.'

Old Mother Kelly nodded. 'Come on then Flo, let's be on our way.'

With a heavy heart, Maureen shut the front door and leaned against it. She'd brought her daughter up to be respectful and kind, so what had gone wrong? To say Susan was a bad apple was putting it mildly. The girl was worse than bad, she was one hundred per cent rotten.

As Tommy and Freddie ran through the corridors, they were filled with a mixture of relief and exhilaration. Not only had they stood their ground with Leroy Wright, they'd frightened the life out of the cunt and done him good and proper.

The fight had been hastily arranged earlier and had taken place in the shower room. It had been all fair and square. Leroy had a mate at Feltham who had been in one of his previous borstals. It was a straight two against two, with a couple of tools included. Tommy had nearly shit himself at first. He'd always been able to handle himself over the years, but that had been with wet-behind-the-ears lads, not the big-league boys.

As Leroy lunged towards him with the lump of wood, Tommy had felt like legging it. Afraid of mugging himself off in front of Freddie, he got a second wind. In a blink of an eyelid, he pulled out the sock containing the pool balls and walloped the motherfucker as hard as he could. As Leroy hit the deck, Tommy clumped him harder and harder. Maybe he was stronger than he'd ever realised. Freddie had done the other lad easily and the feeling Tommy had as he left that shower room would live with him for ever. It was a mixture of happiness, triumph and pure strength.

Finchy saw the two lads running through the corridors. Unbeknown to them, he knew exactly what had gone down and he'd been happy to turn a blind eye to it. Leroy Wright was a screw's worst nightmare. Not only had he clumped a few, but he'd also been the cause of many a riot. Finchy smiled as Tommy and Freddie bolted past him. He could tell by their demeanour that they had been victorious. That thought alone made Finchy an extremely happy man.

Tommy and Freddie tidied themselves up and headed back to the games room. They were finding it difficult to keep the smiles off their faces and were far too excited to carry on playing pool. Sitting in the corner, the two of them spoke quietly.

'You were blinding, Tommy. I thought I'd be doing Leroy and you'd be dealing with his mate. I've gotta hand it to yer. You were summink else.'

Tommy sat back in his chair. He was as proud as a peacock over what he'd achieved. In the past he'd always felt he was second fiddle to Freddie, but not any more. Today he'd proved his worth and now they were equals.

Freddie grabbed his pal's fist in his own and clenched it tightly. 'To us, our friendship and our future.'

Tommy smiled. 'To us.'

NINE

1985 – Ten Years Later

Susan ended the call, replaced the receiver and smiled as she flopped on the bed. It was over four years now since she'd first met her Kev, and he still made her heart race, especially when he was nice to her.

Shutting her eyes, she pictured the night that their paths had crossed. Eighteen she'd been, him twenty-one. It had been a boring Friday night down her local, and on the way home she and Tracey had stopped for their regular doner kebab and chips.

Famished, Susan was too busy shoving rancid pieces of lamb down her throat to notice the two fit blokes enter the shop. Aware of them chatting to Tracey, she plonked herself at a table, carried on eating and took little notice.

'Suze, the boys have invited us to go to a party with them,' Tracey said, nudging her.

Chilli sauce dripping down her chin, Susan glanced around. Locking eyes with the taller one, she suddenly didn't feel hungry any more.

Heart pounding, she tried to sound casual. 'Where is this party then?'

The tall one ignored her, but his mate smiled. 'Whitechapel. It's a mate of ours' twenty-first. Say you'll come, girls. We've got plenty of booze, all we need is the company of some pretty ladies. By the way, I'm Darren and this is Kevin.'

It didn't take much conferring for Susan and Tracey to make up their minds. Chucking their half-eaten take-away into the nearest bin, they smiled at one another and linked arms. The lads in their local were silly little boys and neither of them could believe their luck.

The party was in full swing when they arrived and it didn't take Susan long to realise that the object of her affections wasn't very interested in her. Darren was all over Tracey like a rash, but every time Susan tried to spark up a conversation with Kevin, he gave her one-word answers and quickly walked away. Watching him chat up other girls made her feel physically sick. She couldn't understand why she was feeling the way she was – it was ridiculous, as she'd barely known him five minutes.

As the party dwindled and the smoochies were put on the record player, Susan felt her mood lift as the bird Kev had been chatting up for the last half-hour left with her mate. Beer in hand, Kevin saw her watching him and walked towards her.

'Wanna dance?'

Thrilled that he'd finally noticed her, Susan grabbed him around the neck as though her life depended on it. Determined to snare him, it took her five minutes to get his cock erect and ten to get him in the bedroom. As soon as they hit the sack, Susan knew he was her soul mate. Like hers, Kevin's sex drive was insatiable and they were at it like rabbits all night.

When daylight broke, Kevin leaped up and got dressed. 'Me mum's out tonight. Wanna come round mine for another session?' he asked casually.

Memorising his address, Susan couldn't wipe the smile

off her face. She'd shagged plenty of boys but, for the first time ever, she was hopelessly in love!

Still daydreaming hours later, Susan's thoughts were interrupted by the slamming of the front door.

'Anyone in?' her mother called.

'I was just dozing off. Do yer always have to wake me up?' Susan shouted angrily.

Maureen ignored her daughter's arrogant tone. 'Just puttin' the shopping away. I'm off out again now, so yer can doze as much as yer like. Me and yer nan are goin' up the Roman to choose some paint. We need to decorate the living room before our Tommy comes home.'

Susan didn't bother answering and was relieved as she heard her mother leave the house. Tommy this, Tommy that – she was fucking sick of it. Her brother was due out in just under a month, and her family didn't stop going on about it. Even James had little other conversation.

Desperate to get out of the house before the Tommy fan club returned, Susan decided to get ready early. She was really looking forward to tonight. It was Kev's uncle's fortieth, and all his family would be there. Determined to look her best, she tried most of her wardrobe on. The stretch white Lycra leggings with the matching top won by a mile. She topped her outfit off with red stilettos and a matching red bag. She then blow-dried her hair upside down to give it some oomph, and plastered it with hairspray. Applying the bright red lippy, she smiled at her reflection. Unlike the rest of the world, she failed to notice her rolls of fat, bingo wings and corned-beef legs.

'Kevin, here I come,' she said, blowing a kiss at the mirror.

Unable to drag Tracey and Darren out early, Susan headed to her local alone. The pub was called The Royal Duchess,

73

but no one referred to it as that. Everybody just called it The Duchess. Apart from Kev's mum, she barely knew the rest of the family and was nervous about meeting them. She ordered a glass of cider and sat on the barstool, deep in thought. Tracey, her best friend, had recently fallen pregnant and overnight had changed into Little Miss Perfect.

'We're doing up the nursery, or me and Darren are shopping for baby clothes,' were the excuses she received when she asked Tracey to go out with her.

'Boring cow,' Susan muttered as she sank her pint and ordered another. Tracey might not be able to drink tonight, but she certainly could.

'You look nice, Suze – yer goin' somewhere special?'

Susan smiled. Fat Caz, the barmaid, was desperate to be her friend and had been sucking up to her for ages. She even gave her free drinks when the guv'nor wasn't looking.

'Yeah. Kev's uncle's fortieth. What about you? Off out after yer shift?' Susan replied, knowing full well that Caz had no friends to go anywhere with.

'Dunno, might go clubbing,' Caz said awkwardly.

Susan smiled. The thought of Fat Caz clubbing amused her immensely. She looked at her watch. The party was being held in the Bancroft Arms and was kicking off at eight. Kev, as usual, had told her to make her own way there. She'd begged him to come and get her, but he was having none of it.

'Please Kev, don't make me walk in on my own. I don't wanna schlep there in the dark – say someone jumps me?'

Ever the gentleman, Kev had laughed down the phone at her. 'Fuck off, Suze. You look like a rugby player. Who in their right mind is gonna attack you?'

Smiling at Fat Caz, Susan downed her pint and ordered another. Let Kevin sweat, worry why she was late. He needed to be taught a lesson.

At eight-thirty, Susan decided to make a move. 'I'm goin'
now, Caz. Get a pen and I'll give you me number so we
can go out one night.'

Elated by the invitation, Caz popped the number in
her purse. 'Bye, mate. I'll call you in the week,' she said.

Susan smiled as she walked towards The Bancroft. Caz
might be a moose, but with Tracey up the duff, at least she
was someone to go out with. Kev often went out with the
lads and she was sick of sitting at home. Apart from Tracey,
she had no other mates and beggars couldn't be choosers.

As Susan reached the pub she could hear Tears for
Fears singing 'Everybody Wants to Rule the World'. She
took a deep breath and made her grand entrance. Searching
for Kev, she spotted him in deep conversation with his
mum. She bowled over. 'Get us a drink then, Kev. Where's
Tracey and Dal? Are they here yet?'

Realising that she was half pissed, Kevin shot her a
look. 'They're sitting over by the toilets. Go and sit with
'em, and I'll be over in a minute.'

Annoyed by his cold attitude, Susan ignored him and
went up to the bar. 'I'll have a pint of cider. Actually,
make that two.'

Seething, she downed one on the spot and marched
towards the table with the other. Kev was such a bastard
to her at times. She'd gone to all that effort to make herself
look glamorous and he hadn't even said she looked nice.

'What's up with yous two?' she asked, as she sat herself
down with Tracey and Darren.

Darren rubbed his girlfriend's arm. 'Tracey don't feel
too good. The smoke's making her feel sick.'

Susan let out a deep sigh. This was going to be the
night from hell, sitting with these two. They had faces
like smacked arses, the pair of 'em.

As Wham's, 'Wake Me Up Before You Go Go' hit the

speakers, Susan knocked back her drink and stood up, 'Come on 'ave a dance with me, Trace. It might make yer feel better.'

Tracey shook her head. 'You get up, Suze. Me and Darren'll sit 'ere and watch yer.'

Susan shrugged her shoulders and headed towards the bar. Sod dancing, she needed another drink, and pronto. Eyes darting around the pub, she searched for Kevin. Where the bloody hell was he? He'd barely even said hello to her, and he hadn't come over like he said he would.

As the evening wore on, Susan became angrier and more inebriated. 'I ain't lettin' him treat me like this. I'm goin' to find the cunt,' she told Tracey.

Eyes glazed, she scanned the pub and spotted him. He was standing by the door chatting up two pretty girls. With the familiar pain in her heart that he regularly inflicted upon her, she staggered towards him.

'Whaddya think you're doin'? I'm yer girlfriend and you ain't even spoken to me all night. You've got time to talk to these slappers, though, ain't yer?'

Kevin felt himself blush. Susan was shit-faced and he wasn't about to introduce her as his girlfriend. Talk about showing him up in front of his family. Grabbing Susan by the arm, he dragged her over to where Tracey and Darren were sitting. 'Do me a favour, Dal. When you go home, take this cunt with yer. She's too pissed to walk, so you'll 'ave to put her in a cab. She's a fuckin' embarrassment, she is.'

Realising she'd gone too far, Susan started to grovel. 'I'm sorry, Kev. I was upset because you hadn't sat with me all night. I promise I'll behave meself, I won't show you up, honest.'

Kevin pushed her away. 'You can sit 'ere until Tracey

and Dal leave. I'm goin' up Benjy's with me uncle Paul and his mates and you ain't invited. Now just sit still and shut yer trap, and if yer make a cunt out of me any more tonight, I'm gonna rip yer fuckin' head off. Got it?'

Not wanting him to see her upset, Susan ran into the toilets. He had a habit of making her cry and she was sure that he got a kick out of it.

'I love Kev, he's such a scream. Is he comin' up Benjy's with us?' said a voice from inside the cubicle.

As Susan looked in the mirror, she saw the colour drain from her face.

'Yeah. He told us to leave before him. I think he's gotta get rid of that awful bird first, and he'll meet us up there. Christ knows who she was, but didn't she look a sight in those white leggings?'

Blinded by panic, Susan ran from the pub. She knew the voices in the toilet belonged to the birds Kev had been chatting up. She'd been too busy grovelling to see them go in there, but they were definitely talking about her. She was the only one at the party wearing white leggings. Holding onto the wall, she took deep breaths. She was going to be sick.

Having seen her bolt past, Tracey followed her out. 'Are you OK, Suze?' she asked, rubbing her back.

Susan stuck her fingers down her throat and brought up as much of the cider as she could. She couldn't think straight and she needed to sober herself up.

'Let me go and get Darren and we'll take you home,' Tracey said sympathetically.

Susan shook her head. 'I need to walk, get some fresh air. I'll be fine, honest.'

'I'll ring you tomorrow,' Tracey shouted, as she walked back inside.

As Susan stood on the corner of her estate, she was

livid. She'd always had a feeling that Kevin played around, but how could he be so blatant about it? Unable to face going home, Susan lit up a fag and headed back to The Duchess. Fat Caz would be finishing her shift soon and she desperately needed someone to talk to. She couldn't get the two girls' faces out of her mind. Both were blonde and pretty, but the one with the long hair was stunning – in fact, she looked like Madonna. And as for their conversation, they might as well have stuck a knife in her: 'He's gotta get rid of that awful bird first. I love my Kev, he's such a scream. Christ knows who she was, but didn't she look a sight in those white leggings?' they'd said.

And they were laughing, the fucking slags. Well, she'd give 'em something to laugh about. She was Kev's bird and if four years was about to go up the swanny, she was determined to go out with a bang.

'Suze, you're back! Wasn't the party any good?' Caz beamed, as she approached the bar.

Susan forced a smile. 'Get us a cider and when you're finished, me and you are goin' up Benjy's.'

Unaware that his girlfriend had entered the club, Kevin was enjoying himself immensely. His uncle Paul and his pals had already left. Drunk as skunks, they'd headed off to the nearest curry house and left him with the girls.

'Want another drink, Joanne?'

'Yes, please, I'll have a white wine. Don't bother getting Nat one. She's on the dancefloor with that bloke and she's got two on the table.'

Susan turned her back and hid in the corner as he approached the bar. She was frothing at the mouth and if that slag left the club with Kev, she'd fucking kill her.

'Are you all right, Suze?' a concerned Caz asked.

'No, I ain't. Do I fuckin' look all right? Just let me know when he moves away from the bar.'

As the DJ slowed down the tempo, Joanne was desperately trying to spy on her friend Natalie.

'Thanks, Kev,' she said, as he handed her her drink.

Kev laughed. 'Who yer lookin' at, yer nosy cow?'

Joanne giggled. 'Nat split up with her ex over a year ago and she's never copped off with anyone since. I'm sure she's snogging that bloke. Come and have a dance with me, Kev, so I can spy on her.'

Kevin grabbed her arm. 'Come on then, you pest.'

Susan was horrified as she watched them take to the dancefloor. As Kev put his arms around the Madonna lookalike's waist, her stomach could take no more.

'Hide my drink inside your jacket – we're leaving,' she told Fat Caz.

Filled with anger, Susan marched down the street. 'I can't go home. I'm gonna wait in the alley and confront him as he walks past.'

Caz hated trouble of any kind. Her night out had been awful, and she was absolutely starving.

'Suze, there's a takeaway over the road. I'm gonna get meself a kebab and chips. Do you want anything?'

Susan shook her head. 'Fat cunt,' she muttered as Caz waddled across the road.

As people began to trickle out of the club, Susan kept her eyes peeled. Finally, she spotted him walking towards her. He was alone with the slag, the cheating bastard. Picking up her now empty glass off the ground, she held it firmly in her right hand. She could hear their voices, they were getting closer.

As she leaped from the shadows, she took the pair of them by surprise. 'That's my fella, yer fuckin' slag,' she screamed, as she cracked the glass over the girl's head.

As Joanne crashed to the floor, Kevin laid into Susan. 'Get off of her. You're a psycho, Susan, a fuckin' psycho,' he screamed, as he punched her to the ground.

A group of young lads ran over. 'Oi, leave her alone.'

'Stay out of it,' Kevin yelled as he kicked Susan in the face.

'Whatever's happened?' Natalie screamed, as she saw the blood running down Joanne's face.

'The kebab shop have called the Old Bill,' someone shouted.

Petrified of getting arrested, Kevin grabbed Natalie's arm. 'Look after Jo for me. I'm gonna have to make a run for it, I've got no choice. Say nothin' to the Old Bill, I'll explain later.'

Lifting Susan up, Kevin half dragged her down a side street. 'Try and run, Suze, try and run,' he screamed.

Across the road, Fat Caz stood frozen to the spot. She'd been too busy stuffing her face to see what had started the fight, but she'd seen Kevin beat up Susan.

As Kevin dragged Susan out of sight, Caz knew she had to do more to help her. Remembering that Susan had earlier given her her phone number, Caz searched through her purse and ran back into the shop.

'Give me the phone, quick. He's abducted her and I need to ring her mum.'

Aware of the sirens getting louder, Kevin helped Susan through the back gardens and into a different street. He was fully aware of what led where, as he'd often been involved in bouts of burglary in this neck of the woods. He tried the handle of someone's shed and was relieved to find it open.

'Get in there, Suze, go on, lie down. We're safe here.'

As Kevin handed her a fag, he lit the match and was appalled by what he had done to her face. She was caked in blood and looked like she'd gone ten rounds with Henry Cooper. Susan looked worse than she actually felt and was more bothered about Kevin's infidelity than her injuries.

'Why, Kev? Why did yer cheat on me? Surely the sex ain't as good with her as it is with me? How long yer been seeing her?'

As Kevin held her close, he began to laugh. 'You stupid girl, Suze. I haven't cheated on yer. Joanne, the girl you glassed, is my fuckin' cousin.'

Susan felt nothing but relief as she clung to him. 'I'm so sorry, Kev. Please don't finish with me. I'll never tell anyone that it was you that beat me up. I love you, Kev, I really do. You won't leave me, will yer?'

As Kevin put his tongue in her mouth, all he could taste was her blood. Pulling away, he smiled at her. 'I'm not sure if we're meant to be after this, Suze. I'm gonna need time to think about it, girl.'

Desperate for him to love her again, Susan unzipped his trousers, unleashed his cock, and took him gently into her bruised mouth.

TEN

Tommy Hutton lay sprawled across his bunk with a big smile plastered across his face. Tonight was his last night being detained at Her Majesty's pleasure. From tomorrow he was a free man, his debt to society well and truly paid up.

Unable to sleep, Tommy thought over his ten years inside. When he'd first arrived at Feltham, he was no more than a tearful, frightened kid. Meeting Freddie had been the turning point. Wise beyond his years, his pal had filled his head with knowledge and had taught him how to fulfil his potential. From the day he'd done over Leroy Wright in the shower room, he'd never looked back. He and Freddie had run Feltham from that moment onwards. Neither of them were bullies, but they were the leaders. They never picked on the run-of-the-mill lads and they even looked out for some of the simpletons, or shy kids who couldn't come to terms with the system. The only lads they gave it to were the ones who deserved it. The freaks, the nonces and the pure fucking evil were the ones that always got their comeuppance. Then there were the new boys, the chancers, the ones that arrived thinking they were the next Godfather. Within days they'd be given a good hiding. Most of them got the message there and then, but there were an odd few who tried to get their revenge. They were the ones that suffered the worst, their lives made a misery for the rest of their stay.

Both Tommy and Freddie had a good relationship with the screws. They treated them with a certain amount of respect and received a cushy life and plenty of blind eyes in return. The screws liked a quiet life and Tommy and Freddie helped them keep the other lads in order. The situation suited everybody, especially Finchy, who developed a soft spot for the two tough cast London boys. On many occasions he spoke up for them to the guv'nor and got them out of sticky situations. He was a good bloke, old Finchy, and Tommy would always hold fond memories of him.

At the time, leaving Feltham had seemed awful. As soon as Tommy turned seventeen, he'd been moved to a proper prison. Saying goodbye to Finchy and the lads had been extremely emotional. He'd made many friends there and they even had a little leaving party for him. Saying goodbye to Freddie was probably the hardest thing he'd ever had to do. He'd been desperate not to make a tit of himself by crying, but he hadn't been able to stop the tears rolling down his cheeks. As luck would have it, Freddie had got all emotional as well.

Tommy had begged the guv'nor at the borstal to have a word with the authorities for him. He was desperate to go to a London prison, so he could see more of his family and friends.

He'd been told at one point that he was going to Kent somewhere and he'd been well poxed off about that. His family were still piss poor and, unless he was in London, he'd rarely get a visit.

Freddie had been on Finchy's case to have a word with the guv'nors about getting him into Pentonville. Freddie had an uncle in there, who was aware of Tommy, and would look out for him. Whether it was strings being pulled or just pure bloody luck, that was where he ended up. The journey there was horrendous. It was a really hot day and the van he was shoved into was like a Swedish sauna. The traffic was awful and by the time he reached his destination, Tommy was sweating like a pig.

He was filled with apprehension as he entered his new home. The screws were horrible to him and spoke to him like a piece of shit. He was strip-searched, given his orders and taken to his cell. Walking through the prison, Tommy kept his head down. He'd already come face to face with a couple of the inmates and they were fucking frightening. Great big skinhead types with faces full of hatred and scars. Feltham was full of little boys, the Ville was a different ball game.

Tommy was given a single cell and spent his first night wide awake. By morning he'd made his decision. If anyone gave him any grief, he was gonna clump 'em. Freddie had always told him that this was the best way to deal with matters and he would take his friend's advice. Big, small, black or white – anyone got in his way, he'd give 'em a dig.

Within two days of his arrival, Tommy had grief. He'd seen some fat, tattooed prick giving him daggers at breakfast. Ignoring him, he finished his grub and walked away. At dinner the fat prick went one better. As Tommy walked past him with his food, the geezer stuck out a leg. With a tray in his hand, Tommy had no way of keeping his balance, and went flying. As laughter rang around the hall, Tommy was determined not to look a mug. He stood up, straightened his shoulders, and brushed himself down. Grabbing the fat prick's tray, he smashed it over his head with such force that it took his breath away. Tommy smiled when he noticed his tormentor was not only bleeding, but also had shepherd's pie dripping off his big fat head.

'Leave me alone, you fat cunt,' he said, as he walked away to cheers.

The tattooed one was about to respond, but was stopped in his tracks by the screws' intervention.

'You're dead, kid,' he screamed, as he was escorted from the room.

'Yeah, right,' Tommy replied.

Tommy was punished for his part in the fracas and spent a week in solitary. He didn't care – he was just glad that he'd stood his ground. In a one-to-one fight the geezer would have slaughtered him. The fat cunt was probably treble his weight and could have knocked him out with one punch. Being on his own gave Tommy plenty of time to think. He was a tall lad and, while in Feltham, had shot up to six foot. What he needed now was to fill out a bit, as he was far too skinny to be taken seriously. In Feltham they'd had plenty of exercise, but there were no facilities to lift weights and build up muscle. He knew there was a gym in the Ville and his plan was to use it as much as possible to change his physique.

Within hours of returning to his own wing, Tommy had received many pats on the back. A lot of the older lags had seen a younger version of themselves in him, and Tommy soon learned that the geezer whose head he'd smashed in was a very unpopular inmate called Mark Abrahams, who was nearing the end of a long-term sentence for supplying heroin.

At dinner that evening, Abrahams appeared with a scar across his bonce. Apparently, he'd had a dozen stitches, which had been removed earlier that day. He sat over the other side of the room and not once did he glance across.

Tommy was surprised by this. He'd expected some sort of backlash, even if it was just a threat.

He found out later that evening why Abrahams would be giving him no more trouble. There were two magic words in the prison system. 'Bobby Adams' was an inside form of 'abracadabra' to warn off potential troublemakers, and nobody was brave enough to get on his wrong side.

Freddie had never told Tommy much about his uncle. He'd said he was heavy stuff, a proper chap, and was doing a stretch for robbing a bank, but little else. Tommy was surprised when he first came face to face with Bobby Adams. He'd built a picture in his mind of what Freddie's uncle might look like, but the geezer that stood in front of him was the total opposite of what he'd imagined.

Tall, grey and distinguished, he stood out from every lag in the place. He had an air of authority about him and looked more like a bank manager than someone who robbed the bastard things.

'Bobby Adams, son. Freddie's written to me and told me all about you.'

Tommy shook his thickset hand and smiled. Apart from introducing himself properly, he was at a loss as to what to say.

Bobby noticed his hesitation and took over the conversation.

'You'll have no more trouble from Abrahams. The geezer's a wrong 'un, he's a smack dealer, scum of the earth. He's been warned off you now and he'll be dealt with in due course. Most of these cunts in here are wrong 'uns. About ten per cent are proper, the rest you wouldn't piss on if they were on fire. I'll show you the ropes, teach you who you can trust and who you can't. I've put the word about that you're a pal of my nephew's.

You'll be treated with respect from now on, and you'll have no more grief from the lags or screws.'

Feeling more at ease, Tommy opened up, and spoke fondly about Freddie and their time at Feltham. 'We were the daddies in there, Bobby. I swear we ran the fucking joint.'

Bobby laughed at the kid's stories. He was a young 'un but, like his nephew, the boy had a spark about him. Bobby could spot good potential a mile off. Streetwise kids like Freddie and Tommy could learn more by doing a bit of bird than these clever cunts who opted for university.

Bobby stood up. 'I better go now, kid. Oh, and by the way, well done for cracking Abrahams one. You've earned yourself a lot of respect with some of these lads already.'

Bobby kept an eye on Tommy from that day onwards. At forty-eight, he was too old to spend a great deal of time in Tommy's company, but they often had a good old chat, mainly about Freddie and life in East London. Tommy was hoping that when his pal reached prison age, he'd join him in the Ville. Unfortunately, it wasn't to be, as Freddie got taken to the Scrubs.

Tommy was twenty-one when Bobby Adams was released. Ten years he'd originally got, and he'd served seven and a half.

'Look after yourself, kid. Keep in touch with Freddie and as soon as you get out, we'll meet up.'

Tommy thanked him and said his goodbyes. After years of effort in the gym, his body had now changed completely. Gone was the skinny boy; in his place was a young man full of muscle, and he had no worries about being able to handle himself without Bobby's protection.

Freddie was released a year after his uncle and was doing quite well. He'd visited Tommy on many occasions and was full of stories about the places he frequented and the birds he'd shagged. He'd been working for his cousin, who had a building firm. Freddie loved his freedom, but despised the job.

'I'm just waiting for you to get out, ain't I? As soon as you've done yer bird we'll set ourselves up in business, like we always said we would.'

Tommy lived for Freddie's visits. The thought of doing something with his life, alongside his best mate, was the thing that kept him going through the last part of his sentence.

Tibbsy, Dave Taylor and Benno had popped up to see him a couple of times. He'd been really looking forward to catching up with his old pals, but after two visits from them, he'd been filled with disappointment. None of them worked or had fuck all interesting to talk about. They all still lived with their parents and spent their lives dossing about, drinking and puffing. Six months ago, they'd last come to visit and Tommy hadn't written or sent them a visiting order since. He'd moved up a notch from them now, and he weren't gonna waste his time mixing with tadpoles when there were big fish to swim with.

The only other visitors he had were his family. His mum had aged a lot during his time. She'd had a hard life and the older she got, the more she seemed to be weighed down by it all. His nan was the same old Ethel and even her arthritis hadn't stopped her going out on the thieve. Susan had never visited him once, but he wasn't bothered, as they'd never liked one another. Out of politeness, he always asked after her, but the replies only confirmed that she was still a nasty piece of work. James was a different story. He was a good lad and very intelligent, which pleased Tommy immensely. He didn't want his kid brother to end up with nothing, like the majority of his family. He wanted him to make something of himself and free himself from a life of poverty.

Apart from his uncle Kenny, none of his family had made anything of themselves. The worst culprit was his father, who was a drunken, useless arsehole. In all the years Tommy had been inside, he'd only received one letter from his old man. That had been about a year ago, when he'd asked if he could come up and see him. Tommy had written back, telling him to fuck off. He could just imagine his father staggering in for a visit – that would have done the reputation he'd built for himself a fucking lot of good.

As dawn broke, Tommy sat up. All night he'd lain awake going over his time, and now he couldn't wait to forget it. Prison might be a learning curve, but it was also a bastard. He'd seen it sap the life out of the strongest of men, but luckily for him, he'd survived the system. He'd had help, made friends, while others hadn't been so lucky.

Hearing the wake-up call, Tommy smiled. In the next couple of hours he'd be a free man. Some people might have thought he had wasted ten years of his life, but not him. He'd listened, learned and remembered. As his cell door opened, Tommy took his last trip to the shower room.

Bumping into Brainless Brian, one of the thicker but nicer screws, Tommy shook his hand.

'Good luck on the outside, son.'

Tommy smiled at him. 'I'll let you into a little secret, shall I, Bri? It's not luck that's needed to survive the outside world. All yer need is knowledge.'

'What do you mean? Education and stuff?'

Looking Brian in the eyes, Tommy winked at him. 'You'll have to work that one out for yourself.'

'I dunno where you're coming from. Explain what you mean, Tom.'

Roaring with laughter, Tommy walked away.

ELEVEN

Maureen put the finishing touches to the icing, stood back and proudly admired her cake. 'Welcome Home Tommy' stood out boldly in bright blue writing. She had spent weeks organising her son's homecoming and couldn't believe the day had finally arrived. Thanks to her friends and neighbours, who had all kindly chipped in, she had a fantastic selection of food. Turkey, roast ham, beef – for once they had the works.

Ethel had been her usual light-fingered self and had turned up every day that week with a bag full of goodies. The drink was plentiful, thanks to a fifty-pound gift from uncle Kenny. Knowing Maureen would refuse the gift, he'd sent the money via Ethel. He couldn't make the party, because he and Wendy were on holiday, but he'd sent a lovely card saying that he'd be thinking of them and hoped they had a great night. At the bottom he'd put a PS telling Tommy to ring him and he'd sort him out with a job.

The money Maureen was grateful for, yet it was her son's job offer that made her day. She'd often worried about how Tommy would survive after prison. Would anyone want to employ a lad of twenty-five who had spent over a third of his life in clink?

Over the years the ill feeling surrounding Terry Smith's

murder had died down. His mum, Mary, had left the area yonks ago. Unable to deal with her son's death, she'd moved her family away to make a fresh start. A lot of stories about Terry had surfaced since Mary's departure. He'd had an awful reputation and had made many people's lives a misery. Maureen listened, but never commented on the tittle-tattle. Whatever the lad was, he didn't deserve his bad end at the hands of her son. Nevertheless, she still took some comfort from being told over and over again that her Tommy wasn't to blame.

'Terry Smith was bad rubbish, he was due his come-uppance and he got it,' people said more than once. Even Mary's old pals from the bingo hall were now Maureen's friends again. In fact, most of the stories had come from them. Living in Bethnal Green, they'd known young Terry better than most.

Taking a break from her food preparation, Maureen made herself a well-earned brew. Tommy's surprise party had been all her idea. While inside, he'd changed so much that, surprisingly, she'd become proud of him. He was no longer the obnoxious, skinny little runt he'd once been. He was now six foot tall, handsome, polite and built like a brick shithouse.

While he'd been in Feltham, she'd rarely had a chance to visit him. Kenny had taken her a few times, but the train journey was far too expensive for her to afford on a regular basis. She'd seen much more of him when he'd been moved to the Ville. For the first four years, she'd gone up there once a week. Sometimes she'd go alone, but most of the time either James or Ethel would accompany her.

Her trips to see him had dwindled to once a month after his mate Freddie had been released. Tommy was only allowed one visit a week and, although hurt at first,

Maureen fully understood why he'd rather have his mate's company than that of his boring old mum.

Sipping her tea, Maureen smiled. That Freddie Adams was such a nice lad, and he'd certainly had a positive effect on her Tommy.

'You watch me, Mum. When I get out of here I'm gonna make something of meself. I might even go into business with Freddie. We've often spoken about it,' Tommy told her.

Maureen savoured her last drop of tea. Her Tommy wouldn't have to worry about work now his uncle Kenny had offered him a job. He'd be so pleased, she could hardly wait to tell him. Maybe Kenny would take Freddie on as well. Tommy would love that, he'd be chuffed to bits.

Maureen glanced at the clock. It was ten to twelve and Tommy would definitely be out by now. He wasn't coming straight home. Freddie was picking him up and they were going for a beer first. She wasn't disappointed, she totally understood. Boys would be boys, after all. He'd rung her only yesterday and promised faithfully he'd be home by seven.

'I've got a surprise for yer, so don'tcha let me down, and make sure you bring Freddie with yer,' she told him.

Maureen stood up. She had so much food to prepare that she needed to get her arse in gear. Ethel and the girls were coming this afternoon to give her a hand. Susan had agreed to help as well, although Maureen doubted this, as she was too busy chasing after that no-good bastard who had knocked seven bells out of her. Hours she'd sat up casualty with her. As luck would have it, nothing was broken, but her face was cut to pieces and she was bruised from head to toe.

'Don't you ever have anything to do with him again,'

she threatened Susan. 'In fact, I'm takin' you round to his mother's. I'm gonna show her what he's fuckin' done to yer.'

'Please, Mum, no,' Susan screamed. 'It wasn't his fault, I'm the one to blame. Please, Mum, just leave it.'

Maureen shook her head in disbelief. 'If I find out you're still seeing him, I'll domp yer me fuckin' self. And if I ever come face to face with him, God help me.'

Maureen looked at the clock and tutted. The unreliable little mare said she'd be home over an hour ago. Still, she didn't particularly need any help. She wanted it all done by the time anyone else arrived, so her family and friends could just sit, have a drink and enjoy themselves. They'd all done more than enough already, bless 'em. Maureen sang along happily to the radio as she put the sausage rolls in the oven. Tonight would be her best party ever.

'Excuse me, son. That's twice I've asked you now. Do you have this in my size or don't you?'

The pomposity of the man's voice snapped James out of his daydream. 'I am so sorry, sir. I will look for you immediately.'

James checked through the shirts in the storeroom and, unfortunately for him, came back with the wrong size.

'I've never known such incompetence. Get me the manager, at once.'

Hearing the commotion, James's employer, Mr Cohen, rushed to the rescue. 'You take a break now, James. Make us some coffee and I'll deal with Mr Branson.'

Harold Cohen immediately located the appropriate shirt and handed it to his customer. Full of schmooze, he then talked him into being measured up for one of his most expensive suits. Smiling as he counted the money, he thanked Mr Branson and shook his hand.

Seeing James hover awkwardly in the doorway of the storeroom, Harold waved him over. James walked towards him. He hoped he wasn't about to receive a telling-off. 'I'm so sorry. I was about to . . .' James was stopped mid-sentence by Harold's loud laughter.

'You worry too much, James, my boy. Mr Branson is a *schmuck*, an absolute *putz*.'

James smiled. He might not have been Jewish, but he'd worked for Harold long enough to have picked up a bit of Yiddish. He was no expert, but he knew both *schmuck* and *putz* equalled cock in his own language.

Still laughing, Harold put an arm around his shoulder. 'Now James, I want you to do me a favour. You've been in a bloody trance all day and I'm not telling you off, because I fully understand why. You're excited about seeing your brother and you can't wait to get home to that pretty little girlfriend of yours.'

'She's not my girlfriend,' James insisted.

Harold smiled. James might only be his employee, but he knew him better than he knew himself. Maria, the pretty *shikseh*, had stolen the boy's heart and Harold could sense it a mile off.

'You get yourself home, James. It's quiet now, I'll finish up here. You have a great night, enjoy yourself and you can tell me all about it next weekend. Oh, and by the way, there's an extra tenner in your wages. Get yourself a cab home and treat the beautiful Maria to something nice.'

Waving away James's gratitude, Harold smiled as he dashed out of the shop. It was thirty-two years since his father had retired and he'd inherited the tailor's shop situated on the Bethnal Green end of Roman Road. In all those years, hand on heart, he could honestly say that James was the best employee he'd ever had. He'd worked for him for well over a year now, and although still at school, he did every Saturday and most of the holidays for him.

Harold had lost count of the number of boys he'd employed over the years. At a guess, he'd say it was anything between forty and fifty. The one thing he was sure of was that none of them could hold a torch to young James. Intelligent, polite, eager to learn and a wonderful salesman, James had everything Harold had been looking for.

At sixty-two years old, he was almost ready for retirement. A father to three gorgeous daughters, James was like the son he'd never had, and would make a wonderful successor. He hadn't said anything to the boy yet. He believed in doing things properly and he would talk to the lad's mum before he spoke to him. Deciding to pay her a visit in the next few weeks, Harold happily greeted his next customer.

Head bobbing up and down like a yo-yo, Susan Hutton had a discreet glance at her watch. Seeing it was 5 p.m., she leaped off the bed.

'Kev, I've gotta go. I'm hours late already and me mum'll go apeshit if I ain't home when our Tommy arrives. Not only that, I promised to help her with the food and stuff.'

Kevin shot her a look of pure hatred. 'Don't fuck me about, Suze. I'm ready to come, just finish me off, will yer?'

Knowing that Kevin had not yet forgiven her for the Joanne episode, Susan lay back on the bed. She owed him big time for smoothing everything over. Eight stitches, his cousin had ended up with but, thanks to Kev, hadn't prosecuted. 'I was attacked from behind, and didn't see a thing,' she told the police.

Willing Kev to hurry up, Susan was relieved when he finally shot his load. Swallowing just as he liked her to, she jumped off the bed for the second time.

'Look Kev, I've really gotta go now. I'm sorry you can't come to the party, but yer know how it is. I'll see you tomorrow, yeah?'

Smiling, Kevin handed her her jacket. Susan's mother hated him; he was banned from the house, and if he wasn't allowed to attend the party, he was fucked if Susan was going to enjoy it. Obviously, Maureen had no idea that her wonderful daughter had smashed a pint glass over his cousin's bonce. As usual, he was the bad bastard, the villain of the piece.

'Forget about tomorrow – you're dumped,' he said nastily.

Susan was well annoyed. Twenty minutes she'd just spent sucking his sweaty cock and now he had the cheek to dump her! She'd spent weeks grovelling and pandering to his every whim and she was sick to the back teeth of it.

'What have I done this time?'

Kevin shrugged. 'Nothing really, I just fancy a break.'

Sick of his stupid mind games, Susan walked towards the door. Usually, she cried and begged forgiveness, but not any more. She'd had enough and was physically and mentally exhausted by their fucked-up relationship.

'Go fuck yourself!' she screamed as she slammed the front door.

Kevin was astonished by her little outburst. Years he'd been with her, fucking years, and the odd clump here and there had always stopped her from answering back in the past. It certainly wasn't a case of love at first sight. He hadn't even liked her, and had only copped off with her because he couldn't pull anyone else.

Kevin would never forget that first night with Susan for as long as he lived. His unusually high sex drive was a standing joke to his mates, but Kevin didn't find it funny, as he'd lost so many birds over it. For some reason, once a night seemed to suit the female sex, whereas he needed it at least half a dozen.

Fucking Susan was the biggest surprise of Kev's life. Not only was she a nymph, but she was a dirty whore as well. Eight hours that first session had lasted and it would have carried on longer had his knob not been so sore. From that night onwards, he hadn't been able to keep away from her. Tracey and Darren had fallen head over heels and him and Susan were kind of thrown together due to their love of filthy, non-stop sex.

He'd tried many times during the course of their relationship to get her out of his head. He'd knocked her about, finished with her, shagged loads of other birds, but nothing seemed to erase her from his mind. Even now, four years later, he was sure he didn't love her. It was hard to explain, but she was like a magnet that kept drawing him towards her.

Flopping back onto his bed, Kev stared at the ceiling and thought about life in general. Tracey and Darren had made a nice comfortable nest for themselves. They had a council flat in Bow and a baby on the way. Kevin envied his friend. He loved kids and couldn't wait to have his own. Maybe it was time for him to stop playing games, accept his fate and settle down with Susan.

He smiled as he got dressed. He'd spend one last night with a prostitute and from tomorrow he was all hers.

TWELVE

Ethel burst out laughing when she clapped eyes on the banner. 'Welcome Home Tommy' stood out in enormous green letters and Maureen was asking for help to hang it at the front of the house.

Maureen glared at her. 'What's so funny?'

Crying with laughter, Ethel could barely speak. 'How the fuck have yer got the front to put that up? The whole street knows he was done for murder. Fuck me, that new family that have just moved in opposite will think he's a war hero coming back late from the Falklands.'

Maureen bit her tongue. She loved her mother-in-law more than words could say, but the older she got, the more outspoken she became. She looked at her mates.

'What do you think?'

Brenda paused before answering. 'Look, maybe Ethel's right. Even though Terry Smith was a wrong 'un and what happened is long forgotten, he's still got cousins round here, ain't he?'

Sandra agreed. 'I heard his brother Wayne's moved back to the area. Dunno how true it is, but Rosie's husband saw him in the Duchess last Saturday night.'

As James entered the room, he caught the back end

of the conversation. Seeing his mum's deflated expression, he put an arm around her.

'We don't want no trouble, Mum. Give us it here and I'll put it up in the front room. I don't think Tommy would like it outside, anyway. Yer know what he's like and if Freddie's coming with him, he might feel a bit of a prick.'

Smiling at her son, Maureen handed him the banner.

Tommy Hutton thanked the little blonde bird, rolled onto his back and took off the johnny. Embarrassed that he'd shot his seed in less than two minutes, he apologised and explained why.

'Do you want to do it again?' the girl asked.

He shook his head. 'Thanks all the same, but I've gotta be somewhere.'

Tommy took his time as he got dressed. He didn't want Freddie taking the piss out of him for being so quick, but on reaching the reception, he was surprised to see that Freddie had vanished. The Spanish-looking bird who had taken the money from them smiled at him.

'Your friend, he is in room number six with Chantelle.'

Tommy sat on a chair and shut his eyes. With no sleep the previous night and a gut full of food and booze, he already felt knackered. Being set free had been the best feeling in the world. Walking through the gates after serving ten years of his fifteen was an incredibly special moment, one that only a long-termer would ever understand.

The first person he saw as the fresh air hit him was Freddie, sitting on the bonnet of a white Escort van. They'd literally run towards one another as if they were long-lost lovers, before jumping up and down like nutters.

'Right, what do yer wanna do?' Freddie asked, waving a big wad of dough at him.

100

Tommy was overawed and didn't know what to suggest. 'I'm gagging for a beer. After that, you choose,' he said.

Freddie pulled up at the first boozer they saw. They knocked back a few lagers and spoke endlessly about their time in Feltham. Tommy was the first to change the subject.

'So, how's the building game going? With the wad you're waving about, yer must be doing all right.'

Freddie did a wanker sign. 'It's shit, mate. Me cousin's a prick, he don't pay that well and I knock me bollocks off for next to nothing. I've only stuck with it while I've been waiting for you to get out – that, and to keep me mother off me case.'

Tommy nodded sympathetically.

'What's this?' he asked, as Freddie threw a brown envelope on his lap.

Freddie grinned, 'It's a little present from me uncle Bobby. I think there's two hundred quid in there. Bobby's in Spain for a couple of weeks, but he gave it to me before he went. He said you were to 'ave a good time with it.'

Downing his beer, Tommy smiled. 'If I'm meant to be enjoying meself, best we get out of this shit-hole then.'

The next stop was a restaurant. The dinners in prison had been fucking awful and Tommy was gagging for a good old-fashioned roast.

As he wiped the gravy off his plate with the remainder of his Yorkshire pudding, Tommy swallowed the last piece and let out a satisfied groan.

'Freddie, that was fuckin' handsome. Honestly, it was better than a bunk up.'

Freddie winked at him. 'Funny you should say that, 'cause I've got one of them lined up for yer later. Yer can tell me after you've shot yer load if yer still prefer the roast beef.'

Tommy laughed. He'd had no bird in tow when he'd gone away, but having been sexually active from the age of thirteen, he wasn't going to say no to the offer.

After leaving the restaurant, Freddie wanted to take Tommy to a boozer in East Ham to meet all his pals.

'Not today, Fred. I need to get me head together, and me mum's expecting me home at seven. I can't not turn up, and if we go down your manor, I probably won't get back in time.'

Freddie fully understood where his mate was coming from. He'd been there himself. Walking out of prison was one thing, getting your head together and the family stuff was another. Instead, they'd done a little pub crawl. Nowhere special, just random pubs they liked the look of.

The knocking shop had been the last stop-off. Freddie wasn't one for brasses, but through his friends, he was aware of the big house in Forest Gate that served up sex.

The journey through London was an eye-opener to Tommy. Everything had changed so much. People's clothes, their cars, even their hairstyles were weird.

'I can't believe how much difference ten years can make,' he said repeatedly.

Freddie agreed. He'd felt exactly the same way himself.

'Oi, wake up, you cunt.'

The sound of Freddie's voice jolted Tommy back to reality. He'd obviously dozed off at some point. 'What's the time?'

Freddie laughed at his groggy expression. 'Ten to six. We've got time for a couple more beers and then I'll take you home to mummy.'

James studied himself in front of the full-length mirror. With only his underpants on, he flexed his muscles.

Disappointed that the press-ups he'd been doing hadn't made the slightest bit of difference, he quickly got dressed.

Tall, dark and reasonably good looking, James only had two major hang-ups. One was his baby face, which stopped girls from taking him seriously. 'Aw, he's so cute. Ain't he sweet?' they'd say, pinching his cheeks.

The second was his skinny physique. He'd tried eating more, exercising and all sorts, but nothing seemed to work. His mum insisted he was worrying over nothing. 'You'll fill out in time, son. Look at our Tommy, he was the same build as you at your age and look at the size of him now.'

James just hoped she was right. Grabbing the bunch of flowers he'd bought with Harold's money, he ran down the stairs and dashed next door.

'I've got you a present,' he said, as the door opened.

Maria hugged him. 'You're such a sweetie, James,' she said, then, grabbing his hand, she dragged him upstairs. 'I'm running late, I haven't even had a bath yet. Go and sit in my bedroom and put some music on while I get meself ready. I won't be long, I promise.'

James raised his eyebrows. Maria always took ages to get ready and her 'won't be longs' were legendary. Sifting through her dodgy record collection, which included Wham!, Madonna and even Jason and Kylie, he opted for Duran Duran. Maria was into all that girly shit and he often ribbed her about it. He was more of a fan of early eighties' music. The Jam, Madness and the Specials were his favourites and he'd bought every album they'd ever made. Already sick of Simon Le Bon's voice, James turned down the volume and flopped on the bed. Hearing Maria singing away to herself in the bathroom, he smiled.

Ever since that first meeting across the garden fence when they were five years old, they'd been inseparable.

Even then, Maria had been music mad. She loved to sing and dance and was obsessed with Donny Osmond. Being so young, he'd never taken an interest in pop records, but within a week of meeting her, he'd learned all the words to 'Puppy Love'. That particular song would always hold a special place in his heart, because she'd kissed him once while it was playing. He'd only been six at the time, but remembered it as if it was yesterday.

As the years ticked by and they became teenagers, their closeness stayed intact. A lot of their school friends used to think they were dating, but that was never the case. A couple of kisses at infancy was the furthest they'd ever got to any romance. James had always secretly hoped that one day they'd be together, but as the years ticked on, he'd learned to accept their friendship for what it was.

Maria had been extremely beautiful at the age of five, and at fifteen she was now an absolute stunner. James wasn't stupid – he knew she was out of his league.

She always had different boyfriends. At first, he'd found that hard to deal with, but as they came and went in quick succession, he'd learned to live with it. Her taste in boys was about as good as her taste in music. The types she went for were years older than herself, and they were always wide boys. Over and over again he told her that she was going out with the wrong sort. She always listened to him, even agreed, but then a couple of weeks later, she'd pick a geezer who was a clone of the one before.

She wasn't easy. She told James absolutely everything and he believed her when she said she was still a virgin. She had no reason to lie to him. 'I'm saving myself for Mr Right,' she told him.

She was forever crying on his shoulder and James often wondered if her refusal to have sex was the reason her relationships never lasted. The blokes she went out with were sometimes in their twenties and they probably wanted much more from Maria than she was willing to give.

Although he would always carry a torch for her, James had recently gotten on with his own life. He'd had a one-night stand with a girl he'd met at a party and he'd since slept with another. Neither experience made him feel particularly good about himself. With both girls it had been over in minutes and felt totally meaningless.

Maria ribbed him endlessly about his escapades. 'I can't believe my best friend's turned into the local stud. What was it like, James? Now don't lie to me, I wanna know every little detail.'

James could hardly tell her it was overrated and he hadn't enjoyed it. She'd think he was some kind of weirdo if he said that. Instead, he came out with a load of cock and bull about how great it was and how the girls had begged to see him again.

'And are you gonna see them again?' she asked, giggling.

'Nah, I can't be bothered. I only wanted a bit of fun, you know how it is.'

He felt a right bastard lying to her. He wished he could have told her the truth, that he'd only lost his virginity because of her. At least now, when she lost hers, he wouldn't be so heartbroken about it. Annoyed with himself for thinking such stupid thoughts, James turned his attention to Tommy. He could hardly believe that, after all these years, tonight he and his brother would be sharing the same bedroom again.

Although they'd kept up their relationship over the years with letters and visits, it wasn't the same as actually living together. As kids, even with a ten-year age gap between them, they'd been incredibly close, and James just hoped they could carry on where they'd left off. Tommy had promised him that once he got out, he'd take him to a gym and teach him all he knew about weight training. He also said that they'd go boozing together and go out on the pull. James hoped his brother would stick to his promises. He liked his life, but at times it got boring. His mates were a laugh, but they weren't that into pubs or clubs. At his mother's insistence, he was forever revising, and the only other thing he did was work in Harold's shop. James loved his job, but it hardly filled his days with excitement.

'Well, how do I look?'

Any more thoughts of Tommy or his future were shot to pieces as Maria entered the room. In her slinky black dress, with a silver headband, shoes and bag, she looked amazing.

'You look beautiful, Maria.'

Twirling around, Maria grabbed him by the hand. 'Come on then, stud. Let's go and party.'

THIRTEEN

The journey through the East End was a complete shock to Tommy. Graffiti was everywhere, pubs had closed down, shops had disappeared and the area had become a shadow of its former self. There'd been a few foreigners moving into the East End before he'd gone away, but in Tommy's eyes it had now been overrun by all and sundry and he barely recognised the area where he'd been born and bred.

'Fuckin' hell,' he said repeatedly.

In prison, he'd been told that Thatcher being Prime Minister was a good thing. Looking at his beloved East End, he now wasn't so sure.

Freddie smiled at him sympathetically. He knew what emotions his pal was going through. He'd felt exactly the same about Manor Park when he first came out. Deciding to cheer Tommy up a bit, he tried to make a joke of things.

'If yer think it's bad round here, you wanna take a look around my area. Every time I step out the door, I feel like I'm standing in the middle of Bangladesh.'

Tommy laughed. 'Pull over at that pub on the corner, I need a drink to get over the shock.'

*   *   *

Brenda was the first to spot Tommy arrive. 'Quick Maur, he's here.'

Desperate to be the first to greet her son, Maureen rushed to the front door. While her friends marvelled about how much he'd changed, how handsome he was and what a physique he now had, Maureen proudly threw her arms around her son's strapping shoulders.

Lifting her up, Tommy swung her around and smothered her with kisses. He then moved onto his nan and sister before he turned his attentions to James.

'My little bruvver ain't so little now. Jesus, I can't believe how fucking tall you are,' he said, as he hugged him tightly.

James felt embarrassed. He could see Maria smiling at him and he felt like a stick insect standing next to Tommy. 'Tommy, this is Maria. Maria, this is Tommy.'

Tommy smiled politely. On every visit and in every letter, James had spoken endlessly about Maria and within seconds of meeting her, he could fully understand why. She was extremely pretty and thoroughly enchanting. His brother always denied having designs on her, but Tommy could see through his feelings as clearly as he could see through a pane of glass. James had the hots for his so-called best friend and if Tommy had been a few years younger, he would definitely have felt the same way himself.

By nine o'clock the party was in full swing. Tommy had done the rounds, spoken politely to all the neighbours and friends, and introduced Freddie to everybody. He was now having a quiet ten minutes with his pal in the kitchen. 'I can't believe me mum invited Tibbsy and his loser fuckin' mates.'

Freddie handed him another lager. 'She probably thought she was doing you a favour inviting all your old mates.'

Tommy raised his eyebrows. 'Apart from Tibbsy, Benno and Dave Taylor, I don't know the rest of 'em from Adam.'

'Who's the two macaroons with 'em?'

Tommy shrugged his shoulders. 'How the fuck should I know? The two-faced bastards used to hate the blacks when I knocked about with 'em.'

Freddie smiled. 'Just enjoy yourself, Tom. I know they're pricks, but just suffer 'em. I mean, after tonight you ain't gotta see 'em no more, have you?'

Tommy lit a fag. 'Too fucking right I ain't.'

James hated the music chosen by Maria's friends, so had taken charge of record-player duties. He'd always fancied himself as a bit of a DJ, and tonight was his chance to shine. After he'd played The Jam's, 'Town Called Malice' for the fourth time, Maria walked over to him.

'Put something on that me and the girls can dance to,' she begged him.

James smiled. He'd fly to the moon if she asked him, let alone change the record. He found a party album and started laughing as they all went mental, singing 'Oops Upside Your Head'.

'Come on, James,' Maria screamed, trying to entice him onto the floor.

James shook his head and went in search of his brother. 'The Rowing Song' was girly shit. A few months ago he may have joined in with them, but not now. He needed to start behaving in a more manly way – maybe then he'd be taken more seriously.

Ethel was in fucking agony as she rocked from side to side. With her bad hip, even sitting on the floor was painful enough and to make matters worse, her knickers had disappeared up her crotch and were cutting her in half. With no decorum whatsoever, she shoved her hand up her dress.

Maureen tapped her on the shoulder. 'Mum, for fuck's sake. You're right at the front of the boat, you can't do that. All them young boys are looking at yer and laughing.'

'Let 'em look, the fuckin' perverts. Me drawers are up me crack. What am I meant to do?'

Embarrassed that Tibbsy and co. were in absolute hysterics, Maureen was relieved when 'The Rowing Song' came to an end.

Instead of feeling heartbroken, as she usually did when Kevin dumped her, Susan was having a whale of a time. Usually she took to her bed for days, but tonight was different. She danced, drank loads of alcohol, was happy and had pulled a sexy bloke.

Royston Ellis was a mate of Tibbsy's. Half English and half Jamaican, he had pure white teeth, chocolate-brown eyes and an extremely fit body. Seeing Susan stagger back towards him, he smiled. Usually, she wouldn't have been his type. He liked quiet, petite girls, whereas Susan was plump and common. With his judgement clouded by booze, Royston started chatting her up again. His girlfriend, Mandy, had chucked him recently. They'd dated for three years and he'd given her everything, until she'd dumped him like a bag of old rubbish.

Ignoring his pals taking the piss, Royston led Susan out into the back garden. Then, making sure they were far enough away from the house, he shoved her up against the gate and kissed her passionately. As his hand ventured up her skirt and inside her knickers, Susan let out a groan. There was rarely any foreplay with Kevin, he was more of a wham, bam, thank you ma'am and couldn't care less about her needs. Knowing he'd hit all the right spots, Royston began whispering sweet nothings in her ear.

'You're so beautiful, Susan. I really like you,' he lied, as he placed her hand on his rock-hard penis.

Overcome by lust, Susan led him over the fence and into next door's garden. Rita had a greenhouse and they could do it behind that without being seen.

After sucking him off, Susan took her knickers off and gasped as he entered her. His cock felt enormous inside her, far bigger than Kevin's or any of the other lads she'd been with. Royston came within minutes and quickly zipped himself up. Feeling guilty as he watched the girl he had no intention of seeing again searching around for her knickers, he decided to be a gentleman.

'Do you want me to make you come?' he asked politely.

Susan nodded. Kevin hadn't bothered to make her come since she'd glassed his cousin.

James was putting the black bags full of empty bottles out in the garden when he saw a dishevelled-looking Susan and her new friend walking towards him.

'Excuse me,' he said to Royston, as he dragged her to one side. 'I just need a minute with me sister, mate.'

Grateful for an excuse to make his escape, Royston nodded and left them to it.

'Bloody hell, Susan. Look at the state of you – you're covered in mud and leaves. Where yer been with that black geezer? Mum and Tommy'll go fucking mad if you've been up to no good with him.'

Remembering just how racist her family was, Susan thought up a lie. 'If yer must know, I've just shared a joint with him. As for me clothes, I fell over. It's so dark out here and I've had far too much to drink.'

Relieved by her answer, James tried to brush her down. 'Can you imagine Nan if yer came home with a black boyfriend?'

'Oh fuck off, James. I've been with Kevin for years. I'm hardly gonna run off with Stepney's answer to Michael Jackson, am I?'

111

James shook his head. Smiling at his naivety, Susan walked away.

With most of the youngsters having now gone home, Maureen decided to take charge of the music herself. Ethel and the girls adored the old wartime songs and it was time for a dose of Mrs Mills!

Ethel leaped off the sofa as soon as she heard the first bash of the old girl's piano.

> On Mother Kelly's doorstep,
> Down Paradise Row,
> I'd sit along o' Nelly,
> She'd sit along o' Joe.'

Maureen smiled as all her mates suddenly burst into song.

> She's got a hole in her frock,
> Hole in her shoe,
> Hole in her sock,
> Where her toe peeps through,
> But Nelly was the smartest down our alley.

Laughing, Maureen led them into verse two.

Aware that Maria was flirting with Freddie, James turned his back on her and opened another beer. Tommy put a comforting arm around his shoulder. 'You've got no worries there, Jimmy boy. Freddie likes the older woman, if yer know what I mean.'

James shrugged his shoulders. 'We're only friends, Tom. What Maria does and who she does it with is her own business. I ain't bovvered if she likes Freddie, it's not that. Problem is, she's only fifteen, and when all these older geezers leave her heartbroken, it's left to muggins 'ere to pick up the pieces every time.'

Wondering if he'd got his brother's feelings for Maria all wrong, Tommy smiled at him. 'I can't believe how grown up yer sound. I know you're a nice boy and that, but yer can't spend all your time sorting out Maria's problems, yer need to get on with your own life.'

James agreed. He knew deep down that his brother was right and he probably should have done it years ago. He and Maria were far too close for comfort. For her, it didn't matter, he was just 'good old James', her perfect mate and shoulder to cry on. For him it was different: he was in love with her and, unless he distanced himself, he'd never be able to move on with his life.

He nudged Tommy. 'My mates are so boring. Can't I knock about with you from now on? I'd love us to go out boozing together. We can go on the pull, we'll knock 'em dead.'

Ruffling his hair as though he was five years old all over again, Tommy smiled. 'I'll take you anywhere yer wanna go, Jimmy boy.'

Susan was always happier watching her family enjoy themselves than joining in with them. It had been a funny old day and she needed time to think about it. Splitting up with Kevin, Tommy coming home, meeting Royston, experiencing a fantastic orgasm. The more the drink wore off, the more Susan began to feel guilty. Royston was long gone, thank God. The sex may have been mind-blowing, but she had no intention of ever setting eyes on him again. Kevin might have his faults, but he was the only man she'd ever loved. He'd go fucking mad if he ever found out what she'd been up to. He was ever so racist and would finish with her for good if he knew that she'd been with a black man. Susan just hoped that Royston kept to his word. He'd sworn to her that he'd never tell his pals or anyone else what had happened.

'It's our little secret. No one else ever needs to know,' he whispered as he left.

Racked by feelings of regret, Susan toddled off to bed.

Maria was the next to call it a night. Freddie and Tommy were too drunk and busy enjoying themselves to talk to her any longer and James had ignored her for the majority of the evening.

Dragging her best friend away from his brother, Maria questioned him. 'Have I done something to upset you, James? You've been acting really weird and you've barely spoken to me all night.'

James shook his head. 'Nah, you ain't done nothing. Fucking hell, Maria, I ain't seen me brother properly for ten years. Give us a break, will yer? We're not joined at the hip, you know.'

Maria grabbed his hand and stared into his eyes. 'What's got into you, James? I wasn't chatting up Freddie, if that's what you think.'

Pulling his hand away, James led her outside and spoke sternly to her. 'Get over yourself, Maria. I couldn't give a fuck if you were chatting up Freddie or anyone else, for that matter. I know we're best mates, but my life don't always fucking revolve around you.'

Maria was mystified. 'Don't talk to me like a piece of shit, James. I'd never talk to you like that. Why are you acting like a prick?'

'Me, act like a prick! Well, you'd know all about that, wouldn't yer Maria? I mean, every week you're dating a different prick, ain't yer?'

Maria started to cry. 'What's it got to do with you who I date?'

'Nothing, but next time you get your heart broken, go and bore some other mug,' James shouted.

Seeing her walk away looking so upset tugged at James's heartstrings. Part of him wanted to chase after her and apologise, but the other part of him wanted to take the advice his brother had been giving him all evening.

'What you've gotta remember, Jimmy boy, is all women love a bastard. You can't be too nice to 'em. If you are, they just shit on yer. Treat 'em mean and keep 'em keen. Trust me, it's the only way.'

All the other geezers Maria went for treated her like shit, so maybe that's where he'd gone wrong over the years. Pleased that he'd finally shown some backbone, James took a deep breath, put on a big smile and returned to the party.

FOURTEEN

When she dragged herself out of bed at eight o'clock the following morning, Maureen made the fatal mistake of glancing into the mirror. 'Fucking hell,' she muttered, quickly moving away before she cracked the bastard thing.

Amazed that for the first time in her life she'd woken up fully clothed, Maureen smiled to herself. Christ knows what time she'd gone to bed, but it had been a fantastic bloody party. Her last memory was of singing 'Maybe it's because I'm a Londoner'. After that it was a complete blank. Throwing her housecoat on, she trudged downstairs. She had some tidying up to do, that was for sure.

'Morning, Mrs Hutton.'

The strange voice was enough to make Maureen jump out of her skin.

Seeing her look of shock, Freddie smiled. 'Yer told me I could sleep on the sofa. Sit yourself down and I'll make you a cup of tea.'

Not one to suffer from hangovers, Freddie was only too happy to help his mate's mum tidy up, and within an hour the place was virtually spick and span. Maureen had washed up, vacced and polished and Freddie, bless his cottons, had sorted the rest.

116

'There are a couple of burn holes in the carpet and the curtain rail's fallen down. I've tried to put it back up, but it won't hold. I think it might need drilling or something,' he told her apologetically.

Grateful, Maureen dragged him into the kitchen. 'Sit yourself down there. I'm gonna make yer a nice big fry-up and when you've wolfed it, you can go and wake that lazy son of mine.'

When the smell of fried bacon hit his nostrils, James sat bolt upright. As the night before came back to him, he had a heavy feeling in his heart. Maybe he should go and apologise to Maria, say sorry for the way he'd spoken to her. Deciding not to do anything until he'd asked Tommy's advice, he gently prodded him. 'Should I go and see Maria? Make sure she's OK?'

Tommy lifted the quilt from over his head. 'Don't mug yourself off, play hard to get. Can you fuck off now, James? I've got the hangover from hell and I need some sleep.'

James smiled. He couldn't give a shit that his brother was grumpy. Sharing the same room again after all these years was fantastic, the best feeling ever. As for Maria, he'd play it by ear. Maybe he'd give her time to sweat first, and then he'd apologise.

Unable to deal with the watery sensation in her mouth, Susan ran to the toilet and shoved her fingers down her throat. Flushing away the bile, she washed her hands and face in cold water. Staring into the mirror, she felt nothing but hatred for herself. 'I am never, ever, ever drinking again,' she told herself.

Last night Royston had seemed like a sex god; this morning he revolted her. Remembering that she'd let him lick her fanny, she heaved. The contents of her stomach were finally released by the recollection of the blow-job she'd given him.

After already being woken by his brother prodding him and his sister spewing her guts up, Tommy was almost ready to face the world by the time Freddie gently shook him. 'I'm gagging for a bath. Give us half an hour and I'll be with yer,' he told his pal.

Once Ethel had arrived, Maureen handed her a fry-up and sat down opposite James. 'What are your plans today love? Are yer seeing Maria, or are you working?'

James smiled. It was the school holidays and he was determined to enjoy himself. 'I'm gonna spend some time with Tommy. Harold's given me a few days off, so I'm not due back in the shop until next Saturday.'

Maureen sipped her tea, 'What's Maria doing, love?'

James shrugged, 'Don't know, don't really care.'

Surprised by her son's reply, Maureen guessed they'd had a little tiff. Maybe Maria had met another new boyfriend and James wasn't happy about it.

Feeling ill and incredibly ashamed of herself, Susan went back to bed. Three times she'd managed to doze off, only to find that every time she opened her eyes, it wasn't a bad dream – it had actually happened.

Hearing the first tap on the window, she thought nothing of it. Hearing the second, she removed the quilt from over her head. By the third tap she was convinced someone was out there and was chucking something at her window. Praying it wasn't Royston, she nervously took a peep through the curtains. When she spotted Kevin waving furiously at her, Susan's initial reaction was one of dread. If her mum saw him, there'd be ructions. Her mother had never told anyone, bar her nan, that Kevin had beaten her up.

'If anyone asks, you had a fight with a girl. If the boys find out the truth, there'll be murders, and I won't have them gettin' arrested.'

Convinced she'd been sussed, Susan was relieved to see Kevin looking happy. Wondering if it was just a ploy to get her outside, she opened the window. 'What's the matter?' she asked cautiously.

'Nothing, I just wanna talk to yer.'

Full of suspicion, Susan stayed where she was. 'What about?'

Kevin smiled. 'About us, you div. Come out here, will yer? I can't fucking talk to yer while you're standing up there.'

Susan shook her head. 'I'll only come down if yer tell me what you wanna talk about.'

Pulling out the cheap bunch of flowers he'd hidden behind the wall, Kevin waved them at her. 'Our future, all right. Getting a flat, trying for a baby. Fucking hell, Susan, what do yer want me to do, beg?'

Convinced he was now telling the truth, Susan urged him to wait around the corner.

'I'll meet you outside Old Man Tatler's. Give us ten minutes or so.'

Kevin smiled as he walked away. The prostitute from last night had sucked his knob till it was red raw, but he wasn't going back for seconds. From today onwards, there'd be no more tarts. He was determined to stay faithful to Susan, and make a proper go of it.

'Bye, mum, I'm going round Tracey's.'

'Oi! Come in 'ere and say hello to—'

Maureen's sentence was cut short by the slamming of the front door.

'Ignorant little fucker,' Ethel said, as she slurped her tea.

With James and Freddie upstairs getting washed, Maureen cleared the rest of the breakfast things and sat down opposite Tommy.

'I've got some good news for you, son. I meant to tell you before, but things have been a bit hectic.'

Tommy smiled. 'What's that then, Mum?'

Proud as a peacock, Maureen held his hand. 'Your uncle Kenny's offered you a job. He wants yer to work down one of his scrap yards and he said you're to ring him as soon as he comes back off his holiday next week.'

Annoyed that his life had been organised without his say-so, Tommy stood up. 'I'm not sure that working on the scrap is what I wanna do, Mum.'

Amazed by his lack of gratitude, Maureen tried to make him see sense. 'Whaddya mean, it's not what yer wanna do? Look how successful yer uncle Kenny is. Don't yer wanna be like him?'

Not wanting to upset her, Tommy chose his words carefully. 'Look, Mum, leave it with me and I'll have a think about it. I've barely been out twenty-four hours and I need time to sort me head out first.'

Pursing her lips, Maureen was determined to have the final say. 'It's up to you boy, but remember, beggars can't be choosers. I know you've done your bird, but on paper you're still a murderer, Tom. Employers are hardly likely to be knocking on the door to offer you a job, are they, son?'

Tommy was saved from answering her by the reappearance of James and Freddie. Pissed off by his mother's comments, he cracked open three beers and led his mate and brother into the living room. He glanced at the time, and saw it was eleven o'clock. The pubs would be open in an hour and he couldn't wait to get out of the fucking house.

'Ungrateful little bastard,' Maureen moaned to Ethel. Ethel shrugged her shoulders. She'd had a gut feeling that Tommy wasn't about to turn into the hard-working, reformed young man that his mother wanted him to be.

Kevin sat on the park bench and smiled at Susan. Handing her a can of cider, he spoke honestly. 'Look, I know we're not Romeo and Juliet, but I'm willing to make this work, if you are. I know we've had our ups and downs, what with you glassin' Joanne and me beatin' you up, but let's forget all that. Look how happy Darren and Tracey are with their nice flat and baby on the way. If we stop playing silly games, that could be us, Suze.'

Momentarily lost for words, Susan smiled at him. She'd waited years for Kev to commit and now it was finally happening, she could scarcely believe her luck. Feeling there had to be a catch, she found her voice. 'Of course I wanna be with yer. I'd love us to have kids and move in together, but the only thing that puzzles me is why now, Kev? It was only yesterday that you binned me, so why the sudden change of heart?'

Kevin shrugged his shoulders. 'I dunno really. I suppose you walking out on me made me think about things. I know I'm a bastard to you at times, but I don't wanna lose yer.'

Susan held her head high. For the first time ever it was Kevin doing the grovelling and she was loving every minute of it. 'I'll give it another go on one condition.'

'What?'

Susan looked deep into his eyes. 'That you stop wearing rubbers and we try for a baby straight away.'

Kevin paused before answering, 'OK. But if we're gonna have kids, you've gotta sort things out with your mum. I can't be the father of her grandkids and still be barred from the house, can I?'

Susan nodded. Her mum would come round in time, surely.

Kevin put an arm around her shoulder. 'I think we should get our arses up the council on Monday morning. With all these foreigners moving in round 'ere, we need to move fast. We can stick our name down and as soon as you get up the duff, we'll probably get a flat straight-away.'

Susan agreed. 'Lizzie Manning got one within a month of getting pregnant,' she said excitedly.

Squeezing her hand, Kevin kissed her on the cheek. 'So, how was the party?'

'Oh, nothing special.'

Desperate to change the subject, Susan grabbed the flowers. 'So what are these all about? My nan always says that if a man buys yer flowers for no reason, it's to cover up his guilt.'

Feeling himself go all hot, Kevin opened another can. 'What yer trying to say, Suze?'

Enjoying the wind-up, Susan nudged him. 'Yer didn't get hold of another bird last night, did yer?'

Feeling himself blush, Kevin gulped at his drink, 'Don't be so stupid, course I never.'

Remembering his dad's words that when guilty, attack was the best form of defence, Kevin fronted it out. 'If anyone copped off last night it was you. I sat in watching telly all night, you was the one at a party and you haven't said much about it. If that ain't a sign of guilt, then I dunno what is.'

Sensing her embarrassment, Kevin nudged her. 'Go on, you can tell me. Was he as good looking as me? I bet his cock weren't as big as mine.'

Susan couldn't look him in the eye. 'Stop being crude, Kevin, and don't be so bloody childish. If we're gonna make things work, you have to stop playing silly mind games.'

Kevin handed her another drink. 'Sorry, I was only joking.'

Grabbing the cider, Susan downed it in one.

Maureen had popped up to the shop for some stain remover, and was now taking a fast walk home. She hadn't been able to find her key, so had left the door ajar. As she walked into the hallway, she was greeted by hysterical laughter, but it wasn't until she heard her name and Kenny's that she realised they were the butt of the joke.

'I know Mum means well, but fuck me, I ain't working for no uncle Kenny. He's a nice geezer, but such a boring cunt. I'd hang meself if I had to spend half me life in his company.'

James chuckled. 'What yer gonna do then?'

'Me and Freddie are gonna set ourselves up in business, ain't we, mate?'

Freddie nodded and winked at James. 'We've got plenty of ideas, but it's all top secret at the moment. I promise you one thing, though, we'll earn ourselves a lot of dough.'

Tommy laughed. 'When you're old enough Jimmy boy, you can come and work with us. Fuck all them boring jobs that Mum wants yer to do. Knocking your bollocks off for some other cunt is never gonna get you anywhere.'

Furious, Maureen stomped into the living room. 'You can do what you like with your life, Tommy, but leave James out of it. He's an intelligent boy with a bright future and don't you dare try and lead him astray.'

Tommy stood up. 'Calm down, Mum. I was only mucking about with him.'

Maureen shook her head. 'I've been listening to yer for the last five minutes, and all you've done is take the piss out of me and poor Kenny. That man's been fucking good to you. Many a time he gave up his weekends to ferry us about, so you wouldn't be without a visit. And as for the job he's offered yer, I bet he don't even need anyone. Probably just found something for yer out the goodness of his heart.'

Although he felt a bit guilty, Tommy wasn't about to apologise. How dare she talk to him like a child and make him look a mug in front of Freddie. 'I don't need all this shit, Mum. I ain't fuckin' arguing with yer any more, I'm off down the pub.'

Nodding to Freddie and James to follow him, he stormed towards the front door.

Maureen chased after him. 'You can go exactly where you like, Tommy Hutton, but he's not going with yer. Filling his head with a load of shit and prison talk, I'm not having it. James, get your arse back 'ere now.'

At his brother's insistence, James kept on walking. 'Come on, bruv, we're going for a beer. You're nearly sixteen, for fuck's sake, you need to get a grip on life. Nan, Mum, Susan, Maria, you're surrounded by women. Don't let 'em rule your life. You need to be tougher, start sticking up for yerself.'

Torn between the devil and the deep blue sea, James didn't know what to do. His mum was still calling him and even though he hated disobeying her, he had to stand his ground for once. If he didn't, he'd look a right dick in front of his brother and his mate. Anyway, Tommy was right. He needed to be more of a man if he was gonna turn his life around.

'See yer later, Mum. I won't be late,' he shouted.

While Maureen debated whether to chase James up

124

the road and drag him back by force, Ethel stepped in. 'Just leave it, Maur. Don't make a show of yourself, sort it out later, eh?'

Enraged, Maureen slammed the door. She'd convinced herself that Tommy was a changed lad – how silly was she? He might have looked as though butter wouldn't melt while he was in prison, but in reality he hadn't altered one iota.

Handing her a brew, Ethel tried to calm her down. She wasn't as naive as her daughter-in-law and had seen this coming all along. 'You can't make him work for Kenny if he don't want to, Maur. He's twenty-five years old, a grown man and you've gotta let him make his own choices in life. Chances are, he'll fuck up again, but that's his lookout. You've guided him as far as you can, love, the rest is up to him.'

Maureen sat down and put her head in her hands. Tommy was obviously a lost cause, just like his father, but James needed protecting. Loveable and intelligent, he'd been the light of her life since the day he was born, and she wasn't about to watch him be led up the garden path. Trouble was, he was still wet behind the ears, an easy target, and she didn't want him knocking about with Tommy.

Ethel rubbed her arm. 'Come on, love, don't get all upset.'

Fiercely wiping her tears away, Maureen stood up.

'I'll tell you something now, Mum, and I really fuckin' mean it. One whiff of Tommy leading James astray and I'm kickin' his arse out. That boy's got his exams coming up and a bright future to look forward to. I won't allow him to turn out like his brother. May God be my judge, it ain't gonna happen.'

FIFTEEN

Susan studied the instructions and put them back in the box. Kevin had gone to sign on and she'd best wait for him to come home before she did the actual test. It was three months since they'd first started trying for a baby and now, she'd properly missed a period.

Lying down on her boyfriend's bed, Susan smiled. Ever since that day on the park bench, when they'd decided to give it a proper go, Kevin had been a different person. He'd cut down on his puffing, stopped going out with his mates and even when they did argue, he never knocked her about any more. He still refused to go to work, but had promised her faithfully that when they had a flat and kids on the way, he'd look for a job.

Susan sighed. He was a good 'un, her Kev, and to think she'd nearly fucked things up. The Royston episode was now a distant memory, one she'd thankfully blanked out. She had not seen him since the party, and was sure he'd never opened his mouth. She often bumped into Tibbsy, Benno and Dave Taylor and they'd definitely have taken the piss out of her if they'd had an inkling about what had gone on.

Patting her stomach, Susan wondered if Kev's baby was already inside her. She'd been a bundle of nerves during the first month they'd tried to conceive. Soon after insisting that they try straightaway, she realised that she couldn't remember if Royston had worn a johnny or not. Paranoid, she'd tried to back-pedal.

'Why don't we wait a few weeks, Kev. We need to make sure we're getting on all right and things are gonna work out between us before we bring a poor little baby into our lives.'

Kevin was having none of it. He was desperate for a council flat and gagging for a son.

'Don't fuck me about, Susan. You was the one that wanted kids straightaway, and now I've got used to the idea, yer wanna change all our plans.'

Unable to get out of the hole she'd dug for herself, Susan gave in. She managed to feign a few migraines, stomach aches, that type of stuff, but spent the rest of the month praying for her period to arrive. As luck would have it, God was on her side. A spot of blood had never made Susan dance around the room before, but that month it did. Relieved of her burden, Susan had leaped on Kevin a few days later and they'd been at it like rabbits ever since.

Hearing the door slam, Susan sat up and hid the test behind her back. It was Kev's birthday tomorrow and, fingers crossed, she'd be able to give him the best present ever.

Maureen opened the oven door and put the tray of potatoes in. The rib of beef her Tommy had bought her looked bleeding handsome, and she could hardly wait to dish it up. 'Do you want another cup of tea, Mum?'

Ethel shook her head. 'I can't sit here no longer, Maur. An hour ago she was meant to be here, I'm gonna have to go and look for her.'

127

Maureen felt sorry for her mother-in-law as she trudged off down the road. Her best mate, Gladys, was losing her marbles and her forgetfulness and erratic behaviour were breaking Ethel's heart. It had been Maureen's idea to invite her round for Sunday dinner. Poor old Gladys had no family near by and looked a shadow of her once proud and sprightly self.

Maureen glanced at the clock. The boys had gone to the gym and then onto the pub, but they'd promised to be home by three. Maureen smiled as she thought of her clan. They were no angels but, over the last few months, all three of them seemed to have got their act together. James was in the middle of his exams and revising hard, like a good boy. His future was already mapped out for him. Harold had been to see her recently while James was at school. He wanted her son to work full time for him until he reached eighteen, then James would take over the shop and Harold would retire.

Maureen was gobsmacked. 'He'll never be able to raise the cash. We've got no money and he won't get a loan at his age – he hasn't even got a bank account.'

Harold had waved away her worries. 'The boy's the nearest thing I've ever had to a son, Maureen. I trust him implicitly and all he has to do is pay me off weekly.'

Overjoyed, Maureen had repeatedly thanked him, hugged him and then sat impatiently waiting for her son to come home from school. Her baby, all grown up and running his own business: she could barely believe their luck.

Unfortunately for her, James was less than enthusiastic.

'It's very kind of Harold, Mum, but I'm really not sure. Sometimes it can be so bloody boring and I dunno if I wanna make a full-time career out of it.'

Furious, Maureen had laid the law down to him. 'It's the

offer of a lifetime, James. Other boys would kill to be in your shoes. Just think, at eighteen you'll have your own business, you can take driving lessons, buy a car. You can even go abroad for yer holidays. I'm sure Harold would cover for yer, if yer wanted to go away for a week.'

Knowing her son had been car mad all his life, Maureen prayed that her speech would make him see sense. Fortunately, it did. He accepted Harold's job offer and was due to start full-time work in the shop as soon as his exams had finished. Grinning stupidly, as she always did when she pictured James running his own business, Maureen turned her thoughts towards Tommy.

When he had returned home after their argument, armed with a bouquet and an apology, she'd taken it with a pinch of salt.

'It's all an act, he won't fucking change,' Ethel told her.

At first Maureen had thought her mother-in-law was right, but she'd since had second thoughts. Her son had been a pleasure to be around lately. He'd even got himself a job working on a building site for Freddie's cousin.

'I'm ever so proud of him, he's really starting to turn his life around. He's paid for our new three-piece suite and he's always bringing me home little presents,' she told everyone that would listen.

Ethel thought differently and regularly took the piss out of her. 'You're so fucking gullible. I bet the little bastard ain't even working on no building site.'

Maureen was annoyed. 'Don't be so stupid. Of course he's bloody well working. He leaves the house early every morning and comes home knackered and covered in shit every evening.'

Ethel shook her head. 'I bet you any money you like, he changes out of them clothes as soon as he leaves the house. My mate Lil saw him last week, said he looked a million dollars in a dark grey suit. Glad saw him as well, standing in the betting shop done up to the nines.'

Hearing the names Lil and Glad put Maureen's mind at rest. Both were going senile and were blind as bats. 'I know you're usually right, Mum, but you're wrong this time. He's my flesh and blood and I can sense when he's lying.'

Shrugging her shoulders, Ethel said no more. She knew full well that the little bastard was up to no good, but like all mothers, herself included, Maureen was destined to learn the hard way.

Thinking of her mother-in-law, Maureen smiled. She was too proud to admit it, but for once Ethel had been proved wrong. Last Friday, Tommy had been made foreman at his new job and he'd even given her half of his £200 bonus.

'I'm not taking it, son. It's your bonus, you've worked hard for that. You keep it.'

'Mum, I don't want it. Look, you stuck by me through thick and thin when I was in nick. Now I'm doing well at work, I wanna show yer how grateful I am. If yer don't take it I'll be really annoyed, so please don't insult me.'

With tears in her eyes, Maureen put it in her purse. 'Well? Ain't it time you admitted you were wrong, Mum?' she gloated to Ethel.

Ethel kept schtum. She was too busy trying to fathom out what robbery the lying little bastard had been involved in.

With James and Tommy both sorted with work, Maureen was determined to help Susan find something. Since leaving school seven years ago, her daughter had grafted for the grand total of two weeks. Packing sardines into tins was her only career move to date and she'd been

130

living off the state ever since. But recently Maureen had been flabbergasted by the change in her daughter's behaviour. Gone was the stroppy, nasty little cow and in her place was a nice, polite young lady.

'Have you got a new boyfriend?' she'd asked her a few weeks back.

'Actually, Mum, I wanted to talk to you about that.'

Sitting opposite her, Susan held her hand for the first time since infancy.

'It's Kevin, Mum. We're trying for a baby and we're gonna move in together. He's a changed man, honest.'

Maureen shrugged her shoulders. What was the point of reminding her that he'd knocked her senseless? She wouldn't listen, she never did.

Surprised that her mum hadn't gone into one, Susan carried on talking. 'I swear, Mum, he really has changed. He's gonna get a job to provide for me and the baby, and he'll be a brilliant dad.'

Maureen felt like laughing as she heard the words 'Kevin', 'job' and 'provide' in the same sentence. Her daughter's boyfriend was the laziest bastard ever to walk this planet. Looking at Susan's happy face, she decided not to broach the job conversation. If Susan had decided to try for kids, getting a job was totally pointless anyway. Maureen smiled at her sympathetically. She was a lost cause, bless her, it ran in the family. All the women, including her and Ethel, had ended up with bastards.

'If you're happy, Susan and it's what you want, then I really hope it works out for yer. I'll always worry about him knocking yer about, though.'

'Honestly, he ain't laid a finger on me for ages. I swear on my life, he really has changed. Give him another chance, Mum. If he's gonna be the father of your first grandchild, you've gotta bury the hatchet at some point.

131

Please, Mum, let him back in the house. Even if you can't forgive him, just do it for my sake.'

Not wanting to burst her daughter's bubble, Maureen reluctantly agreed. Unable to forget the six hours she'd sat up in casualty after he'd knocked the shit out of Susan, Maureen barely spoke to Kevin at first. She'd only mellowed the last week or so. He'd tried so hard to be polite and Susan was so bloody happy with him that Maureen eventually called a truce.

'I'll give yer one final chance to prove yourself, Kev, but if you ever lay a finger on my daughter again, I will personally fuckin' kill you.'

Kevin was delighted to finally be forgiven. 'I love Susan and I swear I'll never hurt her again. We're happy now and when she has my kids, I'm gonna be the best dad and boyfriend in the world.'

Enjoying her daydream, Maureen was jolted back to reality by the sound of the front door opening.

'We're early and we're starving, Mum.'

Handing her sons a plate of bread and dripping, she shooed them out from under her feet.

'You'll have to wait for yer dinner, boys. Glad's gone missing again, Nanny's out looking for her and Susan and Kevin ain't arrived yet.'

Tommy smiled. 'As we've missed out on valuable drinking time for no reason, I'm gonna pop up the offie. Do yer fancy a Guinness, Mum?'

'Yes please, love, and James, can you knock next door and speak to Maria while dinner's cooking? Twice today and once yesterday that poor girl's knocked here for yer. I know yer like spending all your time with Tommy now, but you've been mates with her for years and yer can't just dump her like a bag of old rags.'

Feeling incredibly guilty about the way he'd been

treating Maria, James took a slow walk up the path. He'd apologised weeks ago for the argument they'd had, but had avoided her like the plague ever since.

When Maria opened the door, his stomach did its usual somersault. 'All right, mate? I've just got in and Mum said you knocked earlier.'

Elated to see him, Maria's face lit up.

'I wondered if you fancied coming to the pictures with me tonight? I've checked out the films and there's a good horror on. Please say yes, James. We haven't been out together for ages and I know you always enjoy making me jump.'

Wanting to say yes more than anything in the world, James shook his head. 'I can't tonight Maria, I've already made arrangements,' he lied.

Determined not to melt at the sight of her beautiful face, he stared at the ground. It had been two months now since he'd first admitted his true feelings for her to Tommy, and ever since then his brother had forced him on a mission.

'You want her, James, just do as I say and you'll get her. Stage one, stay away from her. Obviously you're gonna see her, 'cause she lives next door, but don't be alone with her at all.'

James nodded. 'What am I gonna say when she knocks and wants to do stuff?'

'You say you're busy, you div.'

Tommy smiled at his brother's naivety. Ten years he'd been locked up, and he could still teach James a thing or two about women. 'Stage two, you start coming down the gym with me, you get that bastard hair cut and you let me take you shopping to sort your wardrobe out. The shell suits need binning, James, you look a knob in 'em.'

133

Not one to take offence, James laughed. 'What's stage three?'

'Stage three's the happy ending. She can't fail to notice how good you look and she'll be missing you dreadfully. Within weeks, she'll be begging to see yer. Obviously you say no, yer need her to realise she was in love with you all along and actually admit it to yer before you give in.'

James had never believed that the plan would work, but when Maria grabbed his hand, he began to think that he would make it to stage three after all.

'Please tell me what's the matter, James. I know you've been spending time with your brother, but I know it's not just that. Have I done something to upset you? Tell me if I have, because I don't know what I've done wrong.'

Eyes glued to the ground, James shook his head. 'You ain't done nothing to upset me, Maria.'

'Please come to the pictures with me. We need to talk, sort things out. There must be something wrong.'

Pulling his hand away, James spoke abruptly. 'I can't, Maria, I've already told yer I'm busy.'

As he went to walk away, he was aware that she was crying. Praying for her to declare her undying love, his heart was in his mouth when she called him back. 'What do you want, Maria?' he asked hopefully.

'I just want you to know that I hate your guts, James Hutton, and I never, ever want to see you again.'

Furious, Maria slammed the door in his face. Shocked by her words, James trudged away, heartbroken.

134

SIXTEEN

'What's the time?' Freddie asked impatiently.

Ignoring the butterflies leaping about in his stomach, Tommy glanced at his watch.

'Half bloody two. I told yer we should have waited a bit.'

Freddie didn't answer. Tommy always got like this before a job; his nerves got the better of him and he'd do nothing but moan in the lead-up to it.

Glancing towards the betting shop, Tommy could feel the sweat running down the back of his neck. So far, him and Freddie had been thoroughly successful in their promising new career. They always worked alone, were careful not to show off any wealth and studied thoroughly any job they chose to do. In reality, today's little number should be a doddle.

An independent bookmakers owned by a simple old boy. They'd been watching the gaff for weeks and, apart from the owner and some drippy bird behind the counter, there were no other staff. The place itself was a gold-mine. The old boy prided himself on giving good odds and, seeing it was situated in the heart of Whitechapel, it was always packed with piss-heads and losers who had nothing better to do than spunk their money up the wall.

Tommy and Freddie had been in there the last couple of Fridays. All suited and booted, they'd quietly placed a couple of bets while watching the old boy's movements. Three o'clock on the dot the owner would count the takings, place the dough in an old blue sports bag and take a nice slow walk towards the bank.

'I can't believe the lack of security. I mean, Whitechapel's full of tramps, junkies and winos. How the fuck don't he get done every week?' Freddie said.

Tommy agreed. They didn't want to hurt the old boy, just planned to teach him a lesson. At three o'clock exactly, the door opened and the man appeared with his blue sports bag.

As cool as a cucumber, Freddie jumped off the back of the bike, threatened the old boy with a replica gun and made a grab for the bag. The old boy clung to his takings for dear life. A war veteran, he wasn't going to be frightened by a bit of a kid and a fake shooter.

'Help, thief!' he screamed as he fell to the ground.

Aware of passers-by, and a have-a-go hero heading his way, Freddie had no alternative but to leg it empty-handed. Leaping on the back of the stolen motorbike, he grabbed hold of Tommy.

'Go, go, go.'

Blissfully ignorant of her son's activities, Maureen was busy preparing dinner. 'Do yer want me to give yer a hand, Mum? I can peel the potatoes or chop the carrots up if yer want.'

Maureen shook her head. 'You sit there and rest, love, I've got everything under control.'

As she listened to Susan gabble on endlessly about baby names, Maureen couldn't help but smile. Truth be known, she was just as excited as her daughter by the news that she was expecting her first baby. Susan had only found out a fortnight earlier that she was pregnant and since then they'd spoken about little else. She was already eating Maureen out of house and home.

'You sure you're not having twins?' Maureen asked jokingly.

'Shut up, Mum. Kevin'll be too frightened to come to me first scan if yer tell him that.'

James and Tommy were both excited by the prospect of becoming uncles. Even Ethel was overjoyed by the thought of being a great-gran.

'Be nice to have a nipper in the family again, won't it, Maur? Shame it's Kevin's, though.'

'Don't say that in front of Susan. She's ever so happy with him now and you'll only upset her if yer open your big mouth,' Maureen said.

Trust Ethel. She always had to say bloody something.

Kevin seemed a changed man since he'd learned he was to become a father. He'd even got a job painting and decorating for a local company. Maureen now allowed him to stay most nights; she even referred to him as her 'son-in-law to be'.

'So whaddya think, Mum? I like Krystal for a girl.'

Putting the lamb stew in the oven, Maureen sat down and smiled. 'What about poor Kevin? Doesn't he get a say?'

Susan giggled. 'We couldn't agree on anything, so what we've decided is that if we have a girl, I choose the name and if we have a boy, Kev picks it.'

'What does he wanna call a boy then?'

'He likes all the old-fashioned names. he wants to call it Sid or Harry.'

Maureen laughed. 'Let's hope it's a boy then, so the poor little mite ain't called Krystal. You know what your gran's like, she'll have a heart attack if yer name it that.'

Hearing the bell go, Maureen went to answer the door.

'Where's Susan?' Kevin screamed excitedly. Waving a letter in his hand, he ran into the kitchen. 'Guess what this is?'

Susan shook her head.

'We've been offered a flat, Suze. Mum opened it and brought it to me at work. They let me have the rest of the afternoon off, so I shot up the council and got the keys.'

Susan leaped off her seat. 'Where is it, Kev? Where is it?'

Handing her the letter, Kevin waited for her reaction. It wasn't perfect because it was in a tower block, but it was only ten minutes from her mum's.

'I know it's in a tower block, Suze, but it's one of the low numbers, so it can only be on the third or fourth floor. I think it's in the same block where Robert King lives. I've been inside his flat and it's well big. He's only got a one bed and they've offered us a two.'

Susan's eyes shone, 'Let's go and look at it now and if it's not falling to pieces, we'll take it.'

James breathed a sigh of relief when Mr Jones called time and collected the papers. Social Studies was his final exam and he was thrilled that his school days had finally come to an end. His mother had been well and truly on his case for the last few weeks. Lectures, revision, early nights – she'd driven him mad. Now it was time for him to enjoy himself, spend some quality time with his brother before he started full-time work with Harold next month. Laughing and joking with his pals, he felt incredibly happy as he left the building for the very last time.

Outside the school gates, he saw Maria climb into the blue cabriolet. Since they'd fallen out, she'd regularly been picked up from school by different blokes. His brother insisted she was doing it on purpose because she always seemed to hang about until she spotted him. They hadn't spoken since the day she'd slammed the door on him. At first he'd been really upset, but he'd since got his head around it. At least now he was leaving school she couldn't rub her conquests in his face any more. Living next door to her wasn't a problem either, because whenever he heard her door slam, he now refused to look out of the window. His brother had come up with that idea, insisting that what James didn't know couldn't hurt him. It had sort of worked and now he felt he had a grip on the whole Maria situation.

'So, James, we're gonna meet in Kate Odder's at seven. We'll have a couple there and, once everyone's arrived, we'll go on a pub crawl.'

James nodded, said goodbye to his pals and headed off home.

Tommy and Freddie sat in a pub they weren't familiar with in Bromley by Bow. They needed to be alone, anonymous, and discuss what the fuck had gone so very wrong.

'I'm telling yer, Tom, the old cunt knew it was a replica gun. That's where we came unstuck.'

'You sure? He looked a simple old fucker to me.'

Freddie knocked back his lager. 'I'm positive. I bet he's some gun expert or something. I swear I saw him clocking the shooter and he knew it wasn't real.'

Tommy lit a fag for both of them. 'I dunno about you, mate, but we were so close to getting caught, it gave me the willies. Maybe we should have a rethink about what we're doing. I'm enjoying me freedom and I really don't wanna go back inside.'

Freddie shook his head. 'Don't fuckin' back out on me

now, Tom. We had a deal, remember? Look, we ballsed up today, 'cause we didn't have a proper gun. Do you honestly think if I'd have fired a shot in the air, Mr Have-A-Go Hero would have chased me?'

Tommy shrugged. 'Probably not, but what happens if we get caught with a firearm? Do we really wanna take that chance?'

Freddie smiled. 'Life's all about taking chances, Tommy. Think positive, we're not gonna get caught. All right, I admit today was a close shave, but that was due to our own naivety. A, we never had the right tools for the job and B, we never thought in a million years that the old boy would put up a fight. We've gotta learn by this and in future be properly prepared.'

Tommy spoke nervously. 'Where we gonna get a gun from? We've gotta be careful, it can only be off someone we trust.'

Freddie moved closer to him. 'Me uncle Bobby's the man for that. I'll set up a meet, we'll go and see him together.'

Tommy was worried. 'I dunno, Fred. It sounds a bit heavy to me.'

Annoyed, Freddie looked him straight in the eye. 'Look, Tom, yer can't let me down, mate. If yer don't work with me, what else yer gonna do? Serve silly cunts in Tesco? Or knock your plums out on a shitty building site?'

Tommy knew his mate was talking sense. He'd loved larging it lately with plenty of money in his pocket and there was sod all else he could do. Desperate to redeem himself, he stood up, full of confidence.

'I'm no quitter Fred. Give yer uncle a bell to arrange the meet. Now, whaddya want to drink?'

Susan couldn't believe her luck as she ran from room to room. The third-floor flat they'd been offered was not only big, but also immaculate. Her mum and nan had accompanied her and Kevin to view the place and even they were impressed.

'I can get yer a bit of material from the market and run you up some curtains,' said Maureen.

'And you can have my old table and chairs, I don't bleedin' entertain any more,' Ethel chipped in.

Susan clapped her hands excitedly at the size of the smaller bedroom. 'I can't believe it doesn't even need decorating, and won't this make a wonderful nursery?' she exclaimed.

Kevin put an arm around her shoulder. 'I'll decorate the nursery properly. We can have the cot over there in that corner, a little wardrobe over there. We'll make it look the bollocks for our little chavvy.'

Seeing her daughter and Kevin kissing, Maureen pushed Ethel out of the room. Dragging her into the kitchen, she turned to her.

'I've never seen our Susan so happy, have you, Mum?' Ethel pursed her lips, 'Let's hope it lasts, eh?'

'Of course it will. They've got a baby on the way, Kevin's working hard, why shouldn't it last?'

Ethel shrugged her shoulders. 'You know the luck the women in our family have, and, don't forget, it was less than six months ago that he was knocking seven colours of shit out . . .'

'Ssh,' Maureen said, as she heard her daughter's footsteps. Ethel was such a pessimist, she could never look on the bright side of life.

Susan's eyes were shining, 'Well, Mum, Nan, whaddya think?'

'We love it, darling, don't we?' Maureen said, nudging her mother-in-law.

'It's very nice, dear,' Ethel said politely.

141

Kevin beamed as he entered the kitchen. His painting job paid cash in hand, so with his earnings, and him and Susan's dole money, they'd be fairly well off. 'We can move in next week if you like, the social will pay the rent for us. The council will be shut now, but if we go down there first thing Monday morning, we can sign the papers.'

Susan threw her arms around his neck, 'I don't arf love you, Kevin.'

'I love you too, Suze,' Kevin replied, and for the first time in his life, he actually meant it.

James had bathed and was scoffing his dinner on the sofa when his brother arrived home.

'Where is everybody?' Tommy asked.

James shrugged his shoulders. 'Mum left a note about going to look at a flat with Susan or something.'

Tommy opened two beers, handed one to James and sat down next to him.

'Well, how did your last exam go?'

James smiled. 'All right I think, but I'm so glad they're all over. Are you and Freddie still coming out with me tonight?'

Tommy shook his head. 'I am, but Freddie can't make it. We had a bit of agg today with a job we were on, and Freddie's got a bit of running around to do.'

James nodded. His brother usually told him everything – between them they had no secrets. 'I'm really glad you're gonna come with us, Tom. Me mates'll love you.'

Tommy ruffled his hair. He didn't fancy going out tonight at all. Weeks ago he'd promised Jimmy boy that he'd go out with him at the end of his exams and he didn't want to let him down.

James put his plate on the table. 'So what happened today, then?'

Tommy got to the bit where they were sitting opposite the betting shop on the stolen bike, but was interrupted by his family returning.

'Keep schtum and I'll tell you later,' he whispered.

With Kevin up the pub, Susan went for a lie down on the bed. She was tired, but far too excited to sleep. To say she was happy was an understatement. The funny thing was, she had never expected happiness to come to her. Up until now, life had confused her. At school she'd never fitted in, she'd always felt inferior to the other girls. She wasn't slim or pretty, so she'd become a bully, just to get herself noticed. At home, she had always felt that her mum and nan had favoured her brothers, and even though she had been shown plenty of love, she'd never been able to return it. Now things were different. She had spent years hating the world and its inhabitants, but finally she felt part of it. A loving boyfriend, a baby on the way; she now had a future to look forward to. All she'd ever wanted was love and security, and at long last she had found it. Picturing the flat, Susan smiled. She had just found the last piece of her jigsaw.

Maureen dished up the lamb stew and listened happily while Ethel rabbited on about Gladys. The boys had already eaten and were now upstairs getting spruced up.

'Oh, look at yous two,' she said as they came down the stairs. 'Don't they look mint in their posh suits, Mum?' she crowed proudly.

Ethel agreed, but inside she was shocked. James had always been her favourite, but for the first time tonight, he no longer looked like a little boy. Standing next to Tommy all suited and booted, the pair of them reminded her of somebody from the past. She racked her brains. Suddenly, it came to her. They looked like a young Ron and Reg. Not wanting to spoil Maureen's happy mood, Ethel, for once, kept her thoughts to herself.

SEVENTEEN

James woke up at midday with only patchy memories of the previous evening. He had no idea how he'd got home, but could remember bits of the argument with his father and getting hold of Ellie Phillips. Feeling as sick as a dog, he went in search of his brother, who was already up and about.

'Christ, you look worse for wear, want me to make yer a nice breakfast?' his mother asked him.

James shook his head. 'I feel too ill to eat. Where's Tommy?'

'He's gone out, love. I dunno where he went, he didn't say. Yous two woke the whole bloody house up when you came in this morning.'

'I can't remember coming home. Was Tommy with me?'

'Yeah, the pair of yer got in about five. Made a right bleedin' racket.'

Changing his mind about breakfast, James lay on the sofa while his mother cooked him something to settle his stomach. He felt terrible as he remembered what had happened with his old man. It had been awful and he didn't know whether to tell his mum or not. Choosing not to, in case he got Tommy into trouble, he decided to pay his dad a visit after breakfast, just to apologise and check that he was OK.

Getting hold of Ellie Phillips wasn't the cleverest move in the world either. She'd been Maria's best girl mate for years until they'd fallen out over some bloke a few months back. James had never particularly liked Ellie. She was a pretty girl, but had a mouth the size of the Dartford Tunnel. She was bound to make sure that Maria found out he'd gone home with her. James felt really bad – he'd only done it out of spite. When he was drunk as a skunk it had seemed a good idea.

Maureen buttered his bread and browned his bacon. He looked dreadfully rough, her baby, and she hoped he wasn't going to make a habit of going out and getting shit-faced with his elder brother. Deciding not to say anything because he'd been studying so hard for his exams, she dished up his grub and took it in to him on a tray.

'You get that down yer neck, darling. I'm popping out with your gran for a bit, she wants me to go and see poor old Glad with her.'

James squirted tomato sauce onto his plate. 'I'm popping out meself in a bit, Mum.'

'Where you off to?' Maureen asked, suspiciously.

'I'm going to meet some girl I was with last night,' James lied.

Maureen smiled as she left the house. She was glad he was into the girls, but deep down she hoped he'd end up with Maria. She'd always liked the beautiful girl from next door and knew that one day she'd make a wonderful daughter-in-law.

James finished his breakfast, had a quick wash and got changed. He felt better for eating, so much so that he managed to run for the bus. From the top deck, he looked out at the gloomy weather and the heavy traffic. He was in no rush to get to where he was going and he needed to plan what he was going to say to his dad.

Last night had been a roaring success – until they'd gone into the Blind Beggar and come face to face with his old man. James had never really hated his father; he didn't know him well enough to have any feelings for him at all. His brother felt differently. He was embarrassed by his dad and despised every bone in his useless body.

Paralytic, Tommy Snr had made a beeline for his two boys. 'Gonna have a beer with yer old dad?' he'd slurred.

'Fuck off before I knock you out,' Tommy Jnr told him.

James was mortified. He'd never told his school mates that his dad was the local dosser. Whenever they'd asked about him, he'd kept his answers polite but evasive. He was aware that a few of them probably knew the score through their parents, but knowing it was one thing and seeing it with their own eyes was another. He could see the shock on his friends' faces, the pity in their eyes.

'He's coming back again,' James whispered to Tommy.

Seeing his brother's embarrassment, Tommy Jnr picked Tommy Snr up by his dirty collar, dragged him outside and gave him a dig. One little punch floored him, and James's last memory as they'd left the pub was of his old man slumped against the wall, crying. Upset by the incident, James kept glancing back at him.

'Shall I go back and make sure he's all right?' he asked Tommy.

His brother dragged him away. 'Leave the useless cunt where he is, Jimmy boy. There's fuck-all wrong with him, I barely fuckin' touched him. He'll live, trust me.'

From there they'd gone on to a nightclub and neither James nor Tommy had mentioned their father any more. It was a closed subject, but they were both deeply affected by the altercation and the pair of them got more drunk than ususal.

It was at the club that James had bumped into Ellie Phillips. Tommy had copped hold of her older sister, Kelly, and they'd gone back to her house. James could remember being in bed with Ellie, but had no idea whether he'd shagged her or not. He just prayed that he'd been too drunk and incapable. Maria discovering he'd gone home with her was bad enough – finding out he'd given her a portion of helmet pie would be totally unforgiveable.

Feeling sick again, James stood up. He was only five minutes from Whitechapel where his father lived, and he'd rather walk than chuck his guts up and make a show of himself. Praying for the doors to hurry up and open, James leaped off and vomited his breakfast up all over the pavement.

'Dirty little bastard,' he heard some old girl say.

Ignoring the comments and stares, he wiped his mouth and walked speedily up the road. Sod his mother and her full English – he'd only wanted beans on toast!

Knowing his dad had drunk in the Horn of Plenty in Stepney for years, but had recently got barred, James suspected that the Blind Beggar was now his new haunt. He knew from his mum and nan that his father was a creature of habit, and he guessed that he'd either be in the pub or at his nearby bedsit. James decided to poke his head around the door of the pub first. There were no more than a dozen or so blokes in there and he spotted his dad immediately. Tommy Snr was sat alone at a table, his hands clutching what looked like a pint of cider.

As James approached him, he noticed Tommy had the same clothes on that he'd been wearing the previous evening. His jumper was dirty and stained with blood and he even had dried blood still encrusted on his face. James didn't know what to say as he sat down opposite him. He didn't really know the man, so went for the obvious.

'Do yer wanna drink, Dad?'

Tommy Snr smiled, showing off his rotten teeth. 'Get me a pint of snakebite, but don't tell 'em it's for me. They've barred me from drinking it, so pretend it's for you.'

James nodded. Leaving the sorry soul sitting alone, he walked to the bar.

Tommy and Freddie sat in the Leonards Arms along the A13. Freddie had wanted to meet with his uncle in East Ham, but Bobby had insisted they meet in Rainham. 'Too many eyes and ears up there, son, everyone knows me in that neck of the woods.'

Freddie ordered two bottles of lager, picked a quiet table and urged Tommy to sit down. They were half an hour early, but it would give them chance to have a chat between themselves.

'So how was your bruvver's do last night?'

Tommy shrugged. 'All right, I suppose. Jimmy boy's mates were a bit young, but they were nice kids. We ended up in a nightclub, pulled two little birds and took 'em home. Mine was a pig, but I shagged it anyway. Jimmy boy was well pissed and I had to sling him over me shoulder to get him home. I dunno if he got his leg over – he was still comatose when I left him this morning, so I didn't 'ave a chance to find out.'

Freddie laughed. 'Where did yer go?'

Tommy chatted happily about the club and the pub crawl they'd been on. He couldn't bring himself to mention the Blind Beggar or his old man. He wanted to forget all about it, pretend it had never happened. He knew he shouldn't have clumped his father, but hadn't been able to stop himself. He'd seen red, lost it with him, and now he felt really fucking guilty.

'How's my two favourite boys?'

Uncle Bobby's arrival ended Tommy's guilt trip. Leaping up, he hugged the man who had been so kind to him on the inside. 'You look well – where yer been to get a tan like that?'

Bobby sent Freddie up the bar and sat down.

'Costa del Sol. I've just bought a little gaff out there, hoping to retire and move there permanently in a few years time, I am. Anyway, enough about me – what you been doin' with yourself?'

Tommy chatted happily about his family and life on the outside. Freddie returned from the bar, joined in the chit-chat and then awkwardly moved in for the kill.

'The reason we asked you 'ere today, Uncle Bobby, is we've been working together, yer know, and, er, we've been using a replica. Last time out we had a bit of grief and we were wondering if you could sort us out with the real thing.'

Uncle Bobby stared at the boys with a serious expression on his face. 'What sort of grief did you have, lads?'

Tommy left all the talking to his mate. As Freddie began to explain about the betting shop, uncle Bobby nearly fell off the chair.

'Don't tell me that was yous two silly bastards that tried to do Old MacDonald's bookies?'

'Who's Old MacDonald? The one we hit was in Whitechapel.'

Bobby roared with laughter. 'That's it, you pair of knobends. The owner's an old army sergeant. I heard about it in Marbella. His son Gary is a proper geezer, lives out there, he does. Good job yer never hurt the old boy – he'd have come home, hunted yer down and strung you both up by the bollocks.'

Freddie glanced at Tommy and shrugged. 'We never knew, we just thought he was some old senile.'

150

Bobby moved closer to both boys. 'You've gotta do more homework, lads. Don't ever hit on anyone until you've checked out the family. Gary MacDonald would throttle yer with his bare hands if he had any idea who you was. You were on a bike weren't yer? Whaddya do with that?'

Freddie smirked. 'We burnt it, thank fuck, and the helmets. We got rid of the lot.'

Bobby sighed. 'Well at least you had the brains to do that. I take it no one else knows it was yous two?'

Seeing Freddie shake his head, Tommy also shook his. He'd told James, but nobody else.

'Look lads, I can get you what you want, but you've gotta up yer game. Don't be wasting your time doing silly shops for a couple of grand. The post offices are the things to do these days. The banks are too hard now, but the post offices are a doddle, if yer know what you're doing.'

Freddie and Tommy nodded. 'When can yer get us a piece?' Freddie asked.

'I'm going back to Spain on Monday. If yer just wanna sawn-off, I can get yer one for tomorrow. If yer want anything else, you'll have to wait a couple of weeks until I get back. I'll go and get us another beer, have a chat and let me know what yer wanna do.'

Tommy and Freddie agreed immediately that a sawn-off would be perfect.

'We'll meet yer tomorrow, Bob, if that's all right. How much is it?'

Bobby smiled. 'Nothing to yous pair, but be fucking careful with it. Give me a ring about six o'clock and I'll tell yer where and when. I won't meet yer meself, I'll send Big Phil or someone.'

Freddie waited until Bobby had left the pub, then turned

to Tommy. 'We're in the big boys' league now, mate. Are yer ready for this, Tommy Hutton?'

Tommy smiled. He might be nervous, but he was also extremely excited. 'Don't you worry about me, Freddie Adams, I'm as ready as I'll ever be!'

Back in Whitechapel, James looked on in horror as his father slid off the chair and fell face first onto the floor. He'd been sitting with him for over an hour and they hadn't even managed to have a proper conversation yet. At his dad's insistence, James had brought him five snakebites and now this had happened. Surely he couldn't be drunk on five pints. Maybe he was ill or something? Trying to lift his dad up was impossible on his own.

'Can yer give us a hand, mate?' James shouted to the barman.

'No I fucking can't. I asked you if the snakebites were for him and you said no. He's a fucking nuisance. You got him drunk, you bastard well deal with him.'

Charlie Venables was sitting at the next table. A sensible old boy, he had no time for Tommy Hutton, but felt sorry for the young lad with the angelic face, who was desperately trying to help him.

'Do you know him well, son?'

James looked at him with pleading eyes. 'I dunno what to do. He's my dad.'

Charlie stood up. 'Come on, lad, he only lives round the corner. You grab one arm and I'll grab the other and we'll drag him home in no time.'

Grateful for the help, James did exactly as he was told. The five-minute walk, lugging his dad, took twenty, but finally they got him there.

'How we gonna get him in? I dunno where he keeps his key.'

Noticing that Tommy had pissed himself, Charlie nodded at James. 'Best you check his trousers 'cause I ain't bleedin' well doing it.'

James found a key in his dad's pissy right-hand pocket. He opened the door and gently laid his father on the filthy mattress. The room stank of a mixture of fags, beer and piss and James gagged as he shut the front door.

'Thanks ever so much,' he said to Charlie.

Noticing how upset the young boy looked, Charlie offered to buy him a pint.

'No thanks, I'd best get going now,' James replied.

Walking away, James couldn't stop thinking of one of his nan's favourite sayings. 'What's bred in the bone will come out in the flesh,' she often said.

Tears streaming down his face, James thought of his dad. He wasn't going to end up like him, not now, not ever.

EIGHTEEN

Once she had finished her make-up, Maureen studied her appearance in the full-length mirror. She barely recognised herself. Her new suit looked smart, proper glam, and her hair had been cut and highlighted.

It was her Tommy that had bunged her a oner, insisting she pamper herself. He'd recently been promoted again. He was manager of the building site now and went to work in a suit most days, instead of his old working clothes. Maureen was ever so proud of him. There weren't many ex-convicts who, within six months of their release, had secured a great career and turned their lives around.

Maureen glanced at her watch. She had plenty of time, nearly an hour before the cab was picking them up. She was nervous about tonight and needed a brandy or two to settle her stomach. It had been Kenny's idea to have a big family get-together. He was paying for the whole evening: the meal, drinks, and the cabs. It had been his fortieth birthday a few weeks back. He and Wendy had been away on a Caribbean cruise and now that they were back, he'd insisted on organising an evening with the family.

James had just received his exam results. Six O-levels,

four As and two Bs the clever little sod had got, and Kenny said they were to use his good news as an excuse for a double celebration. Maureen had been overjoyed. No one in the Hutton family had ever got one O-level, let alone six. She'd told anyone and everyone who would listen. The women up the shops, the girls she sat with at bingo, she'd even stopped a couple of women in the street she barely knew.

Pleased with her new look, she wandered downstairs, and was greeted by her two sons.

'You look really nice, Mum,' James gushed.

'Don't scrub up bad for an old 'un, does she?' Tommy said cheekily.

Maureen walloped him playfully and went into the kitchen to pour herself some Dutch courage. She wasn't used to eating out at posh restaurants. Pie and mash or fish and chips was all she was used to, and she had never felt comfortable in Wendy's company. The woman was so far shoved up her own arse that she was almost bent double, and Maureen knew she looked down her nose on herself and the kids. Maureen could never understand why Kenny had married her. They say when a man picks a wife he looks for a younger version of his mum, but that certainly wasn't the case with him. She imagined Wendy out shoplifting. 'Not on your nelly,' Maureen giggled.

'What yer laughing at, Mum? You ain't pissed already are you?' James shouted.

Maureen was just about to go and clump the cheeky little sod when she was stopped in her tracks by the arrival of Susan and Kevin.

Maureen greeted her daughter and boyfriend warmly. 'You both look ever so smart,' she said proudly.

She'd hardly ever seen Kevin in anything but a T-shirt

and tracksuit bottoms, and he looked different in a shirt and trousers. Susan had made a real effort too, and looked lovely in her floral top and leggings.

'Do I look fat, Mum?' Susan said self-consciously.

'Don't be silly. You're not even that far gone yet. You look gorgeous,' Maureen told her.

Susan smiled at the compliment. 'I'm starving. Tell Kevin what restaurant we're going to, Mum. You did tell me, but I can't remember the name.'

Maureen racked her brain. 'I think it's called Chans or something. It's in East Ham. Kenny said it does a lovely bit of grub.'

Realising time was getting on, Maureen ordered James to go and see where his nan was. 'She'll be late for her own funeral, that woman,' she joked to Susan.

Ethel turned up a few minutes later with a bemused-looking, red-eyed Gladys in tow. 'Go and sit in there and talk to the boys, dear,' she ordered her friend.

Shutting the lounge door, Ethel turned to Maureen. 'She's ever so upset, bless her. I'm gonna have to bring her out with us.'

'Whatever's the matter with her?'

Memory loss had recently really taken its toll on poor old Glad. Maureen was sure she had Alzheimer's, but Ethel wouldn't hear of it. 'Nothing wrong with her, just old age. She's forgetful, not fuckin' doolally.'

Ethel sat down at the table and put her head in her hands. 'You know how much she loves Sooty, her cat?'

Maureen nodded. 'Oh, it ain't got run over, has it?'

Ethel shook her head. 'It's worse than that. She accidently put it in the washing machine and put it on spin dry. Oh, it was awful, Maur. I had to lift the poor little fucker out. You should have seen the state of it.'

'Is it dead?' Maureen asked, shocked.

'Of course it's fuckin' dead. Wouldn't you be if you'd just spent an hour on rinse and spin?' Ethel yelled.

Much to Ethel's annoyance, Susan and Kevin burst out laughing.

'Don't fuckin' laugh, you nasty little bastards. Its tail was rigid with shock and the poor little fucker died with its eyes wide open. I buried it for her in the garden, told her it got run over, I did.'

'Didn't she know she'd put it in there, then?' Kevin asked innocently.

Ethel was fuming. Thick was one thing, brainless was another.

'Of course she fuckin' didn't. She'd just dished it up some tuna and was calling it to come and have its dinner.'

'Poor Sooty,' Maureen said sadly.

Seeing Susan sniggering, Ethel stood up and thumped her.

'Get out my fuckin' sight yous two, and don't you dare say anything to her later, or crack any funnies. As far as you're concerned, the cat got run over. You say one word about what really happened, and I'll marmalise the fuckin' pair of yer.'

Unable to control her hysterics, Susan dragged Kevin out of the kitchen.

Ethel looked at Maureen. 'Wicked little fucker that girl is. Fancy laughing at the terrible death of a poor defence-less animal.'

'She didn't mean it, Mum,' Maureen said.

'Yes she did. She'll make a terrible mother, you mark my words.'

'Cab's here, Mum.' James's voice, luckily, spelled the end of the Sooty conversation.

Picking up her handbag, Maureen shooed everyone out and shut the front door.

* * *

157

Kenny ordered himself and Wendy a drink, 'Cheer up, love,' he said, squeezing her hand.

Wendy smiled falsely. The thought of spending the night with Kenny's family was enough to make a clown look fucking miserable. This time last week they'd been on their lovely cruise ship. Now they were sitting in a shit-hole in East Ham waiting for the Beverly Hillbillies to arrive.

Kenny smiled. 'The food's lovely in here. I've never brought you here before, have I?'

Wendy shook her head. 'East Ham's not really my type of area, is it, dear?'

Kenny was saved from having to reply by the arrival of his family.

'Susan, you sit here, next to Ethel, and James can sit next to Kevin. Sit over there, Tommy, on the other side of Wendy.'

Wendy shot her husband the stare of all stares. It was a look that said, 'Thanks very much for sitting me next to the fucking murderer.'

Seeing her thunderous expression, Kenny ordered the waiter to bring another chair over for Gladys.

'You sit over here next to me, Tom. Let Gladys sit next to Wendy and then your nan can sit the other side of her.'

With the seating finally organised, Kenny ordered a round of drinks. 'Does everyone want wine with their meal?' he asked.

Everyone nodded. Handing the wine list to Wendy, he smiled at her. 'You're the wine expert, dear. Order a couple of bottles of white and a bottle of red.'

Wendy studied the list. She usually prided herself on her choice of fine wines, but not tonight. These rednecks wouldn't know the difference between vintage and bloody

Liebfraumilch. Choosing from the cheaper end of the scale, she handed the list back to Kenny.

Ethel looked at the menu in horror. 'What's all this rice and fucking noodles? Don't they serve potatoes or chips?'

James chuckled. 'It's Chinese food, Nan. I'll order for you, you'll like it once yer taste it.'

Putting her hand up her clout and adjusting herself with one hand, Ethel slung the menu on the table with the other.

'What a load of old shit! I ain't eating anything foreign, it'll play me piles up.'

Wendy glared disgustedly at the old woman. Kenny was too frightened to do or say anything, but the rest of the table roared with laughter.

Ethel cackled as Wendy excused herself to go to the ladies. Ethel purposely had a good old scratch around her ha'ppenny every time she was in her company.

'Stuck-up cow,' she whispered to James.

'Stop it, Nan,' he giggled.

Tommy and James had often eaten in Chinese restaurants and knew exactly what they liked. The rest of the family didn't have a clue, so Kenny ordered a variety of different dishes for them to try.

Gladys stared blankly at the menu and smiled as she put it down. 'I'll have a duck.'

Kenny smiled. 'I've ordered two for us to share.'

'I want a whole one to meself.'

Ethel patted her friend's arm. 'He's ordered you one, dear.'

'Take no notice,' Ethel mouthed to her son.

As a stony-faced Wendy returned from the toilets, Kenny signalled for the waiter to bring over some champagne. Then he gave a small speech about how proud everyone was to have a genius in the family.

'Now, let's all drink a toast to the main man. Well done, James.'

James went red as a beetroot as they all clapped and cheered. Everyone in the restaurant was looking at him and he felt a right nerd. Noticing his embarrassment, Tommy ruffled his hair.

'Who's a clever boy, then?' he said in a parrot-like voice.

'Fuck off, Tom,' James said angrily. He'd spent ages doing his hair, and now his brother had messed it all up.

Thanks to feeling two sheets to the wind before she'd even got to the restaurant, Maureen felt brave enough to give a little speech herself. She stood up.

'I just wanna say a few words. First of all, I wanna say a big thank you to Kenny for bringing us all here tonight – oh, and happy birthday for last week, love. Secondly, I wanna say how proud I am of my family. James might be the brains among us all, but I'm equally as proud of Tommy, who has been promoted once again and is now manager at the building site, and let's not forget Susan, who is gonna make me a very happy granny. Cheers, everybody and good health to us all.'

Ethel nudged James. 'Manager of the building site! Bank robber, more like.'

James shot her a warning glance. 'Ssh, Nan.'

Ethel chuckled. Everyone she spoke to knew Tommy was a villain. Everyone apart from his mother, that was.

'Can I say something now?' Kevin said awkwardly.

'Go on, love,' Maureen urged him.

He stood up. 'I just wanna say how much I enjoy bein' part of this family. I know I've been a bit of a loser over the years, but recently I feel that I've really got my act together. As yer know, me and Suze have had our ups and downs, but we've stuck it out, and now we've got a nipper on the way, we're the happiest we've ever been.'

Grabbing Susan's hand, he dropped to one knee and handed her a ring. 'Me mum had to lend me the money, so it ain't nothin' special, Suze. I love yer so much, babe. Will yer marry me?'

Susan was flabbergasted. 'Yes, yes, yes,' she screamed.

'We need more champagne over here!' Kenny shouted to the waiter.

Maureen burst into tears. 'I'm so happy for both of you,' she cried, as she hugged her daughter.

James and Tommy both shook hands with Kevin.

'Welcome to the family,' Tommy said.

Ethel congratulated them, but said very little. She hoped they would live happily ever after, but very much doubted it. Susan had a habit of fucking things up, and if they even made it up the aisle, it would be a miracle.

Gladys stood up and walked over to Susan. 'Congratulations, dear. Who's the lucky man?'

'Kevin,' Ethel said, pointing him out.

Glad loved a wedding. Tucking her skirt into her bloomers, she broke into song.

> I'm getting hitched up in the morning!
> Ping pong the bells are gonna chime.
> Pull out the stopper,
> He's got a whopper . . .

The restaurant went into uproar as Gladys made up her own lyrics.

Wendy sat with a fixed expression on her face that partly resembled a smile. It was like a circus without the trapeze artist. This family never failed to amaze her. One kid a murderer, one up the spout and now engaged to a retard. Even the old girl was notorious for pilfering and

161

everyone sat there so happy and proud, without a care in the world.

When the food arrived, everybody got stuck in, none more so than Ethel, who piled her plate sky high.

'I thought you didn't like foreign food?' Kenny said, tongue in cheek.

'Seeing as there's fuck all else, I've either gotta eat the shit, or starve,' she replied.

Lifting a pancake off the pile, Wendy delicately spread some hoisin sauce on top. Adding some cucumber and spring onion, she was just about to take a little bit of duck, when Gladys's arm shot out, grabbed the entire bird and started to gnaw at it.

Tommy, James, Susan and Kevin burst out laughing. Annoyed, Ethel glared at them.

'Don't fucking laugh at her.'

Turning to Gladys, she gently tried to coax her to put the bird back on the plate. 'Now, come on dear, put the duck back down and I'll cut you some.'

Gladys held the bird firmly with both hands and shook her head. 'No, it's mine.'

'Now, come on, Glad, put it down,' Ethel said, making a grab for it. Gladys clung on to it for dear life.

'Let her have it, Mum,' Kenny said gently. 'We've got another one over here. There you go, Wendy, have some of that.'

'No thanks, I've gone off the idea now,' Wendy replied curtly.

Kenny nibbled awkwardly on his food. The celebration had turned into a fucking nightmare and Wendy would make his life hell later. Maureen could sense how anxious he was.

'Would yer like some more, Ken?' she said, thrusting a bowl of rice towards him.

Kenny smiled and took some out of politeness.

Once she had finished the duck, Gladys sucked the bones and put them back onto the empty plate. She sipped her wine and smiled at Ethel. 'That was nice, that chicken. What time are we going home? Sooty'll be wondering where I am.'

Ethel looked sadly at Maureen. 'Shut up!' she screamed at Susan, who was laughing like a hyena.

'Sooty's gone on his holidays. You're coming to stay with me, Glad.'

Gladys smiled. 'That's nice, dear. I hope Sooty behaves himself.'

A little while later, Tommy stood up. 'Does anyone mind if me and James shoot off now? Freddie only lives around the corner and we're meeting him in his local.'

Maureen shook her head. 'James has had a lot to drink already. Why don't you go out with Freddie on yer own tonight, love?'

'Oh, leave it out, Mum. I ain't a little kid any more,' James said angrily.

Maureen smiled at him. 'Go on then, but look after him, Tommy.'

As the boys left the restaurant, Wendy urged Kenny to get the bill. 'Order the taxis while you're at it,' she hissed.

Doing as he was told, Kenny was relieved that the cabs arrived quickly. Seeing his family into one, he waved them goodbye. As soon as he got into the other one, he was met by a look of pure hatred.

'I have never been so embarrassed in all of my life. The whole restaurant was laughing at us. Never again, Kenny, and I mean it this time. I would rather divorce you than go through that again.'

Kenny knew she meant it. They did not speak another word to each other for the rest of the journey.

NINETEEN

Maureen made herself a brew and plonked herself down at the small kitchen table. So much had happened recently that she was glad of some peace and quiet. Gladys had moved in with Ethel a week after the restaurant fiasco. Maureen didn't know the full ins and outs because Ethel had kept it rather quiet. She'd had to poke around to get snippets of information. Apparently Gladys had had a little accident and had burnt her kitchen to the ground. The council had then stepped in and insisted she move to a care home. They said she'd become a danger to herself and her neighbours, but Ethel had been furious.

'They ain't carting her off to one of them fuckin' nuthouses, Maur. I ain't having it. She can come and live with me, I'll take good care of her.'

Maureen had begged her mother-in-law to change her mind. 'You've got arthritis yourself, you ain't gonna be able to cope. I know it's sad, Mum, but you've gotta face facts. Glad needs professional help. What if she burns your house down with you inside?'

Ethel was adamant. 'Don't take no notice of all the fuckin' gossip-mongers. She forgot she'd put something in the oven, that was all. We've been friends for over half a century and I know she'd do the same for me. She ain't goin' to one of them loony bins, I won't let it happen.'

Maureen had watched in horror over the next couple of days as Tommy and Freddie had moved all Gladys's stuff that had survived the fire across the road. Ethel could be such a stubborn old cow at times. She wasn't exactly a spring chicken herself and Maureen was sure it would all end in tears. She could understand Ethel's loyalty towards her friend, but not her refusal to admit to the woman's illness.

James had been another problem. He'd started full-time work in Harold's shop a couple of weeks ago. Trouble was, he was living a party lifestyle and she had terrible trouble getting him up in the mornings. His elder brother was becoming a bad influence on him. Before Tommy came out of nick, she'd rarely seen James drunk. Now he was pissed all the time. Last week, when he'd staggered in at six in the morning, she'd had to call in sick for him. A massive row had followed.

'You've gotta pull yerself together, James. You've been given a wonderful opportunity in life; don't fuck it up, son.'

He'd agreed with her at the time, but nothing had changed since. He was still going out every night and coming home at all hours. Maureen just hoped that Harold didn't change his mind about the offer he'd handed James. The silly little sod would know all about it if he lost his job and the business was snatched away from under his nose.

At least Maureen had the one good bit of news. Susan's engagement had come as a bolt out of the blue and her daughter was on cloud nine.

Maureen smiled. The engagement party was this Saturday and she was really looking forward to it. If being a gran wasn't exciting enough, she was now going to be mother of the bride!

Kev's mum worked in a local pub as a barmaid and had organised the party there. The Prince of Wales, in nearby Duckett Street, was better known to everyone as Kate Odder's. Kate, the guv'nor, had agreed to section off half the pub and allow the kids to have it free of charge. Usually Maureen would have held a little do for them around hers, but for once, she was glad of someone else doing all the work. With everything that had been going on, she'd been really stressed out and organising a get-together had been the last thing she needed.

Tommy had been another pain in the arse. People kept dropping hints that he wasn't working on the building site. At first Maureen hadn't taken much notice of the snide remarks, until yesterday, when her two best friends, Sandra and Brenda, had had a quiet word in her shell.

'Look, Maur, we don't wanna be the ones to tell yer this, but someone's got to. Your Tommy ain't working where he says he is. My dad, Archie, says he's hanging about in a pub in Poplar most days of the week. He reckons he's well known in the area, and him and his mate, Freddie, are a pair of villains.'

Maureen's heart sank. Her heart told her that they'd got it all wrong, but her head told her differently. Ethel had always said the same thing and they couldn't all be bastard well wrong. There must be some truth in the rumours – there had to be. She needed to do some investigating, find out the truth. She certainly didn't want James going out with Tommy all the time if he was up to no good. If Tommy got her baby into any trouble, she'd fucking well kill him.

She hadn't said anything to anyone about what she'd been told. She needed proof before she tore into Tommy and went shooting her mouth off. One thing she was sure of, though: if Brenda and Sarn were right, she'd kick his arse out of her house so fast, he'd bounce down the fucking road. Maureen was just about to hatch a plan to catch the bastard out, when she was interrupted by a frantic Ethel.

'Quick, Glad's fallen over. I can't lift her, can yer give us a hand?'

Maureen slammed her cup of tea down and ran out of the house.

'Four thousand and twenty, four thousand and forty.' As he placed the last note on top of the others, Tommy turned to Freddie. 'Four thousand and sixty pounds, me old mucker. Not bad for a morning's work, eh?'

Freddie chuckled. Things had been going incredibly well since they'd upped their game. Three little post offices they'd spun in the last few weeks, which in total had earned them nigh on fifteen grand. They'd left the big towns and cities well alone. There was more money to be earned in them, but with the two of them working alone, they didn't have the manpower. In the bigger offices you needed to be in and out in well under five minutes. Any longer than that and the police would be on your tail.

Freddie's uncle Bobby had given them all the vital information. He'd once made the mistake of hitting busy areas. 'Too many have-a-go Charlies willing to get themselves in the papers as some two-bit hero,' he told them. It had been Freddie's idea to hit the countryside. The money wasn't fantastic, but the jobs were easy peasy.

The owners were naive and the plastic screens that protected them could be smashed with one clump of a baseball bat. Not only that, you could leg it from the building and literally bump into no one. Suffolk, Norfolk and Cambridge they'd hit so far, tiny little villages with more cows than people. Freddie had insisted that they hit a different area every time, so they wouldn't arouse

167

suspicion. They'd even invested in a country wardrobe. When they went to work they wore waxed jackets and corduroy trousers and they looked like any other local until the masks came down and the gun flew out.

After initially being nervous, Tommy now loved the adrenaline of having a real shooter. They'd even fired it in Suffolk, when the old dear behind the counter had refused to hand over the money. Working with a gun had added to his confidence no end, and his nerves had all but disappeared.

Tommy counted out £500, handed half to Freddie and pocketed the rest himself. 'Shall we go out and celebrate, mate?'

Freddie nodded. 'Let's get rid of the dough first, eh?'

Even though they were raking it in, the boys were careful with the money they spent. They always had big wads in their pockets, but steered well clear from buying anything that made them look like big-time Charlies. With both of them still living at home, they'd had no option other than to bring James in on the act. Neither of them had bank accounts and even if they had, they couldn't have used them. James was their bank manager. He hid their money easily for them in the shop. Freddie had been wary about including James, but Tommy had insisted.

'He's as good as gold. He'll be great cover and we can bung him a few quid here and there.'

Freddie opened the door and urged Tommy to hurry up. 'Come on then, Bethnal Green it is. I'll call a cab. We don't wanna walk about with this lot on us.'

Tommy smiled. Life couldn't be any fucking better.

Over in Bethnal Green, James was busy counting shirts.

'James, my boy, I'm off to see that *meshugeneh* in Gants Hill to pick up my money. Then I have to go to the *shikseh*

168

in Aldgate to pick up some shirts. Will you be OK locking up tonight, son?'

James smiled. 'I'll be fine, Harold. You have a good weekend.'

'And you have a nice weekend, too. Enjoy your sister's engagement party and I'll see you bright and early Monday morning. Don't forget to wish her *mazel tov* for me.'

James sighed as Harold left the shop. He was such a lovely man, and he didn't want to hurt him. Feeling guilty, James carried on with the stock check. It was a month now since he'd been working full time in the shop and as much as it upset him to say so, he'd hated every moment of it. Working Saturdays and school holidays had been a different kettle of fish. He'd been a kid then and had thoroughly enjoyed the experience and pocket money. Now that he'd left school, things were very different. He was bored shitless, stuck in the shop day in, day out. The early part of the week was the worst; sometimes they'd go hours without even greeting a customer.

He enjoyed having money in his pocket all the time, but the boredom outweighed the earnings. Giving it up wasn't an option. Harold would be heartbroken and his mum would bloody well kill him.

'All right, Jimmy boy. On your own, are yer?'

James smiled as his brother and Freddie walked towards him. 'Yeah, Harold's gone out for the rest of the day.'

Tommy handed him a big envelope. 'Stash that away for us, will yer?'

James told his brother to keep an eye on the shop while he went out the back. His boss was aware that he put money in the safe for Tommy on a regular basis. A man of the world, he asked no questions. He was a slippery bastard, was Harold, and had bundles stashed in there himself.

'Why don't you put it in the bank?' James asked him one day.

'*Gevalt geshreeyeh*! I can't put it in the bank. What if the wife or the tax man get their greedy hands on it?'

James laughed. A rabbi couldn't be more Jewish than Harold.

As James walked back into the shop, Tommy handed him some money.

'There's a twoer there, Jimmy boy. We're going for a beer now. What time yer finishing?'

'Six o'clock. Where will yer be?'

Tommy shrugged. 'Dunno. I'll ring you on the shop phone at half five and let yer know.'

James watched his brother swagger out of the door. He was so cool, and James wished he could be more like him. Tommy's life was so bloody exciting, whereas his was dull and boring.

Maureen got off the bus and walked boldly towards the crowd of men. Gladys had been OK, thankfully; a sprained ankle was her only real injury. Sitting in casualty had given Maureen a good idea. A builder had come in with a busted nose and as soon as she'd seen him, it had clicked. She knew where Tommy was supposedly working. He'd told her he was in charge of the new housing estate being built in Canning Town. Maureen knew exactly where he meant. Unbeknown to him, her aunt Doris had lived there on the old estate for years before she'd died.

As she approached one of the blokes, she heard wolf whistles. She knew they were taking the piss, because she looked like a packet of hot shit.

'Excuse me,' she said to a man in a bright yellow hat. 'I need to see my son, Tommy Hutton. He's the manager here, apparently.'

The man smiled, 'Never heard of him, darling.'

Maureen felt a shiver run through her veins. 'Is there another estate being built near by? Only, I know he works in this area and he drinks in that pub across the road.'

The man shook his head. 'Not to my knowledge, there ain't.'

'Oi, darling!'

Maureen looked up at the young boy with the big ears. 'What?'

'Fancy a date?' he sniggered. All of his mates were standing behind him, egging him on.

Maureen was annoyed, fucking annoyed. As if her day hadn't been bad enough, she now had a load of dimwits taking the piss out of her.

'Take no notice,' said the nice man in the yellow hat.

Maureen had no intention of taking any notice. Cheeky little blighter – she had a son older than him. Looking back up, she glared at him.

'If yer dick's as big as them ears, I'll be more than happy to go out with yer, love.'

The other lads all fell about laughing. Normally, Maureen would have been pleased by her wondrous humour. Not today, though – she had too much on her plate. She had to find that lying no-good bastard son of hers; she couldn't wait to get her hands on him. She'd give him manager of the building site. Making her look a fool like that: she'd kill him for this, fucking well kill him.

TWENTY

Susan lay back on the bed and smiled as Kevin placed his hand on her swollen stomach.

'He's kickin', Suze. I can feel him moving about.'

Susan laughed. Kev was so positive that they were having a boy, he'd already decorated the nursery blue. She had been a bit annoyed with him when he'd surprised her with it. 'We might still have a girl, Kev, and if we do, I'm not having her sleepin' in a boy's room.'

'You worry too much, Suze. It ain't cost us nothing – I nicked the paint from work. If it is a girl, which it won't be, I'll repaint it pink in no time.'

As Kev stood up, Susan pulled the quilt over her huge stomach. 'Where yer goin'?' she asked him.

'I'm gonna make us something to eat. You have a rest, save yerself for tonight.'

Susan smiled. It was their engagement party tonight, and although she was looking forward to it, she looked and felt like shit. Her pregnancy had been a difficult one. She'd put on loads of weight, had little energy, and often felt hormonal. Kev had been a saint and had treated her with kid gloves. He'd waited on her hand and foot, suffered her tantrums, and even helped out with the cooking and housework. Once the baby was born, she'd make it all up to him. She had twelve weeks to go, and was desperate to feel normal again. Still, it would all be worth it in the end. Together, they were as happy as Larry, but the arrival of their baby would be the icing on the cake.

Maria took off the blue dress and tried the pink one on again. Tonight could possibly be the big turning point of her life and she was determined to look her best. The invite to Susan's party had taken her completely by surprise. Maureen hadn't just asked her to attend, she'd practically begged her.

'Please say you'll come, Maria. I'm so worried about James. He ain't been himself since yous two fell out. He's out guzzling all the time, coming home at all hours. He really misses you, I know he does. Please sort things out with him, even if it's only for my sake.'

Maria agreed and afterwards thought long and hard about Maureen's words. At first she'd been so angry with James that she'd wanted to hurt him. Now she felt differently. She missed him more than words could say and would give her right arm to have him back in her life. She knew now that he hadn't just been her best friend; it was more than that. He was her soulmate, her rock. Why, at the time, hadn't she been able to see what was right in front of her eyes? Years she'd spent dating wasters and dickheads and what for? James had been there all along.

To be honest, she'd never looked at him in a romantic light until recently. It had sort of hit her like a ton of bricks after they'd fallen out. He looked different all of a sudden. His physique, his dress, his hair, everything about him had improved overnight. She'd dated lots of other guys to try and make him jealous but, truth be known, she couldn't bear them near her any more. Luckily, she was still a virgin and just lately even a passionate clinch did nothing but make her think of James. She missed his eyes, his laughter, his stupid jokes and his silly walk. She even missed him taking the mickey out of her and driving her mad with his awful record collection.

Looking at her watch, she knew she'd better get a move on. Deciding to stick with the pink dress, she quickly did her hair. Ever since she was little, James had always said she looked like a princess with her hair chucked up. Finally, tonight, she would have a chance to tell him how she truly felt. She'd debated whether to send him a letter, but would rather speak to him face to face. If he could just forgive her and admit that he felt the same way, then she'd gladly be his girl for evermore.

'Me and Jimmy boy are going for a beer, Mum. We'll meet you at the party.'

Grabbing his younger brother's arm, Tommy pulled him quickly out of the door. His mother had been staring at him with her Russian shot-putter expression all day and he couldn't wait to get out of the house. He was obviously in the dog house over something and, at this particular moment, the wrath of his old lady was the last thing he could be bothered with.

Maureen was glad to see the back of her deceitful son. How she'd kept her mouth shut all day, she would never know. Desperate not to spoil her daughter's engagement party, she'd had to delay ripping his head off for at least twenty-four hours. Tomorrow, he could pack his bags and fuck off as far away as possible. He wasn't leading her up the garden path, or his brother astray, for one minute longer.

'Maur, we're here.'

Maureen told Gladys and Ethel to sit down. 'It's ever

so early. Shall we have a quick drink here before we leave, girls?'

Gladys looked vacantly out of the window. 'Sooty, woof woof, Sooty,' she shouted.

'She seems to have forgotten he was a cat, she thinks he was a dog,' Ethel whispered sadly. 'I'll have a brandy and get her one, as well. It'll do her good to have a drink tonight.'

Maureen did the honours.

Kate Odder's was only around the corner and even though Ethel's arthritis was playing her up, they could easy walk it. Handing the drinks out, Maureen smiled. 'Cheers, girls. To our Susan, eh?'

Ethel lifted her glass. 'To Susan.'

'And Sooty,' Gladys said.

At Tommy's say-so, he and James headed to The Bancroft. It was little Mickey Parks's local pub and Tommy was determined to have a word with the piss-taking little bastard. He'd lent him £100 a couple of weeks ago and the cheeky fucker still hadn't paid him back. Spotting him immediately, Tommy swaggered towards him.

'Oi, Parksy. Where's my fuckin' money?'

Looking sheepish, Mickey Parks dug his hands deep into his pockets. 'I've only got thirty quid on me, Tom. Can I give you a score now and the rest next week?'

Tommy told James to get the drinks in and ordered Mickey into the toilets. Slamming the door, he turned to him angrily. 'Don't take the fuckin' piss out of me, yer cunt. If you've got the dough to stand in here pissing it up, then you've got the dough to pay me. I'll give yer two days and if you ain't got it back to me by Monday, I'm coming round your fuckin' house. Don't forget you've gotta give me one an' a half back, that was the deal we had, remember?'

Shit-scared, Mickey nodded. 'I promise yer, Tom, I'll get it to yer by Monday.'

Tommy smiled as he re-entered the bar. He'd seen the fear on Parksy's face, the mug. He'd get his money by Monday all right, and if he didn't, he'd smash the little prick to fuck.

Tommy dragged James over to the other side of the pub. There was a crowd of good-looking birds standing there and he fancied a bit of a laugh.

'Good evening, ladies. I'm Tommy, this is my brother, James, and we'd like to buy you all a drink.'

'Are you sure?' asked the pretty one with the dark hair.

Tommy winked. 'Absolutely positive, sweetheart.'

Susan felt like a rhinoceros as she walked towards the pub. She'd had no option but to wear black leggings and a baggy top yet again. Nothing else would bloody well fit her.

'I wish I didn't feel so fat and gross,' she moaned to Kevin.

Kevin cuddled her, 'You look beautiful to me, Suze, and I'm the one that's marrying yer.'

Susan looked at him adoringly; the days of him treating her badly were long gone. He'd turned into the perfect boyfriend and she couldn't wait to become his wife. She'd felt guilty earlier when he'd told her that most of his family wasn't coming. 'Word got around that it was you that glassed Joanne. Fuck 'em, it's their loss,' he assured her.

As the loved-up couple entered the pub, they were greeted by the cheering of well-wishers and the sight of decorations and balloons. Susan had taken so long to get ready that they were virtually the last to arrive.

'Kev, Suze,' Tracey and Darren yelled.

Spotting their best friends, Susan grabbed Kevin's arm and made her way towards them.

Tommy and James arrived at the party and headed straight for the bar. Aware of the daggers his mum was aiming his way, Tommy turned his back to her and faced James. He'd taken the phone number of one of the girls in The Bancroft and, unusually for him, was quite taken with her.

'She was nice, that little bird, weren't she, Jimmy boy? Lucy, her name was. I think I might ring her tomorrow and ask her out.'

James smiled. The girl in question had been a timid little sort and certainly hadn't seemed his brother's type. 'I thought she was really pretty, but she seemed a bit quiet for you, Tom.'

Tommy laughed. 'The quiet ones have good wife and breeding potential. All the loud ones are good for is a shag and a laugh.'

Freddie arrived just in time to hear Tommy larging it.

'Anyone would think you were Richard Gere, yer tosser.'

Laughing at Freddie's one-liner, Tommy hugged him. He hadn't been sure if he was going to turn up tonight and now he had, the party could really start.

'Hello, Maureen.'

Looking around, Maureen locked eyes with Kenny. Kissing him politely on the cheek, she smiled at him. 'Hello, love, you on your own? Where's Wendy?'

'She's not well, got a touch of the flu,' Kenny lied.

Maureen couldn't help but smile as she led him over towards Ethel. Wendy had had the flu more times than she'd had hot dinners.

177

'Mum, Kenny's here.'

''Ere he is, me favourite boy. Come and sit here, son, between me and Glad,' Ethel demanded.

Raising his eyebrows at Maureen, Kenny did as he was told.

Rockin' Ronny, the DJ, who had been an hour late due to an accident on the A13, was finally set up and ready to go.

'Hi everybody,' he drawled in a fake American accent.

Susan, who hadn't even noticed him arrive, stared at him in amazement. He was about fifty, with a big quiff, long sideburns and a white suit with tassels.

'Who booked this fuckin' prick?' she said, nudging Kevin.

Kevin shrugged. 'Me mum got him out the paper, I think. Don't say anything, Suze, she paid for him out of her own pocket. Whatever he's like, any music's better than having none at all.'

Susan felt her hormones rise, and stormed off to speak to the freak. She was determined not to have her night spoiled by some delusional dickhead who believed he was Elvis reincarnated.

Kicking off with 'All Shook up', Rockin' Ronny grabbed the mike. He sounded just like his idol and loved to sing along with him. 'Uh huh-uh, uh huh-uh, way-hey.'

Gladys leaped up in excitement, grabbed Ethel's hand, and urged her to follow her.

'Elvis is here, Eth. Quick, come on, let's go and say hello to him. I knew he wasn't dead, yer know, I fuckin' knew it.'

Ethel looked at Maureen and shook her head. Glad truly believed that Elvis had been hiding himself away for years and had decided to resurface in Stepney.

* * *

'Hi James, how you doing?'

James felt embarrassed as he came face to face with Ellie Phillips. He'd carefully avoided her since the night he'd got hold of her and now here she was standing a foot away from him.

'Hello, Ellie, you all right, mate?'

'Why didn't you ring me, James? I thought we were gonna go out.'

Seeing Tommy laughing behind his back, James could feel himself redden.

'I'm sorry, Ellie, I lost your phone number. I would have popped round to see yer, but I've been so busy at work, yer know how it is.'

Happy with his lie, Ellie smiled. 'Never mind, you gonna get me a drink then?'

James stood at the bar like a rabbit caught in the headlights.

Too nervous to make an early entrance, Maria sat in her friend Alison's bedroom and sank yet another glass of wine.

'We'd better go in a minute, Maria, time's getting on and we don't wanna get there too late,' Alison said.

'What is the time?' Maria asked.

'It's half-nine,' Alison replied. She wanted to get her friend there before she knocked any more back.

Maria wasn't about to be rushed. 'We'll leave in twenty minutes and get there for ten. Let's have one more here first.'

Not knowing what to do for the best, Alison agreed. Maria wasn't the best of drinkers and on the odd times she had got drunk, became argumentative and headstrong. Guessing she was in for a night of it, Alison listened politely while a drunken Maria droned on and on about the wonderful James.

*　　*　　*

179

By ten o'clock, Tommy and Freddie were well pissed and throwing shapes across the dancefloor.

'Viva las Vegas,' they yelled as they extracted the urine out of Rockin' Ronny.

James, who had been left at the bar with a gagging-for-it Ellie Phillips, was also steaming.

Hearing the tempo change to slow, Ellie grabbed him by the hand.

'Let's have a dance, James.'

Too drunk to give a shit, James followed her towards the stage.

'Do I still look OK?' Maria asked Alison as she stood nervously outside the pub.

'You look fine, Maria. Now let's get inside, I'm freezing out here.'

As she walked in, Maria had a quick look around, but couldn't spot James.

'Two white wines,' she shouted to the barmaid.

Making her way to a quiet corner, she scanned the place. Finally spotting James, she immediately felt bile rise from her stomach to her throat. He was canoodling with a girl on the dancefloor. It wasn't until James withdrew his tongue from the girl's throat that Maria saw it was none other than her ex-best friend, Ellie Phillips.

Letting out a sob, she made a dash for the exit.

TWENTY-ONE

'Look at our James, the dirty little sod. I didn't know he had it in him,' Ethel chuckled.

Worried, Maureen stood up. She could have sworn she'd spotted Maria come in and run back out. Desperate to find the girl and try to explain James's behaviour, she left the table and went in search of her.

Within seconds of hitting the cold air, Maria's tears were replaced by uncontrollable anger. 'Come on, let's go back inside,' she said, grabbing Alison's arm.

Alison tried to persuade her friend to give the party a miss. 'Boys ain't worth getting upset over, Maria. Let's just go to another pub, shall we?'

Maria refused. She might feel stupid, hurt and let down, but she was also determined to get her revenge. 'I'll show him who the bloody player is, you just watch me,' she said, dragging her friend back inside.

'Oh, there you are. I thought I saw you come in a few minutes back. Let me get you and your friend a drink, Maria,' Maureen said cautiously. She didn't know whether she had clocked James canoodling or not.

Maria put on a false smile and followed Maureen up to the bar. 'I lost my purse on the way in, I went back outside to look for it and, as luck would have it, Alison found it on the pavement.'

Maureen handed the girls their drinks. She could tell Maria was lying, could see it in her eyes. She herself had worn the same false expression and haunted look in the early years of her marriage to Tommy. He'd been a womaniser and even though each affair felt like a knife piercing her heart, she'd put on an act, just like Maria was doing now.

'Where's James?' Maria asked cheerfully.

Seeing that her son was now standing back up at the bar with his brother and Freddie, Maureen dragged Maria towards them. 'Maria and her friend, Alison, are here, boys. Look after them, won't yer?'

Ignoring James, Maria and Alison chatted to Tommy and Freddie. Annoyed, James stormed off. Maria fancied Freddie, he'd always sensed it. Flash, older and good looking, he was just her type. Spotting Ellie Phillips on the dancefloor, he grabbed hold of her again. Fuck Maria, two could play at her game.

As Buddy Holly's 'Peggy Sue' came to an end, Rockin' Ronny picked up the mike. 'Ssh, can I have some quiet please, everybody? As you all know, we're here tonight to celebrate the engagement of Susan and Kevin. Where are the happy couple?'

Well tanked-up, Kevin held his embarrassed fiancée's hand and dragged her towards the stage. 'Is it all right if I say a few words, mate?'

Kevin took the mike and grinned as he gave his speech.

'I just wanna thank a few people for making tonight happen for us. Firstly, I'd like to thank Kate for allowing us to use her pub. Secondly, me mum for helping us organise it and laying on the booze, music and grub. Thirdly, I wanna thank all of our friends and family for coming to celebrate with us. And last, but not least, I wanna thank my wonderful fiancée for making me so happy. Suze, me and you are gonna be great parents. Hand on heart, I love yer to death, girl. Right, now the soppy shit is over – let's all go and get pissed, shall we?'

Susan cried with happiness as the pub erupted in claps and cheers. Kevin had never been much of a romantic, and it was the nicest speech she'd ever heard. He'd said some lovely things on the night he proposed, but tonight meant more, as he'd said it in front of so many people.

As Rockin' Ronny played The Dixie Cups' 'Chapel of Love', everybody felt emotional for the happy couple. Everybody except Ethel, that was.

'I bet it don't bleedin' last. Either Susan'll fuck things up, or he'll start knockin' her about again.'

Maureen looked at her in horror. 'Can't you be nice just for one night, Mum? Jesus Christ, it's their engagement party.'

Ethel nudged Gladys. 'I'm never wrong, you mark my words.'

Gladys, who didn't know what day it was, nodded politely.

At the insistence of the youngsters, Rockin' Ronny halted his beloved rock'n'roll and played some disco instead.

As Kool & the Gang's, 'Get Down On It' blasted out of the speakers, Maria grabbed Tommy's and Freddie's hands.

'Come on, boys,' she said, pulling them seductively towards the dancefloor.

James stood in the corner, watching her out of the corner of his eye. He pretended to listen to Ellie, but he couldn't take his eyes off Maria. She was by far the prettiest girl in the pub, but not only did she know it, she was also acting like a slag. Fuming, he grasped Ellie's hand. 'Come on babe, let's dance.'

Ellie Phillips was in dreamland. Not only was James all over her like a rash, but it was all in front of Maria, the bitch she'd fallen out with.

Maureen watched events unfold on the dancefloor with sadness. Her plan to get Maria and James together had gone well and truly tits up. She guessed that Maria was getting her own back for what she'd witnessed on her arrival, and Tommy and Freddie were as pissed as farts, so it wasn't their fault. If only James hadn't been pawing that tarty girl earlier. If anything, it was his bloody fault for thinking through his dick. He didn't even like the girl, the silly little bastard.

'Do you wanna dance, Maur?'

Maureen smiled as Kenny took her hand and led her onto the dancefloor. He made her feel twenty-one all over again, did Kenny.

Changing the tempo, Rockin' Ronny put on Elvis's 'Love Me Tender' and unable to stop himself, sang along with him. He sounded just like his hero singing this particular track, everybody said so.

As Kenny took her in his arms, Maureen felt like a woman for the first time in years. She knew there was nothing in it – he was married to Wendy, for Christ's sake.

'Do you know what, Maur, I wish . . .'

Maureen stopped him there and then. 'Please don't say any more, Kenny. Come on, I'm not in the mood for this dancing lark. Let's go and get another drink, eh?'

Unaware of the tears in her eyes, Kenny followed her up to the bar.

At Freddie's insistence, Tommy had swapped partners

with him. 'She's all right, that Alison; I wouldn't mind giving her one. You dance with Maria.'

Tommy was quite happy with the swap, as Maria was by far the sexiest bird in the boozer.

Pretending not to look at Maria, James stuck his tongue as far down Ellie Phillips's throat as he possibly could.

Stuck in a time-warp, Rockin' Ronny put on 'Jailhouse Rock'.

Gladys, who had been behaving like a ventriloquist's dummy for the past hour, suddenly broke into life. 'Let's rock!' she screamed, throwing herself onto the dancefloor.

Maureen and Kenny roared as Ethel chased after her.

Rockin' Ronny finished his set with 'An American Trilogy', and called it a night. 'I wanna thank each and everyone of you for being so fantastic,' he said in an American drawl. 'Goodnight, God bless, I love you all.'

Susan was tired, her feet were aching and she had a terrible headache. Kev would be sure to want afters, and she couldn't face a late one.

'Me mum and nan are going, Kev, I think I might go with 'em. I've had three glasses of wine and I can't have no more. You can stay, I don't mind, honest.'

Kevin shook his head. 'I've had more than enough, Suze. I'll come with yer, babe. Why don't you ask your mum if we can have a nightcap round hers?'

Pleased that he didn't want to stay in the pub without her, Susan agreed and went off to find Maureen.

'I've always fancied you, you know. Can't we go somewhere? Just me, you, Freddie and Alison.'

Tommy looked at Maria in amazement. He'd never realised that she had the hots for him. Too drunk to think straight, he glanced around for James. Thankfully, he was nowhere to be seen.

'I'll have a word with Freddie, see if we can go back to his. You OK it with Alison, while I sort something out. Worst ways we can go to a hotel.'

Maria dragged Alison into the toilets. She was so drunk now that she didn't give a damn about anything.

Freddie was drunk, but he could handle his drink more than Tommy.

'We can go to mine. Me mum's gone away for the weekend to me aunt's in Canvey Island. Surely you ain't gonna shag Maria, though. What about James?'

Tommy shrugged. 'Look, James has been with that Ellie bird all night, he's well over Maria, he ain't bothered. Anyway I ain't gonna fuckin' tell him, am I? You was the one that made me swap partners – I'd have been happy shagging your one.'

Freddie smiled. 'We'll go back to mine, then.'

Seeing his brother and Freddie alone, James grabbed Ellie's hand and marched her over to them. He was desperate to know what the score was with Maria. He was just about to find out by pulling Tommy to one side when, to his dismay, Maria returned from the toilet. Unable to look her in the eye, he said the first thing that entered his drunken brain.

'I'm shooting off now, everyone. I'm staying round Ellie's, Tom, so tell Mum I won't be home.'

Dragging Ellie behind him, he marched out of the door.

Maria felt next to nothing as she watched them leave together. James wasn't the person she'd thought he was and Ellie Phillips was just a slag. In fact, they were welcome to one another. Smiling at Tommy, she seductively put her arms around his waist. She'd drunk so much wine that she was desperate for an adventure.

'Are we going back to Freddie's?'

Tommy nodded. He hadn't had a bunk-up for weeks

186

and wasn't one to look a gift horse in the mouth. Most of the birds he pulled were reasonably good looking, but Maria was outstanding. Itching to have his wicked way with her, he turned to Freddie.

'Order the cab, let's get out of here.'

Back at Maureen's, the party carried on where it had left off.

> You made me love you,
> I didn't wanna do it,
> I didn't wanna do it.
> You made me want you
> And all the time you knew it
> I guess you always knew it.

Maureen felt happy as she poured out the drinks. Not only had her family come back, but also Sandra and Brenda. Now all the oldies were being played, she'd never get to sleep. She smiled as she handed Kenny his scotch. He was a different person when Wendy wasn't about. He loved a good drink, and thoroughly enjoyed a singalong. It was such a shame that the woman he'd married had learned the knack of sucking the life out of him.

Kenny smiled at her.

> I want some love that's true,
> Yes I do,
> Indeed I do,
> You know I do.

Maureen joined in with him.

Gimme, gimme, gimme, gimme what I cry for.
You know you've got the brand of kisses that I die for.
You know you made me love you.

As they locked eyes, Kenny tore his away. 'Christ, I didn't realise it was gone two. I'd better ring a cab. Wendy'll be citing for divorce if I ain't home soon,' he joked.

Maureen handed him the phone and carried on singing with the girls. They couldn't stop laughing as Gladys leaped out of her seat and hitched up her skirt.

'My old man said follow the van and don't dilly dally on the way.'

'Bless 'er, she remembers all the words to the songs, yer know,' Ethel said fondly to Maureen.

Maureen squeezed Ethel's hand. 'Glad's fine, she's had a whale of a time tonight. She's living with you now and we're all here to help yer look after her.'

Ethel smiled. 'You're a daughter-in-law in a million, you are.'

'Mum, Maur, me cab's here. I'm going now.'

Ethel gave Kenny one of her famous looks. 'Night, love. You're much better company when yer without that miserable cow by yer side. Let's hope she's got the flu again next time we have a party.'

'Mum,' Maureen said, giving her daggers.

Seeing Kenny out, she apologised. 'You know what yer mum's like, Kenny, she don't mean anything by it.'

Kenny smiled. 'She's right though, ain't she?'

Hugging Maureen, Kenny kissed her on the cheek.

'Thanks for the lovely night, Maur, it's been wonderful, just like old times.'

Maureen waved as he got into the cab. Shutting the

door, she took a deep breath. It had definitely been like old times, too much so for her liking.

Maria let out a groan as Tommy pumped away on top of her. He thought she was showing enjoyment, but she knew differently.

'Ah, baby, you're so fuckin' sexy. Jesus, Maria. Ah, ah, ah.'

Maria felt ill as he rolled off her. What had she done? How could she have been so bloody stupid?

Putting an arm around her, Tommy laid back on the bed. He'd shagged some birds in his time, but it had never felt like that before.

'That was fucking blinding. Was it good for you, babe?'

'It was nice,' Maria said, her voice trembling. It was as much as she could do to stop herself crying.

Tommy wasn't the one she wanted. She was in love with his brother, but now she'd messed things up for good. As Tommy began snoring, Maria started to sob. This was it now, end of. She hadn't just lost her virginity tonight, but also her pride, her best friend and the man of her dreams.

TWENTY-TWO

As soon as daylight broke, Maria crept out of the bed and quietly got dressed. Usually, the sound of the birds singing made her feel happy. But today they didn't; she felt dirty and disgusted with herself.

Finding her knickers, she sat on the bed and slipped them on. She couldn't wait to get home, have a bath and scrub away the smell of Tommy Hutton.

Aware of her movements, Tommy opened his eyes and sat up. 'What yer doing? What's the time? You ain't going home already, are yer?'

Unable to bring herself to look at him, Maria finished getting dressed. 'It's nearly seven. I've gotta go, me mum'll be worried sick.'

Reaching towards her, Tommy grabbed her arm. For the first time in his life, he was well loved-up. 'Stay another hour, come back to bed and we'll have a little cuddle.'

Maria shook her head; she couldn't think of anything worse. 'I don't want to, Tommy. I've got a headache, I feel ill, and I just wanna get home.'

Surprised by her abrupt manner, Tommy leaped out of the bed and walked towards her.

'What's the matter, babe?' he said, taking her hands

in his. 'You're not worried about James, are yer? He's with that Ellie bird now, he'll be all right. Anyway, if we're gonna be seeing one another regularly, I'll break the news to him gently.'

Maria looked at him in horror. Seeing each other regularly! Was he having a laugh, or what?

As he put his arms around her and tried to kiss her, she smelt his beery, stale breath and felt her body go rigid. His touch made her feel ill and she had to put him straight.

'Look Tommy, we were both very drunk last night and we made a stupid mistake. I really like you as a friend, but I don't wanna relationship with you. You're far too old for me, anyway. I need to meet someone nearer my own age.'

Tommy couldn't believe what he was hearing. Cheeky little mare, who the fuck did she think she was? Annoyed that he'd mugged himself off, he did his best to sound cool. 'I don't give a shit if we see one another again or not, Maria. You know what I'm like with birds, I usually love 'em and leave 'em anyway. I was just being kinder to you 'cause we live next door to one another,' he lied.

Maria forced a smile. She wanted sod all to do with him, but she didn't want to make an enemy of him, either. 'Well at least we both feel the same way, Tommy, eh? Can we keep this a secret from James? If me and you was just a one-off, there's no point in him finding out about it, is there?'

Tommy shrugged. 'Fine by me.'

Maria picked up her clutch bag, 'I'll see you around, then.'

Shocked by her rejection of him, Tommy tried to contain his anger, but couldn't resist a parting shot. 'I promise, Maria, I won't say a word about last night to anyone.

You were nothing special anyway, girl, so why would I wanna brag about yer?'

Maria opened the bedroom door. 'The feeling's mutual, Tommy,' she said, as she closed the door behind her.

Fuming, Tommy flopped back onto the bed. He was used to birds falling at his feet, not giving him the fucking brush-off. Remembering the shy bird, Lucy, he'd met in the Bancroft, he decided to give her a call later. Fuck Maria, there were plenty more fish in the sea!

James woke up just before midday. Thankful that he was in his own bed, he sat up and rubbed his eyes. His stomach lurched as he remembered all that had happened the previous evening. He'd made a right prick of himself in the pub – he didn't even like Ellie Phillips and now everyone, including Maria, thought they were a couple. Thank God he'd had the brains not to shag her when he'd taken her home. He hadn't even gone in her house, he'd kissed her goodnight at the gate and staggered off home.

Seeing Maria flirting with Tommy and Freddie had really done his head in. Looking at his brother's empty bed, James wondered what had happened after the party. Surely Tommy hadn't got hold of her. He often stayed out all night, but the thought of him being with Maria made James feel physically sick.

Hearing his mum clattering about in the kitchen, he decided to go downstairs. If he stayed in bed, he'd only drive himself mad imagining the worst. Tommy loved him, they were brothers and he'd never betray him in a million years. Remembering the black bag episode, James tried to push it to the back of his mind.

He didn't recall much about being five years old, but he remembered lugging that bag about as though it were

192

yesterday. He'd been so bloody frightened, he didn't like to think about it, even now. Tommy hadn't mentioned it for years. He probably thought James had forgotten all about it, and maybe he would have done if he hadn't checked out his brother's case via the newspapers in the local library a few years back. The evidence that had convicted Tommy had been found hidden in a black bin bag in the alleyway that led round the back of Gladys's old house. James had gone cold as he read it. It was a journey he'd never forgotten. There were two questions he would have loved the answers to. How could his brother have got him involved when he was only five years old? And was his failure to hide the bag as well as he should have the reason Tommy had got caught?

After a lot of deliberation, he decided not to mention any of it to Tommy. Some skeletons were best left in the closet, so they say. Trouble was, this Maria thing was bringing it all back to him. It made him wonder if Tommy was as loyal and trustworthy as he made out.

'Christ, you look like something the cat dragged in. Shall I make you some brekkie, love?'

'Please, Mum.'

Maureen put a sausage and a couple of rashers on and sat down opposite him. 'I've got a bone to pick with you about last night. I invited Maria so that you and her could sort things out. You are a silly sod, 'cause just as the poor little cow walked in, you were groping that tart with the big tits. Maria loves and misses you and if yer can't see that, James, you're sillier than I thought.'

James felt himself go cold. 'I weren't groping Ellie when she came in, I only copped off with her 'cause Maria was all over Freddie and Tommy.'

Maureen shook her head. 'You were snogging her on

the dancefloor when Maria walked in. I clocked you, so did she, and I saw her run back out. I went out to find her and could see that she'd been crying.'

James stood up. Suddenly, he wasn't hungry any more, just angry. 'Why didn't you tell me all this last night?' he shouted.

'Don't have a go at me, it ain't my bleedin' fault. I would've told yer last night if you hadn't been so rat-arsed.'

Furious that he'd been so stupid, James grabbed his jacket and ran out of the house.

Next door, Maria was just as miserable as James.

'I'm gonna make us some lunch. Are you all right in there, love?' Janet asked.

Maria tried her best to sound cheerful, 'I'm fine, Mum, I'll be out in a minute.'

Janet went downstairs to prepare the lunch. Her Maria was acting really strange lately and she wished she could get to the bottom of it. She'd had a right go at her this morning when she'd stayed out all night without asking permission.

'Don't you ever do that to me again, madam. All night I laid awake. I even knocked Maureen up at half three this morning to see if you were in there.'

Maria burst into tears and ran to her room. She then refused to come out and had since locked herself in the bathroom for Christ knows how long.

Feeling a bit guilty, Janet added some salad to the cheese sandwiches. It had hit Maria hard when her dad left home and sometimes Janet blamed herself. She'd caught Alex having an affair and had kicked his arse out. For months he'd begged her forgiveness, but Janet was having none of it. She was far too proud even to give him the time of day, let alone forgive the bastard. At first

Maria had missed her dad terribly, but as time passed, her own bitterness had somehow rubbed off on her daughter.

'I don't want to see dad any more,' Maria announced a few months ago.

At the time Janet was secretly pleased. Serve the bastard right, she thought. That'll teach him to keep his dick in his pants. Recently, though, she'd felt differently. For all Alex's faults, he'd always been a good dad and she should have done what any decent mother would have done, encouraged contact.

Cutting the sandwiches in half, Janet sat down to wait for her daughter. They always ate lunch together and today would be no different.

Sinking his fourth and final pint, James stood up and walked out of the pub. He needed to be brave, should have done it years ago. Maria needed to know the truth of how he felt about her. Breaking into a run, he headed towards her house. It was now or bloody never.

Chucking a tenner at the cab driver, Freddie waved goodbye to Alison and went back into the house.

Tommy wasn't amused. 'About fucking time. Why didn't you get rid of her earlier? I've been sitting here like a prick waiting to go for a beer.'

Freddie laughed at his pal's annoyance. 'It ain't my fault if birds find me irresistible. She wouldn't leave me alone. All night and then again this morning – she was begging me for more.'

'Just hurry up,' Tommy said agitated.

Freddie grinned. 'Fucking hell, did you get out the wrong side of the bed or what?'

Tommy shook his head. He was still fuming over the

way Maria had treated him, but he wasn't about to tell Freddie.

'Nah, I'm just gagging for a beer. I fucked Maria off this morning, I thought you'd do the same and we'd be out by now. I'm bored, that's all,' he lied.

Grabbing his keys, Freddie pushed Tommy towards the door. 'Come on then, let's go, and you can tell me all about the lovely Maria.'

Tommy forced a grin. He had to lie to Freddie, he'd look a right fucking idiot if he told him the truth. 'She was OK, nothing special, mind. I've got a feeling it was her first time. I did ask her, but she denied it. Then again they always do, don't they?'

Freddie grabbed him in a headlock, 'A virgin, you lucky bastard. You seeing her again?'

Laughing, Tommy pushed him away. 'Nah, can't be arsed. I promised I'd ring her, but I won't bother. I was thinking about what you said, yer know, about telling James. I don't think he needs to know, so let's just keep it between ourselves, eh?'

Freddie nodded. 'I ain't gonna say anything, am I?'

Clocking the first pub he saw, Tommy dragged Freddie towards it. 'Enough about birds – let's talk business.'

Freddie smiled. Birds came and went; money was far more important.

Maria sat down gingerly. She was tender down below and the soreness was a constant reminder of her terrible night.

Janet handed her a sandwich, 'So where did you stay last night, love?'

Maria couldn't look her in the eye, 'I was at Alison's. I got a bit drunk, that's why I never came home.'

'Was it a good party?'

Maria was saved from answering by the doorbell.

'I'll get it,' she insisted. She thought it might be Alison and wanted to clue her up on what to say to her mum. As she opened the door, her heart leapt when she came face to face with James.

'Can we talk, Maria? There's something I need to say to you. Please, just hear me out.'

Maria's first thought was that he knew all about Tommy. Relieved that he didn't sound angry, she invited him in.

'Mum, I'm going upstairs to talk to James. Don't disturb us, will you?'

Janet smiled as she covered Maria's sandwich in cling-film. If James was back on the scene, it would explain Maria's strange behaviour. Janet adored James and would love him as a boyfriend for her daughter. Trouble was, Maria liked the bad boys. Many had been to the house to pick her up and Janet had never liked any of them. Praying that her daughter had finally come to her senses, she made a start on the ironing.

James was petrified as he walked into the bedroom. As Maria sat on the bed, he decided to sit next to her. At least that way he could say what he wanted, without seeing the rejection in her eyes. Clearing his throat, he began his speech.

'Look Maria, you're probably not gonna like what I'm gonna say, but I have to say it anyway. Ever since we were kids and shared our first kiss to "Puppy Love", I knew you were the girl for me. Deep down, I knew I was never your type, but I still lived in hope. As the years ticked by and you went out with bloke after bloke, all I became was your shoulder to cry on. Watching you waste your time with all them losers broke my heart and I had to keep a wide berth from yer for me own sanity. I knew you didn't want me, so I tried to get on with me own life, meet other girls and stuff. Them other girls, including Ellie Phillips, mean nothing. You're the one I want, you always have been, Maria.'

Overcome by emotion, Maria threw her arms around his neck. She was crying now, her tears a mixture of joy and guilt.

'Oh James, I wished you'd have told me ages ago. We've been so stupid and wasted so much time. I never really liked any of them boys I went out with, I didn't understand what we had until we fell out. I missed you so much when we weren't talking, and I sort of realised you was the one.'

Having waited a lifetime to hear such words, James started to cry too. Feeling a right wilf, he fiercely wiped his eyes. 'We're a right pair, ain't we? What are we like?'

Maria smiled as she hugged him. She felt so safe in his arms, it all just felt so right. Why the hell hadn't she seen what was in front of her eyes all along?

Tilting her chin, James gently kissed her lips. 'You still got that Donny Osmond record? he asked jokingly. He didn't think for a minute that she'd still have it.

Maria nodded. 'I've played it a lot lately, it reminded me of you. Shall I put it on?'

'Yeah, I wanna dance with yer to it.'

James held her close as 'Puppy Love' began. It was their first ever dance and they were both swept away with the romance of it all.

Staring into her eyes, James smiled at her. 'I really love you, Maria.'

Maria felt too guilty to speak, 'I love you too, James,' she managed to mumble.

She turned her head away from him. She couldn't look him in the eye, she didn't deserve him. As she sobbed,

James placed her head on his shoulder. Bless her, it's all been a shock and she's overcome by emotion, he thought. Obviously, he had no idea that the tears soaking his shirt were tears of pure guilt.

TWENTY-THREE

Kev took the piece of paper out of his pocket and checked the door number. 'This is it, number thirty-one.'

Susan looked at the six cats perched on the windowsill and felt herself shudder. Susan had never liked cats and the woman obviously had a house full of them. 'I don't wanna go in there, Kev. It's filthy, and I don't wanna catch something in case I harm the baby.'

Kevin laughed. Susan had been dead against visiting Mad Molly in the first place.

Susan allowed him to lead her up the garden path. She had a bad feeling about this, she really did. She'd done the ouija board once with Tracey, years ago, and the glass had flown off the table and smashed. Her mother had gone apeshit when she found out that she'd done it indoors.

'Yer silly little cow. Don't fuck with stuff yer know nothin' about. You're messin' with fate, and Christ knows what else.'

Ever since that day, Susan had held a fear of anything to do with the spirit world. But Kev, being Kev, was so desperate to confirm they were having a son that she'd allowed him to drag her to the most famous clairvoyant of all time. Molly Muggins was a part of East London folklore, and even though she was now eighty-eight, still had a reputation for getting anything she was asked spot-on. Rumour had it, the mad old bat had even predicted the Second World War.

As the front door opened, Susan felt the hairs on her arms stand up on end. A wizened woman with black teeth, Molly Muggins had a hump on her back like a camel.

'Would you like a cup of tea?'

Too scared to speak, Susan nudged Kevin. 'No, we're fine, thanks. All we want is a quick reading,' he replied.

Molly smiled. 'Come into my special room, then.'

As Susan walked in, she punched Kevin's arm. The room was painted black, with pieces of silver foil decorating the walls. The foil had been made into the shapes of the sun, moon and stars, and they were dotted everywhere. A little table was positioned in the centre of the room, with a large crystal ball sitting on top of it.

Susan sat gingerly on the sofa. There were too many cats to count, but all she could feel was their eyes penetrating her. Unable to stop herself freaking out, she stood up. 'I feel sick, Kev. You do the reading and I'll wait outside in the fresh air.'

Knowing that his mother was on the warpath, Tommy managed to avoid her for a few days by staying at Freddie's. Unable to outstay his welcome any longer, due to Freddie's mum returning from Canvey Island, he finally headed home late on Tuesday afternoon. Not brave enough to face the wrath of his old lady on his own, he decided to stop off at the pub for a pint. He wanted to check if that shit-bag Mickey Parks had his money and, also, he could ring James at the shop and get him to meet him there.

He had terrible trouble finding a phonebox that was working, but finally he found one.

'All right, bruv? Do us a favour will yer? Meet us at The Bancroft so I can come home with yer. Mother's got the knives out for me, ain't she?'

James agreed. 'She's definitely got a cob on with yer over something, but she ain't said what. I'll lock up now and meet you in about half an hour. I can only stay for a couple, though, I've got a date tonight. It's all been happening Tom, I've got loads to tell yer.'

Tommy smirked as he replaced the receiver. His little bruv must be loved up with Ellie, the bird with the big knockers.

James locked up the shop and ran for the bus. Thanking the driver for waiting, he sat down and smiled. The last few days had been pure heaven and he'd never felt so happy. He'd taken Maria out for a meal on Sunday and they'd properly discussed their future. He didn't want any secrets between them, so he'd had to come clean about Ellie Phillips.

'I never went home with her the night of the party, Maria, but I did go round there once. I honestly don't think I slept with her, but I was too bladdered to remember. Apart from the two girls that you already know about, there's been no one else that I've had sex with. I only got hold of Ellie to get back at you – I swear that's the truth.'

Maria smiled. She was hardly in a position to have a go at him. 'Forget Ellie, it doesn't matter now that we're together.'

'What about you?' James asked. The pair of them needed to start on a clean slate and he'd rather know now if she'd slept around.

'There's been no one,' Maria told him. 'Obviously I've done stuff with boys, but I've never gone the full way.'

James breathed a sigh of relief. He'd have accepted the situation if she had slept around, but he was so glad that she hadn't. He would be her first and hopefully her last.

James had no intention of rushing the sexual side of things between them, but he came up with a suggestion. 'I'd like to take you away for a weekend, Maria. It will be so nice, just the two of us and you can choose where we go.'

Maria was ever so excited. She told him that she liked the seaside, but he was to choose the destination. He didn't have a clue about seaside resorts and had asked Harold's advice. His boss had suggested Brighton and had shown him how to book it. He couldn't wait to tell Maria that it was all booked and they were going Friday week.

On hearing that Parksy had dropped the money round to his mum, Tommy bought him a pint. He didn't particularly like the geezer, but he wasn't one to hold grudges.

'I need to speak to me bruvver now, Mickey, I'll see you around,' he said, excusing himself.

As he walked over to James, he smiled. 'Fuck me, you look happy. Been giving Ellie some welly have yer, Jimmy boy?'

James laughed. Ordering his pint, he explained his good news. 'Me and Maria are going out properly, Tom. It's real serious and we've sorted out all the shit we went through. I love her so much and I can't tell yer how happy I am.'

Tommy couldn't help laughing. This was a wind-up, it had to be. 'Don't muck about, Jim. Go on, tell us about Ellie.'

James shook his head. 'Nothing happened with Ellie, I swear I'm not mucking about. Me and Maria are a couple, we're well loved up. We're even going away to a hotel for the weekend.'

Realising that his brother wasn't joking, Tommy excused himself. 'I'm just going to the khazi. I'll be back in a minute and you can tell us all about it.'

Tommy entered the toilets and fiercely punched the wall. He was absolutely fucking fuming. What the hell was Maria playing at? She was taking the piss, that's what she was doing. He would have given it a go with her, but no, she'd chucked him and come on to his little brother instead. He had to pull her to one side, have a quiet word. She wasn't going away with Jimmy boy, he wouldn't allow it. Dousing his face in cold water, he plastered on a smile and headed back to his sibling.

As his brother rambled on, Tommy tried his hardest to sound pleased for him, but unable to stand his obvious euphoria, he urged James to down his drink.

'Sorry, Jim. I am really happy for yer, but I might not seem it, 'cause I'm dreading facing mother.'

As they walked towards home, James asked him the one question he'd been too frightened to ask Maria.

'You know the other night, Tom, at Susan's party? What happened when I left, yer know, with Maria?'

Tommy put an arm around him. 'Nothing, you dick. All she was doing was trying to wind you up. She ain't got no interest in me or Freddie and, in any case, she's miles too young for us. We wouldn't be looking for birds that age, especially ones that me bruvver likes.'

James grinned. 'Thanks, Tommy, I thought you'd say that.'

Maureen checked the dumplings. They had stew for dinner tonight. Ethel had been on the thieve again this morning and had turned up with a rabbit.

'It's Glad's birthday today and it's her favourite. Will

yer cook it for us, Maur? Me old legs are playing me up again.'

Maureen smiled. She was such a lying old cow. Her legs never played up when she was out on the rob, but when she couldn't be bothered doing ought, her arthritis suddenly appeared. Informing her mother-in-law that she wasn't bloody stupid, she offered to cook the stew, and do a spotted dick for afters.

Maureen began dishing up. Hearing the door slam, she called out to her son.

'That you, James? Your dinner's ready, love.'

Tommy pushed his brother into the kitchen and walked in meekly behind him.

'All right, Mum?'

Maureen had to stop herself from throwing the hot saucepan at him. She hadn't said anything to Ethel about her trip to the building site; she wasn't in the mood for her 'I told you so'. She needed to get Tommy on his own, have his guts for garters, and she wasn't about to do it in front of James.

'I suppose you want some dinner?' she snapped at him.

'Please, Mum,' he said angelically.

She got another bowl out of the cupboard. She'd give him 'please, Mum'. She'd knock his fucking block off.

'There's plenty of stew left over. Why don'tcha knock next door, James, and ask Maria in for her tea?'

Maureen was over the moon that they'd finally got it together.

'I'll give her a knock,' Tommy offered, as James ran upstairs to get changed.

Maria was in her dressing gown when the doorbell rang. Her mum, bless her, had made herself scarce for the evening. Thinking that James was early, she excitedly ran down the stairs.

'You're early,' she giggled, as she opened the door.

Tommy barged in and slammed the door shut. Seeing her cover herself with her dressing gown, he smirked.

'Don't bother doing that, darling. I've seen it all before, remember?'

Feeling threatened, Maria tried to hold her nerve. 'What do you want, Tommy?'

Tommy peered towards the kitchen. 'Is your mother in?'

Maria nodded. She had to lie because she didn't want him to know that she was in the house alone. 'She's upstairs in the bath.'

Tommy sneered at her. 'Whaddya think you're playing at, Maria? What's all this about you and Jimmy boy?'

Maria looked away, 'I love him, Tommy, and I want to be with him.'

Grabbing her, Tommy shoved her up against the wall. 'You didn't love him last week, did yer? I ain't gonna let you fuck my bruvver about and break his heart. I want you to finish it with him.'

Maria looked at him in astonishment. He was jealous, she could see it in the bastard's eyes.

'I will do no such thing,' she exclaimed.

Tommy moved his face an inch away from hers. 'If you don't finish with him, I'm gonna tell him all about me and you.'

The smell of fags and beer on his breath made Maria feel sick. He revolted her and she realised there and then what a nasty piece of work he was. 'Tell him then, Tommy. He'll probably forgive me – we weren't even together at the time – but I'll tell you something, he'll never forgive you. If you wanna lose your brother for good, then go ahead and tell him.'

Tommy was stopped from answering by the knock on the door. 'All right,' he said, as James walked in.

'What yer doing, Tom? Your dinner's gettin' cold.'

Tommy smiled. 'I was just trying to entice your girl-friend indoors for some of mum's world-famous rabbit stew.'

'I've already eaten, James,' Maria said nervously.

Tommy smirked at her, 'Can't we tempt you with some spotted dick, Maria? That's your favourite, isn't it?'

Ignoring his sarcasm, Maria squeezed James's hand. 'Yous two go and have your dinner while I finish getting ready.'

Aware of an atmosphere between his brother and girl-friend, James shooed Tommy out.

'Tell Mum I'll be a couple of minutes,' he said.

He shut the door and held Maria tightly. 'Are you OK?'

Maria clung to him, 'I'm fine, James, just embarrassed. I thought it was you at the door and I was mortified when I stood there in my dressing gown and it was Tommy.'

James smiled. She was so sweet, that explained things. 'Why don't you quickly get dressed and come in. I'll wait for you.'

Maria refused. 'I haven't even done me make-up yet. Go and eat your dinner and hurry up back. Mum's gone out for the evening and I've got us a bottle of wine and a video.'

James kissed her and left. Even in her dressing gown she looked stunning, and being her boyfriend made him feel like a million dollars.

Sat on the wall, Susan grinned as Kevin walked towards her. The fresh air had worked wonders, and the panic she had felt earlier had all but disappeared. 'Well, how was your reading? What did she say? Are we havin' a boy?'

Kevin snatched her hand and pulled her off the wall. 'Come on, let's get out of 'ere,' he said.

Susan could see he looked as white as a ghost, and she was frightened to ask what was wrong. 'Did she say we're having a girl? Is that why you're upset?' she managed to say.

About a hundred yards from the house, Kevin stopped and took her in his arms. 'You was right, Suze, we shouldn't have gone. She went all weird on me. She really freaked me out, she did.'

Susan held his hands. 'What did she say?'

Kevin shrugged. 'Well, she said that we're 'aving a boy, but then she started rambling on about tears and sorrow. It made me paranoid. She was talking as if the baby was gonna be born disabled or have an illness or something.'

Susan was really annoyed. 'I told yer not to go, didn't I? She's off her head, the nutty old cunt. Take no notice. She's nearly ninety, for fuck's sake – what do you expect?'

Kevin still looked worried. 'Everyone says that she's always right though, Suze. Say our son's got Down's syndrome or something?'

Susan slapped him around the face. She didn't hit him hard, but she had to make him see sense. 'Look, Kev, if our baby had something wrong with it, the doctor would know. We can't spoil what's meant to be the happiest moment of our lives because we're worried about what some senile old woman's predicted.'

Kev nodded. 'I know you're right, but she kept goin' on about tears and sorrow. She even started wailing herself, and then the cats joined in.'

Susan shook her head. 'She's talkin' bollocks. She's probably got our future mixed up with our past. I mean, we had loads of tears and sorrow then, didn't we?'

Kev nodded. 'I suppose she is old. Maybe she looked in her crystal ball and saw the way we used to be.'

Susan carried on. 'She probably saw me glass Joanne, and you beat me up. There was plenty of tears and sorrow that night, wasn't there?'

Kev forced a smile. 'Let's not think about it any more. As you said, she's a nut-job. You were right though, we should never have gone to see her.'

Susan grinned. 'Well, best you listen to me in future, eh, Kev?'

Tommy was too wound up to enjoy his rabbit stew. He'd thought the bitch would fold, but instead she'd called his fucking bluff. Deciding he needed to get Maria out of his head once and for all, he borrowed his mum's phone and rang Lucy, the bird he'd met in The Bancroft. As he knew she would, she jumped at the chance of going out with him, so he took her address and arranged to pick her up at half eight.

Maureen kissed James goodbye and took the dirty bowls and plates into the kitchen. Shutting the lounge door so Ethel couldn't hear her, she went upstairs to see Tommy.

'How's the job going?' she asked, as she barged into his room.

Not knowing if she was on to him or not, Tommy was relieved to see her smiling. 'Yeah, it's going really well, thanks, Mum.'

'Yer lying little fucker,' Maureen screamed, as she laid into him.

Partially dressed, Tommy held his hands over his meat and two veg.

'What yer doin'? You gone off your head, or what?'

Maureen pushed him onto the bed. Wagging her finger in his smarmy mush, she gave him what for. 'I've been down to your building site and no one's ever fuckin' heard of yer there. Don't take me for a fool, Tommy. I've heard all the rumours about what you're really doing; now tell me the fuckin' truth.'

Tommy sat there like a naughty little schoolboy. She obviously had him by the short and curlies and if he told her that he was on a different building site, she'd only trot down there as well.

'I didn't tell yer the truth, Mum, 'cause I didn't wanna worry yer. I've been working with Freddie. It's nothing heavy, just a bit of this and that.'

Maureen clipped him around the head. 'What exactly is this and that, Tommy?'

'You know, just bits and bobs. A bit of thieving, that kind of stuff.'

Pulling his case from the top of his wardrobe, Maureen slung it at him.

'I want you to pack your stuff, son, and get out of my house. I will not have you disrupting your little brother. Through thick and thin I've stuck by you and this is how you repay me. I'm disowning you, Tommy Hutton. From today, me and you are finished.'

'Don't do this, Mum, please. Look, I'm sorry. I'll get a job, I'll make you proud, I promise. I'll . . .'

Maureen shut him up mid-sentence. 'I've given you enough chances, Tommy, but no more. You're no good, son. You're like yer fuckin' father. Just pack yer stuff and go. I want yer gone before James gets home.'

Totally unaware of what was going on next door, James was snuggled up to Maria. 'Can't we turn this girlie shit off and watch a proper film instead?' he asked, tickling her.

Maria forced a giggle. Tommy turning up earlier had completely ruined her evening. She hadn't realised that

210

he was so nasty and vicious, and she was worried about the lengths to which he'd go to spoil what she and James had. Sleeping with him was the biggest regret of her life. Part of her wanted to tell James the truth; maybe she should blame the drink and come clean. Twice tonight she'd tried, but the words just wouldn't come out. The thought of losing him was too much of a risk for her even to contemplate.

James topped up her glass. 'You're ever so quiet, babe. You're not bored with me already, are yer?'

Maria kissed him tenderly. 'I will never be bored with you, James. I love you too much for that.'

Beaming with pride, James turned back to the girlie film. He'd watch any old shit, as long as it made her happy.

Tommy dragged his case down the stairs and made a couple of phonecalls. He literally had nowhere to stay. He rang Freddie, and was told that he was out. Not wanting to ask Freddie's mum if he could doss there, he replaced the receiver. Apart from a hotel or a B & B, he was well and truly fucked. Remembering he was meant to be taking Lucy out, he rang her to explain and cancel.

'I've got my own flat, Tommy. You can stay here tonight, if you've nowhere else to go,' she said immediately.

Tommy was shocked. She'd only looked young and he'd assumed that she lived with her parents. He immediatcly took her up on the offer. It was dark now and he didn't fancy wandering about like a prick with his case.

'I'll ring a cab and see you in a bit,' he told her.

Sitting on the stairs, he thought things through. He didn't know sod all about this Lucy bird. Beggars can't be choosers and all that shit, but for all he knew, she could be a psycho.

Deciding to have one more crack at his mum, he walked morosely into the kitchen.

'Look, Mum, I'm really sorry. Please don't chuck me out.'

Hearing the cab toot, Maureen remembered the envelope that the junkie-looking boy had brought round. Grabbing it from the drawer, she slung it at him.

'Goodbye, Tommy. Take your dirty money and good fuckin' riddance.'

TWENTY-FOUR

Maureen took the tea bag out of the mug and threw it in the bin. She put up her deck chair, made a quick sarnie and took the tray into the garden. It was such a nice day, sunny with a lovely breeze. Finishing her lunch, she tilted back her head and took in the warmth. As she shut her eyes, she thought about James, and as usual she couldn't stop smiling.

It was less than a month ago that he'd come home with Harold in tow to tell her that he'd be taking over the tailor's shop earlier than expected. Harold had done most of the explaining.

'*Gloib mir*, your son to me is *bracha*. My health is none too good, Maureen, and I'm going to allow the boy to do his own thing. He's as good as *mishpachas* to me, and he's that good a salesman, my dear, all I do is sit on my *tuchis* all day. So, from next Monday young James is the proud owner of Cohen and Son. James, open the champagne,' he urged.

Maureen joined in with the toast. '*Mazel tov*,' she repeated after Harold.

When Harold left, she turned to James. 'I've guessed you're taking over the shop on Monday, but I never understood the rest. Doesn't he talk funny, that Harold?'

James smiled. 'He said that I'm a godsend and as good as family, Mum. *Mazel tov* means congratulations.'

Maureen looked at her son in awe. 'How do yer know what he's saying?'

James laughed. 'He speaks Yiddish. I've picked it up so well that I can now speak it better than he can.'

Maria had also been a positive change in James's life, and Maureen had never seen him so happy. To say they were inseparable was an understatement. They were totally in love and the tenderness they shared sometimes brought tears to her eyes. God had obviously looked down on her son and his girlfriend, as they had found that special something most of the world could only dream of. She was sure it would last between them. Having been best friends for years, they knew one another inside out. They were far too well suited and loved up for things to go wrong and, hopefully, one day they'd get married, have kids and live happily ever after.

True love was hard to find, she knew that only too well. Once she'd felt the real thing, the passion, but it wasn't to be. Not wanting to dwell on the past, she thought about her Susan. She still wasn't due for a couple of months, but her pregnancy was now taking its toll on her. She was ever so miserable, her feet were swollen and she was struggling with back pain. Maureen had done the best that she could. Most days she popped round Susan's flat and helped her with the shopping and housework.

'It'll all be worth it when you're holding that beautiful little baby,' she kept telling her.

'I'm never having any more, Mum,' Susan wept.

Maureen was doing buttons for her first grandchild to arrive. She'd knitted some beautiful little baby coats and was always picking up bargains on the market.

Ethel was a regular visitor to Mothercare. 'I've never

known an easier store to thieve out of,' she exclaimed. 'They're a load of divs that work there. I could walk out with fuckin' armfuls and no one would notice.'

With two of her kids sorted, Maureen still worried about the third. The night she'd chucked Tommy out, she'd been determined to wash her hands of him for good. Trouble was, as hard as she tried, she couldn't. She didn't like him very much, but having spent hours in labour giving birth to him, she couldn't hate him either. They were on speaking terms again, just. She didn't see much of him, but he popped in here and there to say hello. How he earned his money was a subject they no longer spoke about. He seemed to be doing OK, though. He had a girl-friend, whom she'd met once, called Lucy, and he was renting a flat with Freddie in Ilford somewhere.

It had been James who had begged her to resume contact with him. At first she'd refused, but he'd kept on and on at her until she'd agreed.

'Please, Mum, for my sake. Tommy adores you and the only reason he lied about the building site was 'cause he didn't want you to worry.'

James had always known how to wind her round his little finger. This time it was his persistence and doleful expression that did the trick.

'Bring the no-good bastard round, then,' she told him.

Although James was still in regular contact with his brother, they rarely went out drinking together any more, which pleased Maureen immensely. James had gone off the rails a bit when he'd been out boozing with Tommy and now he was with Maria, he'd sorted himself out. Maureen couldn't help turning her thoughts back to her youngest. She was so proud of him running that posh tailor's shop on his own. Her baby, the businessman – who would have ever believed it?

Feeling the first spots of rain, Maureen opened her eyes. She'd been so busy daydreaming that she hadn't realised the sky was as black as coal. Grabbing her deck chair, she ran inside. As she was about to put the kettle on, she heard the doorbell. Her family, all bar Tommy, had keys, so she guessed it was either Sarn or Brenda.

The sight of the two Old Bill was the last thing she was expecting.

'Are you Mrs Maureen Hutton?'

She nodded.

'Do you mind if we come in?' they asked, removing their hats.

With her heart in her mouth, she led them into the living room. It had to be to do with her Tommy, it couldn't be anything else.

'You might want to sit down, Mrs Hutton.'

Heart beating like a drum, Maureen flopped onto the chair. She knew it was serious by the look on their faces.

'What's my Tommy done now? Has he been arrested?'

The male officer did the talking. He told her his name, but she was in such a state that she couldn't even remember it.

'I'm afraid we have some bad news for you, Mrs Hutton. Your husband, Thomas, has been found dead at his home address in Whitechapel. We don't think that there were any suspicious circumstances, but unfortunately his body is rather decomposed. It seems he may have been dead for quite a while, so it may take some time to conclude the postmortem.'

Maureen nodded. Part of her felt relieved and part of her guilty. The relief was that it wasn't Tommy Jnr and the guilt was because she was glad it was her husband.

She turned to the coppers. 'Although we were still legally married, we'd been separated for years.'

216

The female officer stood up. 'Would you like me to get you a glass of water or a hot drink, Mrs Hutton?'

Maureen nodded, 'A cup of tea would be nice, dear.'

Shrugging her shoulders, Maureen smiled at the policeman. 'You probably think I'm weird, or wondering why I ain't crying, but truth is I ain't had nothing to do with him for years. Don't get me wrong, I wouldn't wish this on him, but he was a terrible husband and an even worse father.'

The officer smiled compassionately. This type of reaction was common in this neck of the woods. The women in Stepney were as tough as old boots.

'I understand,' he said sympathetically.

Maureen sipped her tea in a daze. She hadn't given a thought to poor old Ethel and didn't have a clue how to tell her the news. Like herself, Ethel had sod all to do with Tommy, but he was still her bloody son.

'His mum lives opposite me. Shall I go and get her?' Maureen asked.

'You're still in shock. Why don't I give her a knock?' the policewoman said, moving towards the door.

'No,' Maureen shouted. Ethel had a flat full of hooky gear, and would have a heart attack to see uniformed police standing at the door.

'I'll ring her and get her to come over,' she said.

Ethel arrived shortly after, with Glad in tow.

'Sit down, Mum,' Maureen urged.

Ethel eyed the Old Bill suspiciously. She had no time for the filth whatsoever.

'Tommy senior's dead, Mum. They found him in his bedsit in Whitechapel.'

Ethel wasn't good at showing her feelings. Her life had been too bloody hard for that. Not knowing how to react, she shrugged her shoulders.

'I can't say I'm shocked. He's been an accident waiting to happen for years.'

The two officers glanced at one another. The women of Stepney strike again, they both thought.

Gladys started to cry. 'Have you seen my Sooty?' she asked.

The police looked at her in amazement. Who the fuck was Sooty?

Seeing their puzzled expressions, Maureen couldn't help but laugh.

'Take no notice, it's her cat,' she explained.

The male officer stood up and urged his colleague to do the same. He had to get out of this nuthouse as quickly as possible. He couldn't believe the reaction they'd got to the poor man's death. The mother had shrugged, the wife was laughing, and the other old bird was more worried about the cat.

Maureen said goodbye to the coppers and shut the door. Taking a deep breath, she went into the kitchen and poured three large brandies.

''Ere, drink this,' she said, handing a glass to both Ethel and Glad.

Sipping her own, she thought of her children. Whatever Tommy had been, he was still their dad.

'I suppose I'd better ring the kids, get 'em to come round later.'

Ethel nodded. 'Kenny's working away in Birmingham. I'd better ring him and tell him what's happened.

Maureen got in touch with James at the shop. She didn't tell him what had happened, just told him to come straight home after work. She then got in touch with Susan and told her to come round at six. Tommy was the hardest to get hold of: she rang a few pubs he drank in, but couldn't track him down. As luck would have it, he popped into the shop to see James, who told him to come home.

Susan was the first to arrive, 'This better be important, Mum. I feel terrible.'

Maureen sat her down and made her a cup of tea. She wanted to tell the kids together, not separately.

James and Tommy arrived shortly after. Sitting all three of them on the sofa, Maureen sat in the armchair opposite.

'I'm afraid I've got some bad news for you. The police turned up earlier. Your dad's been found dead.'

James's lip began to wobble and as Susan burst into tears, he hugged her. Tommy showed no emotion whatsoever.

'Go and get 'em a brandy, Mum,' Maureen told Ethel.

James managed to pull himself together, but Susan couldn't stop sobbing. Seeing as she'd never been close to her father, or even liked the poor bastard, Maureen guessed it was just her hormones playing up.

The doorbell rang and she went to answer it. Seeing Kenny standing there was a shock, because she knew he'd been working away.

'I got here as soon as I could,' he said kindly.

'Go and see your mum, Ken, she's in there. I'll get you a brandy, love.'

As Kenny hugged Ethel, her eyes welled up. 'I'm OK – go and sit down,' she urged him as she fought to stop her tears.

Hearing his sister wailing, Tommy looked at her in contempt. 'For fuck's sake, Susan, get a grip, will yer? You didn't even like him, and yer ain't seen the tosser for years, have yer?'

Maureen stuck up for her. 'Leave her alone Tommy, she's pregnant.'

Tommy stood up. 'I ain't sittin' here listening to this shit. Everyone's got their fuckin' head in the clouds. Let's be honest, shall we? None of us wanted him dead, but none of us will miss him. He was a shit husband and a crap father, he was a loser and a drunk, so why are we all sittin' here fuckin' mourning him?'

No one replied. Tommy might be callous, but everyone knew he was telling the truth.

He turned to James. 'You coming out for a beer, Jimmy boy?'

James stood up, 'I could do with a pint, I'll just knock next door and let Maria know what's happening.'

As the boys left, Kevin arrived. He'd taken on a bit of private work, and had been busy all day painting some old dear's khazi. 'Are you all right, Suze?' he asked, hugging her.

'My dad's dead,' she wailed.

Maureen, Ethel and Kenny all glanced at one another. She was definitely overdoing the dramatics.

'How much is that doggy in the window? The one with the waggly tail.'

Everyone looked at Gladys in amazement. She picked her times and places, bless her. Maureen was the first to burst out laughing and soon everyone joined in. Even drama queen Susan was unable to keep a straight face.

Tommy and James stood at the bar in the Horn of Plenty. It seemed an appropriate place to go, seeing as their dad drank in there for many years. Both lads were in a quiet mood, neither really knew how to react to the news. Tommy had calmed down a bit now, and he was making James laugh with the old memories he had of their father.

Seeing Tibbsy, Benno and Dave Taylor walk in,

Tommy's stomach lurched. 'This is all we fuckin' need,' he muttered to James.

'All right Tommo? All right Jimmy boy?' Benno said.

Tommy looked at his old mates as though they were something bad he'd trodden in. Not only were they drunks and druggies but, if you listened to the grapevine, they'd also got into burglary and had mugged a couple of old ladies. Tonight, of all nights, Tommy really couldn't be doing with them.

'Look, lads, I hope yer don't mind, but I just wanna have a quiet drink with me bruvver. We've just found out that me old man's dead and we've got shit to sort out and stuff.'

Tibbsy grinned like a Cheshire cat. 'I saw your old man a couple of months ago. He was propped up in the corner of the Blind Beggar. He'd pissed and shit himself, the dirty bastard, and everyone was cracking up.'

As Benno and Dave Taylor burst out laughing, Tommy saw red. Grabbing Tibbsy by the neck, he shoved him up against the wall.

'See you, yer mug. Don't you ever, ever, disrespect me or my family again.'

Knowing he'd said the wrong thing, Tibbsy tried to turn his comments around. 'I'm sorry, Tommo. I didn't think you liked your old man. I would never disrespect you, you know that.'

Silencing him with a knee in the bollocks and a head butt, Tommy watched him slump to the ground.

'Whether I liked him or not is none of your business. He was my dad and if anyone's gonna slag him off, it'll be me.'

Seeing Tibbsy crumpled up in pain, Tommy snorted and spat on him. Turning around, he nodded to his brother.

'Come on Jimmy, we're out of 'ere.'

TWENTY-FIVE

The day of the funeral was wet and dismal, which matched everybody's mood perfectly. They'd found out only the day before that Tommy senior had been dead for over three weeks before his body was found. It was the postman who had alerted the police. He'd noticed a nasty smell, had looked through the letterbox and seen the room swarming with flies.

As the funeral cars headed towards the City of London Crematorium, the rain fell by the bucketful. It had been Ethel's decision to have Tommy cremated. In the past, all of her family had been buried.

'You bury treasure and burn rubbish, my dear old mum used to say,' she said.

Ethel had thought long and hard about her choice. No one would tend to his grave, so it was best to say goodbye once and for all.

Kenny led the family into the chapel. He'd been pretty choked up over his brother's lonely death and, for once, Wendy had been very supportive.

'I'll come to the funeral. He was your brother, after all,' she insisted.

Surprisingly, the chapel was quite full. There were a few distant cousins, a couple of aunts and uncles,

Freddie was there and all of Maureen's and Ethel's friends had turned up to offer their support. Tracey and Darren were the only ones who couldn't make it – they were on holiday in Spain.

'All right, son? How are you?'

James didn't recognise the grey-haired man at first.

'Charlie Venables. I helped you take your dad home from the Blind Beggar that time.'

James shook his head. 'Thanks for coming, Charlie.'

The service was short and sweet, and Kenny arranged a free bar and a bit of grub in the Horn of Plenty as a tribute. Tommy had been barred from the pub in the latter part of his life, but prior to that, had nigh on lived there.

Maureen had offered to do the honours. 'There's no point wasting your money in a pub, Kenny, I'll do it at home. There's hardly gonna be any people there, anyway.'

Kenny had refused. 'Look, Maur, it's a bad enough day for you as it is. Let the pub sort it, it'll cost peanuts and it's not worth the agg.'

'What's the matter, Mum?' Maureen asked, as she handed Ethel a brandy.

Ethel's eyes filled with tears. 'Oh I dunno, I was just picturing my Tommy as a little un. He was such a cute kid – all the neighbours loved him, yer know. He had this big gappy smile and was such a cheeky little sod. Once he found alcohol, that was it for him. It was his poison; he could never say no.'

Maureen hugged her. She'd never seen Ethel really cry before. 'He's at peace now, Mum,' she told her soothingly.

James looked at his watch: Maria should be here by now. She'd offered to take the day off work to come to the funeral, but he'd told her not to bother. She'd recently started a job in a hairdresser's not far from his shop and he didn't want her to get into trouble.

'Look, Maria, you've only been there for a fortnight and you can't ask for time off yet. Anyway, you never even met my dad. I'll be fine, honest. All my family will be there with me. Just come to the pub when you finish work, that's when I'll need you the most.'

Tommy ordered his brother another pint, 'What's up with you? You waiting to go home or something?'

James smiled. 'Nah, Maria's coming, she should be here soon.'

Tommy left James talking to Freddie and went to the payphone.

'Hi Lucy, it's me. The funeral went OK, and I'm in the Horn of Plenty now. Come down and 'ave a drink, will yer? I need a bit of TLC. Freddie's here, so bring one of yer mates. Ask that Sarah bird, she'll be right up Freddie's street, she will.'

Lucy agreed to come straightaway and, feeling pleased with himself, Tommy went back to the bar.

Seeing Wendy walking towards her, Ethel lifted her dress up. Clocking her look of horror, she winked at Maureen.

'Look at the boat race on Lady Penelope,' she said loudly.

Wendy turned to her husband. She'd spent all day playing the caring wife and now she'd had enough. 'Can we go soon, Kenny?'

Kenny glared at her. Didn't she realise this was his brother's funeral? 'No, we fuckin' can't,' he told her bluntly.

Susan was sat at a table with Kevin, sipping a glass of wine. Carrying a sprog wasn't all it was cracked up to be, and she felt as if she'd been pregnant for ever. 'Cop a feel of your son,' she said, putting Kev's hands on her belly.

Kevin's face lit up. 'Fuckin' hell, feels like he's kickin' and punching. Maybe he's gonna be a boxer, Suze.'

Susan laughed. Thankfully, they had virtually forgotten about their visit to the fortune teller. They'd made a pact that day not to tell anybody or mention it again, and they'd stuck to it. Susan was positive that their baby was fine. She should know – it was dancing about inside her morning, noon and night.

As Kev went up to the bar, Susan spotted a blast from the past that made her stomach lurch.

'What's up?' Kevin asked as he sat back down.

'Billy Barnard's over there with his mum. I feel really bad: I used to pick on him when I was young.'

Kevin shrugged. 'We've all done shit we regret when we were kids. Don't worry about it, Suze.'

Susan stood up. 'I need to go and speak to him. I know he ain't all the ticket, but I still have to apologise.'

Billy grabbed his mother's arm as Susan walked towards him. Her face brought back so many terrible memories that he was unable to control his emotions. 'Please don't let her hurt me. Tell her to go away, Mum.'

Mrs Barnard stroked Billy's arm. 'It's OK love, sssh. No one will hurt you while I'm here.'

Unable to look at Billy's panic-stricken face, Susan spoke directly to his mum. 'I just wanna say that I'm so sorry for the way I used to treat your Billy. I was a horrible person when I was younger, and I hate myself for it.'

Mrs Barnard nudged her son. 'Susan's saying sorry to you, Billy. She wants to be friends with you.'

Billy shuffled his feet and looked at the floor.

'Be a good boy and shake Susan's hand,' his mum urged.

Susan smiled as Billy held out his podgy hand. 'I'm sorry, Billy. Truly sorry.'

*   *   *

225

Maria felt really nervous as she walked towards the pub. She'd managed to avoid Tommy since the day he'd come barging into her house. She'd been on top of the world when she'd heard his mother had kicked him out. It was such a relief not to have to worry about him knocking on her door, or seeing his smarmy face.

James still saw him a few times a week. Now and again they had a boys' night out on a Friday but, other than that, he only saw him at work. She knew that Tommy often popped into the shop. He'd obviously never said anything about their night of debauchery, but she didn't trust him as far as she could throw him. She could sense he was an evil bastard, and the thought of seeing him tonight was making her feel sick to the stomach.

As she reached the pub, she took a deep breath. James needed her and she had to be there for him.

Sandra and Brenda were the first to start the singalong. It was a ritual in this neck of the woods, especially after a funeral. 'Daisy, Daisy, give me your answer do! I'm half crazy, all for the love of you!'

Wendy was in total disbelief as the rest of the pub joined in. They were at a funeral, for Christ sake, and these low-lifes were acting as though it was a bloody party.

'Hello darling.' James hugged Maria as though he'd never let her go. He might not have ever been close to his dad, but he'd found the whole day upsetting all the same. 'You're well late, but I'm so glad you're here,' he told her.

With his arm casually slung around Lucy, Tommy watched the tender moment between his brother and Maria with interest. She was looking at him adoringly and clinging to him like a fucking leech. He couldn't help

226

smiling as he turned back to Lucy. As special as Maria thought she was, he'd been the first to penetrate that tight little fanny of hers.

He walked towards her and politely kissed her on the cheek, 'Hello Maria. How are you? This is Lucy, my girlfriend.'

'I'm fine thanks, Tommy. Nice to meet you, Lucy,' Maria said, relieved that he had a girlfriend in tow.

Maria tugged James's arm. 'Where's your mum?'

'Over there with me nan.'

Maria smiled. 'Shall we go and sit with them?'

'If you want,' James replied.

Ethel spotted her first. ''Ere she is, me little darling. You come and sit over 'ere with me.'

Wendy moved up and ended up sitting next to Gladys. If things weren't already bad enough, she was now lumbered with the nutty old bat that swallowed whole ducks.

Gladys smiled at her. 'How much is that doggy in the window? The one with the waggly tail.'

Wendy stood up. She'd had enough. Searching for her husband, she found him up at the bar.

'Kenny, I've tried, but I can't stand this one minute longer. Can you call me a cab, please?'

Tommy was spot-on about Freddie liking Sarah. He was all over her like a rash, the dirty bastard.

'Looks like we'll be going out in a foursome from now on,' he joked to Lucy.

Lucy agreed. 'I'm just popping to the little girls' room, I'll be back in a sec.'

Tommy smiled as she walked away. She had a cute little arse and he liked the way she wiggled it. He couldn't quite put his finger on how he felt about Lucy. She'd been bloody good to him, that was for sure. He'd barely known her at all when his mum had chucked him out, but she'd let him stay there for a week and treated him like a god at the same time. She was three years older than he was and worked as a receptionist up town. She was no man's fool and he did really like her, but that special spark wasn't there. He fancied her all right, though. She was slim, blonde and stunning, but she was a bit too quiet; he liked them feisty.

Maureen and Ethel were more than ready for a singalong.

> Pack up all my care and woe,
> Here I go, singing low,
> Bye bye blackbird.

Susan tried to join in, but couldn't. The baby kept kicking and bringing tears to her eyes.

Noticing that her daughter looked as white as a ghost, Maureen stopped singing. 'Are you OK, love?'

Susan forced a smile. 'I think I'm having a footballer, Mum. It's got to be a boy, he don't stop bleedin' kickin' me.'

Maria giggled as James joined in. He knew every word to every bloody song.

'How do you know all these oldies?' she asked him.

James smiled. 'I was brought up with the bloody stuff. My nan drummed every word into me from the age of two onwards.'

Extremely drunk, Kenny was relieved that Wendy had now gone home. She did his head in sometimes and, as much as he loved her, he could never quite relax in her company.

'Ssh, it's my turn now to choose a song,' he demanded.

'Go on, my son,' Ethel urged. Her Kenny had such a lovely voice.

Kenny stood up. 'Who's sorry now? Who's sorry now? Whose heart is achin' for breakin' each vow.'

Maureen stood up. She desperately needed another drink.

Watching her mother walk away, Susan grabbed hold of the table. She was fucking sorry now, that was for sure. The baby was giving her gyp and when the little bruiser finally arrived, it would definitely be her first and last.

Enjoying the singsong, James told Maria to shout up some more drinks. The ramp in the Horn of Plenty was round and centred in the middle of the pub. Seeing Maria standing opposite, Tommy excused himself from his present company and walked over to her.

'How's it goin'?'

Maria felt like running back to the table, but decided against it. She wasn't going to let him think he had the better of her.

'Things are going great, thanks. What about you? Lucy seems nice.'

Tommy smiled. 'She is, and she's far better in the sack than you.'

Looking around to make sure no one had heard, Maria snarled at him. 'We need to forget the past, Tommy. I'm with James now, you're with Lucy, so why can't we just be friends?'

Seeing James walking towards them, Tommy slyly pinched her arse. 'Of course we can, Maria.'

Debating whether to feign a migraine and ask James to take her home, Maria was stopped in her tracks by the commotion at the table. 'Whatever's goin' on?'

James shrugged, 'I dunno.'

Unable to help herself, Susan let out a scream. This

229

was more than just the baby fucking kicking. 'Mum, help. I think me appendix has burst or something.'

Kevin was standing over the other side of the pub with his mates. Seeing his Susan in distress, he darted towards her.

'Are you OK? What's wrong with you? It's not the baby, is it?'

Gasping for breath, Susan lay on the seat. She felt like something out of a freak show as everyone stood gawping at her, but she was in so much pain, she didn't care.

Glad looked at Ethel and nudged her. Ethel nodded. They might have spent most of their life aborting babies, but they were the only two to notice when one was on its way. Ethel was the first to pipe up. 'Move back, she's in bleedin' labour – her waters have broken.'

Kevin was hysterical. The baby wasn't even due yet. 'Don't just stand there! Ring a fuckin' ambulance!' he yelled at the barmaid.

The ambulance arrived within minutes.

Aware of the paramedics getting the hump with Kevin's behaviour, Maureen took him to one side.

'Me and Ethel'll go with her in the ambulance. You follow in a cab and for fuck's sake, calm yourself down. They'll chuck you out of the hospital if you behave like that, yer know.'

Kevin was desperate to be a daddy, but he had a terrible phobia of pain, blood and everything else that went with it. He was one of the old school, and believed men shouldn't be involved with those things. Looking up Susan's fanny was certainly not on his 'must do' list, and seeing her actually push the kid out would put him off sex for life. Seeing the state of him, James and Tommy offered to accompany him to the hospital.

'Please come, Maria,' James begged her.

Maria refused. She blamed getting up for work in the morning, but really she was repulsed by the thought of sitting in a confined space alongside Tommy. Lucy opted not to go either. She was quite shy and didn't fancy being at such an important event with a family she barely knew.

'I'll drop the girls off home and I'll keep an eye on Glad until you get back,' Kenny offered.

The London Hospital was literally minutes away, in Whitechapel. Susan's contractions were fast and furious and she was rushed straight into delivery. Ethel and Maureen donned surgical gowns and stood beside her.

'Aah, I'm fuckin' dying!' Susan screamed. 'It hurts so much, Mum,' she cried.

'I hope everything's all right. She ain't 'alf early,' Maureen whispered to Ethel.

Ethel squeezed her hand. 'She'll be fine, they've just got the dates wrong, the soppy bastards.'

Maureen smiled. 'God works in mysterious ways, don't he? We've just said goodbye to Tommy Snr and our first grandchild chooses to arrive on the very same day.'

Outside, Kevin was pacing the corridor like a madman. He could hear Susan screaming and it was doing his head in.

'There's something wrong in there, I know there is,' he said, over and over again.

James put an arm around him. 'Everything'll be fine, Kev. Just sit down and drink your coffee, it'll all be over soon.'

'I can see the head, Susan,' the midwife said. 'You're doing just fine. Now keep on pushing, deep breaths.'

Maureen and Ethel squeezed each other's hand. They were both emotional and even Ethel had tears in her eyes. A little baby in the family; they couldn't wait to spoil it.

'You're nearly there now, Susan. One more big push and baby will arrive.'

Susan took one last deep breath. 'Aaaah!' she screamed.

Spellbound, Maureen and Ethel looked at one another.

'It's a boy,' the midwife announced happily.

Ethel was the first to snap out of her trance. She had forgotten her glasses and her eyes must be deceiving her. Taking a closer look at the child, she jumped back in shock.

Frozen to the spot, she grabbed Maureen's arm.

'Gawd, stone the crows! Either I'm going off me rocker or me blinkers are playin' me up, 'cause I'm tellin' yer now, Maur, as God's my judge, that baby looks fuckin' black!'

TWENTY-SIX

Temporarily struck dumb, Maureen took a closer look. There must be some mistake; there had to be. She stared at the child and shook her head in disbelief. Compared to Kevin and Susan, it was as black as a raven's wing.

Finding her voice, she turned to Susan. 'What have yer been doin'? Yer dirty little whore. Poor Kevin's standing outside. What am I meant to tell him, eh? You've pulled some strokes in the past, Susan, but mark my words, yer brothers will disown you this time. Rip the family to pieces, this will.'

Not knowing what to do for the best, the midwife tried to defuse the situation by handing the screaming baby to Susan.

'It's not mine. I don't want it. Get it away from me,' Susan shouted. Thinking back, Susan realised that although she'd spotted, her periods hadn't been normal ever since she'd slept with Royston. If only she'd gone to the doctor. She could have aborted the bastard kid without anyone knowing.

'Do you want to hold him?' the midwife asked Ethel.

Ethel shook her head. 'No, I fuckin' don't.'

* * *

Kevin paced up and down the corridor. All he could think of was his reading with Molly Muggins. 'I'm sure I heard the baby cry ages ago. Do yer think there's something wrong? Why ain't no one called for me?' he said, holding his head in anguish.

Tommy and James glanced at one another. They were both thinking the same as Kev, but neither wanted to admit it.

As the baby let out another scream, Tommy smiled. 'Boy or girl, it's got a pair of lungs on it. You're gonna have some sleepless nights with that racket,' he joked.

Kevin flopped onto a nearby chair. The waiting was playing havoc with his mind. He turned to James. 'Go in there for me. I can't take any more of this. Just find out what's goin' on, will yer? I'm dying to know if it's a boy.'

James nudged his brother. 'I don't wanna see Susan with her legs up in the air. You're the oldest, you go in, Tom.'

Tommy stood up. Somebody had to do the honours. He walked towards the delivery room and poked his head around the door. 'What's happening? Kev's pullin' his hair out. Is everything all right?'

Susan's sobbing and his mum's and nan's stern faces answered his question. 'You're gonna have to wait outside,' the nurse told him.

Tommy ignored her. He wasn't moving until he found out what was wrong. He heard the baby cry and walked towards the cot.

'Don't look at it, Tommy,' his mother said, pushing him away.

'Let him fuckin' see it. Let him see what his dirty whore of a sister has been up to. We can't bleach it and pretend it's fuckin' white, can we?' Ethel shouted.

Tommy felt sick as a pig as he peered into the cot.

Unable to control himself, he lunged towards Susan. 'You fuckin' slag. Who's the father, you fuckin' whore?'

The nurses tried to stop him as he grabbed Susan by the hair and tried to drag her out of the bed. 'Get security,' one screamed.

'Stop it, Tommy. You're hurting her,' Maureen yelled, as she grabbed him from behind.

Afraid for Susan's safety, Nurse Zokora leaped into action. She was of African origin herself, and was more than used to the racist comments and behaviour that she was seeing and hearing. 'Please, let us stop this fighting. We have a beautiful baby boy here. The child needs his mother and his family; he needs love, bless his soul.'

Ethel shook her head. 'He's one of yours, darlin', not one of ours. I ain't bein' seen with a kid that's as black as Newgate's knocker. Imagine takin' it out in a pram? We'll be a laughin' stock, us Huttons, the talk of the fuckin' town.'

As two security guards rushed past, Kevin stood up. 'What the fuck is goin' on?' he shouted, as he followed them into the room. 'Susan, where's my baby? Is it a boy? What's wrong with him? Is he dead?' Kevin screamed, as Tommy walked towards him.

Ethel was the first to answer. 'He ain't your son, Kevin. The baby's as black as fuckin' soot. It's in that cot; look for yerself.'

Maureen shot her a look. She could be so tactless at times.

Kevin looked at Tommy. Ethel was winding him up, she had to be. Tommy shook his head. 'Let's talk outside, Kev.'

Kevin pushed Tommy out of the way and looked into the cot. 'No, Susan, no,' he sobbed, as he sank to his knees.

'I'm so sorry, Kev. It was one night, I was drunk. Please

forgive me, I'll get it adopted and me and you can have another baby. Don't leave me, Kev, please, I love you.'

'You have to leave now. Only birthing partners are allowed in here,' the security guard told Tommy and Kevin.

'Touch me again and I'll knock you out,' Tommy shouted, pushing him away.

Maureen bent down and urged Kevin to stand up. 'Come on, love, let's get you out of here.'

Still sobbing, Kevin felt a bolt of anger surge through him. 'What is my mum and mates gonna say? I've been taken for a right cunt, and it's all that slag's fault. Fuckin' black man's meat, she's a fuckin' whore. I'll kill you for this, Susan, fuckin' kill yer. Molly Muggins was right: sadness and tears, she said. When you get out of this hospital, you're dead, you nigger-lovin' slag.'

As he was led from the room, Kevin completely lost the plot. 'I'm gonna fuckin' kill some cunt,' he screamed, as he pushed over the drinks machine.

Being no more than eighteen stone between them, the security guards were well out of their depth. 'Call extra security,' one shouted to the other.

As Kevin continued smashing up the hospital, Maureen and Ethel walked outside. Distraught, they sat on a wooden bench. 'I can't believe this is happening. What are we gonna do, Mum?' Maureen asked.

Ethel shrugged her shoulders. 'Don't ask me. I suppose it's best all round if she has it adopted.'

Maureen shook her head. 'She can't do that. No matter what colour it is, it's still our flesh and blood.'

Ethel stood up. 'Well, it ain't my flesh and blood. I'll never be able to show me face down the bingo or the market again. I'm goin' home now. Need a lie down, I do. I want nothin' more to do with Susan or the fuckin' kid.'

Maureen watched her walk away. Part of her wanted to do the same, but she couldn't.

Unable to stop Kevin taking his temper out on the hospital property, Tommy and James could only watch as the police arrested him and led him away.

'Poor bastard,' Tommy said, as they sat in a nearby pub drowning their sorrows a couple of hours later.

'I wonder what's gonna happen to the baby. Do yer think she'll keep it?' James asked his brother.

'Fuck knows, but I ain't having nothin' to do with it, and neither are you, Jimmy boy. I could kill our Susan – talk about trash the family name. I wish I knew who the father was: I'd kill the black cunt.'

James kept quiet as he sipped his drink. He remembered seeing Susan and Royston together. They'd both looked dishevelled and Tommy's welcome-home party was about nine months ago. He decided to say nothing. Tommy was a loose cannon, and James didn't want him to get himself locked up again. He changed the subject. 'Where's Mum, Tom? Did she go home or stay at the hospital?'

About to answer, Tommy was aware of laughter coming from the bar area. He turned around and came face to face with Tibbsy, Benno and Dave Taylor. 'What's funny?' he said.

'We hear your Susan had her baby. What did she have?' Tibbsy asked, nudging the others.

Tommy looked at James. News travelled fast in the East End, and he needed these goons like he needed a hole in the head. He never used this boozer himself, and had he known his old pals did, he would have gone elsewhere. 'Why don't you fuck off, you losers,' Tommy told them.

Dave Taylor was very drunk. Killing himself with

laughter, he decided to be brave. 'I heard she had a golliwog.'

Tommy jumped up and smashed Taylor in the face with his pint glass.

'I'm calling the police,' the barmaid screamed.

'Leave it, Tom, they ain't worth it,' James shouted, trying to break up the fracas.

As Tibbsy and Benno joined in, Tommy went mental and all hell broke loose. Desperate to stop his brother from getting nicked, James could do only one thing to stop the fight.

'It's their mate's kid, Tom. It belongs to Royston Ellis.'

As the sound of sirens echoed in the distance, Tommy spat on the ground and brushed himself down.

'You called yer own mate's kid a golliwog, yer fuckin' two-faced mugs. Grass me up, and I swear I'll kill all of yer.'

As Tommy and James left the pub, Benno, Tibbsy and an injured Dave Taylor were totally lost for words.

Maureen opened her eyes and for a second wondered where she was. She quickly remembered. After the chaotic scenes earlier, Susan had been moved to a little room of her own.

'Why don't you stay with her? Help her bond with the baby,' the nurse had told Maureen.

Susan had been in a terrible state. Totally exhausted, she had finally sobbed herself to sleep.

Maureen checked that Susan was breathing OK and stood up. She'd dozed off on the chair, and her neck was as stiff as a board. The baby was nowhere to be seen, and Maureen felt guilty as she thought back to earlier.

'Get it out of my sight. I hate it – it's ruined my life. I never want to see it again,' Susan had screamed at the nurse.

As the door opened, Maureen smiled. Nurse Zokora had been so nice to her. 'Would you like a cup of tea or coffee?'

Maureen nodded. 'I've got a mouth like a camel's arse, a cup of tea wouldn't go amiss. Where's the baby?'

'I'm looking after him in another room. He is so beautiful; why don't you come and see him?'

Maureen followed her into the nicely decorated room. As she looked into the cot, she was surprised to see him wide awake.

'Would you like to hold him?' the nurse asked.

Maureen automatically nodded. Half of her wanted to touch him, the other half was telling her not to form too close a bond.

The nurse handed her the child. 'I won't be long. I'll go and get your cup of tea for you.'

Maureen stared at the child. He was big for a newborn, and had striking features. She sat on a chair and stroked his cheek. 'We're goin' to have to think of a name for you soon,' she whispered.

As he clenched her little finger, she felt the tears roll down her cheeks. 'You look like a Johnny to me, but I'll have to check with your mum if that's OK first.'

He gurgled and she held him close. It didn't matter what colour he was, he was her grandson and he needed her. She smiled at him.

'I won't let you be adopted. If yer mum doesn't want yer, then Nanny'll take good care of yer.'

Nurse Zokora stood outside listening to the conversation Maureen was having with herself. She smiled. These racist people were all the same and, apart from the odd one, they all came round in the end.

TWENTY-SEVEN

Maureen lifted her grandson out of his cot, and tenderly fed him his bottle. 'We're gonna have to get our arses in gear and sort his birth certificate, Susan. Shall we register him as Johnny? Or do yer wanna choose something else?'

Susan stared at the television. 'Call him Mistake for all I fuckin' care! As I've told you a hundred times already, Mum, I don't want him. He'll have a much better life if we put him up for adoption.'

Maureen threw her a look of evil. 'Over my dead body will you farm him out. You made your bed, Susan and, believe me, you will fuckin' learn to lie in it.'

'How am I meant to love a child that's taken away everything good that I had in my life?' Susan sobbed. 'Kevin's left me, Tracey called me a dirty fat slag and told me never to ring her again, Tommy and Nanny hate me. At least if I gave him away, I could make a fresh start. If he was white I could manage, Mum, but how can I bring up a black kid round here?'

Maureen put her grandson in his baby chair and sat next to Susan. She'd been staying with her daughter since she'd left the hospital. The nurses had been worried by Susan's behaviour, and Maureen had promised she would look after the baby herself.

As Susan sobbed, Maureen awkwardly put her arms around her. 'I know things are hard Susan, but you can't shut the barn door after the horse has bolted, love. Little Johnny needs you, you're his mum, and give it time, things will get easier for yer. People's attitudes will change. Look at James, he's already mellowed and in the future Tommy and Nan will do the same. Look at him, Susan, he's gorgeous – how can people not love him, eh?'

Susan said nothing. Her mother meant well, but was doing her head in. She needed to get rid of her fast, and if acting like a doting mother herself was the only way, so be it. She smiled. 'You're right, Mum. Bring him over here and let me hold him.'

Royston Ellis stood nervously outside the Horn of Plenty. Jan, the barmaid, had rung him to tell him the Huttons were having a lunchtime tipple. It had been just over a fortnight now since his pals had informed him that he was the father of Susan's child, and he'd been shitting himself ever since. He'd fled the area as soon as he'd heard, and had stayed at his cousin's in south London. He'd had no plans on coming home, but his mother had turned up yesterday with other ideas.

'You disappoint me, Royston. I brought you up to be a man, and if you've fathered a child, you get your arse back home and face the music. I want you to go and see the family and ask for some proof. If it turns out to be yours, you have no choice other than to financially support it.'

As Royston entered the pub, James clocked him immediately. 'Tom, look,' he said, nudging his brother.

As the pleasant-faced lad stood in front of him, Tommy felt no hatred. He'd done a lot of homework on Royston, and from what he'd heard, he was a cut above Tibbsy,

241

Benno and Dave Taylor. He occasionally drank with them, but was no petty crook like they were.

'Can I have a quiet word with you?' Royston asked nervously.

Aware that the pub had fallen silent and all eyes were on him, Tommy did what any brother of a white East End family would do. 'Yer cheeky black cunt,' he said, as he gave him a right-hander.

James grabbed hold of his brother. 'Leave him, Tom. Let's go outside, see what he has to say. Kickin' shit out of him ain't gonna solve anything, is it?'

Grabbing Royston by the neck, Tommy shoved him out the door.

Thrilled that Susan was showing more enthusiasm, Maureen stepped up her plan. 'Why don't we put Johnny in the pram and take him out for a walk? We can't stay cooped up in here for ever, we all need some fresh air.'

The thought of facing the outside world filled Susan with dread. Everyone knew that she and Kev had been an item. How was she meant to explain her baby being born fucking black? Desperate for her mother to move back home, she agreed. Being seen out with the bastard child was the last thing she wanted, but once her mum got off her case, she could do as she pleased.

Maureen smiled as she handed Susan her coat. 'We fit?'

Susan forced a smile. 'Walkies, Johnny,' she said sarcastically.

Ethel was deep in thought as James told her about Royston's visit to the pub.

'When he first walked in, I thought Tommy was gonna marmalise him, but when we got outside, he seemed to

242

calm down a bit. Royston said that he'll definitely support Johnny if it's proved he's his. Tommy seemed OK about that – well, he must have been 'cause he's still going out clubbing tonight with Freddie. I know it's awkward, Nan, but I don't think Royston deserved a clump. I know he ain't white, and he'll never be one of us, but he don't seem a bad bloke. At least he had the balls to come and see us and try to sort things out.'

Ethel handed James his dinner. 'I never thought I'd see the day when I felt sorry for Kevin. How long had they been at it for? Do yer know?'

James shrugged. 'Royston reckons it was just a one-night stand. He said they were both drunk and it just sort of happened.'

Ethel shook her head. 'The dirty little whore, and don't you worry about Tommy, he did the right thing. Black and white don't mix, James. If we were all meant to live in fuckin' harmony, God would have mixed us all together in the first place.'

James said nothing as he polished off his lamb stew. He'd had a couple of black mates at school, and he couldn't fully understand his nan's and brother's attitude. He handed his nan her dish back. 'That was handsome: I'm gonna shoot off now, Nan.'

'Where yer goin'?' Ethel shouted, as he grabbed his coat.

'Me mate's,' James lied.

He wasn't, really. He was going to see his mum and baby Johnny. Black or white, that kid was his nephew, and no matter what anyone else said, he wanted to be part of Johnny's life.

Maureen held her head high as she pushed the pram along-side Susan. Old Mother Kelly and her sister were heading their way and she was determined to put up a front.

243

'Lovely day, isn't it? Would you like to see my grandson?' she said boldly.

Old Mother Kelly peered into the pram. 'He's a big boy, ain't he? I heard he was a darkie, but he's lighter than I thought he'd be.'

Maureen linked arms with Susan. 'Dark, light, pink or blue, he's my first grandchild and we all love him dearly. Such a shame you never had children yourselves – it's a wonderful feeling to become a nan,' Maureen said sarcastically.

Old Mother Kelly and her sister nodded a curt goodbye and walked away. Maureen smiled at Susan. 'Never had a man between them, those two. Always lived together as well. Rumour has it they're a pair of old lesbos.'

Susan smiled politely. Her mum might have more front than Marks & Spencer, but she couldn't wait to get home. Taking Johnny out was embarrassing, and she wished the pavement would swallow her up.

'Oi, yer fuckin' slag! You've got some front showing yer face round 'ere. My Kevin's moved up north because of you.'

Maureen could only look in horror as Kev's mum, Sheila, ran towards them and grabbed Susan by the hair. Susan let out a sob and fell to the ground. As Sheila kicked Susan in the face, Maureen shoved the pram into someone's front garden and lunged towards them.

'You think your Kev's so fuckin' perfect then, do yer? No wonder she fancied a change. Beat her to a pulp, he did, on one occasion. I should know – I sat up casualty with her all fuckin' night.'

With Susan rolled up like a ball on the ground, Sheila turned her anger towards Maureen. 'You soppy, naive mug,' she said, pushing her against a nearby wall. 'He told me all about it, and do yer know why he did it, well, do yer?'

Maureen shook her head. 'Because she glassed my sister's daughter. Ask her, go on, ask the fuckin' slag, outside Benjy's it was, and do you know what? We all forgave her and covered up for her. It was Kev that stopped her gettin' arrested, and half my family still don't talk to us now 'cause of it.'

Walking away, Sheila spat on the ground. 'Scum you are, the lot of yers. My Kevin's best out of it; he'll meet someone far better than that fuckin' slag.'

Maureen helped Susan to her feet, and hurriedly pushed the pram towards home. 'Are you sure you're all right, love? What was Kevin's mum talking about? She said you'd glassed someone. Yer never, did yer?'

Susan didn't feel like acting, but had no choice. 'It's all bullshit, Mum. What do you expect? Everyone was lookin' at her – she had to say something,' she lied.

Two weeks later, Susan's acting finally paid off. 'Wave goodbye to Nanny,' she said, moving Johnny's little arm towards her mother.

Maureen smiled. Susan was genuinely besotted with the child and all her hard work had paid off handsomely. 'Now if there's anything yer need, just ring me. I'll pop back on Sunday, make sure you're coping OK.'

Susan smiled. 'Thanks for everything. But don't worry, me and Johnny will be fine, Mum, honest.'

As Susan shut the door she breathed an enormous sigh of relief. Her mum had left her £20 for emergencies, and getting off her head was an emergency of top priority.

Susan weighted up her options. Bella, who lived below, was a white single mum, with a mixed-race kid. Kevin had never liked her, he'd said she was a slut and a junkie. Susan wrapped Johnny in his blanket. She needed a friend, and beggars couldn't be choosers.

As Susan neared the flat, she could hear the voice of Jimi Hendrix. She had to knock hard just to make herself heard.

Bella opened the door an inch. 'All right, Suze? What are you doing here?'

Susan felt awkward. She could hear voices, lots of them. 'Sorry, I didn't know you had company. I've got a spare £20, I fancied gettin' pissed and stoned, but I'll pop back another time if yer like?'

Bella smiled as she fully opened the door. 'I always thought you were a stuck-up cunt. Stick the nipper in the bedroom with my Aaron, then come and join the party.'

Two hours later, Susan was the happiest she'd felt in ages. The reason why? She had just injected her very first needle.

TWENTY-EIGHT

1995 – Ten Years Later

'I've got to go home for me dinner now, Johnny. Shall we meet up again later?'

Johnny shrugged. 'I dunno, I might have to go round me nan's for dinner. If me mum's got money, I'll go to the chippy and give you a knock. If not, I'll see you tomorrow.'

With his beloved football shoved under his right arm, Johnny trudged towards the flats. The word dinner had reminded him just how hungry he was, but he knew he'd get no food indoors. His mum was very different from all of his friends' mums, you see. They all shopped at Tesco and Sainsbury's, and cooked nice dinners, unlike his, who bought the odd loaf and can of baked beans, and spent every other penny she had on drugs, fags and booze.

Johnny kicked his ball against a nearby wall. His friends were well aware of his situation, but he still told them as little as possible. Whatever she was, she was still his mum and he loved her dearly.

With Led Zeppelin blaring out of the speakers, Susan took the needle from Bella and desperately tried to find a vein. Having no joy with her arm, she cursed herself and shoved it in her foot. As the heroin entered her body, she relaxed, closed her eyes and smiled.

Johnny put his key in the lock. 'I'm home, Mum.'

He walked into the living room. Benno, Tibbsy, Dave Taylor and Bella were all regular features in his mother's flat, and it was no surprise to see them there.

''Ere he is, shoeshine boy,' Dave Taylor said nastily.

Johnny ignored him and crouched down next to Susan. 'Mum, I'm hungry. Can I get some chips?' he asked, shaking her.

Susan opened one eye, 'Anyone got fifty p?' she slurred.

No one answered. Barely able to focus, Susan propped herself up against the sofa. 'You'll 'ave to eat round Nanny's. I cash me book tomorrow, yer can 'ave chips then. Before yer go, Johnny, do us a favour. We're out of booze, go down to Old Man Tatler's, and nick us some wine.'

Johnny averted his eyes and stared at the filthy carpet. His mum regularly asked him to thieve, and he hated it. Over the years he'd become an expert at it, his mother had made sure of that. Only once had he been caught, and he'd been six years old at the time.

'Don't make me do it, Mum. Can't one of them do it?' he asked, nodding at Tibbsy, Benno and Taylor.

'Shoeshine boy, you know you're our slave,' Dave Taylor said, laughing.

'Don't call him that,' Bella said, punching him playfully on the arm.

Susan pulled herself together, stood up and gave Johnny a cuddle. Benno and Tibbsy were OK, but Dave Taylor could be a proper racist bastard at times. 'Take no notice of him. Please Johnny, go and get some wine. Do it for me today, and I promise I won't ask yer no more.'

Johnny nodded. His mother forgot her promises as often as she made them, but what could he do? Unconditional love equalled blackmail in her eyes. He might only be ten years old, but he was old enough to know he was a victim of loving his mum too much.

He returned to the flat fifteen minutes later. ''Ere yer go,' he said, handing her two bottles of cheap plonk.

Susan grabbed him in a bear hug. 'You're a good boy for your old mum, ain't yer?'

Johnny kissed her, picked up his ball and left the flat. Football was his passion, his main reason for getting up in the mornings, and his PE teacher said that he possibly had the talent to play professionally one day. That thought alone gave Johnny hope. If he was rich, he could look after his mum properly. He could buy her a nice house and help her get better.

Johnny played keepy-uppy as he walked towards his nan's house. Aware of his stomach rumbling, he ran the last part of the way. His nan wouldn't let him take the key home with him, so he fished around under the plant pot to find it.

'Your mother and her junkie friends will clean the fuckin' house out. Leave the key in the garden under the pot, Johnny, and for fuck's sake, never tell anyone where I leave it.'

Maureen was washing the kitchen floor as the door opened. She put the mop down and hugged her grandson tightly.

'Are you hungry, darling?' she asked. She knew that he would be, the poor little sod always was.

Johnny sat himself down. 'I'm starving, Nan.'

Maureen handed him a glass of orange juice. 'How do yer fancy eggs, chips and beans?'

Johnny smiled. 'Can I have a sausage as well?'

'You can have anything you like, me little china. You're filthy dirty, you been playing over them fields again?'

Johnny shook his head. 'I've been playing football over the park. The dirt's from yesterday. I tried to wash it off this morning, but there's no hot water indoors and Mummy can't cash her book till tomorrow.'

Ordering him to go upstairs and have a bath, Maureen started on his dinner. The poor little mite had no life with that mother of his and the sadness of it all broke her heart. Many a time she'd asked him to live with her permanently, but he wouldn't.

'If I move out, there's no one to look after Mum,' he insisted.

Maureen couldn't force him to live with her. She'd often felt like contacting social services and telling them the truth, and if she could, she would legally adopt him. She always stopped herself from ringing them, though. Say they felt she was too old to have him and took him into care? If that happened, she'd never forgive herself.

Johnny was very mature for a ten year old. His life had never been easy and he'd been forced to grow up fast. Looks wise, he was as handsome as they come. With his light brown skin, chocolate eyes and cropped hair, he looked like a child model.

Obviously things had been very different ten years ago, when the poor little sod had first arrived into the world. The day he was born she remembered like it was yesterday. How could she ever forget it? They'd caused chaos at the hospital, and their family were the talk of the neighbourhood for weeks after.

James had accepted Johnny almost immediately, but it had taken years for everybody else to get over their racist beliefs and change their tune. By that time, people's attitudes had improved and England was considered to be a multicultural community.

A happy, sunny-natured child, little Johnny was very

difficult not to love from the word go. The colour of his skin was hardly his fault and, as he grew into a toddler, his smile would light up a room. Things were very different now. Time had proved a great healer and he was loved by them all, including Ethel, who doted on the child as though he was her own.

Royston had insisted on a paternity test to confirm that he was Johnny's father. He'd paid child support ever since, but had very little to do with the lad. He lived in Kent now, with a wife and family of his own, and only visited Johnny a couple of times a year. He'd turn up like a bad penny on the lad's birthday or a couple of days before Christmas.

Susan was a terrible mum from the word go, but somehow couldn't help herself. She tried to take care of Johnny, but didn't have it in her. In her eyes, she couldn't love and look after a child who had lost her everything worthwhile in her life. In her selfish heart, she blamed Johnny for the whole fiasco.

'If only he'd been born white,' she'd often say in front of her son.

Her drinking and drug-taking had started when Johnny was only a few weeks old. Getting out of her box was the only way she could cope with losing Kevin. Puff, ecstasy, crack, sleeping pills, cider, vodka, heroin – anything would do, as long as it made her forget.

Over the years it had escalated to a point of no return. She drank daily, from the moment her eyes opened in the morning, until she passed out later in the day. Maureen had done her best to help her over the years, but no one could stop her self-destruction. Twice Maureen had taken her to the doctor and got her on a methadone and alcohol programme. Twice, Susan had started it and failed miserably within days. Maureen had since given up. Susan had far too many junkies and alcoholics hanging around her to be able to straighten herself out.

Her flat was always packed with low-lifes. None of them went to work; instead they spent all day, every day getting out of their heads. Maureen rarely went to her daughter's home any more. There were always people crashed out on the floor and she found visiting Susan too upsetting. The flat stank to high heaven, it was an absolute shit-hole and to call it filthy was an understatement. She'd cleaned it a few times over the years, gone over it top to bottom but, within weeks, it was the same as before.

It was a tragedy, but Susan was too far gone for any help that Maureen could offer her. Maureen's only priority now was to take care of Johnny. She was forever buying him clothes, doing washing and ironing for him and making sure he was fed well. He stayed with her most weekends and she'd give her right arm to have him in the week as well.

'Is my dinner ready yet, Nan?'

Maureen scooped him into her arms and hugged him tightly. 'Go and sit yourself down in front of the telly and Nanny'll bring it in to yer.'

As she took in the tray, she heard the front door open and close.

'It's only me, Maur,' she heard Ethel shout.

Poking her head around the door, she smiled at Johnny. 'How's my favourite boy today?'

Johnny giggled, 'I'm fine, Nanny Ethel.'

'You hungry, Mum?' Maureen asked.

Ethel nodded. Since Glad had died, she rarely cooked for herself any more. She hated eating alone and much preferred coming over to Maureen's. It had taken her a long time to get over her best friend's death. Glad had spent her last couple of weeks in the London Hospital, but up until then Ethel had cared for her at home. Still, she'd done all she could for her and at least the poor old cow hadn't suffered the humiliation of being carted off to one of them funny farms.

'Is a drop of lamb stew and apple pie and cream all right?'

Ethel smiled. 'Sounds handsome. You're a good girl to me, Maureen, an absolute diamond.'

Less than a mile down the road, Susan was on a comedown. As Tibbsy, Benno and Dave Taylor re-entered her flat, she smiled like a cat that was about to get the cream.

'What yer got?' Susan asked, a hint of desperation in her voice. Her last hit had long worn off and she was clucking like a chicken.

Tibbsy pulled a bag of wraps out of his pocket. Up until recently, he'd been just a user, but now he was a dealer as well. He'd been forced to start selling the stuff to support his own ever-increasing habit.

'I've got loads of temazepam eggs and some twenty-quid rocks, Suze. If you ain't got the readies, you'll have to give me your book.'

Susan agreed and handed it to him. He regularly gave her stuff on tick and then cashed her social book himself. She went in search of an empty plastic bottle. She usually had them already prepared, but someone banging on the door earlier had sent her and her friend, Bella, into a state of paranoia and they'd slung them out of the window. Finding an old Diet Coke bottle on the landing, she quickly set herself up.

She burnt a hole in the side with a fag, stuck a straw in and put some used chewing gum around the edge, so that no air could escape. On the top of the bottle she put some foil and tightened it with an elastic band. With a needle she pricked some holes in the foil and carefully laid some ash on top. She shook with excitement as Tibbsy put some crack on top of the ash and handed her the lighter. Smiling, she set fire to the rock and inhaled deeply through the straw.

The hit was immense, pure joy, and, as she passed the bottle to Bella, she felt a feeling of total elation. Drugs made all of her problems disappear and Susan couldn't get enough of them.

Little Johnny spent a happy evening playing cards with his gran and great-gran. Seeing him yawn, Maureen urged him to stay.

'Don't go home tonight, darling. You've got no school tomorrow, have yer? Stay here with us and Nanny'll cook you some nice egg and bacon for breakfast, and then tomorrow, I'll take you out for the day.'

Johnny wanted to stay, but instead shook his head. 'I didn't tell Mum I was stayin' out. She'll be worried if I don't go home.'

Maureen glanced at Ethel. Both women knew that Susan wouldn't give a shit if the boy disappeared for a week.

Maureen stood up. 'I'll walk back with yer then, Johnny, it's dark now and you're not walkin' home on your own.'

'There's no need Nan, I'll be fine,' he said, picking up his ball.

'No, I'm coming with yer,' Maureen insisted.

Susan still lived in her old flat, which was less than a ten-minute walk away.

As they stood outside, Maureen smiled at him. 'I'll wait down here, Johnny. Wave to me when you open the door, so I know you're in all right.'

'Bye, Nan, thanks for me dinner,' he said, running towards the entrance.

Johnny opened the front door and waved goodbye to Maureen.

'Mum, I'm home,' he shouted.

Usually the flat was full of people and noise, but tonight he was greeted by silence. Bounding into the lounge, he saw his mother lying face down on the carpet. She'd obviously been sick, because her hair was matted with vomit.

He crouched down and gently tried to wake her. 'Mum, it's me, Johnny. Please wake up, Mum.'

There were three empty cider bottles beside her, a syringe, the funny-coloured things she called eggs and an empty bottle with foil on that she used as a pipe. Spotting the discoloured foil with the brown stuff on it, Johnny started to cry. He hated her smoking the brown stuff and injecting the eggs. She went all goofy and funny afterwards and they often made her sick.

She was too heavy for him to lift, so he propped her head up against the sofa, and went and got a bucket of cold water. There were no cleaning products in the cupboard, so he made do with an old sponge and a bar of soap.

Susan woke up as he was desperately trying to wash her hair. 'Where am I, Johnny? What yer doin'?' she slurred.

'You're indoors, Mum, you haven't been well, but don't worry 'cause I'm here to look after you now.'

'I wanna go a bed,' Susan mumbled.

Johnny helped her up and led her towards the bedroom. He sat her on the edge of the bed and did his best to undress her.

'I'll tidy up the lounge for you, Mum,' he said, covering her with the quilt.

He waited until she fell asleep and then started on the cleaning. The room was a tip, but he tidied it up the best he could. He put all the empty cans, bottles and drug evidence into two black sacks and dragged them straight out to the chute. They were too heavy for him to lift, so he asked the next-door neighbour to put them in the chute for him. He then found an old brush and did his best to scrub the sick off the threadbare carpet.

Satisfied he'd done all he could, he put on his pyjamas and got in his mum's double bed. Usually, she had men sleeping in there and it was nice to have her all to himself for once. Seeing her eyes flicker open, he kissed her on the cheek.

'Goodnight, God bless, love you Mum.'

TWENTY-NINE

James counted the last of the money. Putting the three piles into separate bags, he handed one to Tommy and one to Freddie.

'It works out eighteen grand each, boys.'

Tommy and Freddie smiled at one another. Easy pickings was putting it lightly.

It had been Bobby Adams's idea to get involved in the wonderful world of cannabis. He'd moved to the Costa del Sol in the late eighties and had soon got his foot in the door with the locals. Knowing that armed robberies were now a thing of the past, he'd invited Freddie and Tommy over to have a little chat with him.

The villa he lived in was the bee's knees, and from the moment the lads had stepped off the plane, they had visions of living the life that Bobby had made for himself. On the third night of their stay, he sat them down next to the swimming pool. Opening a bottle of vintage champagne, he handed them both a glass.

'I invited you over here because I've got a business proposition for you. That game you're in has had it. You need to ply your trade elsewhere and I've got the perfect solution for you. I want to start bringing cannabis into England by boat and I need someone trustworthy to collect it for me. There'll be two drop-offs a month at a seaside resort on the south coast. The Old Bill there are on my payroll, so you'll have no grief with them. Once you've picked up, you'll take it to a pal of mine's warehouse. The people who are buying it will collect from wherever you say. All you've got to do is unload the stuff off the boat, arrange and meet the buyers, and collect and look after the money. The profits we'll split down the middle, fifty–fifty, minus the cost of the drug itself.'

Tommy and Freddie decided within minutes that they were willing to give it a go. That was now three years ago, and since then they'd never looked back.

'Yer coming for a celebratory drink, Jimmy boy?'

James shook his head. 'I can't, Maria's got some running around for me to do.'

Tommy and Freddie both did a wanker sign as they got in the car. Maria had him well under the thumb, but it was his stag night on Friday, and they were determined to give him a night to remember. They'd wanted to take him abroad for the weekend, but he was having none of it.

'You can fuck right off, I know what yous two are like. You ain't getting me off me head and leaving me stranded in some foreign country.'

Both Tommy and Freddie knew that that was just an excuse. The real reason he didn't want to go away was solely because of Maria. She wasn't a big fan of his involvement with them, and it was obvious that she thought they were a bad influence on her beloved James. Many a time they'd got him so pissed that he'd stayed out all night. Maria had gone mental every time it had happened, so much so that she'd banned James from socialising with them any more.

James smiled as he started up his new sports car. He'd

only bought the Mazda recently and was in love with it. The traffic was at an absolute standstill and it gave him plenty of time to think about his forthcoming nuptials and life in general. He'd been with Maria for over ten years now, and he loved her more as each day passed. They'd been living together for the past two years in the flat above the tailor's shop.

He still owned the shop, but business was anything but booming. Times had changed and an old-fashioned tailor's shop was now a thing of the past. He no longer worked there himself, he had a guy called Martin running it for him. Once Martin had been paid, there was virtually no profit left at all, but he kept it going for reasons of his own. He'd finished paying Harold back a couple of years ago, and even though his old boss knew that business was crap, he'd still be devastated if the shop that had been in generations of his family were to be closed down.

James was still very close to his old boss. Harold's health wasn't great now and James always vowed to himself that he wouldn't close the shop down while Harold was still alive. Another reason he liked to keep the shop running was that it kept his mother off his case. She knew he was up to other bits and bobs, and he told her that he'd expanded into wholesale. The only thing he'd forgotten to tell her was that he was wholesaling cannabis, rather than suits.

His desperation to give Maria the life she deserved had forced him into a life of crime. Maria worked as a hairdresser, but even with a bit of private work on the side, her wages were poor. Both their mums were skint, and Maria still wasn't speaking to her dad, so unless they saved for their future themselves, there wouldn't be one. James's hard work had paid off handsomely and, in ten days' time, Maria would become his wife and get the wedding she deserved. He'd also promised her the dream move to Essex that she so badly wanted. 'We need to move to a nice area before we have children, James. The East End's a shit-hole now and I'm not bringing kids up around here,' she insisted.

It had been about three years ago when he'd decided a change of career was needed. The shop had been taking peanuts and he'd been barely able to scrape Harold's money together, let alone earn anything on top. It was around about the same time that Tommy and Freddie had started a new business venture. Seeing the money they were chucking about made his eyes water and, as luck would have it, they told him they needed an extra pair of hands.

Having never lied to Maria in all of the time they'd been together, James made the decision to tell her the truth from the start. She hadn't been happy at first – in fact she was worried sick – but, as time ticked by, her worries eased. Having children and a nice house with a big garden was their dream. Both he and Maria hated living in the cramped flat in Bethnal Green and, thanks to his new-found career, their dream would very soon become reality.

Parking in the alleyway behind the back of the shop, James turned off the engine and picked up the brochures. He'd changed the honeymoon location only this morning. Maria thought they were going to Majorca, and he couldn't wait to see her face when he told her the truth – that they were heading for the Caribbean. Laughing, he locked up his car.

Tommy and Freddie's celebratory drink lasted only a couple of hours. Both lads had families now and at nine o'clock they said goodbye and went their separate ways.

Freddie was the happiest of the two. He'd met Sarah in the pub after Tommy's dad's funeral and had been with her ever since. They had a five-year-old daughter, Daisy, and were currently trying for another. They weren't married, but had recently moved to Hainault in Essex. Freddie didn't particularly like the area. After living in Manor Park for years, he found it far too quiet and, if it hadn't been for his daughter, he wouldn't have moved at all. The day his Daisy had come home from nursery reciting 'Baa Baa Black Sheep' in Hindu was the final push that he'd needed.

Tommy swung his BMW into the pub car park. Bowling into the boozer, he ordered a large scotch on the rocks. Pleased he had chosen a pub where no one knew him, he ignored the admiring glances from the barmaid, and stared at the football on telly. The game was one–all and near the end, but he had no interest in it, he just didn't want to go home.

Unlike his brother and best pal, he wasn't all that happy with his lot. He was still with Lucy, but he wasn't with her by choice. She'd trapped him, it was as simple as that.

At the time, she'd sworn blind she was on the pill, but had mysteriously fallen pregnant within months of them getting together. He'd been furious with her: he was only twenty-five, and he demanded she got rid of it. She'd refused, and then, like most dads, he'd taken one look at his son, and had wanted to be with him. Lucy wanted to name the boy after him, but he was adamantly against it. He didn't want the kid to have the same name as his piss-head grandfather.

With his father's alcoholism and his own murder rap, the name Tommy Hutton was a fucking curse. Desperate for his son to have a good start in life, he called him Alfie.

Alfie was nine now, a cheeky little fucker he was, and

the apple of Tommy's eye. He now had another one on the way as well, but fuck knows how he'd managed that. He rarely shagged Lucy any more and, amazingly, she'd managed to conceive while taking contraception once again.

He didn't hate her. She was a good mum, a loyal partner and their house in Chingford was spotless. She was also a fantastic cook and worshipped the ground he walked on. The problem was, he didn't love her. He'd tried, but he couldn't. He envied his brother and Freddie because they had both found the one thing that eluded him. He'd give his right arm to be in their shoes, he really would, but that was never going to happen, not with Lucy. That's why he fucked about, shagged anything and everything. It didn't make him feel better about himself, but he did it out of frustration.

Picking up his mobile, he dialled his landline. 'All right, Luce? I'm on me way home. Do yer want me to pick up a Chinese?'

'I've done you a nice roast, Tommy, but I don't mind if you'd rather have a takeaway.'

Tommy sighed as he ended the call. She was so keen to please him that she agreed to anything. No man could respect a desperate woman, including himself. He liked spirited birds with a bit of fire in their belly. Picturing Maria, he finished his drink and picked up his keys. It was time to go home.

'So, what's my surprise, then?' Maria asked, excitedly.

As James chucked her the brochure, Maria's eyes lit up. She'd always longed to go to the Caribbean and James had promised to take her there some day.

'Have you booked it? When for? Next year?'

James smiled at her. 'I've cancelled Majorca. Only the best for my bride – we're going there on honeymoon.'

262

Maria squealed and threw her arms around him. 'James Hutton, I love you so, so much.'

James kissed her passionately. Feeling himself getting hard, he rubbed himself against her. 'Any chance of you showing me your gratitude?'

Maria giggled. Grabbing his hand, she led him towards the bedroom.

Over in Chingford, Tommy walked dejectedly through the door.

'Daddy!'

He scooped his son into his arms. 'I bought us a Chinese. You hungry, boy?'

Alfie nodded. He was always hungry.

Lucy jumped up from the sofa. Men were no good at dishing dinner up, they just threw stuff onto a plate. 'You sit down, I'll do that.'

Taking two trays into the living room, she handed it to her two favourite boys.

'I'm gonna have a quick bath while you're eating. I won't be long.'

As the water ran fiercely through the tap, Lucy sat on the toilet seat and cried. From an outsider's point of view, her life seemed idyllic. All the girls up the school were in envy of her. In their eyes she had the nice house, the handsome husband, the perfect family life. She hid the truth well; it was the only way that she could cope.

Behind closed doors, her life was a complete shambles. Tommy had never loved her, she knew that. He'd stayed with her because of Alfie, and the only way to keep him there was to have another. Trapping him had been the only answer, because he would never have agreed to have kids with her. He would have met someone else, left her and moved on. The thought of him having kids with another bird would have finished her off. She loved him so much that she felt that her heart would break at times. If only she could make him love her like she loved him. Over the years she'd tried her best, but she knew it was never going to happen. She knew he had other women – she could often smell them on him – but as long as he met no one special and came home to her, she would always turn a blind eye.

Patting her rounded stomach, she stopped crying and forced a smile. 'You'll help me to keep daddy at home where he belongs, won't you, darling?' she whispered.

Back in Bethnal Green, the bed was rocking. 'Aah, I love you, oh Maria!' James shouted as he came. He then used his fingers to make sure that she shouted his name. Pleased that she was satisfied, he rolled onto his back and smiled.

'I don't suppose you've cooked us any dinner, Maria, have you?'

Maria giggled. Her culinary skills were a standing joke between the two of them. She hated cooking and he ribbed her rotten over her culinary attempts.

'Whaddya fancy?' he asked her.

'I wouldn't mind a curry,' she replied.

James leaped out of the bed and slung on his clothes. Sex always made him hungry and tonight was no exception. The local Indian was only four doors away, and it was easier to walk there than order it over the phone.

'Don't tell me: chicken tikka masala, pilau rice and naan bread.'

Maria laughed. She had the same thing every time they got a takeaway.

As he shut the door, she flopped back onto the bed and sighed. She was about to become Mrs Maria Hutton and she couldn't bloody wait.

Their relationship over the years had gone from strength to strength. At first, she'd been wary, as she truly believed that Tommy would open his big mouth and spoil their happiness, but as the years passed, she'd stopped worrying so much. Tommy had his own family now and he was hardly likely to blurt out the details of their one-night stand when he had so much to lose himself.

Maria hated him and had as little to do with him as possible. Lucy was nice, Maria liked her, but apart from the odd unavoidable family get-together, James and Maria had very little to do with them socially. Maria knew James worked with his brother – that couldn't be helped – but she'd stopped their drunken nights out.

'I'm not having you rolling home pissed at all hours,' she told James firmly. 'If you want to get married to me and have children, then you have to start acting like an adult, James.'

Thankfully, he had taken her advice. She wouldn't have cared if he was out with anybody else; she just didn't trust Tommy. There was always a chance he could put his foot in it, or get James drunk and encourage him to stray.

Although Tommy was settled in his family life, she knew deep down he was jealous of her and James. She could see the deep-rooted envy in his vicious eyes. If James wanted to work with Tommy, fine, but otherwise, she'd ordered him to keep well away.

'Why don't you like Tommy?' James often asked her.

'I can't put my finger on it, but I don't trust him. Just do what you have to do and come straight home,' she insisted.

As the door opened, Maria started to chuckle. Every time he went to the Indian, he came back mimicking their voices.

'Your chicken tikka has arrived, madam. Would you

like me to dish it up for you, my lazy one?' he said in his best Indian accent.

Throwing on her dressing gown, she smiled. He was one in a million, her James, and she loved him more than life itself.

THIRTY

The stag and hen parties were arranged for thc following Friday, a week before the wedding. Maria had insisted on this. Getting James legless and leaving him in the middle of nowhere was the type of vicious plan that Tommy would hatch, given the opportunity, and Maria wasn't taking any chances on him spoiling their big day.

There'd been nothing major arranged in either camp. The boys were meeting locally, probably going on a pub crawl and ending up God knows where. The girls were more civilised; they'd booked a Greek restaurant and were looking forward to a meal, some plate-smashing and a disco.

'Cor, you look fuckin' gorgeous. Keep away from them waiters, or I'll have to come down there and knock 'em all out,' James joked, as Maria made her grand entrance into the lounge.

She'd chosen a long red dress for her special night and looked a million dollars. Seeing James looking handsome in his black suit, Maria punched his arm.

'Don't worry about me, you worry about yourself. If I find out you've even set foot in a strip club, I'll have your guts for garters.'

James grabbed her and swung her around. 'There's only

one bird I wanna look at naked and I can't wait to marry her.'

Maria laughed. 'Put me down, you'll crease me dress.'

James kissed her gently. 'We ready to make tracks?'

Maria nodded. It may have been their so-called last night of freedom, but they were still sharing a cab.

The girls were meeting in The Duchess, the boys in the Horn of Plenty. The pubs were virtually in spitting distance of each other, so it made sense to travel together.

James ordered the driver to drop Maria off first.

'Have a wonderful night, darling. I won't be too late, I'll see yer later.'

'Behave yourself and try and steer clear of anywhere Tommy and Freddie wanna drag you off to,' Maria told him.

James waved her goodbye and got the driver to spin around and drop him over the road.

'Here he is, the condemned man,' Tommy shouted, thrusting a glass of champagne towards him.

James greeted his friends and family. About a dozen of his old school pals had turned up, and even Harold and his uncle Kenny were there.

'What's the plan? Where we going after here? We going on a pub crawl?' he asked his brother.

Tommy handed him a pint glass. 'It's a surprise, Jimmy boy, now get this down your neck.'

James gagged as he drank the foul-tasting drink. Christ knows what was in it, but he felt it go straight to his head. Tommy laughed. His plan was to get his brother well and truly plastered, and by the look of him, it was going to be easy.

Maria sat giggling at the top end of the table. There were about fifteen of them altogether. Most of them were friends, but she was overjoyed that her mum, Maureen and Ethel had agreed to come, too.

'Ain't you got any last-minute doubts or nerves?' asked her cousin Coleen.

Maria had never liked Coleen. She was a jealous bitch. Maria shook her head, 'None whatsoever. James is the love of my life, and I can't wait to marry him.'

'Get me a bucket, will yer?' Coleen said nastily.

The sarcastic banter continued as dinner was served. As Ethel's plate was put in front of her, she looked at it in horror. Poking about with her fork, she opted for her loudest tone. 'What's this shit? It looks more like dog than fuckin' lamb!'

The look of disbelief on the waiters' faces made the table rock with laughter.

James sat at a table having a quiet chat with his uncle Kenny and Harold. He felt a bit drunk and had got away from Tommy and Freddie. The concoctions they'd plied him with had made him feel well ropey.

'Hi, Jimmy boy, I have a big surprise for you.'

James looked at the big bird standing in front of him. He was sure he didn't know her, she was tarty-looking and old. Wondering if it was one of his mum's friends, he smiled at her.

'Do I know you from somewhere?'

'You don't, but you're never gonna forget me, lovey.'

Releasing her gigantic breasts from under her jacket, Juicy Julie whacked them straight in his face. As the pub erupted in laughter, James could barely breathe. Embarrassed beyond belief, he had no choice other than to join in with her antics. He'd have his brother for this – he'd fucking kill him.

'*Oi vei*! Look at her *tuchis*, James!' Harold exclaimed as Juicy Julie bent over.

Tommy and Freddie egged her on.

'Get his clothes off, grab his cock, make him suck your tits,' they yelled.

By this time, apart from a silver necklace, Juicy Julie was totally naked. James glanced down as she rubbed his hand around her nether regions. Her noony felt horrible, like a pig with its throat cut.

The fun came to an end when she pulled down his trousers and got his cock out. Seeing the look of horror on his nephew's face, uncle Kenny stepped in and rescued him.

'Enough's enough, come on. Thanks, love,' he said to Juicy Julie, as he led James away.

'What's a matter with yer? Yer boring cunt,' Tommy yelled.

Kenny shot him a look. He could see that Tommy was well pissed and probably beyond reasoning with. Ignoring him, he helped James get dressed.

'Are you OK?'

James smiled. 'I am now and thanks for that.'

Annoyed with Kenny's interference, Tommy decided it was time to move on. Ordering some cabs, he grabbed James to one side.

'We're going to a nightclub now. Surely you ain't got the hump? It was only a joke.'

James hugged him. 'Of course I ain't got the hump. I dunno if I fancy clubbing though, I may just stay here for a bit. You go, Tom, and I'll stay with Kenny and Harold.'

Tommy shook his head, 'Don't be a boring cunt, Jimmy boy. I know Maria's got you under the thumb but, fuck me, you're entitled to go out and enjoy yourself on your stag night.'

Feeling belittled, James tried to argue his way out of it.

'It's nothing to do with Maria. I just feel a bit pissed that's all.'

Tommy spoke with contempt. 'What are you? A man or a fucking mouse? It's your stag night, you're meant to be pissed.'

Desperate not to look a wimp, James smiled. 'All right, I'll come.'

Tommy smirked. His little brother always danced to his tune, had done ever since he was a baby.

Back in the Greek restaurant, Ethel's arthritis had miraculously vanished. She'd never drunk ouzo before and it had a wonderful effect on her aches and pains. Grabbing hold of Nick, the handsome young waiter, she swung him around.

'Whoaa!' she screamed as she grabbed his arse.

Maureen, Maria and the rest of the table were in hysterics at her antics. When she lifted her skirt up, showed her bloomers and tried to teach him the can-can, they nearly wet themselves.

Maureen nudged Maria, 'She'll regret this tomorrow. I bet she's that stiff, she won't be able to move for a week.'

Maria giggled. The hen night had been a fantastic success and she'd enjoyed every minute of it. She adored James's mum and gran and, coming from a small family herself, it was wonderful to be a part of something bigger. Seeing her mum yawn, she glanced at her watch. Talk about time flies when you're enjoying yourself, it was half past bloody one! Debating whether to order some cabs, she thought about James. With a bit of luck, he'd be home when she got there.

As the waiter walked towards her with six bottles of champagne, Maria thought there was some mistake.

'We haven't ordered those – we're going in a minute,' she said.

The waiter shook his head. 'You must stay. A man telephone us, he buy these for you, he say a gift for Maria from Tommy Hutton.'

Maureen smiled. He might be a bastard at times, her eldest, but he had a heart of gold. 'Ain't that thoughtful of him, Maria?' she said.

Maria felt sick. The bastard was miles away, yet he'd still managed to spoil her evening. The worst thing was, she knew he'd done it on purpose.

Listening to James and Freddie ramble on about their wonderful fucking girlfriends, Tommy moved away. The nightclub was buzzing and he didn't need to be suffocated by other people's happiness.

He thought of his phone call to the restaurant and smiled. He'd done it to piss Maria off, and it was worth the money the champagne had cost to imagine the sickly smile wiped off her face.

Noticing a little blonde bird eyeing him up, he smiled at her. She looked up for it, and if there was nothing better about, it might be her lucky night. Deciding to make his way towards her, he was stopped in his tracks by a foreign-looking bloke who looked vaguely familiar.

'Tommy Hutton. Long time no see.'

Racking his brains, Tommy was sure he knew him, but couldn't place him.

'Mustapha Osman. We were in the Ville together.'

As the penny dropped, Tommy hugged him. Mustapha had been a weedy little kid on the inside, but now he looked a million dollars.

'Fucking hell, you ain't half changed. I would never have recognised yer.'

Mustapha grabbed his arm. 'I'm part-owner of this club. I'll get us some champagne and we'll go in the VIP lounge.'

Tommy was well impressed. Mustapha couldn't have been thirty and he part-owned this fucking joint. He looked the part as well. His suit, shirt, watch, his aftershave; he had pure wealth stamped all over him.

Sitting alone in a cubicle, they caught up on old times. 'So what you up to now?' Mustapha asked him.

Knowing his friend was one of his own, Tommy was coy but truthful. He excluded details, but explained he imported cannabis and was doing all right out of it.

Seeing people falling over themselves to say hello to Mustapha and shake his hand, Tommy couldn't believe this was the same little squirt he'd been inside with. Impressed wasn't the word, and he was desperate to know what had happened to him.

'Come on, then, you know my story. Spill the beans: how did yer get all this?'

Mustapha laughed, 'I'll tell you later,' he said, as some dark-haired beauty sidled towards him. 'Camellia, go and get Roxanne and you can both join us.'

As the two stunners sat at the table, Mustapha introduced them, 'Camellia, Roxanne, this is a very good friend of mine, Tommy, and tonight we're all gonna have some fun.'

As the girls giggled, Tommy winked at them. Now this was what you called a fucking good night out!

Happy, drunk and tired, Freddie was ready for the off. 'Where's your brother gone? He would have said if he was going home and we can't just leave him here.'

James picked his beer up. 'He's probably pulled some bird. Come on, we'll have a walk round, see if we can find him.'

After walking around for ten minutes, Freddie spotted Tommy through the glass in the VIP lounge.

'I need to see me mate, I won't be a sec,' he told the doorman.

The doorman shook his head. 'No pass, no entry.'

Freddie was annoyed. He hated fucking doormen at the best of times, and this fat foreign prick thought he was Rambo. Agitated, he stood his ground.

'Look, I'm his business partner, this is his brother, and we ain't leaving here till we fuckin' speak to him.'

Seeing that Freddie meant business, the doorman ordered someone to go and tell Tommy he was wanted.

Seeing his pal walk towards him, Freddie craned his neck. 'What yer doing in there? Who you with?'

Tommy grinned. 'An old pal I was in nick with.'

Freddie peered through the glass. 'Do I know him?'

'No, you don't,' Tommy replied.

Seeing James stagger backwards, Freddie grabbed hold of him. 'Me and him are fucked, Tom. It's three o'clock – you coming with us?'

Tommy shook his head. 'I'm gonna stay here with me mate. I'll bell yer tomorrow.'

Freddie said goodbye and led James out of the club. It was unlike Tommy to be evasive with him, but he'd certainly been cagey about the friend he was with. Spotting a black cab, he flagged it down.

'Bethnal Green and Hainault, mate.'

Noticing James swaying, the driver was dubious. 'He ain't gonna chuck up on me, is he, mate?'

Freddie shook his head. 'It's his stag night; he's only going to Bethnal Green. He'll be fine, I promise yer.'

Maria lay in bed, wide awake. She couldn't sleep, not until James got in safely. Hearing the downstairs door go, she sat up. 'James? You all right?'

The cold air had knocked James senseless. Dragging him up the stairs, Freddie unlocked the other door.

'I've got your fiancée here, Maria,' he shouted.

Throwing her dressing gown around her, Maria went to help out. She didn't care that he was drunk, as long as he was home.

'The bleedin' state of him! How many's he had?' she joked.

Freddie grinned. 'He's been as good as gold. He's been standing with me at the bar singing your praises all night and, apart from a roly-poly strippergram, he ain't as much as looked at one other bird.'

Ordering Freddie to chuck him on the bed, Maria thanked him, said goodbye and snuggled up to her fiancé. Thank God he was home in one piece.

Accepting the offer of another fat line, Tommy grabbed the straw and indulged in the hit. Roxanne was a babe and the blow-job she'd given him was a work of art.

Ordering the girls to make themselves scarce, Mustapha sat down opposite him. 'You enjoying yourself, Tommy?'

Blown away by it all, Tommy threw his arms across the back of the leather sofa. 'I'm curious, Mustapha. How the fuck did you come out the Ville and get all this?'

Mustapha leaned his elbows on the table. 'You can have what I've got, Tommy. I'm always looking for sensible business associates. Do you want what I've got? Do you wanna earn lots of wonga?'

Tommy sighed. 'You bet I do. What am I gonna be doing, then? What's the magic word?'

Mustapha smiled. 'Heroin, Tommy. The magic word is heroin!'

THIRTY-ONE

Johnny grabbed his sports bag, shouted goodbye to his pals and rushed towards home. His uncle James was getting married this afternoon and he was ever so excited. He'd never been to a wedding before, and his nan had brought him his first ever suit. She'd also bought him a posh shirt, tie and shiny new shoes. Even his mum had a smart new outfit, thanks to Maureen's generosity.

James had asked him to be pageboy, but his nan had insisted that if he accepted the offer, he had to stay round hers and go to the wedding from there. He'd refused, knowing full well that his mum would never get to the church on time without his help. Also, he hated being the centre of attention, and was more comfortable to just watch the wedding than have to walk down the aisle behind Maria.

He'd had a football match this morning, and his mum had promised him that she wouldn't drink or take any drugs while he was out. He didn't want her showing him up, today of all days. She looked nice in her new outfit, and he wanted to walk in holding her arm, and be able to feel proud of her for once.

'I'm home, Mum.' Johnny's heart sank as he heard the voices of her friends.

'Shoeshine boy,' Dave Taylor shouted.

Johnny ignored him, and walked over to his mother. She was asleep on the carpet and as soon as he saw the empty syringe lying beside her, he knew that she wouldn't make the wedding. With tears in his eyes, he walked away. His nan had been right, as usual.

'Yer better off comin' with us, Johnny. Yer mother's so fuckin' unreliable. What's the betting she gets out of her box and you end up having to make your own way there?'

Johnny had been adamant that she wouldn't let him down. 'She's wearing her new outfit, Nan, and she's really looking forward to it.'

Thankfully, his nan had forced him to take the address of the church and some cab money, just in case. Annoyed with himself for not listening to his nan, Johnny wiped his eyes and ran himself a bath. The water was cold, so he decided to stand up in it, and wash the mud off that way. Satisfied he was clean enough, he released the dirty water, and dried himself with a towel.

He ran into his room and looked in his wardrobe. His suit, shirt, tie and shoes were nowhere to be seen. His heart lurched as he frantically searched for them. His mum had sold stuff of his in the past, but surely even she wouldn't sell his wedding outfit. He chucked on his tracksuit and went into the living room.

'Mum, Mum, where's me clothes for the wedding? Have yer put them somewhere else?'

Susan struggled to focus. 'Dunno where they are,' she slurred.

Dave Taylor burst out laughing. 'Some little boy's probably strolling down the road in them as we speak. Poor little shoeshine boy won't be goin' to the ball after all.'

Johnny burst into tears, and ran from the flat as fast as his legs would take him.

As Maria walked into the room, her mum, Maureen and Ethel gasped. Most brides looked beautiful, but Maria looked sensational. With her tiny figure, perfect make-up and dark ringlets, she looked more like a princess than a bride.

As the three women crowed and complimented her beauty, Maria stood nervously waiting for her car to arrive. Marrying James was her dream; it was the thought of spending the day with Tommy that was giving her the jitters.

She'd begged James not to have him as best man, but he'd been adamant, and brushed away her fears. 'Look, I know you don't like him, but he's my brother and, apart from you, he's my best mate. He's got a good heart, Maria. Please give him a chance.'

She'd left it at that. What could she say? She didn't want James to become suspicious. Trouble was, Tommy had done it again. At the hen party, he'd got himself involved, just to spoil her night. Now she had to say 'I do' to the man she loved with that bastard handing over the rings and smirking at her.

Seeing the car pull up, she took a deep breath. She had to put on a brave face and somehow get through today. Tomorrow they would be on their honeymoon. She would be James's wife, Mrs Maria Hutton, and finally she could relax and enjoy herself.

James stood nervously at the front of the church. She was a stunner, his Maria, much better looking than he was, and he couldn't believe that after all these years, she was about to become his wife. What if she changed her mind and realised she could do better? Annoyed with himself for being so stupid, he pulled himself together. She loved him, they were soul mates and she would never hurt him like that.

Seeing the vicar smile and nod at the organist, he breathed a sigh of relief. She was here and ready to marry him.

As the 'Wedding March' began, he glanced around. The sight of her took his breath away. He'd been five years old when he first fell in love with her and, twenty years later, he couldn't believe that they were about to be joined in matrimony. Her beauty brought tears to his eyes. She'd always been the prettiest thing he'd ever seen, but the sight of her in her stunning white wedding dress made him feel like he'd been struck by lightning.

Maria's mum had urged her to let her dad give her away, but Maria had been dead against it. 'He broke your heart, Mum and he left us skint and in shit-street. I don't want him or his old tart anywhere near us at my wedding,' she'd insisted.

Instead she'd chosen her grandad, Ted, who was now hobbling along beside her on a stick. As she reached him, James grasped her hand, smiled, and turned to the vicar.

Unable to see Susan or Johnny, Maureen nudged Ethel. 'I knew it. I fuckin' knew our Susan would let that boy down and break his little heart.'

Ethel nodded. Johnny was a glutton for punishment, bless him.

While the vows were being recited, Tommy ruffled Alfie's hair and glanced at Lucy. All tearful and gooey, she was, silly cow. She kept on at him lately, now they had another one on the way, to make an honest woman of her. She had no fucking chance – he'd rather marry his nan! Half a bottle of Jack Daniels and a gram of gear he'd drunk and snorted this morning, and he was still having trouble getting through the day.

He hated happy people, they pissed him off and as for that slag, Maria, she didn't deserve his brother. Many a time he'd nearly slipped up and told James the truth: but what was the point? He'd probably forgive the fucking slut anyway.

As he was called to hand over the rings, he felt like spewing his guts up. His mum, nan, Freddie, Sarah, everyone had stupid grins on their faces. Unable to resist a smirk at Maria, he walked away. Let them all believe in true love. Only he knew the truth: Maria was a fucking whore.

'You may now kiss the bride.'

The church erupted in tears and cheers as James did the honours.

'*Mazel tov*,' Harold shouted, as he squeezed his wife's hand. She might now be twenty-two stone, but he still loved her, and remembered his own wedding as if it was yesterday.

The reception was to be held in the Horn of Plenty. It was usually dead on a Saturday night and the guv'nor was only too pleased to close it to the general public and earn some proper money. James had offered Maria the works, but she'd knocked it back. 'Pick somewhere cheap, James. I'd rather spend our savings on a nice house in Essex than the actual wedding,' she said.

James had chosen the venue with care. A spit's throw from home, it was so easy for everyone to get to. It was also his dad's old local, where they'd held his funeral. He may not have known his old man that well, but he often thought of him, and by choosing the Horns, he felt as if he was including Tommy senior in the celebrations somehow. James and Maria had paid for the wedding themselves, but Kenny had insisted on paying the bar bill.

'I'm doing it as a present from your dad. He was a good man, James, before the drink got hold of him, and it's what he would have wanted,' he said.

Kenny had wanted to book a meal in a posh hotel, but both Maria and James had said no. He'd already done more than enough and they decided on pie and mash and fish and chips being brought to the pub instead.

James had decided against a disco and had chosen the music with his mum and nan in mind. George and Brian were once legends on the East End circuit. A bit like Chas & Dave, they did all the old stuff. He'd also booked Roy Davis, another well-known local singer, to perform in the interval.

As the guests began to arrive, the music started. Wendy stood next to Kenny with a look of disdain. He'd begged her to come today, and the promise of a weekend away for her and her friend at the new posh health club that had just opened was too good to refuse.

Kenny smiled at her. 'It's my favourite nephew's wedding – please try and enjoy yourself for once.'

Gritting her teeth, Wendy smiled sarcastically. She'd avoided his scumbag family like the plague since the last turn-out, but tonight she would get very drunk and put up with the dregs of society, just for his sake.

Sitting next to Maureen, Ethel sang along to the oldies with Brenda and Sandra. It was at times like this that she missed her Gladys. There wasn't a day went by when she didn't think of her best friend, and even though Glad had been senile, Ethel would still give her right arm to be looking after her again.

'You all right, Mum?'

She smiled at Maureen. 'Just thinking about Glad. I always do when all these old songs are played.'

Maureen grabbed her hand. 'Come on, let's have a dance.'

'Nanny.'

Spotting little Johnny, Maureen picked him up. 'Where was you and Mummy? You missed the wedding. Where's yer nice suit? Why you wearing that old tracksuit?'

Johnny clung to her, 'I couldn't find my new clothes. I didn't want to come to the church in a tracksuit,' he sobbed.

Maureen was furious. Her Susan was a fucking disgrace. Hiding her anger, she kissed him, 'You're staying with me tonight, young man.'

Johnny smiled. He was happy again now. He loved staying at his nan's house – she spoilt him rotten. He waved at Nanny Ethel, and ran towards her.

''Ere he is, me favourite boy. Where yer been? Where's yer whistle and flute?'

Maureen shook her head to warn Ethel not to say any more. 'He's mislaid his new clobber,' Maureen said kindly.

Guessing that his no-good mother had flogged his clothes for drugs, Ethel decided to cheer him up. 'Yer remember that nasty Auntie Wendy? She keeps looking at us. Why don't me and you go and say hello, and when Nanny scratches her snatch, you scratch your cobblers, got it?'

Johnny giggled. He knew exactly what he had to do.

'All right, Wendy? Enjoying yourself are yer?' Ethel asked sarcastically.

Wendy was drunk by now, extremely fucking drunk, and for once, even though it was horrendous and the people were vagrants, she was quite enjoying herself. As her nasty mother-in-law scratched her crotch and the foreign-looking grandson scratched his bollocks, she

282

smiled. The old girl had taken the piss out of her for years and two could play at that game. Lifting her Karen Millen dress, she shoved her hand as far up her kilt as it would go.

'Must be something in the air, Ethel, I've got an itch as well.'

Ethel couldn't stop laughing. Who would have thought it, eh?

Walking back from the toilet, Kenny stared at his wife in horror.

'Stop it, Wendy. What are you doing?' he said, pulling her dress down.

'You told me to enjoy myself. You've always wanted me to join in with your family, so now I am. Come on Ethel, let's dance.'

Seeing Kenny's shocked expression, Wendy carried on dancing. Seeing as he was always working, it was nice to have his attention for once. She loved him, she always had, but their problems had reached breaking point. All her friends had kids and she resented him for them being childless. Low sperm count equalled not fucking capable and she was sick of living a lie. Wealth meant nothing if you weren't happy, and there were times when she certainly wasn't.

As the 'Hokey Cokey' started, she smiled to herself. For years he'd begged her to join in with his appalling family and now she was ready. As everyone stuck their right foot in, she pulled the neck of her dress down.

'You stick your right tit in, Your right tit out, In, out, in, out, and shake it all about,' she screamed, flashing her bare breast.

Kenny grabbed her top and put her tit away. Appalled by her behaviour, he marched her out of the door.

* * *

283

At ten o'clock, James gave the signal to the singers and barman. He'd already arranged what was going to happen.

'The groom would now like to say a few words.'

Taking the mike off the singer, James took a deep breath. He wasn't one for the spotlight and he certainly wasn't one for speeches.

'Hi everybody. There's a few people that I'd like to thank for today. Firstly, I'd like to thank my mum and nan for all their help and support. My uncle Kenny, who I think has gone home, for paying for the reception. My brother, Tommy, for being my best man and I'd also like to thank all of yous for coming. There are two more people I want to mention. As most of you know, my dad had a lot of problems and drank in this pub for many years. Well, whatever he was, he was still my dad. I'm part of him and I loved him. Last, but definitely not least, I want to thank Maria. I was five years old when I first met this girl and I fell in love with her then. She looked over the garden fence at me and I was so taken with her, I fell off me pogo stick.'

As everybody laughed, he urged Maria to join him on the stage. Seeing Tommy glaring at her, she chose not to.

'You carry on,' she mouthed to him.

James blew her a kiss. 'She may be too shy to join me on the stage but, thankfully, she wasn't too shy to marry me. Maria, I can honestly say you've made me the happiest man alive.'

Nodding to the barman to play the CD, he took her in his arms to the sound of Donny Osmond singing 'Puppy Love'.

As the pub cheered, he kissed her gently. 'This will always be our song, you know.'

Maria smiled at him, 'I love you so much, James.'

*   *   *

Tommy sat with his own family and Freddie's clan, but had no interest in their mundane conversation. Unable to take his eyes off the happy couple, he gritted his teeth. What the fuck did James have that he didn't? He was better looking, had a better body, he had much more money, yet the fucking slag had blown him out and married his brother. His true feelings always surfaced when he was drunk and tonight he really was drunk. He'd never admit to liking her when sober, but he had liked her, really liked her. He remembered fucking her like it was yesterday. Them soft tits, that tight pussy. Birds rarely affected him like that, but she had.

'Daddy, can I have some crisps?'

Tommy pulled himself together, and smiled at his son. The past was the past, this was the present, and now he hated the fucking whore.

With her arm around young Johnny, Ethel was having a field day over Wendy's outrageous behaviour. Maureen, Brenda and Sandra roared as she repeated the story for the third time.

'She put her hands right up her ha'penny, she did, and had a good old scratch.'

Johnny giggled. 'And she showed her big boobies.'

Ethel kissed his head, 'You scratched your bollocks in front of her, didn't yer, boy?'

Johnny laughed. 'Yes, Nanny, you told me to.'

Maureen playfully punched her arm. 'Fancy telling him to do that, Mum.'

Ethel laughed, 'I've hated that miserable cow for years, but tonight I actually quite liked her.'

Maureen shook her head. 'Poor Kenny, he never re-appeared, did he?'

Hearing the start of 'Ballin' the Jack', Ethel forgot

about Wendy and leaped off her seat. Dragging Johnny up, she lifted her skirt up to show him the moves.

> First you put your two knees close up tight.
> You swing them to the left
> And then you swing them to the right.

Grabbing Maria, James dragged her towards his nan. He loved this song – it was his childhood favourite.

> Spread your lovin' arms way out in space.
> You do the eagle rock with such style and grace.
> You put your left foot out and then you bring it back
> Now that's what I call ballin' the jack.

Seeing Tommy staring at the newlyweds, Freddie nudged him.

'I know it's a bit awkward with what happened between you and Maria, but you're gonna have to get up and say something,' he said.

Tommy glared at him, 'What the hell am I meant to say? Shall I tell all the guests that I fucked the bride?'

Aware of the girls coming back from the toilet, Freddie shushed him.

'You're the best man, Tom. You've gotta say something: it'll look well funny if you don't,' he whispered.

Tommy went to the toilet. Drugs weren't normally his scene, but tonight he needed the shit. Mustapha had suggested the idea and provided him with the stuff.

'Pure cocaine,' he assured him. 'It's the shit they mix it with that fucks you up. This stuff's proper: it'll get you through the day.'

He hadn't meant to tell Mustapha about his problems,

but they'd all come tumbling out last night. He'd been dreading the wedding and had got steaming drunk with his new pal.

'Take this, snort it and forget the slut,' Mustapha advised.

Since meeting Mustapha just over a week ago, Tommy had been out with him a few times. Freddie was all familied up now, and his new pal was a breath of fresh air. Freddie was wary and had been asking lots of questions.

'What does he do, Tom? You must know what he does.'

Tommy had kept schtum. 'He ain't really said. I think he just sells a bit of gear, like we do.'

Freddie didn't like the sound of him. 'Do yourself a favour and don't get too involved. That nightclub must be worth millions and you don't earn money like that from selling a bit of puff. The Turks are always involved in the brown – you ask my uncle Bobby. Heroin dealers they are, the lot of 'em.'

Entering the cubicle, Tommy shoved as much gear up his nose as he could fit. Feeling it run down the back of his throat, he unlocked the door. Looking in the mirror, he admired himself. He was one handsome bastard. Smiling, he ran his fingers through his hair. Time for his speech!

As Tommy grabbed the mike, Maureen poked Ethel. 'He's giving a speech, bless him. I know he's a bit of a rogue, but he ain't all bad, is he?'

Ethel snorted. She'd heard many a story about her eldest grandson and none of them were nice. He was trouble, a fucking wrong 'un, but there was no point telling Maureen. One day she might take off her rose-tinted glasses, but for now she was still wearing them.

Maria looked on in horror, as Tommy smirked at her. Surely he wasn't going to ruin their wedding day? Please God, no.

Tommy cleared his throat.

287

'Being chosen as my brother's best man is a wonderful honour for me and it's my duty to say a few words. Jimmy boy and I have always been close – he's the best brother a man could wish for. Now he's married, flown the nest and is gonna spend the rest of his life with the classy, beautiful, loyal Maria.'

Hearing the viciousness and sarcasm in his voice, Maria shot to the toilet. He had a dangerous expression on his face and if he was going to blurt out Christ knows what, she couldn't be present.

Seeing her bolt, Tommy smiled. Gutless, fucking slag, he thought.

'And all I've got left to say is congratulations and good luck for the future. Jimmy boy and Maria make a wonderful couple and I'd like everybody to raise their glasses for a toast.'

Seeing Maria come out of the toilet, Tommy smiled at her.

'To the happy couple.'

THIRTY-TWO

Susan was busy sucking Dave Taylor's penis as the front door opened and closed. 'That you, Johnny?' she shouted, as she covered his hard-on with the quilt.

'Don't fuckin' stop, I was just about to come. Tell shoeshine boy to fuck off and come back later,' Dave Taylor said venomously.

Ignoring her boyfriend's nastiness, Susan put on her old dressing gown and walked out of the bedroom. 'Johnny, be a good boy. Me and Dave never get much time to ourselves. Can't yer go and play football for a bit and come back later?'

Johnny shrugged his shoulders, 'I've been playing footy all day, Mum. I'm starving, I need something to eat.'

Susan found £2 in her purse and handed it to him. 'Go and get something from the chippy, and nick us some drink on the way back.'

'Do I have to, Mum?' Johnny asked sulkily.

'Do as yer fuckin' mother says. You've just taken our beer money for yer grub,' Dave Taylor shouted.

Johnny felt close to tears as he left the flat. His mum and Dave had recently become an item and his home life had gone from bad to worse. Whenever he went home they seemed to be in bed together, and he often heard them having sex, which made him feel ill. He'd walked in on them last week. His mum had been making terrible noises and he'd thought Dave Taylor had been beating her up. The sight of his mum with her legs wide open, and Dave Taylor licking her mary-ann would live with him for ever. Annoyed with himself for being unable to stop thinking about what he'd seen, Johnny broke into a sprint and headed for the chippy.

Susan handed the joint back to her boyfriend. She propped herself against the pillow and stared at his handsome face. 'Why don't yer move in properly, Dave? I mean, yer stay here most nights anyway, so it'd make sense if yer moved all yer stuff in.'

Dave Taylor sat himself up, and reached down the side of the bed for his cider. He took a swig and turned to face Susan. 'Yer know I like yer and all that, Suze, but I've told yer before, I ain't bringing up no black kid.'

Susan kissed him. 'Oh please, Dave. I mean he's not that black, and Royston was yer mate years ago.'

Dave Taylor shook his head. 'I've never had black mates. Tibbsy and Benno were pals with him, I barely spoke to the cunt. I mean it, Susan, I won't live with him. It's your choice: me or the kid, understand?'

Susan nodded. She understood perfectly.

As the plane landed on British turf, James squeezed Maria's hand. Sun, sand, sea, sex, their honeymoon in the Caribbean had been amazing. Maria hadn't wanted to come home at all.

'I wish we could stay here for ever, James,' she kept saying.

'We have to go back to reality, babe, build for our future,' he told her.

They'd talked and talked and planned and planned while away. It had been a joint decision for Maria to come straight off the pill; they'd discussed that before the wedding. Both of them wanted kids and felt more than ready to start a family sooner rather than later. The only thing they couldn't quite agree on was whether to buy a house just yet. Maria was desperate to move to Essex as soon as possible. With the shop and her job, they could easily get a mortgage, but James would rather they bided their time instead of jumping in feet first.

The takings in the shop were shit, but it was handy to keep as a cover. With the cannabis selling like hot cakes, Bobby had been talking about adding an extra run here and there. James and Maria had spoken at length about this and they both agreed that the extra money would be a blessing, as it would enable them to move sooner.

'As soon as we get home, I'll sort it,' James assured her.

Nice houses cost money and he was determined to buy Maria the best that he could afford.

Tommy Hutton counted the ten grand, shook hands with the Indian bloke and walked away happy. Mustapha had been dead right – the big money was definitely in heroin. He'd only been punting the stuff for the last ten days and he'd earned far more than he earned in a month from selling puff.

Mustapha had advised him not to include James and Freddie in their business arrangement.

'Work it yourself. All you need is a lackey to carry it. Find yourself someone half sensible, you'd be mad to share the profits.'

Tommy had agreed. He had no intention of including

anyone on this particular little money-spinner. Deep down, he knew that James and Freddie would be dead against it. Selling puff was one thing, flogging smack was a different ball game. He couldn't risk telling Freddie or James, and Bobby Adams would have a cardiac if he knew. He'd given the smackheads a real hard time in nick and he hated the dealers with a passion.

'Fucking scum they are. One level behind the nonces,' he'd voiced on numerous occasions.

Tommy'd found a runner to work for him. Jason was a bit of a plum, but seemed trustworthy enough.

Looking at his watch, he saw he was running late. Picking up his phone, he rang Mustapha's number. 'I'm stuck in traffic; I'll be about forty minutes.'

'Hurry up. I've got four beautiful women and as much cocaine as you could possibly snort.'

Tommy smiled as he ended the call. Mustapha had introduced him to the high life and he was loving every fucking minute of it!

Within a month of returning home from honeymoon, James met with Freddie and together they set up the extra run with Bobby. He'd flown home in person to sort out the details and they'd met at an Essex restaurant.

'Never trust talking on any kind of phone, boys. They fucking bug 'em, I'm telling yer. There's been many a good man caught out by the art of technology. Now, where's Tommy? Is he running late?'

Not wanting to get him in trouble, James and Freddie said as little as possible. 'He ain't been home all night – probably with some bird,' James joked.

Bobby was furious. He'd managed to make the meet on time and he'd come from the Costa del fucking Sol. Tommy lived within spitting distance and in Bobby's eyes was taking the piss. 'I take it he knows where we're meeting? Bird or no bird, business comes first. Give him a ring and tell him to get his arse in gear.'

As he saw his uncle's nose turn red, Freddie turned away. Bobby's hooter always gave a warning of what was to come and when it spread to his cheeks, he lost it completely. Thankful that the waitress appeared, Freddie smiled at her.

'Shall we order?' he asked his uncle.

Bobby nodded. He wasn't about to go hungry on account of some cunt who couldn't be bothered to turn up. 'Have you rung him yet?' he asked Freddie.

Pretending he had no signal, Freddie went outside with his phone. He was in a dilemma and didn't know what to do for the best. Tommy had been on the missing list for three days now, his bird and son were frantic and Lucy had been ringing him non-stop.

'I don't know what to do, Freddie. I've rung all the hospitals and all the pubs he drinks in. What if he's been arrested or he's lying dead in a ditch?' she sobbed.

Freddie felt sorry for Lucy. She was a nice girl, she was pregnant, and she didn't deserve to be treated like dirt. Tommy was a cunt to her. He was always messing about with other birds behind her back, and when he was at home, he spoke to her like shit.

Ringing his pal's mobile, Freddie wasn't surprised to hear it go straight to answerphone. It had been like that for the last three days. Running his hands through his hair, he debated what to do for the best. His uncle Bobby was a powerful man and he dare not lie to him. It wasn't just that: they worked together, had a tidy little earner and he couldn't risk them all getting arrested by Tommy's stupidity.

His pal was bang on the gear, he knew that. Ever since

he'd met that Mustapha geezer, he'd changed completely. He hadn't even turned up for their last job; him and James had done it alone. Obviously, they hadn't told Bobby. He'd have gone apeshit, so they covered his arse.

Taking a deep breath, he walked back into the restaurant. Blood was thicker than water, and it was time to tell Bobby the truth.

James sat in silence as Freddie did all the talking. He needed this job desperately for his and Maria's future. If Bobby got the hump and called a halt, he'd be well fucked financially, that was for sure.

With Tommy being his best pal, Freddie tried to play down the situation as best as he could. 'He met this new mate a couple of months back and I think he's gone off the rails a bit. No one's seen him for the last few days and we ain't got a clue where he is. I know he ain't happy at home. He was planning on leaving Lucy, but she got up the duff again. He feels a bit depressed and trapped, I think.'

Bobby was concerned. He didn't deal with anyone off the rails and he certainly didn't want them working for him. 'Is he doing drugs?'

Freddie shrugged his shoulders, 'He's been doing a bit of coke, but only recently, since he met this new mate. He can't be hooked – he's only been taking it for a couple of months. He was never on it before, when he was knocking about with me.'

Bobby lit a cigar. 'What's the geezer's name he's knocking about with?'

'Me and James have never met him. All we know is that his name's Mustapha and he met him in the Ville.'

Bobby's nose went bright red when he heard the name. A fucking Turk, wonderful! He hated the bastards and didn't trust them as far as he could throw them.

'I don't remember any Mustapha when I was in the Ville. Don't you know anything about him?'

Freddie shook his head. 'Not really.'

James knew more, but kept schtum. His brother had told him that Mustapha owned the nightclub they'd gone to on his stag night. He had no choice but to keep quiet. His brother was in enough shit without him sticking his oar in.

Freddie was relieved when their food arrived. He'd hated telling tales on his pal, but Tommy had left him with no choice.

Finishing his meal, Bobby paid the bill.

'Right, I'll tell you what we're gonna do, lads. Yous two carry on with business as usual and I'll sort the rest out. I'll delay my flight, do a bit of detective work. It won't take me long to get the lowdown on our dear fucking Turkish friend. Once I get the vibes of what's going on, I'll know how to deal with it.'

James didn't like the sound of 'deal with it'.

'You ain't gonna hurt Tommy, are you, Bob?'

Bobby smiled at him. He was a good kid, was James. 'Of course not, I've gotta lot of time for your Tommy,' he said, with a hint of sarcasm.

Bobby stood up. 'Best I get going. I'll be in touch.'

Freddie and James looked at one another as he left the restaurant. Both were worried and neither knew what to say.

'I had to tell him, James. I know he's your brother, but I had no choice. Believe me, I love him as much as you do. Bobby ain't a man to fuck with, James. He's premier league and not a man to be lied to.'

James smiled. 'You don't have to explain yourself to me. I fully understand, honest I do.'

As his phone rang, Freddie handed it to James.

'It's Lucy again, she keeps fuckin' ringing me and I dunno what to say to her. You talk to her, James.'

As James answered the call, he was greeted by hysterics. 'No, it's not Freddie, it's James. Calm down, Lucy, I can't understand what you're saying.'

'Help me! I don't know what to do, I think the baby's coming, but it's not due for ages. I'm all alone with Alfie. Please help me, James, please.'

James did his best to calm her down. 'Ring an ambulance, Lucy. Me and Freddie are on our way, we'll be about twenty minutes.'

'Please hurry, please!' Lucy screamed.

Freddie drove to Chingford as fast as the traffic would allow. Stuck behind Hinge and Bracket in the fast lane, he kept his hand on the hooter.

'Fucking Sunday drivers, I hate 'em,' he said, as he finally dodged past.

James sat quietly during the journey. He'd promised Maria he'd be home early. It was her mum's birthday and they were supposed to be visiting her. He'd rung her and told her the score, but she wasn't happy.

'Your brother is a fucking arsehole, James. As usual, he's nowhere to be seen and everyone else is rallying around, sorting out his problems.'

'Get a cab to your mum's, Maria. I'll be there as soon as I can, I promise.'

'Whatever,' she said, as she slammed the phone down.

Freddie tried to ring Lucy to make sure she was all right, but got no answer.

'When is your brother's baby actually due, James?'

James shook his head. 'I dunno. He ain't had much interest in it; he's never spoken about when it's due.'

Freddie spotted the ambulance as he pulled into the turning.

'Thank fuck they're here! I had visions of me and you delivering the kid.'

As they leaped out of the car, they couldn't help but hear Lucy's screams.

'You go in first,' Freddie told James, pushing him up the path.

'Fuck off, I don't wanna see her with her legs in the air,' James replied.

'You're family, just fuckin' go in first, will yer?'

A nervous James poked his head around the open door. 'Are you OK, Lucy?'

He was ushered out of the room by a paramedic, who told him, 'Just wait outside.'

Freddie and James glanced at one another. Neither of them was Einstein, but it was obvious that something was very wrong.

As Lucy was taken from the house on a stretcher, a paramedic approached them.

'Which one of you is James?'

'I am.'

Leading him away from Freddie, the paramedic spoke to him. 'I know you're a relative. I take it Lucy is your sister-in-law?'

James nodded. 'Yeah, she's me brother's bird.'

'I'm very sorry, but the news isn't good. Your sister-in-law had already given birth by the time we arrived. Unfortunately, the baby was premature and stillborn. We did our utmost, but we couldn't revive her.'

James felt himself go cold. 'Did you see her? Was the baby a girl?'

The paramedic nodded. 'Your sister-in-law wants you to look after your nephew – he's next door, at number fourteen.'

James thanked the paramedic and watched him walk

297

away. He was dreading telling his mum. No one had known the sex of the baby, and his mum had been rambling on for months about having a granddaughter.

'Too many men in this family,' she'd joked. 'We need a little girl to dress up and spoil.'

Freddie walked towards him. 'I take it the baby's dead?'

Tears pricked James's eyes. 'Not only have I gotta tell me mum, but I'm gonna have to find Tommy and tell him as well.'

Freddie kicked the wall in temper. He was dreading telling Sarah; her and Lucy were best buddies. 'Don't worry about Tommy, this is all his fuckin' fault, James. It's the stress of him treating her like shit and not comin' home for days on end that's caused this to happen. He may be my best pal, but the geezer's a cunt. He never wanted this kid and now he's got his fuckin' wish.'

James walked up the path of number fourteen and knocked at the door. Thanking the neighbour for her help, he took Alfie by the hand.

'Where's Mummy and the baby gone?'

James didn't know what to say. He wasn't good in this type of situation.

'They've gone to the hospital in the ambulance.'

Smiling, Alfie skipped along happily. 'Have I got a brother or a sister?'

James glanced at Freddie. 'I don't know, Alfie. I tell you what, we'll go and see Nanny Maureen, she'll know more than me and she can tell you everything.'

THIRTY-THREE

As the blonde bird nuzzled away at his ear, Tommy did another juicy fat line and offered the straw to Mustapha.

He'd spent the last few days at his pal's luxurious Docklands apartment. To say they'd had a party was an understatement; a drug-induced orgy was a better description. Tommy had lost count of the number of birds he and Mustapha had rumped, but was sure they'd made it into double figures.

Pushing the bird away from him, he sat up and put his head in his hands. All of a sudden he felt ill, really fucking ill.

'I've lost track of time. What day is it?' he asked.

Mustapha laughed. 'It's Saturday, you prick.'

'I need to get home and sort meself out,' Tommy moaned.

The blonde girl knelt down in front of him, pushed his legs astride and took his limp dick into her mouth.

'Just get off me, will yer?' he said, kicking her as hard as he could.

He was fucked and couldn't raise another gallop if his life depended on it.

As he gingerly got dressed and searched for his keys, Mustapha couldn't stop laughing.

'You are fucking lightweight, Tommy Hutton.'

Tommy left the flat and clambered into his BMW. He was dreading going home to face Lucy. What he was going to say, God only knew, and his head wasn't clear enough to think of any feasible excuses. Starting the engine, he headed towards Chingford. It was time to face the fucking music.

Maureen sat her grandchild on her lap and did her best to comfort him.

Unlike Johnny, who was round at hers on a daily basis, Maureen rarely saw Alfie. Their lack of contact didn't stop her thinking the world of the cheeky little bugger and it broke her heart to see him so upset. The news had been an awful shock to her and Ethel, but they were trying to hold it together for the sake of the child.

Seeing that his tears had now subsided, Maureen smiled at him. 'Shall Nanny get you a nice bowl of ice cream?'

Alfie nodded. 'Can I have chocolate?'

Ethel followed her into the kitchen. James had left to go in search of Tommy, but he'd told them the score before he'd gone.

'No one knows where Tommy is. He's been on the missing for a few days. Lucy's been frantic and Freddie reckons that's why she went into labour so early.'

Ethel closed the door. She didn't want Alfie to hear what she had to say. 'That son of yours needs a fucking good doughboy. Surely even you ain't gonna stick up for him this time?'

Putting the ice cream back in the freezer, Maureen turned to her. 'We don't know what's happened to him yet. Say he's been arrested, or something?'

Ethel shook her head. 'Don't talk bollocks. We'd have heard if he'd been banged up. He's out enjoying himself,

300

probably with some old scrubber. When are you gonna wake up and admit what he's really like, Maur?'

Saved by the bell, Maureen answered the door and was shocked to see a dishevelled-looking Susan standing there. Johnny was stood next to her, with two bin liners, one in each hand.

'What the fuck do you want, Susan? I thought I told you never to darken my door again.' Selling Johnny's wedding outfit had been the final straw for Maureen.

'Mum, I'm in trouble. I owe people money and they're threatening to hurt Johnny. I need you to take him until it's sorted. He'll be safer with you.'

Johnny let out a sob and clung to his nan. As Maureen ushered them inside, she noticed that Susan looked terrible. She couldn't have weighed more than seven stone, her teeth were beginning to blacken and she had dark rings around her eyes.

'Go and sit in the kitchen for a minute, while I go and check on Alfie.'

Seeing that Alfie had crashed out, and was sound asleep on the sofa, Maureen put his ice cream on the table beside him and quietly shut the door. 'Go upstairs and have a bath, Johnny, while I talk to Mummy,' she ordered.

Ethel explained to Susan what had happened with Tommy's baby, but she was far too wrapped up in her own problems to be bothered with anyone else's.

Seeing the lack of interest written across her face, Maureen changed the subject, 'How much do you owe, Susan? And who do you owe it to?'

Susan looked at the floor. 'Three hundred pound to a bloke called Frank. I used to buy me gear off him and I ran up a tab.'

Maureen thought long and hard about what she should do. She had about £500 hidden in a tin box under her mattress. It had taken her years to save for a rainy day and maybe that day had just come. She made her decision and turned to face Susan.

'If I give you the money to clear your debt, I need you to promise me something.'

Susan looked hopeful, 'I'll promise you anything, Mum.'

'I want you to promise me that Johnny lives permanently with me. Tell him whatever you've got to tell him, but I don't want him at your flat no more. It's not safe for him living in your world. He's a lovely kid and I can offer him a much better life than you can.'

Susan readily agreed. This was turning out to be much better than she'd expected.

As Maureen left the room to fetch the money, Ethel turned to her granddaughter. 'Yer might fool her, but yer don't fool me. There is no debt, is there? You just wanna buy drugs, don't yer?'

Susan looked her in the eye and shook her head. She'd become that good at lying, she could look God in the eye if she had to. 'I'm telling the truth, I swear,' she said.

'Lying little cunt,' Ethel spat at her.

Maureen returned and handed her the money. 'Promise me, Susan, you won't go back on your word. If you wanna see Johnny, you can visit him here.'

Susan snatched the money and stood up. 'I promise. He's all yours, Mum.'

As she left the house, Ethel looked at Maureen in amazement. 'You're so gullible, she ain't in no trouble. She'll inject that three hundred quid by tomorrow, you mark my words. If she was a daughter of mine, I'd knock her into next week.'

Maureen shrugged. 'The money's a small price to pay if it means Johnny can live here. At least he'll be looked after and safe with me.'

Ethel shook her head. 'What type of mother sells her own son for three hundred quid? It makes me wonder what we've raised between us, Maur. Susan and Tommy are both fuckin' wrong 'uns. All I can say is, thank God for James.'

Susan ran towards home with a massive grin on her face. It had been Dave Taylor's idea to spin the yarn about the debt. She'd known that her mother would take the boy, but she'd never expected to get the money out of her as well. She couldn't wait to tell Dave – he'd be over the moon. What a result!

As Tommy opened the front door, he was shocked to be greeted by silence. 'Lucy! Alfie!' he shouted.

Maybe she'd had a gutful of him staying out and left him. He was such a bastard to her sometimes, he wouldn't blame her if she had.

Running upstairs, he checked the wardrobe. All her clothes were still there, so she hadn't gone far. Checking Alfie's room, he was relieved to see that all his stuff was still intact. He went back downstairs, took a beer out of the fridge and walked into the lounge. As he saw the stain on the carpet, he froze. It was blood, he was sure of it. Guessing that Alfie had had an accident, he frantically searched for his phone. Locating it in his jacket pocket, he stuck it on charge. The bastard thing had been dead for days and he was annoyed with himself for not charging it at Mustapha's. He hadn't bothered at the time, as he knew Lucy would be on his case.

Downing his beer, he immediately opened another. He was desperate to mellow himself out, he still felt out of his head. Overcome by paranoia, he feared the worst. If Alfie was critically ill or dead, he'd never forgive himself.

Hearing the doorbell go, he ran to answer it. 'All right, Jimmy boy? What you doin' here? Do yer know where Lucy and Alfie are?'

Clocking the state of his brother, James pushed him into the hallway. His pupils were dilated and he stank of a mixture of booze and sweat. 'Do I know where Lucy and Alfie are? You having a laugh, you cunt? Shall I tell you where they are? Shall I?'

Tommy nodded. He'd never seen James so angry before.

'Your son's at Mum's house. The poor little fucker had no one to look after him, and Lucy's in hospital. The worry of you goin' missing sent her into an early labour and she gave birth on the carpet in the living room.'

Tommy sank to his knees. 'What did she have? Is the baby OK?'

James glared at him. 'She had a little girl and she died, and do you know what? It's all your fuckin' fault, Tommy. Look at the state of you. You've got a lovely family and you've fucked things up this time, big style.'

Tommy stood up. It wasn't his fucking fault that the baby had arrived prematurely and died. How the fuck could it be? Fuming that James was speaking to him like a mug, he punched his fist against the wall. 'What hospital's she been taken to?'

'Whipps Cross, and don't ask me to come with you 'cause I can't. I was meant to pick Maria up hours ago. It's her mum's birthday and we were supposed to celebrate it with her. As usual, my life's put on hold while I run around like a blue-arsed fly, covering up all your mistakes.'

Seeing red, Tommy grabbed him by the neck, shoved him against the wall and head-butted him. 'Who do you think you're fuckin' talkin' to? My kid's just died, remember? Go on, fuck off and enjoy your meal, go and spend your evening with that slag, Maria.'

The sound of Maria being called a slag made James feel physically stronger than ever before. His nose might be throbbing and pouring with blood, but for once he didn't give a shit. Lifting his leg, he kneed Tommy as hard as he could in the bollocks, and followed up with a swift right-hander.

As Tommy hit the deck, he stood over him with a look of contempt. 'Don't ever speak about my Maria like that again. Do you hear me?'

Tommy laughed. It wasn't a pleasant laugh, it was false and vindictive.

James opened the front door. He had to get away before he lost it completely.

'Ask darling Maria what sex with me was like. You think you're so clever, Jimmy boy. I took her virginity, you mug. I stuck my big cock right up that tight little pussy of hers.'

James stood transfixed. Tommy was lying – he had to be. Knowing he had to get out of the house before he hurt Tommy badly, James forced his legs to walk away.

'Ask the fuckin' slag, go on, ask her!' he heard his brother screaming.

Breaking into a run, James reached the car. Unable to think straight, he started the engine and drove off like a maniac.

Susan took a lug of the crack pipe and handed it over to the man who had brought the sunshine back into her life. After Kevin had left her, she never thought she'd find love again but, thankfully, with Dave she had, and she was willing to do absolutely anything to keep him. He'd been thrilled earlier when she'd taken him in the kitchen and waved the £300 in his face.

'Keep it schtum,' he told her.

Within minutes, he'd slung all of their friends out of the flat. 'Me and Susan wanna spend some time on our own,' he lied. The truth was all of their mates were skint and he didn't want to share their windfall with them.

As soon as they left, he lifted Susan up and swung her around. 'You're a top bird, you are. Do you know that?'

He then went off to stock up on all their favourite goodies. 'Don't spend it all, Dave. Hold fifty quid back for emergencies,' she told him.

He didn't listen, but then again, he never did.

As he handed the pipe back to her, she smiled at him. 'Now I've got rid of Johnny, will you move in with me properly?'

Dave nodded. His mother had chucked him out last week and he was at a loose end anyway.

Susan threw her arms around his neck. Their relationship had always been turbulent because of Johnny and, now he'd gone, they could really make a go of it.

'I love you, Dave,' she said.

Dave Taylor smiled, but said nothing. Susan wasn't really his type, but she'd do for now. As soon as something better came along, he'd be off like a shot.

Maureen carried Alfie upstairs and put him to bed. Johnny kept firing questions at her about Susan and she was glad of some breathing space. Should she tell him the truth or shouldn't she? Maybe it was time to come clean. She smiled as she walked back into the living room and saw Ethel plonked on the floor playing snakes and ladders with him. As usual, she had little decorum and sat with her legs wide open, showing all her clout.

'Mum, for goodness' sake. You're showing Johnny what you've had for dinner.'

Ethel roared. Not used to much laughter indoors,

Johnny quickly joined in. 'Nanny's got white knickers, Nanny's got white knickers,' he sang.

'I can't bleedin' help it. It's me arthritis and I can't sit any other way,' Ethel said, defending herself.

Maureen was glad to see that Johnny had cheered up a bit. He'd been very downcast earlier and she hated seeing him like that, as he was usually so bubbly.

'I can't fuckin' get up. Help me up, Maur.'

Maureen laughed as she struggled to help her mother-in-law move her fat arse off the carpet. 'I'm bleedin' knackered. I'm gonna love yer and leave yer now,' she said.

'Night, Nanny Ethel,' Johnny said, kissing her.

Maureen saw her to the door and watched her go across the road. 'Night, Mum.'

Ethel opened her front door and waved.

Maureen went back into the lounge and sat next to her grandson. 'There's something I've got to tell you, Johnny. I had a chat with Mummy earlier and we've both decided that it's best if you come and live with me.'

Johnny shook his head. 'I have to live with Mum. She gets ill when I'm not there and she'll have no one to put her to bed. Dave Taylor's horrible – he won't help her when she gets sick.'

Maureen felt a lump in her throat as she looked at his genuine little face. 'You shouldn't have to put her to bed, Johnny. She's the adult, you're the child, she should be looking after you, but unfortunately, she's not capable.'

'But I love her.'

Maureen ruffled his hair. 'I know you do, darling, and you'll still see her. She'll come and visit you 'ere.'

Johnny looked at her pleadingly. 'If I ask you something, Nan, will you tell me the truth?'

Maureen nodded. 'Of course I will, darling.'

'Mum doesn't love me and doesn't want me, does she?'

Maureen was choked as she looked at him. She'd lied for her daughter for years and now she had to be cruel to be kind. 'No, darling, she doesn't,' she replied honestly.

As his eyes brimmed with tears, she held him to her chest. 'Nanny wants you to live with her, Johnny, and she will always love and take care of you.'

Johnny looked at her dubiously. He didn't know whether to believe her; he was too used to his mum's lies. 'Do yer promise never to give me away, Nan?'

Maureen smiled. 'Cross my heart and hope to die.'

THIRTY-FOUR

James sat in the corner and stared at his empty glass. After leaving Tommy's, he'd stopped at the first boozer he'd come across. The place was empty, a shit-hole, and it matched his mood perfectly.

Going straight home to Maria after what Tommy had just said was totally out of the question. He needed to sort his head out, work out whether to confront her or not. He felt ill, sick to the stomach. Standing up, he walked back to the bar.

'Give us another brandy, and make it a treble this time.'

The fat, tattooed barmaid smiled at him. The blokes that usually came in were pig ugly; James was a bit of eye candy and she was desperate to get chatting to him.

'You having a bad day, love?'

James shook his head. The last thing he needed was polite conversation. 'Nah, I'm fine.'

'You don't look fine. What you done to your face? You been fighting?'

James usually prided himself on being polite to all and sundry. Today, was an exception though. 'Just give me the fucking drink, will yer?' he yelled.

Surprised by his own rudeness, he snatched the glass, apologised, and quickly sat back down. This whole situation was fucking his head up and he needed some answers quickly.

Maria was fuming as she studied the takeaway menu. So much for their big night out at a posh restaurant. They'd be lucky to get a few manky leftovers from the local chinky at this time of night. Throwing the menu down in temper, she tried James's number once again. His phone had been switched off for hours and each time she tried to get through to him, she became more and more infuriated.

'How dare he turn his fucking phone off? He makes himself look such a knob, chasing around after Tommy like some fucking Joey. I'm not putting up with it any more, Mum. I swear on my life, I'm putting my foot down from now on.'

Janet put an arm around her daughter. 'Now calm down, Maria. James has got a heart of gold, and if Lucy's gone into labour and Tommy can't be found, then he's bound to help out. You've got to remember, he didn't know that you'd booked the restaurant. He just thought we were eating at home.'

Maria burst into tears. She'd planned tonight with such precision. Her big news would be delivered on her mum's birthday, in the beautiful restaurant, and now, thanks to Tommy, everything had been well and truly fucking ruined.

As Bobby Adams pulled up outside Tommy's house, he was surprised but pleased to see his car on the drive. He hadn't been able to contact him by phone, the bastard hadn't been answering. Bobby was well pissed off with Tommy and he'd had visions of driving around all night looking for him. Thank God he'd struck gold by trying the house first.

Bobby banged on the door and waited patiently for an answer. It didn't come, so he looked through the lounge window. Seeing Tommy sprawled face down on the sofa made his blood boil. Probably out of his nut again, he thought angrily. Getting more wound up by the second, Bobby pounded on the glass with his fist and caught his diamond ring against the lead.

'Tommy, I know you're in there. Answer this fucking door before I break the bastard thing down.'

Bobby Adams was not a man to be kept waiting.

As Tommy opened his eyes, he wasn't sure where he was. He could hear banging and shouting and wondered if he was still at Mustapha's. He sat up, rubbed his eyes and recognised his own living room. Seconds later everything came back to him. Lucy, James, the baby – he remembered the whole caboodle. Guessing that James had come back to either kick off again or apologise, he staggered to the front door. Seeing Bobby Adams sent shivers through his spine.

'You took your fucking time,' Bobby said, as he pushed him into the lounge.

About to tell him to fuck off, Tommy noticed the colour of his face and shut his mouth. Bobby's nose and cheeks were beetroot red and that was never a very good sign.

'What's up, Bob?' he said, in a grovelling voice, as he was shoved onto the sofa.

With a look of pure disgust on his face, Bobby stood over him sneering. 'Look at the fucking state of you, and you've got the cheek to call yourself a man, Tommy Hutton? You had everything, boy, and you fucked up big time. You're now a junkie. How clever are you, eh?'

Tommy shook his head. He needed to dig himself out of this one, fast. Arms spread in innocence, he tried to excuse himself.

311

'You don't understand, Bob. Me baby was born today, it was premature and it died. A little girl, it was, and we lost her.'

Bobby stared at him with revulsion. How dare he blame the poor baby? The cunt had been out of his nut for months and hadn't given his unborn child a second thought. 'I've no time for sob stories, Tommy. In fact, I don't care if you've lost your mum, nan, or virginity. I've come here tonight for one reason only and that's to tell you you're out of the fold. I don't want you working for me any more – you're a fucking liability.'

Tommy was shocked. He might have fucked up a bit lately, missed a couple of runs, but he'd always been loyal to Bobby, fucking loyal. Knees shaking, he stood up to face the man.

'Look Bob, I know I've messed up a bit recently, but I'll get meself sorted. Why are you binning me? What have I done to deserve that?'

Unable to stop himself, Bobby grabbed his neck with his goalkeeper-sized hands and shoved him against the wall. 'Don't take me for a fool, Tommy. Did you really think I wouldn't find out that you were knocking about and selling smack with that filthy fucking Turk?'

As he squeezed Tommy's neck, Bobby laughed at his fear. 'Well, answer me. Did you?'

Tommy could barely breathe, let alone talk. As Bobby let him go, he slid down the wall.

'I'll make it up to you. I'm sorry,' he croaked.

Bobby shook his head and walked towards the door. As he opened it, he turned around. 'Oh, and there's a couple of other things. Number one, don't even think of grassing us up, 'cause I've changed the whole set-up and, number two, stay away from Freddie.'

Tommy was shell-shocked. 'Whaddya mean, stay away from Freddie? He's me best fuckin' mate.'

Bobby smiled. 'Not any more, he ain't. I mean it, Tommy, stay away from my nephew. If I find out you've been within ten foot of him, I promise you, I will fly back from Spain and personally kill you with my bare hands. Understand?'

Tommy nodded. He didn't have the guts to disagree.

Cursing that the kitchen door was locked, James gave a gentle tap. After half-a-dozen large brandies, he'd realised that the only person in the world he wanted help and advice off was his mum. Knowing that Maria was probably still next door, he'd parked his car in the street behind and hopped over the fences. He couldn't face seeing her, not yet anyway. He'd toyed with the idea of ringing Freddie and demanding if he knew the truth, but he decided against it. Freddie had been friendly with Tommy ever since their Feltham days and it wasn't fair to put him in such an awkward position. Not only that, James wasn't sure whether he wanted to know, or could handle the truth himself just yet.

Having put Alfie and Johnny to bed earlier, Maureen was unable to concentrate on the telly and had chosen to have an early night herself. It had been a truly awful day, full of drama and upset. Even now, her mind couldn't rest. She'd spent the last hour tossing and turning. Hearing a noise outside, she sat up. She'd heard something a few minutes ago. She was about to get up and investigate, when there was a thud against her window that sounded like a stone. Nervously, she peeped through the curtains.

James stood by the big plant, frantically waving his arms at her. She opened the window, 'Whatever's the matter, love?'

'Ssh,' he said, holding his forefinger to his lips. 'Open the door, I need to talk to yer,' he whispered.

Maureen put on her dressing gown and did as she was told. Surely there wasn't another drama on the horizon. With the day she'd had, she couldn't bloody stand it.

As she opened the door, she saw the state of his face. His forehead was red raw, his nose looked as though it had taken a clump and his eyes were starting to blacken. In fact, he looked like he'd run into a brick wall.

'Oh, James, my poor baby. Whatever's happened to you?'

The tenderness of her voice and the concern in her eyes was all too much for James. Throwing himself against her chest, he clung to her and sobbed like the baby she had just called him. Maureen stroked his hair as though he was a little boy all over again. Her James had never been a fighter and she hadn't seen him cry for bloody years. She knew whatever had happened to him was serious, and she dreaded hearing the truth.

James felt a right wuss as he pulled away from her. He was twenty-five years old, and here he was crying like a fucking newborn.

Maureen forced a smile. 'I'll make us a nice cup of tea, shall I?'

James shook his head. 'I need something stronger, Mum. Beer, brandy, whisky, anything'll do.'

Maureen handed him a lager. She didn't want to encourage him to drink spirits.

Sipping his beer, James launched into the story from the very beginning. He told her about Lucy giving birth to the baby, about the ambulance men who did their best to save the child and about Lucy's piercing screams on hearing her daughter was dead.

As his mum wiped her eyes and blew her nose, James changed the subject. It was time to tell her about Tommy.

'You should have seen the state of him, Mum, when he answered the door. He looked like a fuckin' tramp, he was totally out of his head. I took one look at him, saw red, and gave it to him. I told him his fortune and he lost the plot. He went mental, he did, and started head-butting me.'

Maureen gasped. She'd never imagined in a million years that James's injuries came from his brother. How could his own flesh and blood do that to him?

'I'll never have him darken my door again, James, and I mean it this time. I can't believe he's done this to yer. If I get my hands on him, I'll fuckin' marmalise him.'

James carried on – he needed to get to the Maria bit. 'I wasn't gonna hit him back, Mum. I was gonna walk away, but he started calling Maria a slag and I went apeshit and clumped him. It was awful Mum, really awful.'

Maureen rubbed his arm. 'I'm glad you fuckin' hit him and I hope you walloped him hard. He's no good James, he's . . .'

'Shut up, Mum, let me finish. When I was about to leave, he was laughing at me, then he said he'd slept with Maria. He said she'd lost her virginity to him and he started saying some really nasty stuff about her. I'd have killed him if I'd have stayed there, so I ran out, jumped in the car and went straight to the pub. I couldn't think straight and I needed a stiff drink to calm meself down.'

As tears began to roll down his cheeks, Maureen held him close. For years she'd had a feeling that something had happened between Maria and Tommy. She'd clocked the atmosphere, heard the remarks and smelt the hatred. She'd never said a word, not even to Ethel, but she'd always, always known.

'How am I gonna find out the truth, Mum? Do I confront her? Beg him to tell me? Ask Freddie? What should I do?'

Taking the brandy out of the cupboard under the sink, Maureen poured two large glasses. Lager was no use to the poor little sod with the shock he'd just had. Handing one to James, she sat opposite him and sipped her own. 'Do nothing, boy. If Tommy was drugged up he was probably talking rubbish. Can you imagine how poor Maria would feel if you went home and accused her of something she'd never done? It could ruin your marriage, love.'

'But I need to know if it's true, Mum, I can't live a lie.'

Maureen took a large gulp of brandy. She'd lived a lie for years and was an expert on the subject. 'Only you can decide what to do, James, but my advice would be to let sleeping dogs lie. It's just Tommy being vindictive, that's all it is. If I was you, I'd forget all about it.'

James sipped the rest of his drink in silence. Part of him wished he could take his mum's advice, but he knew he couldn't forget. He had to know the truth and the only person who could provide him with that was Maria. He finished his drink and stood up.

'I'm going next door, Mum, and if she ain't there, I'm going home to ask her. She'll tell me the truth, I know she will.'

Maureen plastered on a fake smile. 'You do what you think is best, love.'

Wishing him luck, she shut the front door. It was time to cry her own tears now.

Maria put her book down and stared at the ceiling. She'd left her mum's and come back to the flat hoping that he'd be there, but he wasn't. Her mum's birthday surprise had been totally ruined. She wasn't worried about that any more; she wasn't even annoyed. Something had happened, she could feel it in her bones. It was so out of character for James not to contact her. Even if he was still at the hospital with Lucy and his phone was dead, he'd have called her from somewhere.

Her eyes followed a fly leave the ceiling and walk down the wall. Either he'd had an accident or Tommy had opened his poisoned mouth; there was no other explanation. Guessing it was the latter, she prepared herself. She couldn't lose James – not now, not ever.

As she heard his car pull up, her stomach lurched. Hearing the door open, she took a deep breath. One look at his face told her all she needed to know. He knew.

'I'll make us a coffee and you can tell me all about Lucy and the baby,' she said brightly.

James waved away the offer of the coffee and walked towards her. 'I need to talk to you, Maria. I saw Tommy earlier and he said something about you and him. He –'

Maria had no choice other than to interrupt him. She had to drop her bombshell before he could drop his. 'Guess what, James?'

'Can't you just let me finish for once, Maria?' he said angrily.

She shook her head. 'No, I can't. Whatever you've got to say is not as important as what I've got to say, and I've been waiting all day to say it. I'm pregnant, James, me and you are gonna have a little baby.'

James felt like he'd been shot in the back. Rooted to the spot, he was totally unable to show any emotion.

Maria smiled at him. 'Well, say something, then.'

James was dumbstruck. He could hardly drop the accusation that Tommy had made now.

Maria threw her arms around his neck. 'I thought you'd be ecstatic. Please say something, James.'

317

James responded to her hug and held her tightly. With tears in his eyes, he smiled at her. 'Ecstatic is putting it mildy – I'm over the bloody moon!'

Maria looked him straight in the eye. 'Now, what did you want to tell me that was so important?'

James shook his head. 'I can't remember now.'

Maria smiled. 'Well, it obviously wasn't that important in the first place, then.'

James turned his head away. If only she knew.

THIRTY-FIVE

2005 – Ten Years Later

'So, what you doing tonight, Johnny? There's a crowd of us going down to that new soul club in Ilford, if you fancy it.'

Johnny stepped out of the communal shower. 'Nah, I've got plans for tonight. Let us know if you're going out again next week.'

'I'm sure he's got some little bird on the go,' one of the lads shouted.

'I bet she's a right fat minger. Go on, admit it, Johnny, you're dating a dog,' shouted another.

Johnny smiled as he dried himself off. He was used to his team-mates ribbing him. Banter was a part of their match-day ritual, and he always gave as good as he got.

'See yer later, tossers!' he shouted as he left the changing rooms.

'Wanker!' the lads yelled back.

Johnny got into his van and drove out of the car park. The lads were right in one sense: he was seeing a bird, but what they didn't know was that bird was his mum. None of his current pals knew much about his upbringing. They knew he lived with his nan, but little else. In his eyes, his past was his past, and it was no one else's business.

* * *

Unable to concentrate on the film because of Ethel's snoring, Maureen decided to tackle the ironing. As she walked into the kitchen, the phone rang.

'All right, Nan? I'm just shooting round me mate's and then I'm going straight round Mum's. I'll probably stay there the night. We're gonna have a couple of beers and a takeaway.'

'OK, Johnny, I'll see yer when I see yer. How did the game go, by the way?'

'We won and I scored two goals. I'll tell yer about it properly tomorrow. I wanna hurry up and get round Mum's before *The X Factor* starts.'

Maureen smiled as she replaced the receiver. She was so pleased for Johnny's sake that his mum had finally got her act together.

Susan had been clean for just over a year now, and was doing really well. She'd come to Maureen for help after a prison stint for shoplifting. Maureen had been dubious about trusting her at first – another false dawn was the last thing that Johnny needed. Maureen had gone to the doctor with her, not holding out very much hope, but her GP had been fantastic and had got her into rehab. On completion of her treatment he had demanded that the council move her away from her old area and temptation. The authorities were told that she had a son who wanted to stay with her, and after deliberation with Barking and Dagenham council, she was offered a two-bedroom house in Becontree Heath.

Maureen offered to view the property with Susan and they had both fallen in love with it on sight. The corner house of a cul-de-sac, it was in immaculate condition and had a pretty little garden.

'Oh, Suze, it's beautiful. You've gotta take it,' Maureen insisted.

'I love it, Mum. I'm gonna be so happy here; it'll be a new start for me,' Susan crowed.

Maureen was delighted that Susan had managed to kick the heroin habit that had blighted so much of her life. She looked an entirely different person without the sallow eyes and haunted expression. Her sparkle returned, along with rosy cheeks and a hint of laughter.

Obviously, life without hard drugs wasn't all plain sailing, and within weeks of leaving rehab, Susan was indulging in the odd drink and joint. Maureen was furious with her. 'Yer silly little cow. What did yer drugs counsellor tell yer, eh? He said once yer start takin' soft drugs, you'll be back on the hard stuff before yer know it.'

Susan stood her ground. 'I can't live like a fuckin' nun, Mum. I swear on my life, I'll never touch the brown again. I'm clean as a whistle and you're just gonna have to trust me.'

On accepting the council's offer, James and Freddie had decorated the house as a surprise for Susan. Maureen brought curtains, cushions, ornaments and new bedding. The fewer reminders of her past and the flat in Stepney the better, her counsellor advised.

Once her daughter had moved in, Maureen made sure that she visited her a couple of times a week. She often found Susan half-pissed or stoned, but overall there seemed nothing major to worry about. She seemed happy and content and had even made friends with her next-door neighbours.

Maureen was thrilled that finally she'd managed to get away from Dave Taylor. An arsehole, waster and junkie, he'd done nothing but drag Susan down with him. For ten years she'd been with him on and off, and in that time he'd lived with five other birds, fathered three kids and repeatedly broken her heart.

321

'Good riddance to bad rubbish,' Maureen kept reminding her.

The most pleasing aspect of Susan's new life, for Maureen, was that she'd managed to rebuild her relationship with her son. Once her brain was no longer bamboozled by smack, she saw Johnny for what he really was – a polite, intelligent, loving young man.

Having finally seen the light, Susan often had attacks of guilt and only recently had broken down and poured her heart out to Maureen.

'I don't deserve him, Mum, and I can't believe, after the way I've treated him, he still wants to know me – let alone loves me. What about the time I sold his wedding outfit?' she sobbed.

Maureen cuddled her. 'The past is the past, Susan, don't dwell on it. You've got years of catching up to do with Johnny. Just enjoy it, love.'

Susan had taken her advice on board, and Johnny often visited and stayed with her on a Saturday night. It was a special kind of bonding for both of them. They'd get a takeaway, sink a few cans, and laugh and cry as they watched *The X Factor* together.

'Maur, I'm fuckin' wastin' away in 'ere. Make us some grub, girl.'

Ethel waking up spelled the end to Maureen's daydream. Sighing, she switched off the iron and switched on the cooker.

Maria stepped off the treadmill and drank her bottle of water. She'd joined the gym a few months ago in the hope of making new friends. So far, apart from the odd hello and goodbye, she hadn't had much success. Maria didn't miss living in the East End at all, but she did miss the friendliness of the people. Essex was quite snooty, and the people who lived there seemed very shallow.

'Excuse me, my friends and I are about to participate in a well-earned glass of wine at the bar, if you care to join us.'

Maria looked around to make sure the woman was definitely talking to her. Seeing no one standing behind her, she held out her hand. 'I'd love to, and I'm Maria, by the way.'

The woman accepted her handshake. 'I'm Lavinia. Now, shall we get that drink, Maria? Follow me and I'll introduce you to the other girls.'

Maria was as pleased as punch as she was led into the bar area. She'd noticed Lavinia and her friends when she had first joined the gym. Out of all the girls there, they looked the in-crowd. She was in no rush to get home. James was away for a couple of days, doing a run with Freddie, and her mum was indoors looking after the girls.

Maria couldn't stop smiling as she sipped her wine and listened to the chit-chat. She was finally part of the Essex girls' gang.

Tommy counted the money and handed the guy the keys and the logbook. As he watched his beloved Merc disappear into the distance, he went back indoors and slammed the door. He opened a can of lager, shoved some gear up his nose and lay down on the carpet. How the fuck had his life ended up like this? Everything had been cushy up until last year. He and Mustapha had led the life of Riley. They'd had birds, drugs, flash motors, vintage champagne and anything else they wanted, coming out of their arseholes.

Tommy's world had crashed the day Mustapha got

himself arrested. Over the years, they had ended up being partners in crime. They got on like a house on fire, and had trusted one another with their lives. Tommy was away on holiday with Alfie when Mustapha got spun. Any other time, he'd have been with him. But instead, he was caught with Emre, his pal who owned a kebab shop in Tottenham High Road. They were caught with a fair old lump. The filth would have a field day once they totted it up. Then again, the police always made it sound worse than it was. Instead of adding it up in ounces or kilos, they got a kick out of adding it up in £10 deals.

Mustapha and Emre were both currently in Belmarsh awaiting their court case. Twenty years plus, the poor bastards were looking at. Tommy had tried to carry on with the business, but hadn't had much success. He'd never actually met the Mr Big who supplied Mustapha. The boss had always refused to meet Tommy. Apparently, he didn't trust the English, and would only deal with his own. With very few other contacts, Tommy tried his luck with some south London Turks he'd met through Mustapha. They were having none of it – in fact, they had tried to kill him.

'One week you go away and Mustapha get arrested. You fucking English grass,' they shouted, as they chased him down the road with a machete.

Tommy had had to run like a greyhound to get away from the bastards. He could understand their loyalty, though. Even he had to admit, it looked fishy that he'd been on holiday when Mustapha had got caught.

With no major supplier, Tommy had no choice other than to buy small and deal on the streets again. After a lot of debating, he decided against it. He'd been a big fish for years and wasn't ready to mug himself off by selling £20 wraps. He also had Alfie to think about now, and didn't want to drag him into anything untoward. With little else on offer, he'd decided to take a break and see what cropped up. Trouble was, nothing had, and his money was disappearing fast and furious. His own drug problem hadn't helped. He'd recently sold a property he owned in Ilford to help get him by, and had snorted and smoked the proceeds in under six months.

All he had in the world now was the house he lived in and the £18,000 from the motor he'd just sold. Tommy thought of his Merc and sighed. He'd loved that car, it had been a beauty to drive. Depressed, he went in search of his crack pipe.

Johnny pulled up outside his mum's house. He grabbed the beers and takeaway from the footwell and walked up the path. He rang the doorbell three times before it was finally answered. One look at his mum's face told him something was definitely amiss.

'You OK? What's happening?' he asked.

Susan looked sheepish. 'Can yer pop back tomorrow, love,' she whispered.

'Who's that? It ain't me old mate Johnny, is it?'

Johnny looked at his mother in horror. Dave Taylor's voice had haunted him for years, and he recognised it immediately. 'Why is he here, Mum? You know he's bad news.'

Dave Taylor staggered towards the door. 'Oi, shoeshine boy, who you calling bad news?'

Johnny grabbed him by the neck of his scruffy T-shirt. 'You leave my mum alone, and if you ever call me shoeshine boy again, I'll fuckin' kill yer.'

Susan pushed Johnny up the path. 'Don't start, son. Just go, for my sake. I'll ring yer tomorrow, OK?'

In a temper, Johnny slung the Chinese and beers up the path. He ran to his van, leaped in and drove off like a loony. Unable to see straight because of his tears, he angrily bumped the van up a kerb. His nan would know what to do for the best.

Maureen's heart sank as she took the phonecall. How could Susan be so bloody stupid? 'Forget her, Johnny, she's not fuckin' worth it. Now stop crying, love, just get yourself home.'

As Maureen stood at the bedroom window waiting for his van to pull up, she had plenty of time to reflect. Since Johnny had moved in with her at the age of ten, she had had a special closeness with him.

She'd been struck down with breast cancer within a couple of years of him moving in. The chemo had made her tired and Johnny had been her little helper. He hadn't understood the seriousness of her illness, but he'd been her bloody reason for fighting the dreaded disease. Thanks to her grandson, Maureen had been extremely positive about her illness from the word go.

'Nanny will be fine,' she assured him.

Even when she lost her hair, they made a joke of it. He helped her choose a wig and they'd roared with laughter as she'd tried on numerous funny ones.

'You look like Scary Spice, Nan,' he'd giggled, as she put on an afro.

Thankfully, the chemo had worked and she had since been given the all-clear.

With her three having long ago left home, she'd brought Johnny up as though he was her only child. After his shit start in life, he'd done so well for himself. He'd worked hard at school, gone to college and was only months away from finishing his apprenticeship and becoming a fully qualified electrician. Unlike with Tommy and Susan, she'd done a good job of bringing up her grandson. He was a normal, down-to-earth lad who played football on a Sunday, and liked a couple of pints and a flutter on the horses. He even had the occasional girlfriend, but nothing too serious. Johnny reminded Maureen of James. He was good natured and kind hearted, just like her youngest.

Out of all of her children, James was, and had always been the apple of her eye. He was still married to Maria and, thankfully, they were now happier than ever. The Tommy episode was now long forgotten. In fact, James had never mentioned it since the day he'd turned up in bits around her house.

Apart from that one hiccup, Maria was the perfect daughter-in-law and Maureen couldn't thank her enough for making her son so happy and producing the two most beautiful granddaughters in the world.

Tara, nine, and Lily, six, were Maureen's other pride and joy. Maria's mum, Janet, still lived next door and the girls spent many weekends being spoilt and fussed over by the pair of them. They had their own bedrooms in both houses; on Fridays they stayed at Janet's, and on Saturdays they slept at hers.

James and Maria had now moved out to Ingatestone in Essex and the girls went to an excellent local school. They spoke ever so posh and Maureen loved the fact that her family had gone up in the world. They never discussed how James made his money. The tailor's shop had been shut down five years ago, shortly after Harold's death. Apart from knowing that her son was in partnership with Freddie, Maureen had very little idea about what he actually did.

Tommy was no longer part of their family circle. Both James and Freddie had nothing to do with him whatsoever and Maureen could count the times she'd seen him over the last couple of years on one hand.

Splitting up with Lucy was the worst thing that could have happened to Tommy. She'd given him a stable home life and, to a certain extent, had kept him on the straight and narrow. His son, Alfie, was nineteen now and Maureen rarely saw him either. A chip off the old block, he'd left home at eighteen and moved in with his father.

Lucy had been, and still was, distraught. She'd been a bloody good mother and couldn't understand why Alfie had chosen to leave her. She had heard that Tommy was bang on the gear and was desperately worried about her son. She was still in regular contact with Maureen, but the pair of them were at a loss as to what to do about the situation. If a nineteen-year-old boy wanted to live with his father, in reality, there was sod all you could do about it.

Lucy had rung Maureen recently, telling her that she'd bumped into Tommy. 'He looked awful. He's lost so much weight and was out of his nut,' she told her. Maureen hadn't slept a wink that night.

'We've got to help him, James, someone's got to look out for Alfie,' Maureen told her youngest the following day.

James shook his head. 'Me and Freddie have both tried, Mum. He's a crackhead, he's too far gone.'

Unable to rest, Maureen had spent a week visiting all his old haunts to find out his home address. Not wanting to involve James, she'd asked Kenny if he would drive her there.

Kenny's one-time undying love for Wendy had turned into a form of hate over the years and he was only too glad of an excuse to get out of the house.

Pulling up outside the house in Leytonstone, Maureen was surprised to see a well-kept, nice-looking property. She was even more surprised when Tommy opened the door, looking a damn sight better than Lucy had described.

'I've been worried about you, Tommy. Lucy said you'd lost a lot of weight and looked really ill.'

Tommy laughed. 'I ain't surprised, Mum. I'd been out partying for three days solid when she saw me.'

On accepting the offer of a quick cup of tea, Maureen was relieved to see Alfie sitting on the sofa happily munching beans on toast.

'How are you, love? Are you enjoying living with your dad?'

Alfie nodded. 'Me and Dad have a right laugh. He's not on my case all the time like Mum was.'

Maureen gulped her tea, made Alfie promise to ring his mum more often, said goodbye to Tommy and left. The inside of the house was untidy and in need of a good clean but, other than that, there was nothing much to worry about. At least the visit had put her mind at rest, if nothing else.

Maureen's thoughts were interrupted by Ethel. 'Maur, hurry up. Quick, I need the toilet.'

Ethel was eighty-six now and, apart from suffering from severe arthritis in her legs and hips, was still as strong as an ox. She no longer lived in her flat over the road. Three years ago, Maureen had insisted that Ethel give it up and move in with her. Ethel kept falling over, so, to stop herself worrying, Maureen had offered to care for her. Stubborn and independent, Ethel had flatly refused at first.

'There's fuck-all wrong with me, I don't need bleedin' looking after.'

An especially bad fall, which had resulted in a month in hospital, had forced her to change her mind. James had brought her a top-of-the-range sofabed to sleep on, and a commode. By day the lounge looked normal and at night it reverted to Ethel's toilet and bedroom. Apart from needing help getting in and out of bed, Ethel managed to get about indoors with the aid of a frame. If Maureen took her out, they used a wheelchair. Her legs might have packed up, but her mind was still as sharp as a knife. Mentally, she hadn't changed one iota over the years and, as Maureen pushed her around Tesco, she would still be on the thieve, hiding her haul under her blanket.

'Maureen. Quick, I've crapped meself.'

Johnny arrived home just as Maureen was shovelling up shit. 'Don't come in the living room, love. Nanny's had a little accident, and I'm just sortin' her out.'

'I'm not stoppin', Nan. I've only come back to change me shoes. I'm going clubbing with the lads from football.'

'Are you OK, love?'

'Yeah, I'm fine,' Johnny shouted, as he slammed the door.

Maureen sat Ethel back down and went to make a cuppa. Susan never failed to disappoint her. If Dave Taylor was round there, she was bound to be tempted to take whatever he was on.

'If she goes back to her old ways, I'm never having anything to do with her again,' Maureen told Ethel, as she explained the story.

Ethel said nothing as she sipped her tea. She'd had this same conversation with Maureen so many times over the years that she couldn't be bothered to answer her any more. Maureen had had the wool pulled over her eyes so many times, it was a miracle that she could still fucking see!

Johnny stood quietly in the the corner of the club. All of his mates were mucking about on the dancefloor, but he had too much on his mind to enjoy himself. Seeing his mate, Gazza, walk towards him, he forced a smile.

'What's up, Johnny?'

'Nothing. I'm all right.'

Gazza put an arm around his shoulder. 'You're not all right. I might not be a psychiatrist, but I know when me mates have got problems.'

Johnny was fairly drunk, and the alcohol, mixed with Gazza's concern, made his eyes brim with tears. Feeling a right prick for showing his emotions, he dragged his mate towards the exit.

'We'll talk outside, but promise me, Gazza, you won't tell the rest of the lads?'

Gazza held his hands up. 'Scout's honour.'

Gazza shook his head in disbelief as Johnny spilled the beans. His pal was so nice and normal, he couldn't believe his mum was a smackhead.

'Look, I'm driving tonight, 'cause I've gotta work tomorrow. I'll tell the other lads that we're shooting off early and I'll take yer round your mum's. At least if yer knock and make sure she's OK, it'll put your mind at rest.'

Johnny hesitated. 'What if that cunt Dave Taylor's still there?'

'Fuck him. Even if he is there, at least you can see if your mother's out of her nut or not.'

Johnny nodded. 'You tell the others we're going, and I'll wait here. Tell 'em I don't feel well or something.'

The journey to Becontree Heath was only a short distance from Ilford, and they were there within ten minutes.

'Do yer want me to come with yer?' Gazza asked.

'Nah, I'll be all right. Just sit in the car and watch me back in case Taylor starts.'

Johnny walked up the path and rang the bell. The house was eerily silent. Getting no answer, he pushed the letterbox open.

'Mum, it's me, Johnny. Open the door.'

331

Wondering if she'd gone out, he peered through the window. The curtains were closed and he could see very little other than that the lights were on. He walked back to Gazza's car.

'I can't get no answer. I know she sometimes leaves the kitchen door open, so I'm gonna climb over the fence and try round the back.'

Gazza stepped out of his vehicle. 'I'll come with yer. You might need a leg-up.'

Johnny could feel his heart pounding as they scaled the fence. 'It's open,' he said, as he tried the handle.

'Mum!' Johnny shouted as he walked into the kitchen.

As he stepped into the living room, he saw her legs first. They were poking out by the side of the sofa. She was lying face down. There was no sign of Taylor.

'Mum!' he shouted, as he turned her body over.

An empty syringe lay beside her, and her hair was covered in vomit. She was cold and as white as a sheet.

Johnny frantically shook her, 'Mum, please wake up. Mum, Mum!' he cried.

Gazza bent down and checked for her pulse. There wasn't one.

He looked at his pal. 'I'll ring for an ambulance. I'm so sorry, Johnny, but I think she's dead, mate.'

Johnny sobbed as he knelt down beside her. He took her lifeless hand in his.

'I loved you so much, Mum. We had our whole lives ahead of us. Why did you have to take that shit? Why, Mum, why?'

THIRTY-SIX

Maureen turned on the lamp and glanced at the alarm clock: 4.30 a.m. and she hadn't slept a bloody wink. Debating whether to get up, she chose not to. The day ahead was going to be the most difficult day of her life and she certainly didn't need to lengthen it.

To bury one's own child was the most horrendous feeling in the world. Losing parents, relations and friends was soul destroying, but life went on. Being told that your child is dead is a different ball game. No mother on earth expects to outlive their kids and Maureen was no exception. Feeling a tear roll down her cheek, Maureen turned the lamp off. She had to try to sleep. It was the only thing that could temporarily take her pain away.

Johnny lay wide awake in the room next door. He'd barely slept since he'd found his mum dead. The nightmares were the worst, as every time he shut his eyes, all he could see was his mum's lifeless body. The police had turned up just after the ambulance. They hadn't been very sympathetic and Gazza had had a go at them.

'Have some respect – Johnny's her son, you unfeeling bastard,' he'd told one officer, when he'd referred to Susan as a junkie.

The postmortem confirmed that his mum had been

dead for hours, and had died of an overdose of heroin. The tragedy was, the coroner said, that had she still been a regular user, the amount she had taken wouldn't have killed her.

Johnny told the police that Dave Taylor had been round his mum's earlier that day and had almost certainly supplied her with the heroin that had killed her. The police went looking for Taylor, but were told he'd left the area.

'She probably OD'd while he was there and, instead of calling an ambulance, he panicked and did a runner. We'll put a warrant out for his arrest,' the copper told him.

Johnny hadn't bothered answering. To the Old Bill, his mum and Dave Taylor were just a pair of smackheads, and even though his mother was now dead, they weren't gonna break their necks looking for her partner in crime. In Johnny's eyes, Taylor was a murderer, the lowest of the low. In the coppers' eyes, he was nothing more than his mother's supplier.

Feeling his eyes well up, Johnny got out of bed. He'd been acting like a wimp and, today of all days, he needed to be a man.

As her daughter's body arrived at the house in a coffin, Maureen let out a loud sob and was quickly comforted by Sandra and Brenda.

'Now, sit down for a minute next to Ethel and I'll pour you a nice brandy to steady your nerves,' Brenda told her.

Maureen was only too grateful for the kindness of her friends. They'd been absolute bricks and, without their help, she didn't know how she would have managed.

Over the last week or so, she'd experienced every emotion going. The guilt was the worst. She knew that when Susan was a kid, she'd always favoured Tommy and James.

'You never favoured the boys purposely. I'm not speaking ill of the dead, but if you remember rightly, Susan was a spiteful little toerag as a kid,' Ethel reminded her.

Her mother-in-law's harsh words had made her feel better, temporarily at least.

James stood in the front garden, talking to Maria and Freddie. He'd been keeping a watchful eye on his mum through the window. Seeing her get upset again, he asked Maria to go inside and sit with her. Women were much better at that type of stuff than blokes were.

Tara and Lily were next door being looked after by Nanny Janet. Both James and Maria felt that they were far too young to experience life's harsh realities by attending a funeral. They'd barely known Auntie Susan anyway. With her lifestyle and problems, she'd been the last person James had wanted his precious daughters spending time around.

With Maria inside the house, James turned to Freddie. 'Well, he ain't here yet, is he? Do you reckon he'll come?'

Freddie shrugged his shoulders. Telling his wife, Sarah, to go inside with Maria, he turned to his pal. 'I dunno, I thought he'd have been here by now.'

For very different reasons, both men were dreading having to spend the day in Tommy's company. With James, it was the Maria obstacle. Since his brother's accusations and their fisticuffs years ago, things had been incredibly difficult between them. They'd never socialised since that day and on the odd occasion they'd bumped into one another, their conversation had been stifled and stilted. Their lives had taken two completely different paths and while James's had gone upwards, his brother's had taken one almighty dip. The last time James had seen him was just over six months ago. He'd heard the rumours that his drinking and drug-taking had got well and truly out of hand and was worried about Alfie living with him. He had gone to see his brother at his local and got a barrage of abuse for his trouble.

'Who do you think you are, you cunt? Coming in here, telling me how to live my life. Fuck off back to your bum-chum Freddie. Fucking Judases, the pair of yer. Go on, fuck off.'

Head bowed, James had walked away. He could understand Tommy's bitterness, but he only had himself to blame. He'd had the world at his feet at one point and if he hadn't self-destructed, would probably still be on top of his game.

Freddie's concerns were very different. He knew his ex-best pal considered him a wrong 'un and, in a way, he didn't blame him. They'd been through so much together and now they were enemies for no reason. It would have been better if they'd had a fight or a row; Freddie would have felt less guilty if that had been the case. Instead, he'd walked away on the insistence of his uncle Bobby.

'If I find out you've had any more to do with that junkie scumbag, then you're out the firm as well,' he was told.

In a nutshell, he had had no choice but to erase Tommy from his life. James had replaced his old pal as his business partner and best friend. They worked well together and trusted one another implicitly. They were still in the import and export business with uncle Bobby. The whole set-up was extremely tight knit, which was why it was still going strong. They brought in much more now than when they'd first started years ago. The money was very good and, all in all, cannabis had provided them and their families with a very pleasant life. Obviously, there was always a chance of getting nicked, but neither Freddie nor Tommy ever spoke about the risks.

'Do yer want another fag?'

James waved the box in front of Freddie's face. Neither of them smoked on a regular basis, they only bought a box when they were pissed or nervous. Today they were suffering with their nerves and, with Tommy due to turn up any minute, both of them had good reason to puff like fucking dragons.

Alfie sat awkwardly at the table. His dad was knocking back one large scotch after another. They were in a pub in Leytonstone and the quick one that his old man had insisted they stop for had now turned into six.

Having lived with his father for the past year, Alfie was more than used to his dysfunctional behaviour. If he wasn't drinking, he was snorting coke, and if he wasn't snorting coke, he was smoking crack. Alfie didn't mind him kicking the arse out of whatever he did, but not today, not at Auntie Susan's funeral.

'What time are we going, Dad? I think I should ring a cab. It's half-eleven now and the service starts at twelve.'

Tommy nodded and went to the toilet. He needed a livener before he went anywhere. Checking his nose for telltale signs, he studied himself in the mirror. His party lifestyle had certainly ravaged his looks. He looked gaunt, old and his hair had started to thin. He doused his face in cold water. He was dreading today, and didn't know if he'd be able to control his anger.

He wasn't bothered about the actual funeral. He and Susan had never been close and the fact that she was now brown bread hadn't affected him in the slightest. There was no way he couldn't attend, though. Whether he liked her or not, she was still his bloody sister.

Anyway, Freddie, James and Maria would be ecstatic if he didn't show his face and he wasn't gonna give them the satisfaction. Facing his arse-licking little brother, his ex-cunting best friend and the slag with the tight fanny filled him with hatred, but he was gonna front it, he had to.

Straightening his tie, he took a deep breath. Time to face the enemies.

Maureen sat at the front of the chapel and glanced around. It was filling up by the second and, seeing as Susan had never been the most popular person on the planet, she was surprised at just how many people had turned up.

The East End was a very special community and a lot of people had probably turned up to support her and the family. Whatever their reasons, it was better to have a full chapel than an empty one.

As the service began, Johnny, who had barely said a word all day, began to sob. Both Maureen and James, who were either side of him, did their best to cuddle him and offer whispers of comfort.

The service itself was very moving. The vicar hit the nail on the head when he said that Susan's death was a dreadful waste of a young life. Johnny, Maureen, Maria and even Ethel all cried a few tears at the truthfulness of the eulogy.

Knowing that his mum and Johnny wouldn't be able to, James had offered to get up and say a few words. Taking his folded-up piece of paper out of his pocket, he began.

'My sister Susan's life was full of ups and downs. I'm sure everybody here today is well aware of the problems that she faced. What most of you are probably not aware of is that for a year prior to her death she was totally clean and had really moved on with her life. In that time she made amends with her family and, most importantly of all, built a wonderful relationship with her son, Johnny.'

Seeing his nephew sobbing his heart out, James tried his best to carry on. Unable to see through his own tears, he handed his speech to the vicar to finish.

Susan had always insisted that she would hate to be buried and Maureen granted her her final wish. In time, Susan's ashes would be buried with a plaque remembering her in the grounds. Seeing as her father had had a similar send-off in the same crematorium, Kenny said it would be a nice idea to put Susan near her dad.

'I know they weren't close, but at least she'll have company and won't be alone,' he said kindly.

As the service came to an end, Led Zeppelin's 'Stairway to Heaven' played while the curtains closed. Johnny had chosen the song, saying that his mum played it endlessly in the flat when he was a kid.

'What's this load of fuckin' shit?' Ethel complained.

'It was Mum's favourite song of all time,' Johnny said, annoyed. He loved his nan, but she never knew when to keep her mouth shut.

Tommy and Alfie arrived just in time to see the end of the service. They'd waited ages for a cab and the traffic around Manor Park had been at a virtual standstill.

'I told you we should have left earlier – we've missed it,' Alfie complained.

'Just shut up and stand in the corner,' Tommy hissed at him.

As the music ended, the front row stood up to leave. Being pushed in her wheelchair by James, Ethel had no need to look straight ahead like the others. Glancing to her right, her eyes met Tommy's and she nodded at him in acknowledgement.

As they hit the cold air and stood by the flowers, she called Maureen over. 'Tommy's here. He was standing in the corner at the back.'

Maureen breathed a sigh of relief. She'd been so angry thinking that he hadn't turned up. Poor sod, he probably felt awkward because Freddie and James were sat in the front row, so he'd purposely stayed at the back.

Telling Alfie to walk on ahead of him, Tommy went in search of a toilet. He desperately needed a line to lift his mood after the scene he'd just witnessed. How dare that cunt Freddie sit alongside the family, as though he was part of it? Wasn't it enough that he'd stolen his brother from him?

Feeling the gear hit the back of his throat, he sat on the toilet seat. He desperately needed to get his head together. None of this would be so bad if his own life wasn't so fucking terrible.

Hearing footsteps outside, Tommy pulled the chain and walked out.

'There you are, I've been looking everywhere for yer. Alfie said you'd be in the toilets.'

Tommy gave Maureen a hug. 'Hello, Mum. Nice service weren't it? How you bearing up, girl?'

Maureen clung to him. 'All the better for seeing you. I'm so glad you came, Tommy. At one point I thought you weren't going to.'

Pulling away, Tommy held both of her hands. 'Susan was my sister, I wouldn't miss it for the world.'

Maureen smiled. Whatever his faults, he was a good lad, deep down. 'We're holding her wake in The Bancroft. Kev's mum works there now. She rang up, she did, said we should let bygones be bygones. He was devastated, Kevin. Apparently, he's here today. Come all the way from Manchester. Ain't that nice of him, Tom?'

Tommy nodded. 'Poor old Kevin; she broke his heart, did our Susan.'

'Oh, that was years ago. Anyway, Kev's mum has laid on a load of food for us and James is paying for all the drink. Please come, Tommy, you've got to say goodbye to your sister properly.'

Tommy grinned. Extremely high, he'd forgotten about his earlier worries and was more than ready for a party. James, Maria, Freddie: they'd be sick as pigs at his arrival and he was looking forward to watching them squirm.

'Oh, I'm coming, Mum, and not only that, I promise I'll stay till the end.'

Maureen was thrilled as she led him towards the rest of the mourners. If only her kids could settle their differences. She'd already lost one child and it made her realise just how important family was.

'Look, James and Maria are on their own, over by that brick wall. Go and say hello to them.'

Sauntering towards them, Tommy saw the look of fear on their faces. 'So, how is my wonderful brother and his charming wife, then?' he asked sarcastically.

James and Maria glanced at one another. Neither of them knew what to say. James found his voice first.

'All right, Tom? How you doing?'

Tommy smirked. 'I'm good – and do you know what? I'm all the better for seeing yous two.'

THIRTY-SEVEN

Back at The Bancroft, Johnny felt a tap on his shoulder.

'All right, son? How you holding up?'

Johnny was shocked to see his father. He hadn't seen him for yonks, and certainly hadn't expected him to turn up at his mum's funeral.

'I'm all right, Dad. I didn't see you earlier, did you go to the service?'

Royston nodded. 'You were with all your family, so I didn't come over. I stood at the back, I felt it was the right thing to do.'

Johnny felt awkward. He was pleased his dad had come, but at the same time, he didn't really know what to say to him. Royston sensed his embarrassment.

'I'll get us a couple of pints, eh? Grab that table, Johnny, and we can have a proper chat.'

Maureen sat at one of the tables next to Ethel in her wheelchair. They were both discussing all the old faces that had turned up. All of Maureen's old pals from the bingo were there, along with Tracey and Darren, Fat Caz, Tibbsy and Benno; even Lenny Simpson and his brother Matty had come to pay their respects. Dave Taylor was nowhere to be seen. Apparently, he was still on the run. Maureen had vowed to stick a knife in him had he shown his face. In her eyes, he'd murdered his daughter, and she'd do life over him if she ever clapped eyes on him again.

Maureen was surprised to see Mary Smith's sister and cousin at the chapel. It had been Mary's boy, Terry, whom Tommy had murdered many moons ago. The people of east London were a different breed from anyone else; they lived by their own set of rules.

'Where's Johnny?' she asked Ethel.

'He's sitting over there with his dad.'

Maureen looked around in amazement. Royston Ellis was the last person she'd expected to see today. Seeing Johnny laugh at something he said, Maureen nudged Ethel.

'He might be a shit father, but at least he's done the right thing by turning up today. Johnny looks much brighter than he did earlier, don't he?'

Ethel nodded and pointed to the bar. 'Look, Kevin's over there.'

Maureen stood up. She'd meant to talk to him earlier, but she couldn't find him at the crem.

'Hello, love, how are you?'

Kevin smiled. 'I'm fine thanks, Maur. I'm so sorry to hear about Susan. How you been managing?'

Maureen's eyes filled up with tears. Seeing Kevin brought back so many memories. She'd despised him initially when they'd first got together, but once he'd matured, he'd provided her daughter with some of the happiest times of her life.

'I miss her dreadfully, Kev. She'd really started to get herself sorted and then that arsehole Dave Taylor got his claws into her again. He's to blame. I'll kill him if I ever get my hands on him.'

Kevin didn't agree, but said nothing. He knew Susan better than anyone. She was a fool to herself and the only person to blame for her downfall was her.

Wiping her eyes with a tissue, Maureen smiled at him. 'So, what you up to now? You're looking well. Your mum said that you're happily married with a couple of chavvies.'

Kevin nodded. 'I married a girl called Jane. We've got two boys, Harry and Sid. Life's pretty good at the moment, I suppose.'

Seeing Wendy plonk herself down next to Ethel, Maureen hugged him and said her goodbyes.

'I'd better get back to Mum – you know how much she loves bleedin' Wendy. I'm glad that everything worked out for yer, Kev, and thanks ever so much for coming. It means the world to me and I know if our Susan's looking down, it'll mean the world to her as well.'

Wendy sat down next to Ethel and tried her best to be polite. She could see Kenny watching her from the bar and she didn't want to upset him. Over the years the worm had turned in their house. Once she'd become too old to have children, she had kind of accepted her fate. The problem was, by then, she realised Kenny hated her with a passion. For years he'd treated her with kid gloves, surrendering to her every whim, while she treated him like shit. Now he avoided her like the plague.

There wasn't a day went by when she didn't worry about him leaving her. His change of attitude made her realise just how much she loved and needed him. She would curl up and die if he left her; without him, life would seem worthless. To help her cope with her paranoia and panic attacks, she drank lots of alcohol. At first it was just a couple of glasses of wine a night to help her sleep, but over the last few years it had escalated to a couple of bottles. Alcohol made her feel good, it eased her worries and temporarily took away her problems.

Looking at Ethel, she forced a smile. 'Would you like me to get you some food from the buffet?'

Pinching Maureen, Ethel smiled back at her. 'No thanks. I need a shit, I can feel it poking out.'

Horrified, Wendy ran from the table. As much as she tried, she could never like Kenny's family. Ethel in particular revolted her – the woman was as vulgar as they come.

Ethel roared at the quickness of her departure. Her cackle was infectious and Maureen couldn't help joining in with her.

'Oh, you are terrible, Mum. You shouldn't wind her up, she was trying to be nice.'

Ethel pulled a face. 'Fuck her, shame she never tried to be nice years ago, the stuck-up whore.'

James, Maria, Freddie and Sarah sat quietly at a table. None of them felt particularly comfortable with Tommy just a few feet away. Aware that he was loud, drunk and giving them the eyeball, James and Freddie both averted their eyes. Seeing Tommy take yet another trip to the toilet with Benno and Tibbsy, Freddie nodded to James to follow him up to the bar. Out of earshot from the girls, he turned to his pal.

'I dunno about you, James, but I don't like the look of this. He's gonna start, I can see it in his eyes. I know you can't leave early and I don't mind staying with yer, but how about we send the girls home? If it's gonna kick off, I don't want Sarah involved and I'm sure you feel the same about Maria.'

James shrugged. 'I know what you're saying, but I'm not sure if Maria will wanna go. Her mum's having the kids for the night and I think she'll wanna stay with me. I can ask her, but you know how headstrong she is. If she wants to stay, she'll just tell me where to go.'

Freddie wrestled with his conscience. He was worried that Tommy would blurt out he'd fucked Maria – that

345

would really put the cat among the pigeons. For years he had tortured himself over his knowledge of that evening, and if he could have told James without breaking his heart, he would have come clean. But, how can you tell your best mate that the woman he married was shagged senseless by his brother? It was impossible.

Unlike James, Freddie wore the trousers in his household. As much as he loved, respected and listened to Sarah, it was a case of what he said went. Pulling Sarah to one side, he insisted it was time for her to go. He could tell that she wasn't too happy about it.

'I'll explain later,' he said, as he saw her safely into a cab.

As James had predicted, Maria was going nowhere. With two young daughters to look after, she rarely got out, and wasn't going to change her plans because of Tommy fucking Hutton.

'I'm staying here with you, James. It's been ages since I've had a good drink and, seeing as it's your sister's funeral, I feel that I need one.'

No longer was she intimidated or scared of what Tommy might say. He was a pathetic piece of shit and she certainly wasn't going to be bullied by him.

As Freddie returned to the table, she smiled at James. 'I'm gonna leave yous boys to talk business. I'm gonna go and sit with your mum and nan.'

Little did James know, as he squeezed her hand and watched her walk away, that he wasn't the only one watching her. Seeing that firm little arse move across the pub brought back pleasant memories to Tommy.

Turning to Benno and Tibbsy, he decided to give it the large. He hadn't spoken to them for years and they were so grateful to be in his good books today, they were hanging on to his every word.

346

'You see her, Miss Prim and Proper, that married my bruvver?'

Benno and Tibbsy nodded.

Tommy smirked. 'I shagged her till she screamed. She was a virgin, had the tightest pussy you could wish for.'

Benno grabbed him round the neck, while Tibbsy punched him playfully.

'What, you shagged Maria? Really, Tommo? Tell us more.'

Benno and Tibbsy listened in awe as Tommy told them the story. 'Honestly, she had the tightest fanny I've ever poked,' Tommy said, as he headed to the khazi. It was time for another line.

Although his mum's funeral had most definitely been the saddest day of Johnny's life, sitting with his dad and cousin, Alfie, all day had eased the pain somewhat. His dad had been really interested in his football, and the conversation was now flowing nicely.

'Shall I get us all another drink?' he asked chirpily.

Royston shook his head. 'I've got to go in a minute, son. I came by train and I've gotta get back to Kent, remember?'

Johnny felt sad. He never got to spend any quality time with his dad and even though the circumstances were awful, he'd thoroughly enjoyed his company.

'When am I gonna see you again, Dad? Why don't you come and watch me cup game? Or I can always come and visit you in Kent?'

Royston looked sheepish. His wife hated him spending time with Johnny. 'You've got two children here that need your attention and love. The past is the past, Royston, forget the white woman's son and concentrate on your daughters,' she always said.

Royston felt awkward as he stood up. His wife had bigger bollocks than him and he couldn't promise the boy anything. 'I'll give you a call in the next couple of days, Johnny. Take care, son.'

Without a backward glance, he walked away.

Clocking Kenny looking at her, Maureen smiled at him. As he glanced at Wendy and raised his eyebrows, she did the same. Wendy had been knocking back the wine like there was no tomorrow. Ethel was having a whale of a time at her daughter-in-law's expense. Rarely had she seen the stuck-up bitch make a tit out of herself and she was loving every minute of it.

'Tell the barmaid to turn the music up,' Ethel shouted.

As Wendy stood up to do 'The Loco-Motion', Ethel egged her on. 'Go on girl, give it some welly.'

Too drunk to realise that her husband's family were taking the piss out of her, Wendy went for it. Grabbing the nearest bloke, she rubbed herself up and down his leg.

Ethel nudged Maureen. 'Well, who would Adam and Eve it? Look, she's hawking her fuckin' mutton now, the dirty whore.'

Wendy was in her own little world. 'Way-hey,' she screamed, as she lifted her skirt and flashed her black knickers.

Ethel roared. This was more like it.

Tommy stood at the bar staring at the family table. As Maria laughed, her pretty face shone out like a beacon. He hated to admit it, but she was as fit as a butcher's dog. What she was doing with his wimp of a brother he could not imagine. Noticing that James and Freddie were deep in conversation over the other side of the pub, he sauntered towards her.

'Enjoying yourself, are yer?'

As he sat opposite her, Maria looked at him coldly. 'How can I be enjoying myself? I've just been to your sister's funeral.'

Maureen clocked the hatred in Maria's eyes. The atmosphere between her daughter-in-law and eldest son you could cut with a knife. She stood up and excused herself to go to the toilet. She'd always known that there was history between Tommy and Maria, but tonight it stood out like a sore thumb. Poor James, she thought as she washed her hands, at least what he didn't know couldn't hurt him.

Looking into the mirror, she studied herself. She looked old, fucking old; Susan's untimely death seemed to have aged her ten years. The gap between a death and a funeral was the longest gap ever and the relief when it was finally over was indescribable. That's why everyone got so fucking drunk, it was such a release. Tomorrow, reality would hit home and the sadness would return, but tonight Maureen was determined to enjoy herself. Susan deserved a good send-off and Maureen wasn't going to spoil it by being miserable.

As she walked out of the toilet, Chubby Checker's, 'Let's Twist Again' was blaring from the speakers. Seeing Ethel waving her arms in the wheelchair and Wendy leaping up and down next to her, Maureen decided to join in. As the old saying goes, 'If you can't beat 'em, join 'em'.

Wendy falling flat on her face spelled the end of her evening. Pissed as a fart, she was unable to get back up. Kenny was livid as he dragged her out of the pub and into a cab. All night she'd made a complete show of him and when she sobered up tomorrow, he'd have her guts for garters.

As Maria walked to the toilet, Tommy checked that no one was watching him follow her. Coked up to the eyeballs, he felt brave now, really brave.

James was drunk and extremely annoyed. Tommy had been sitting at the same table as Maria for ages now and he felt like the biggest mug ever. His mum, nan, Sandra, Brenda, they'd all been fucking laughing, and he just hoped they weren't laughing at him.

Freddie had left the wake half an hour ago. 'Sarah's got a mask on, I'd better sort it out,' was his excuse.

James decided to move tables so he had his back to Maria, and he was now sat with a drunken Johnny and his mate Gazza.

'I know my mum weren't the best in the world, but I loved her, James, really loved her.'

James nodded. He loved his nephew very much, but tonight Johnny kept repeating himself and it was doing his head in. Normally, he'd try to comfort him, but at this precise moment, he had far too many problems of his own.

Maria was putting on her lipstick when Tommy barged into the ladies and stood against the door.

'Sprucing yourself up for me, are yer?' he asked nastily.

Startled, Maria turned to look at him. How the fuck did he have the nerve to follow her in here, in front of a packed pub? 'What do you want, Tommy? Just fuck off and leave me alone.'

Tommy smiled. It wasn't a pleasant smile, more of a sarcastic smirk. 'I'll tell you what I want, shall I? I wanna know why you blew me out and then married my loser of a bruvver. I wanna know why my big, hard cock wasn't enough for you, Maria. I've wanted you since the moment I set eyes on you, and me and you together, we could have made it big. Why did you do it, Maria? Why?'

As he gabbled on, talking crap, Maria was shocked. She'd always known he was a self-obsessed arsehole, but she'd never realised he was an absolute nut-job. Not

350

knowing what to do for the best, she allowed the alcohol to answer for her.

'Shut the fuck up, Tommy, and listen to me. See you, you're nothing to me. You never was and you never will be. Watch my lips. I love your brother, he is everything you are not. Why can't you just get a life and leave us alone?'

Realising the declaration of his feelings had got him precisely nowhere, Tommy tried another tactic. Grabbing her beautiful, long dark hair, he yanked it towards him.

'What about the sex, Maria? What about that night we had together? You can't have forgotten that, I was your first, remember?'

Ignoring the pain he was inflicting upon her, Maria grabbed his shoulder and tried to look him in the eye. 'The sex was terrible, Tommy, and you were fucking shit in bed. Do you know how many times I've regretted that terrible night I spent with you? Well, do you?'

As the toilet door opened, Tommy let go of her hair and ran out. Unable to hide his fury, he pushed past his mum and barged his way out of the pub. High as a kite, he sprinted for what seemed like miles. As he reached a bus stop, he put his hand on his knees to catch his breath. Noticing a poster of Girls Aloud, his fury returned. Maria was a ringer for that Cheryl Cole. Unable to control himself, he lunged at the advertising board.

'Bitch, whore, slut, slag!' he screamed, as he punched and kicked it. Losing all sense of reality, he ignored the other four girls and focused solely on Cheryl Cole's face.

'See you, Maria. Who do you think you are? Talking to me like a piece of shit. You're not fit to lick my shoes, you cunt. You think you're so good with your perfect life and your perfect fuckin' family. But I'll have the final say, Maria, you just wait and see. The last laugh will be mine, I promise.'

THIRTY-EIGHT

Over the next seven days, Tommy's madness reached new heights. As a rule, getting out of his face on drugs blotted out all of the bad stuff, but the sight of James, Maria, Freddie and Sarah playing happy families was eating away at him, like maggots. Apart from Alfie, he had nothing. No bird, no money coming in, no close family, Jack fucking shit. While everybody else's lives were so wonderfully fucking happy, all he had to thank God for was his best mate being locked up and a poxy cocaine addiction.

With his mood and behaviour at an all-time low, he demanded Alfie go back to his mum's for the time being.

'Please, Dad, I don't wanna live with Mum. Please let me stay with you.'

Tommy refused and made him pack his stuff and leave immediately. He knew he was losing his sanity and he didn't want his son to witness it. He hadn't washed, shaved, or changed his clothes for days – all he'd done was drink, smoke and snort.

With Alfie out of the way, he ordered up some crack. He rarely smoked the pipe in front of his boy any more. Snorting coke he could get away with, but inhaling rocks was heavy shit. With his first lug, he shut his eyes and smiled. He felt better now and was ready to make plans.

Maria was a trappy cow and he was determined to shut that pretty mouth of hers once and for all.

James sat in the Harvester with Maria and the girls. They often ate at the same restaurant, as it was Tara's and Lily's favourite.

'Can I have some more salad, Daddy?' asked Lily, thrusting her bowl his way.

Maria and James both burst out laughing. She was only six years old and went through more lettuce than a fucking rabbit. James took her hand and led her back to the salad bar. Lily was a proper Daddy's girl, whereas Tara was all for Maria. The girls' personalities were chalk and cheese. Tara was very feminine and loved anything girly, while Lily was the complete opposite. Unlike her sister, she took no interest in dancing, fashion and pretty dolls, and was more into climbing trees and playing football with the boys.

'Is that enough for yer?' James said, showing her the bowl.

Studying the contents, she put her hands on her hips. 'You haven't put the pink sauce on, Daddy.'

James laughed at the annoyance in her voice. His mum had got her spot-on: 'I'm telling yer now, James, she's six going on sixteen. You'll have your hands full with her; she's a cowson, you mark my words,' she told him.

Maria smiled as father and daughter returned to the table. She loved eating out with James and the girls, and her family life was everything that she'd dreamed it would be. James was a great provider, a wonderful dad and she was so bloody happy with him. They'd recently decided to try for another baby; it had been his idea and, even though he hadn't admitted it, she knew that he was desperate for a boy.

'I need to go for a pee,' Lily announced.

Telling Tara to take her sister to the toilet, Maria turned to James.

'What time you off tonight?'

James sighed. 'About ten.'

Maria said nothing, but he knew what she was thinking. He hated leaving his family for days at a time, just as much as Maria hated the situation. They'd spoken about his choice of career a lot lately. The money had been fantastic over the years, but they'd both agreed it was probably time for a change.

'You're not gonna get away with it forever, James. One of these days your luck's gonna run out and I'll be visiting you in prison,' Maria said.

He'd taken her words on board and had spoken to Freddie about his dilemma. Surprisingly, Freddie felt exactly the same way. 'Sarah's been on my case for ages – I'm so glad you said something, I wanted to tell you I'd been having doubts, but I didn't know how to broach the subject.'

It had been decided that they would have a proper chat about their future on their next trip. Both had money behind them and if they pooled it together, they'd hopefully have enough to set up a decent, legitimate business. With contacts in the building trade, they'd had a vague chat about becoming property developers. Nothing was set in stone yet, but they had some good ideas of how to get things started.

'I think we should get Christmas out of the way and tell Bobby our decision in the New Year,' James told Freddie.

Freddie hadn't said much about the subject since, and James knew the reason why. Telling his uncle wasn't going to be easy; Bobby Adams was not gonna be a happy bunny.

*   *   *

354

Over in Stepney, Maureen had problems of her own. 'Johnny,' she shouted as she knocked on her grandson's bedroom door. 'Dinner's ready, love. I've cooked you your favourite, spag bol.'

Johnny lifted the quilt from over his head. 'Thanks, Nan, I'll have it later.'

Not knowing what to say to entice him out of the room, Maureen walked away. She knew that he wouldn't eat it later – he'd throw it in the bin, like all the rest of the dinners he kept pretending to eat. Not hungry herself, Maureen dished a plate up for Ethel.

'I've done you some dinner, Mum.'

Ethel looked at the tray in horror. 'I ain't eating that shit, it looks like a plate of fuckin' worms.'

Maureen put it on the sofa beside her. The old cow would eat it in a minute, she'd put her house on it.

Face etched with worry, Maureen sat opposite her. It was a week now since Susan's funeral and Johnny had barely eaten or come out of his bedroom. The job that he usually adored had gone by the wayside as well. It was as though he'd put his whole life on hold.

Seeing Ethel tuck into her plate of worms, Maureen smiled for the first time in days. Ethel might be a cantankerous old fucker, but she had a way of cheering Maureen up. As Ethel wolfed the lot, Maureen took the empty plate away from her.

'Nice was it? I thought you didn't like spaghetti bolognaise?'

Ethel eyed her with sarcasm. 'It was fucking rotten,' she insisted.

Maureen got a cloth and wiped what she'd dropped off her cardigan. 'With a mouth as big as yours, I'm surprised you can miss it,' she said sarcastically.

Ethel playfully walloped her. She loved her Maureen

more than anyone in the world, and without her she'd be shunted off to God's waiting room. She hated them fucking homes. Poor old souls, all sitting there in their own shit and piss, waiting to die.

Maureen poured her a Guinness and sat down next to her. 'What we gonna do about Johnny, Mum? His boss keeps ringing up and he's gonna have to go back to work next week. He still won't come out of his room, I don't know what else to do to help him.'

Ethel knew exactly what to do. 'Ring his fucking father; it's about time he stood up to his responsibilities. 'Ere, give us that phone, I'll ring the no-good bastard for yer.'

Maureen refused to give Ethel the phone, but thought about her idea. Johnny needed guidance and Royston should bloody well take responsibility for once.

She smiled at Ethel. 'Do you know what? I think you might be right, Mum. I'll ring him tomorrow morning – hopefully he'll be at work then. I don't wanna ring him while he's at home with his family; she's a funny one that Jamaican bird he married.'

Sipping her drink, Ethel had a smug expression plastered across her wise old face. She might no longer be a spring chicken, but she was always fucking right.

Tommy didn't bother going to bed that night, he was far too excited to be able to sleep. He looked at the clock: 5 a.m., which meant he still had three hours to kill. Opening up the piece of foil, he chipped off another piece of rock and set it up on top of the bottle. Setting it alight, he inhaled deeply through the straw. As he felt the cocaine flow through his body, he lay on the carpet and pictured Maria's face.

Last night he'd done a bit of spying and he knew that

James had gone away. He'd borrowed his mate's work van and had hidden in the back of it. The windows were blacked out to stave off thieves nicking any tools that may be inside. In other words, you could see out, but couldn't see in.

Tommy was on cloud nine as he watched his brother load the sleeping bag and all the camping equipment. It was obvious that he was going on a run and, from past experience, Tommy was sure that James would be away for a couple of days at least.

Smiling like the Cheshire Cat, he'd clambered into the front seat and calmly driven away. Once back home, he'd got his thinking cap on. He wasn't exactly sure what he was going to do to Maria, but obviously he'd have to wait until she'd taken the kids to school and was indoors alone. He wasn't planning on physically hurting her. He just wanted to frighten the living daylights out of the foul-mouthed whore, or watch her beg in terror for a couple of hours – that would be good enough revenge. At least then she wouldn't be so fucking cocky in the future. As long as he didn't lose his temper and mark her, she would have to keep his visit quiet.

There was no way she'd say anything to James. How could she? She'd be far too worried about her sordid past coming back to haunt her.

Pouring himself another large scotch, Tommy smiled to himself. He couldn't wait to see the look of horror on that pretty little face of hers. Fucking bitch. What goes around comes around.

'Look at the bloody state of you, Lily. What have you been doing?'

Lily said nothing. She'd been playing outside in the garden, but daren't admit it, as she was banned from going out there of a morning. Unfortunately, she had fallen into a puddle of mud, hence her mother's anger.

'Go upstairs and quickly get changed. Hurry up, else you'll be late for school.'

Exasperated by her tomboy of a daughter, Maria turned to Tara and smiled. 'Do you want me to plait your hair while we're waiting for madam?'

'Yes please, Mummy.'

Maria was deep in thought as she brushed her daughter's hair. She loved the girls equally, but wished Lily would be more feminine, like Tara. It would save her an awful lot of washing and ironing, as she was such a dirty little mare.

'I'm ready, Mum.'

Looking at Lily, both Maria and Tara burst out laughing. She'd changed her school uniform, but still looked like a bundle of shit tied up ugly. With one sock up and one down, one bunchie in and one out, she looked like Orphan Annie.

Maria straightened her out and cuddled her. 'What am I gonna do with you, eh?'

Lily shook her head. 'I don't really know, Mummy.'

Maria saw the girls into the back of the four-wheel drive and checked that their belts were on. Hearing them giggle and chat was her favourite part of the journey. For complete opposites, they got on extremely well together and rarely ever argued. Glancing into her mirror, she smiled as she hit the accelerator.

Tommy watched with interest from the back of the van. Sneering to himself, he pulled faces as they drove past. They couldn't see him, obviously, with the blackened windows, but secretly mocking them made him giggle.

Crouching down behind the two front seats, he opened his goody bag. He'd come well prepared: he had scotch, lager, puff and cocaine. He hadn't brought the pipe, just the powder. Preparing a couple of lines, he did them and took a swig from the whisky bottle. She'd be back soon, the slag, and then the party could really start.

Maria had her own little routine of a morning and, after dropping the girls off, would regularly head off to her local gym to participate in a class or two. Today she'd done body combat and, having sweated like a pig for the past hour, she couldn't wait to get home and have a nice soak in the bath.

Usually, she had a coffee and a chinwag at the gym, but today she was in a rush, as she'd invited her newfound friends over for lunch.

Last week she'd had lunch at Lavinia's beautiful home. Now it was time to return the offer and she was determined to get it right. She'd always hated cooking and wasn't very good at it but, determined to impress, she'd bought a recipe book. She didn't want to attempt anything too difficult, and with James's input and advice, she'd decided on garlic mussels for starters, salade Niçoise for main and fresh fruit salad for dessert. Desperate to get things spot-on, she'd spent ages choosing the wine.

'How fucking much?' James joked as he footed the bill.

She laughed. These women served up the finest of everything in their houses and she was determined to follow in their footsteps. She may not have been brought up in or around class, but it was never too late to learn. As her mother always said, 'When in Rome, do as the Romans do.'

Pulling up on her drive, Maria grabbed her bag and ran up the path. Her guests were due to arrive in less than two hours and she needed to get her arse in gear.

As Tommy watched her go into the house, he noticed

that he was sweating with nerves. He knew what the problem was: too much coke always made him feel paranoid and, as usual, he'd overdone it.

Rolling a joint, he lit it and knocked back the scotch. He needed to bring himself down before he did anything. Two joints and half a litre later, he felt the coke wear off and the paranoia leave his body. Checking that nobody was about, he crept out of the van.

He walked up the path and rang the doorbell. There was no answer, so he rang it again.

'Who is it?' he heard the bitch shout.

Smiling, he said nothing.

'Is that you, girls?' he heard her say.

'Yes,' he said imitating a girlie voice.

'Hang on a sec, I'm just getting out of the bath.'

Tommy couldn't believe his luck. He'd sounded like the big bad wolf in 'Little Red Riding Hood', and the silly tart was probably half naked as well.

As her footsteps moved nearer, his heart began to beat faster. When she opened the door, he smiled at the look of horror on her face.

Barging his way in, he kicked the door shut and put his hand over her mouth to stop her screaming.

'Surprise, surprise, you fuckin' slag.'

THIRTY-NINE

Tommy had prepared himself for Maria being shocked; what he hadn't prepared himself for was her physical strength.

'Ouch,' he yelled, as she bit his hand.

Her screams were loud, very loud. For a petite bird, she could really give it some welly.

As the blood ran down his wrist, he kneeled on her chest and squeezed her cheeks together with his hand. His blood dripped onto her face.

'See what you've done, you fuckin' bitch.'

Unable to speak or breathe properly because of the way he was holding her, Maria struggled to make herself heard. Realising that she was trying to tell him that he was hurting her, he moved closer to her face.

'If you scream, we'll be back to square one,' he said, as he released his grip on her cheeks and took his knee off her chest. Straddling both legs across her, he sat on her hips to stop her from moving.

Maria didn't know what to do. The house was big and detached and even if she did scream, chances were no bastard would hear her. She was furious with herself for opening the door. If only she had unlocked the bedroom window, she would have seen the identity of her caller.

Rarely did anybody ever call at the house in the day, but because the girls were coming for lunch, she'd stupidly surmised that they'd arrived early.

Feeling Tommy's eyes gawping at her barely concealed breasts, Maria shivered. She only had her bathrobe on and the fact that it could be so easily undone made her feel naked and vulnerable. In all the years Maria had known Tommy, she'd never been physically afraid of him before. She'd been scared that he might open his big mouth and ruin her happy marriage, but that had been about it.

As she looked into his glassy eyes, she realised that she'd seriously underestimated him. He was a definite fucking loony tune, with danger stamped all over him.

Her voice shook with fear. 'What do you want, Tommy? James will be back soon and he'll go mad if he finds you here.'

Tommy knew that she was talking bollocks and he started to laugh. 'You must think I'm stupid, Maria, Jimmy boy's away and you're all alone. Don't you think I've done my homework, you silly fuckin' bitch?'

Unable to look at the psychopath's face, Maria averted her eyes.

Tommy stood up and ordered her to stand. 'I'm thirsty. You got any scotch?'

Maria nodded. Her arms and legs were shaking so much that she could barely move.

Clocking her fright, Tommy pushed her against the wall and tilted her chin. Kissing her gently on the lips, he smirked at her. 'Not so trappy now, are you, sweetheart?' he said, as he pulled away.

Repulsed, Maria began to cry. His breath was unwashed, tasted stale, and made her want to vomit. She retched and spluttered as she swallowed.

Tommy poured himself a large scotch and ordered her to sit on the sofa. Sitting opposite, he watched her intently.

'You got any knickers on?'

Unable to find her voice, Maria shook her head. As she saw the big smile spread across his twisted face, she began to lose control. Her worst fears were confirmed as he walked towards her, grinning. 'Undo that dressing gown and show me them pert little tits,' he ordered.

More scared than ever before in her life, Maria let out one almighty scream.

Unaware of his wife's ordeal, James was thoroughly enjoying his ham, egg and chips.

Ruby's Café was a favourite of his and Freddie's and, whenever on the south coast, they always popped in for a snack or two.

James nodded at his pal. 'Pass us the tomato sauce, mate.'

Freddie handed it to him and smiled. Sitting waiting for their load to be dropped off the previous night, they'd had a good old heart to heart about their future.

James had already been to view the run-down property they were considering putting a bid in for. The house in Shenfield was owned by an old lady with no family. She'd recently gone into a care home and was wanting to sell the property cheaply and quickly to a buyer with no chain, who wasn't going to mess her about. The house was going for peanuts, taking into account the size of it and the area it was in. It needed a hell of a lot of work done, but it was perfect for James and Freddie to start their new venture with.

'It might take us six months to a year to put it right, but we should make at least a hundred and fifty grand on it,' James insisted.

After a long discussion of what exactly needed doing and who they were going to get in to help them, Freddie agreed that it was just what they were looking for. The building work they could do themselves, and all they had to really pay out for was an electrician and a plumber.

Full of beans about their new set-up, Freddie couldn't stop talking about it. He'd been sick of looking over his shoulder for ages now and he couldn't wait to go legal. Wiping the last of the yolk off his plate with his crusty bread, he leaned towards James.

'Do you know what? I don't think we should wait till after Christmas. If we put a bid in when we get home tomorrow and the old bird accepts it, what do we wanna keep doing this for?'

James nodded. They didn't want to chance their arses if they didn't need to any more.

'I know where you're coming from, Fred, but we're gonna have to give Bobby some notice.'

Freddie laughed. 'What fucking notice? We ain't working for NatWest bank. We're doing this for ourselves and our family and the quicker we go straight, the better.'

James smiled. 'Look, you know what I mean. He's gotta find someone else to take over from us, we can't leave him in the shit.'

Freddie bit his lip nervously. 'Will you do us a favour, James? I'm dreading telling him and I can't talk to him properly on the phone. If this comes off with the old girl's property, will you fly out there with me and we'll tell him together?'

James thought over the request for a minute or so and nodded. Bobby Adams had been bloody good to them over the years. A top bloke, he was as honest as they come and an absolute joy to work with. The least he deserved was a face-to-face explanation from the pair of them.

Freddie was relieved. 'I'm going outside to ring Sarah and tell her our news,' he said happily.

James looked at his watch. Maria should be back from the gym by now and he couldn't wait to tell her their decision. She'd be well pleased; it would be such a weight off of her mind. He rang the landline and got no answer. About to try her mobile, he suddenly remembered that she was having the girls over for lunch. Not wanting to spoil her street cred, he decided to ring her later. She'd be far too busy impressing her new pals to be able to talk to him.

Back in Ingatestone, Maria certainly was not enjoying herself. Tommy was still tormenting her and even though she'd punched him and slung a vase at his head, he'd proved far too strong for her. Completely drained by her ordeal, she'd now lost all of her fight and was doing as he asked.

'Open them again wider this time. I want you to finger yourself and look at me while you're doing it,' he demanded.

Unable to stop herself from sobbing, Maria spread her legs and looked at his vulgar face. She hated him with a passion and had never felt so degraded in the whole of her life.

'Just do it, you slag. Remember, whatever I ask yer to do, I've seen it all before,' he callously reminded her.

As she did as he asked, she heard his breathing quicken.

'Now, I want yer to take yer dressing gown off and show me that tight little pussy of yours. Lay on the floor and spread your legs as wide as you can,' he demanded.

'I can't do this any more. Please leave me alone, Tommy. Please, I beg you, I swear I won't tell James. If you leave now, I promise I won't tell anyone you were here.'

Tommy walked threateningly towards her. 'Shut up, you lying fuckin' slag. Just do as I say, or I'll rip them pretty little legs of yours open meself,' he yelled.

Petrified of him touching her, she once again did as he requested.

As she played with herself, Tommy couldn't take his eyes off her. He was that rock hard, he felt that his cock was about to burst. That pretty face, gorgeous hair, her nakedness, she made him throb more than any woman he'd ever known. He'd never forget that night they'd spent together, even if he lived to be a hundred.

Thoroughly enjoying himself, Tommy ordered her to kneel on the floor with her arse facing him. 'Now, lean against the sofa and spread the cheeks of your arse. I wanna look at you from the rear.'

As the doorbell rang, Maria screamed. 'Help! Help me! Ring the –'

Tommy leaped on top of her and shoved his hand over her mouth. He moved her to the side of the sofa so no one could see them through the window. Maria fought and struggled, but couldn't move him. The arrival of her lunch guests was the only chance she'd had of getting away from the bastard. As the doorbell rang three more times, she heard their voices calling her.

'Maria, it's us. Open the bloody door. We're parched and frozen stiff standing out here.'

Finding some inner strength, she wriggled like an eel as she tried to unclamp his hand from over her mouth.

'Stay there. I swear, Maria, if you say or do anything, I'll fuckin' kill yer.'

Maria's friends didn't know what to do. They thought they'd heard her shout, but they didn't know her well enough to intrude into her private life. Maybe she was arguing with her husband.

As Maria heard the footsteps fade away, she wailed like a wounded animal.

Dragging her up with him, Tommy peeked out of the curtain. The coast was clear. Turning to her, he smiled and gently moved her hair out of her pretty face. Her eyes were red raw and her vulnerability made him, all of a sudden, love instead of hate her.

'I'm sorry for what I made you do earlier, Maria. I'm sorry for the names I called you as well. I don't hate you, I love you, I always have. Leave James and we'll run off together. I'll treat you like a queen, I promise.'

Maria couldn't stop shaking. He was completely off his head.

Being an inch away from her was too much for Tommy to bear. He could smell the cleanness of her skin, feel her heart beating in rhythm with his. Dragging her back on to the floor, he ripped his own clothes off and smothered her in kisses.

'You know you want it,' he panted.

In spite of her wildly flailing arms and legs, Maria was unable to get him off her. As he forced himself inside her, she screamed with anger and pain.

'No, Tommy, no! Why are you doing this? Please, Tommy, don't do this to me, please, I beg you.'

Tommy hadn't planned to rape her, but couldn't stop himself. He had to feel himself inside her once again, as he had done many moons ago.

'Tell me I'm better than James. Tell me you love me!' he screamed, as he came like a steam train.

Maria lay perfectly still while he pulled himself out of her and stood up. He'd done the worst thing that he could possibly do to her and her life was ruined, she was sure of that.

Aware of the look of disgust on her face, Tommy calmly

finished his Scotch and got dressed. 'I'd best be going now,' he said politely.

She didn't answer, she couldn't.

He crouched down next to her. 'You'd better get dressed and pull yourself together. What time you gotta pick the kids up?'

Remembering her daughters, Maria turned her head and glanced at the clock. She didn't have to pick them up until three. The time was now half past one and her ordeal had lasted for over two hours.

Tommy tried to help her up.

'Leave me alone,' she said viciously.

He shrugged his shoulders. 'Look, let's not be enemies, eh? It's not as though we haven't done it before, is it?'

Maria huddled her knees to her chest and turned her back to him. Was he that fucked up in the brain that he didn't realise he'd just raped and tortured her for the past two hours?

'Just go, will you?' she said.

Tommy walked towards the door. Pausing, he leaned against it. 'Let's not make this awkward, Maria. You broke my heart and took my bruvver away from me, so let's call it quits now, shall we? I won't bovver you any more, I promise.'

Maria looked at him in amazement. She was waiting for him to laugh, but the nutter was actually serious. Feeling her inner strength return, she snarled at him, 'I hate you, Tommy Hutton, like I've never hated anyone before. And do you know what? I hope you rot in fucking hell.'

Tommy knew she wasn't joking. Determined to have the last word, he walked towards her and crouched down beside her.

'A word of warning, sweetheart. One word to Jimmy boy and I'll tell him everything. Not only will I tell him that I took your virginity, I'll also tell him that you've been gagging for a repeat performance for years and you begged me to come round here today. Understand what I'm saying, Maria?'

Maria gathered some spittle in her mouth and spat it straight in his face.

'Drop dead, you sicko.'

FORTY

As the front door slammed, Maria stood up and put on her dressing gown. A tear rolled down her cheek, and she fiercely wiped it away. The girls had to be picked up soon and she had no time to wallow in self-pity. She quickly tidied the room. Picking up the broken vase, she plugged in the Dyson and vacuumed the carpet.

Satisfied that every sign of his visit had been wiped away, she poured herself a large glass of wine. She couldn't stop shaking and her hands wouldn't do as they were told. She ran a bath and tested the temperature. The water was boiling, but she didn't care – the hotter it was, the cleaner she'd feel. She was desperate to get rid of the scent of him, her skin smelled of his sweat. She winced as she lowered herself in. Picking up James's rough sponge, she covered it with liquid soap and ferociously scrubbed herself. The pain was immense, but it was much better than smelling that bastard on her. She thought about James. She couldn't tell him or anyone else what had happened. She would keep it a secret and try and carry on as normal.

Hearing her phone ring, she jumped out of the bath. It was probably her friends wondering why she hadn't been at home.

'Hello.'

'All right, babe? How did the lunch go? Are the girls still there?'

The sound of her husband's wonderful voice was too much for Maria to deal with. Aware of the tears streaming down her face, she tried to put on the most normal voice she could muster. 'Can I call you back later, James? I'm really busy at the moment.'

'No probs, babe, ring us back when you've picked the girls up from school.'

James ended the call and smiled at Freddie. 'She sounded a bit weird. I bet she's got half-pissed with her mates and don't want me to know. She's turning into a right Essex girl, she is.'

Freddie chuckled. 'Who was coming round for lunch?'

James shook his head. 'Fuck knows. Some old birds she met down the gym, I think. I don't take a lot of notice, they're right up their own arses where we live. You know what women are like, though. Maria's desperate to impress. She's driven me mad all fuckin' week; I've had to help her decide on the menu, pick the wine and all sorts. I wouldn't mind: she's a terrible cook, she'll probably fucking poison 'em.'

Freddie laughed. 'Sarah's the same. With us being the breadwinners, these women have got too much time on their hands.'

James agreed. 'I'm gonna put me foot down, cut her allowance back so she has to curb it,' he joked.

Maria poured herself another drink and mentally checked her story. The girls needed an explanation and she had to quickly think of one. She didn't want to lose the only local friends she had. Picking up the phone, she rang Lavinia.

'Lavinia, I am so, so sorry. I had one drama after

another this morning and I had to rush out to deal with a family crisis. Not thinking straight, I forgot my phone, which is why I couldn't call you to cancel.'

Lavinia didn't believe a word. She'd heard Maria's voice and she'd heard noises coming from inside the house. Furious at being lied to, she decided to make things as awkward as possible for her so-called friend.

'Maria, your car was on the drive and I heard somebody inside the house.'

Maria bit her lip. Fuck, she thought. What was she meant to say now? She hadn't prepared herself for this bit. Thinking of the first thing that came into her mind, she blurted out any load of old rubbish.

'My cousin was indoors. She's a complete lunatic, an alcoholic. Her son's teacher had been on the phone, he'd broken his leg at school and been rushed to hospital. My cousin was too out of it to sit with him, so I took her car and went there for her. I rang her from the hospital payphone to get her to call you, but she was that drunk, she couldn't find my mobile. I'm really sorry, Lavinia. Could you explain what happened to the other girls for me? Families, eh? Who'd have 'em?'

Lavinia said her goodbyes and ended the call. Within seconds, she rang her friend, Polly. 'The lying fucking bitch,' she said vehemently.

Maria chucked on a tracksuit and blow-dried her hair. She had no choice other than to put today out of her mind and act as though nothing had happened. Maybe God was paying her back for not being truthful to James. She'd hidden the truth for years and had always expected to receive her comeuppance one day. She checked her appearance in the mirror. Satisfied that she looked fairly normal, she grabbed her handbag. It was time to pick the girls up from school.

* * *

In the heart of the East End, Maureen was also having a stressful day. She'd caught young Johnny drinking and smoking what looked like wacky baccy in his bedroom that morning. Furious, she'd read him the riot act.

'I'm not having you living under my roof if you're gonna go down the same slippery slope as your mother. You've got a great future in front of you, Johnny, and I know you're upset about your mum, but acting like her ain't gonna bring her back. For fuck's sake, pull yourself together.'

Not used to his nan shouting at him, Johnny felt sorry for himself. 'It's no wonder I'm going off the rails, is it? Look at my parents. A dead, junkie mum and a dad who promises to ring me, then doesn't. All I've got is you, and you ain't gonna live forever, are you?'

Maureen hugged him and tried to cheer him up by turning his question into a joke. 'Thanks a bleedin' lot. What am I? On me way out, or something?'

Johnny calmed down. 'Sorry, Nan.'

'I know it's hard, love, but you must try to get back to normal. Promise me you'll go back to work next week. And what about your football? You ain't even been training. You're the star player; just think how the team must be missing you.'

Johnny nodded. 'I know you're right. I'll ring me boss and tell him I'll be back on Monday and I promise I'll go football training tomorrow night as well.'

Maureen smiled. 'That's my boy. Now, you can't stay cooped up in this room forever, so why don't you go out and get some fresh air or pop round and see one of your mates. He was a lovely boy that Gazza who came to the funeral. Ring him and go out for a pint with him.'

Johnny nodded. 'I'll ring him now.'

Maureen stroked his cropped hair. 'You best have a

bath before you go anywhere – you're chucking up a bit, and so are those bedclothes.'

Johnny sniffed under his arms. 'You're right, I am chucking up. Thanks, Nan, for everything.'

Relieved that she'd finally gotten through to him, Maureen went downstairs to make some lunch.

Ethel was upset over Johnny. 'Poor little fucker! As soon as he goes out, you wanna ring that no-good old man of his and give him a right fucking earful.'

As Johnny walked down the stairs, Maureen warned her to keep her big mouth shut.

'Oh, look, look at him, don't he look mint?' Ethel crowed.

'You look all handsome again now,' Maureen told him. 'I'll make you a nice clean bed up while you're out.'

Embarrassed by all the attention, Johnny couldn't wait to get out of the door.

'I'm going round Gazza's. I won't be late.'

Within a minute of him leaving, Maureen was on the phone to his father. 'That boy needs you, Royston, and I don't care how busy you are, you get your arse down here at the weekend to see him.'

Royston sighed. 'It's not that I don't wanna see him. I've told you before that things are awkward with Candy. She's already made plans for us and she'll make my life hell if I disappear at the weekend.'

Sitting next to Maureen on the sofa, Ethel was able to hear his reply. ''Ere, give us that fuckin' phone,' she said, as she snatched it out of her daughter-in-law's hand.

'Royston, it's Ethel. Now, you listen to me. If you don't get your arse down 'ere this weekend, Tommy or James will come to your house and fuckin' drag you down feet first. Do you understand what I'm sayin', boy?'

Royston understood all right. 'I'll be down on Sunday morning. Tell Johnny I'll pick him up at eleven.'

Ethel winked at Maureen. 'And don't just think this is a one-off Royston – you'll be seeing him regularly from now on, if yer know what I mean.'

Royston took a deep, nervous breath. 'Yes, Mrs Hutton.'

As Ethel ended the call, she roared with laughter. 'That told the bastard, didn't it?'

Maureen shook her head. 'He's our Johnny's dad – yer shouldn't have threatened him, Mum.'

'Fuck him,' Ethel cackled.

Over in Leytonstone, a paranoid Tommy was sitting alone in a pub that he rarely used. After attacking Maria, he'd bought some more gear and gone home to celebrate the occasion. Problem was, when he got there, he couldn't relax. Deep down, he was 99 per cent positive that Maria wouldn't tell James, but there was always that 1 per cent chance that she would. Suddenly, he felt worried by what he had done. Hatching a plan, he rang his mate, Colin.

'All right, Col? I need to get away for a while. Is anyone using your caravan?'

'No, mate, it's empty. I'm indoors, come and pick the keys up, if you like.'

Tommy breathed a sigh of relief. A trip to Clacton would sort his head out. If the shit hit the fan, he'd rather find out by phone than by someone hammering at his door.

Finishing his drink, he stood up. For the first time ever, he realised that he was a bit wary of his little brother. Annoyed for thinking that way, he quickly got a grip on himself.

As he walked down the road, he spoke to himself out loud. 'Forget Jimmy boy, he's nothing. You're the main man, Tommy, always have been and always will be.'

*　*　*

As Tara and Lily ran towards her, Maria hugged them tighter than ever before. Lily quickly pulled away. She wasn't the cuddling type, not unless they were cuddles from her dad.

'Get off, Mummy, all my friends are watching,' she complained.

Maria got the girls into the car, belted them up and did her best to sound chirpy. So far, so good, she thought, as they chatted happily about their day.

'How was your lunch with your friends, Mummy?' Tara inquired.

Maria felt a shiver go down her spine. 'Mummy had to cancel the lunch. I wasn't well, but I couldn't tell my friends why. I was so embarrassed, I couldn't get off the toilet, so I pretended to them that I had to go out somewhere.'

Tara and Lily couldn't stop laughing. 'Mummy had the poo-poos,' Lily sang.

Maria forced herself to join in with their laughter. She felt like bursting into tears, but that wasn't an option.

Back at their lock-up, James and Freddie counted their money, shook hands and said their goodbyes.

'I'll ring the old dear tomorrow and let yer know when yer can look at the house,' James yelled as he drove away.

Clocking the time, James turned down the stereo. Maria must have been pissed earlier, as she hadn't rung him back yet. He pressed speed dial for his home number and smiled when she picked up.

'Oi, I've got a bone to pick with you. I ain't having you lunching with these posh old birds if you're gonna forget all about your husband,' he joked.

The love and kindness in his voice was too much for Maria. Unable to stop herself, she let out a sob.

'I'm only joking, Maria. Whatever's the matter?' James asked, his voice full of concern.

Aware of her legs shaking, Maria slumped down on to the armchair. 'Oh, take no notice of me. I haven't been well, that's all and I had to cancel lunch.'

Worried, James pulled up in a lay-by. 'Whaddya mean? Not well? What's wrong, darling?'

Grabbing a tissue, Maria blew her nose. 'I think I've had food poisoning or a tummy bug. It was awful, James, I couldn't get off the toilet. I felt sick and was far too ill to entertain, so I had to cancel.'

James's heart went out to her. This lunch had been so important to her and she'd been desperate to impress her new friends.

'Look, I'll be home soon. Shall I get a takeaway?'

'Yes, please,' Maria said, her voice was no more than a whisper.

'I'll be about half an hour. Have a lay down, eh?'

'OK. Bye, James.'

James had the number of their local Chinese in his phone.

'Make sure it's ready by half past. Me wife ain't well and I'm in a rush,' he told Mr Chong.

As he drove towards home, he was worried. Maria had rarely been ill in all the years he'd known her and she certainly wasn't a cry-baby.

Hearing the door open and close, Maria took deep breaths. Please God, don't let him know I'm lying, she prayed.

'You all right, babe?' James asked, crouching down beside her.

Maria smiled. 'I think I'm on the mend. I was so ill, James, the pains in my stomach were awful,' she lied.

Lily giggled. 'Mummy's had the poo-poos.'

Seeing Tara burst out laughing, James couldn't stop himself joining in with their banter.

'Did you tell your posh friends that you had the shits, dear?'

Maria shook her head. 'Of course not, I came out with some cock and bull about an imaginary cousin in a crisis.'

James laughed. 'Have you rearranged the lunch?'

'No, I felt that ill, rearranging was the last thing on my mind.'

James stood up. 'I thought you put the phone down on me sharpish earlier. Was you on your way to the khazi then?'

Maria forced a laugh. 'Yeah, I was, now stop taking the piss and dish the dinner up, will you? Don't bring me any in, I couldn't face a thing.'

As the girls followed James into the kitchen, Maria breathed a sigh of relief. He believed her; she'd got away with it. Thank God, her family had been spared the awful truth. What had happened was entirely her own fault and her penance was to live with that knowledge for ever.

FORTY-ONE

James chucked his tools on the floor and opened the back door to let in some air. 'I dunno about you, Fred, but I've had it for today, mate. Me mouth's like a camel's arse, and I could kill for a cold beer.'

Freddie didn't need much persuasion to stop work. Both he and James had spent the last few months literally working their bollocks off.

'Let's go to that little boozer down the road, eh? I'm starving and they do a nice bit of grub in there.'

On entering the pub, James flopped on the nearest bench seat and sent Freddie up to the bar. Renovating the house was good fun, but bloody hard work. Three months on, it had begun to take shape and both lads were overjoyed with their efforts. With little experience, they'd been a bit dubious in the beginning, so much so that on their first day they'd stood looking at one another like a pair of lemons.

Freddie had been the first to break the ice, 'Come on, clever clogs. Seeing as all this was your idea, where the fuck do we start?'

Laughing, they'd got stuck in and had hardly come up for air since.

They'd been shitting themselves on their trip to the

Costa del Sol. The thought of telling Bobby Adams that they were giving up the drug run filled them both with dread. They'd fully expected him to go apeshit but, surprisingly, he'd been fine and had taken their decision on the chin.

'Obviously I'm disappointed, but I fully understand your reasons. You've both been fantastic to work with and I wish you all the luck in the world with the property venture.'

James and Freddie felt a mixture of relief and joy by Bobby's reaction and, on his insistence, had stayed with him for a couple of days and had a whale of a time.

'Now, remember, don't be strangers. You're always welcome to stay at mine any time you like,' he said, as he dropped them at the airport.

James smiled as Freddie sat down opposite him.

'You took your bleedin' time.'

Freddie nodded. 'They're so slow in these country boozers. The Foster's ran out and they had to change the barrel.'

As the two ploughman's lunches were brought up to the table, both lads attacked them hungrily.

'So, how's Maria?' Freddie asked, between mouthfuls.

James shook his head. 'She's still tearful and biting me head off.'

Maria's behaviour over the last few months had been odd, to say the least. At first, James had thought she had a cob on because he was working seven days a week, but now he wasn't so sure. She seemed to have gone off him, so much so that she didn't even want him to make love to her any more.

'You don't reckon she's bored with me, or met someone else, do yer?' James asked Freddie.

380

Spitting his pickled onion back onto the plate, Freddie shook his head. 'Never in a million years – she's not the type. Think back over all the years you've known her. Has she ever gone off the boil with yer before?'

James racked his brains. 'Only when she was pregnant. She was tearful then and didn't want me anywhere near her, with both the girls.'

Freddie smiled. 'Well maybe that's your answer then. You've been trying for another one, ain't yer? Maybe she's up the spout.'

James shook his head. 'We ain't had sex for fuckin' months and if she'd missed a period, she would have told me.'

Freddie shrugged. 'If I was you, I'd get a test and make her do it. Sarah didn't know she was pregnant with Daisy until I made her do the test.'

James ran his fingers through his hair. Maria was certainly acting all hormonal, so maybe she was up the duff.

He smiled at his pal, 'Right, I'll get us another beer and then we'll go and find a chemist.'

Back in the East End, Maureen was all of a fluster. First, Kenny had rung up and invited himself round for dinner, then Johnny had phoned up from football informing her that his dad would be joining them for Sunday roast as well.

'I'm gonna have to pop to the supermarket, Mum. The leg of lamb's big enough, but I ain't got enough fresh veg. I'd better get some wine and some beers as well. All we've got is Guinness, and we can't offer 'em that.'

Much to Maureen's annoyance, Ethel insisted on going with her.

'Can't yer stay here? I'll be quicker on me own. It'll take

us a good hour or so if I have to push yer around in the chair.'

Ethel was having none of it. 'Don't be so fuckin' wicked. I ain't had no fresh air for days – anyone would think you were trying to kill me off.'

Maureen tutted. Ethel drove her mad at times. 'Don't be so bloody stupid. I was just thinking of the time. Kenny said he'd be here at one and it's half eleven now.'

Ethel sneered. 'Bollocks to Kenny! He only wants to come and see us 'cause he's probably had a row with Lady fucking Penelope. Now pass me me blanket. Like it or not, I'm comin' with yer.'

Over on Hackney Marshes, Johnny coolly placed the ball onto the penalty spot. If he scored this, it would secure his hat trick and, hopefully, win his team the game.

'Go on, Johnny, you can do it!' he heard his dad shout.

Staring into the keeper's eyes, Johnny sent him the wrong way and blasted the ball into the roof of the net.

'Well done, son.'

Running to the touchline where his dad was standing, the hat-trick hero threw himself onto the grass. As his team-mates joined in the celebrations, Johnny's smile lit up the overcast skies of Hackney.

A few miles way, Maureen pushed Ethel around the supermarket as fast as she could. Satisfied that she'd gotten all that she needed, she made her way to the checkout.

'What's a nipper like you doin' stuck 'ere on a Sunday? You should be out enjoying yourself,' Ethel told the pretty young cashier.

'I need the money to help out with my education. I'm still at college,' the girl said, smiling.

Ethel shook her head and laughed. 'Education, what a

load of old bollocks! I could teach you more in a day than you'd learn at any bleedin' college in a year.'

Maureen put her change in her purse. 'Sorry, love, take no notice,' she whispered to the shocked girl.

On reaching the exit, Maureen stopped to hang the bags on the handles of the wheelchair.

'Excuse me.'

As a huge arm grabbed her shoulder, Maureen swung around and came face to face with a rather tall security guard.

'What's the matter?' she asked impatiently.

The security guard spoke in a strong Nigerian accent. 'I need you to come back inside the store. I believe you have shopping that you haven't paid for.'

Maureen pulled her receipt from her purse. Surely Ethel hadn't been on the rob? She'd fucking kill her if she had.

Inside the manager's office, her worst fears were confirmed, as a fresh chicken, a packet of strawberries and a tub of double cream were pulled out from under her mother-in-law's blanket.

'I forgot they were there – it's me Alzheimer's,' Ethel said indignantly.

As luck would have it, the manager was a pleasant chap.

'I'm so sorry. She's eighty-six and not all the ticket,' Maureen kept repeating.

'Just pay for the items and we'll forget all about it,' the manager said kindly.

Embarrassed, Maureen shoved a tenner at him. 'Is that enough?'

The manager led them back to the checkout. 'You'll have to pay here, the items need to be scanned.'

The young girl who had served them before smiled. 'Back again?'

'Mum forgot to pay for her shopping,' Maureen said, wishing the ground would open up and swallow her.

Outside the shop, she gave Ethel what for. 'Next time you wanna go to the supermarket, don't ask me to take yer. Why did you nick a chicken when we've got lamb for dinner?'

'I thought we could have it in sandwiches for supper.'

'We've got ham for sandwiches,' Maureen said, fuming.

Ethel couldn't stop laughing, 'Cheer up, Maur, we got away with it, didn't we?'

Maureen was really pissed off. 'I swear on my life, Mum, I'm not bringing you out no more – that's your lot. Never again will yer show me up, and I mean it this time.'

Over in Ingatestone, Maria was also cooking a Sunday roast.

'I'm starving, Mummy. Is it ready yet?' Lily asked impatiently.

Maria put the chicken back into the oven. 'Don't drive me mad, Lily. Go and sit in the other room with your sister, and as soon as Daddy gets home, I'll dish up.'

Lily scowled at her mum, pouted her lips and walked away.

'Mummy is so horrible lately,' she complained to Tara.

Tara said nothing, but nodded in agreement. Their mum used to be happy and laugh a lot; now she was sad and shouted all the time.

Maria poured a glass of wine and sat at the kitchen table. She hadn't felt well lately; she was always tired and had no energy whatsoever. Wondering if her fatigue was caused by her newly found friendship with alcohol, she pushed the thought to the back of her mind. A couple of glasses of wine never hurt anyone and at the moment it was the only thing that got her through the day.

She'd tried her best to forget about Tommy's visit, but it was hard – bloody impossible, in fact. Many a night she woke up in a sweat as images of his evil face interrupted her dreams. She knew that James was worried about her and she hated herself for that. He was working so hard to secure a better future for them; the poor sod deserved better than to put up with her moods.

Determined to try and be more cheerful from now on, Maria poured herself another drink. For the sake of her family, she had to try and snap out of it.

Back in Stepney, the house was full of high spirits. Ethel nudged Maureen as Johnny's hand shot out for yet another helping of roast potatoes.

'Bless him, I do like to see a growin' lad eat well. Ain't he got his appetite back?' Ethel said.

Still smarting from earlier, Maureen ignored her and began to clear the dinner plates. There was no doubt that Johnny had come on in leaps and bounds since his dad had appeared in his life. In all honesty, Royston wasn't a bad lad. Polite and well mannered, he was a good influence on Johnny and someone for him to look up to.

Once a week Royston drove up from Kent to spend the day with his son. His wife had hated the arrangement at first, but once he'd begun to alternate the Saturdays and Sundays, she'd kind of accepted the situation.

'Who wants dessert? I've got apple pie and custard or strawberries and cream,' Maureen said, shooting a look at Ethel. She wanted to remind her that she still had the hump with her.

Ethel chuckled. 'They're my treat, the strawberries and cream.'

Guessing what the joke was, Kenny looked at Maureen. 'Please tell me she didn't thieve 'em?'

Maureen shook her head. 'Don't ask – sore subject.'

Kenny turned to Ethel. 'Ain't you ever gonna learn to behave yourself, Mother? I know you used to chore when we were kids but, fuck me, you're eighty-six years old. You must be the oldest kleptomaniac in living history.'

Ethel pursed her lips. 'If it wasn't for me givin' birth to yer, yer wouldn't even be 'ere, so mind your own business. Anyway, how comes you've invited yourself round for dinner? Had a row with Lady Penelope, have yer?'

Kenny shook his head. 'Her sister and husband are over for the weekend; they were doin' my head in and I had to get out of the house.'

Maureen laughed. 'I bet Wendy weren't too pleased when you said you were going out. Did you tell her you were comin' here?'

Kenny took a mouthful of apple pie. 'I didn't say where I was going. Cor, this is handsome, Maur,' he said, cleverly changing the subject. 'Did you make it yourself, girl?'

Maureen blushed with pleasure. 'Of course I did, it's a recipe me mum taught me when I was knee high.'

Ethel watched her daughter-in-law with interest. Maureen glowed whenever her Kenny was about. The way she felt about him stood out like a sore thumb.

Over in Essex, Maria was trying her hardest to be jolly.

'Can I have some chocolate ice cream, Mummy?' Lily asked her.

'I want banana split,' Tara demanded.

'Neither of you are having any dessert until you've eaten all of your vegetables,' Maria said, smiling at James.

Seeing his wife pour herself yet another glass of wine, James nudged her.

'Follow me out to the kitchen. I need to talk to you alone for a sec.'

Feeling awkward, Maria followed him. She hoped he wasn't going to tell her off about her drinking again.

'What's the matter?' she asked uneasily.

James handed her the paper bag and waited for her reaction.

Maria laughed as she took out the pregnancy test. 'What's this for? I'm not pregnant, James.'

James leaned against the worktop. 'Well, I think you are.'

Maria shook her head. 'I'm sure I haven't missed me period and I've had no morning sickness. I know all the signs, James, and I'm tellin' you, I'm definitely not pregnant.'

'Just do the test. Please, Maria?'

Maria shrugged. 'OK, I'll do it in the morning.'

James smiled. 'The woman in the shop said that there were two tests in the box. Do one now and you can do the other one in the morning. Please, Maria, do it now for me?'

Maria read the instructions. 'All right, I'll do it in the toilet.'

James didn't want to miss out on the excitement. 'Let's give the girls their desserts and then we'll go and do it together. I didn't wanna say anything in front of them, in case it was a false alarm.'

Maria nodded and took the ice cream out of the freezer. When she'd been pregnant with the girls, she'd had sore breasts and been as sick as a pig for nine months. Frantically trying to remember when she had last seen her period, she felt herself go cold. She couldn't remember; her mind had gone blank. Surely not, she thought. Please God no, not after what had happened with Tommy.

Ten minutes later, James snatched the white stick from her and hid it back in the box. 'The instructions say that it takes five minutes. Let's time it and then we'll look at it together.'

Maria said nothing as he hugged her tightly. Her insides were in knots and all of a sudden she felt sick to the stomach. Say she was pregnant? What could she do about it?

James looked at his watch. 'That's it, the five minutes are up. Are you ready?'

As he picked up the box, Maria prayed silently. Please God no, please God no, please God no.

James's ecstatic scream confirmed that God hadn't listened.

'There's a blue line. Look, Maria, look. I knew it, I fucking knew it – you're pregnant, we're having another baby.'

Over the moon, James picked her up off the floor and swung her around. 'Let's go and tell the girls and then I'll ring me mum and Freddie. You better ring your mum, Maria, she'll be so excited.'

Unable to stop herself, Maria let out a wail of pure sorrow.

FORTY-TWO

Staring at the screen, the sonographer averted her eyes and smiled at the happy couple. 'Your baby looks just fine, everything is as it should be.'

'Thank God for that,' James said, squeezing Maria's hand. He'd been ever so worried because of Maria's alcohol intake. It wasn't her fault: she wouldn't have been drinking if she had known she was pregnant.

'Most women have cravings for ice cream or doughnuts. Not my old woman – she was necking the wine,' James joked.

The sonographer laughed, but Maria didn't. She knew what the next question would be and she was absolutely dreading the answer.

'How far gone is she?' James asked, squeezing his wife's hand.

Maria had been insistent that they didn't tell a soul until they knew how far gone she was.

The sonographer looked intently into the screen. 'Approximately thirteen weeks.'

Maria's heart lurched: the timing couldn't have been any worse. Thirteen weeks ago, she'd been having regular sex with her husband, but it was also the same time that she'd been raped by his brother.

James kissed her on the forehead. 'Good job for your sake it was thirteen weeks.'

'What do you mean?' Maria asked nervously.

'Well, if it was any less, I'd have had to beat up the milkman.'

Maria tried to smile, but couldn't. The way she felt at this particular moment, she could never imagine smiling again. As the scan came to an end, James helped Maria stand up.

'Thanks ever so much,' he said, shaking the sonographer's hand.

'Good luck and don't worry, everything's fine.'

James was annoyed as they left the hospital. The woman that scanned Maria had been lovely, but Maria hadn't even thanked her or said goodbye. Even when they learned that the baby was fine, she hadn't cracked a smile.

'I'm getting sick of your moods, Maria. You were really rude to that woman in there, you didn't say fuck all to her. We know that the baby's OK, so what's your fuckin' problem? Is it me? Don't you love me any more?'

Maria started to cry. 'It's not you James, I love you more than life itself.'

'Well, what is it, then? You've got me doting on you, two beautiful daughters, a nipper on the way. We've no money worries, so what the fuck is your problem?'

Maria couldn't stop apologising. 'I'm so sorry, James, I think I'm just hormonal. Once the baby's born, I'll be fine, you'll see.'

James shook his head. 'I'll tell you something, Maria, best you try and lighten up, because I ain't putting up with another six months of this.'

Sobbing, Maria ran after him as he stormed out of the building.

*   *   *

Over in Stepney, Ethel was hungry and restless. Maureen was no company these days – she was always asleep. 'Maur, Maur, wake up for fuck's sake. You still ain't done me any lunch yet, and I'm sitting 'ere wasting away.'

Maureen rubbed her tired eyes. Ethel had the appetite of a carthorse and there was more chance of Elvis turning up alive and well than her wasting away.

She stood up. 'Whaddya fancy?'

Ethel took her false teeth out of the cup and popped them back into her mouth. 'Do us that other pair of kippers. Bleedin' handsome they were, them ones I had yesterday.'

Maureen looked at her in horror. 'What have I told you about putting your teeth in the cups? It's disgusting, Mum, people have to drink out of them.'

Ethel shrugged her shoulders. 'I can't help it if these new gnashers hurt me. What am I meant to do? Sit here in fuckin' pain?'

Maureen ignored her and went out to the kitchen. Looking after Ethel was getting her down lately and she was struggling to wait on her hand and foot. The tiredness had started a couple of months back. She couldn't put her finger on it: she didn't exactly feel ill, just listless all the time.

'Probably old age catching up with me,' she convinced herself, as she slung the kippers in the frying pan.

Thinking of Kenny's visit the previous week, she smiled to herself. She'd certainly perked up while he was here. Maybe that's what she needed, a few more visits from Kenny.

'Hurry up! What you doin'? Catching the bloody things?' Ethel shouted.

Maureen shook her head. As much as she loved the

old girl, sometimes she could quite happily ring her bloody neck.

Tommy opened his front door and bent down to pick up the post. Glancing at it, he lobbed it on the stairs – all he ever got sent to him was fucking bills. Checking his answerphone, he was relieved that there were no messages from James. The slag had obviously kept her mouth shut, then. He went to the fridge and cracked open a beer. A long break in Clacton had done him the world of good. He'd had a good drink while away, but had left the gear alone. He felt much better for it, his head was a lot clearer.

Going over his messages again, he felt a pang of guilt. Alfie had left loads. 'Dad, where are you? Please pick the phone up if you're there. I really miss you and I wanna come home. I'm worried about you, Dad. Please ring me back so I know that you're all right.'

Tommy had taken his mobile away with him, but hadn't spoken to a soul. Alfie had left tons of messages on that as well.

He pressed speed dial and smiled as his son answered his phone. 'All right, Alfie? I'm sorry I didn't call you, son. I went away to sort me head out, but I'm back now and feel much better, so you can come home if you want.'

Alfie was overjoyed. 'That's blinding, Dad. I've been so worried and I've really missed you. I'll be round within the hour.'

Tommy cracked open another can. Some people in life had no one; he was lucky, he had a son who loved him. Thinking of Maria, he smiled to himself. Retribution was the greatest feeling in the world and now he'd gained his, he could finally move on.

* * *

With James barely speaking to her, Maria left her dinner untouched and walked out of the room.

'Where are you going, Mummy?' Tara asked, concerned.

'You haven't eaten your vegetables,' Lily said sarcastically.

'Just shut up and eat your dinner,' James told his daughters. His temper was getting shorter by the second.

Sitting on her bed, Maria felt more alone than ever before. She needed to spill her guts to someone and get some much-needed advice. Debating whether to speak to her mum, she quickly decided against it. Her mum would get too involved and would probably take her anger out on Maureen, with Tommy being her son. Desperately racking her brains for an answer, she struggled to find one. The problem was, whoever she told, she would have to come clean about her fling with Tommy. Who could she trust? Suddenly the answer came to her.

'Maureen,' she whispered.

Her mother-in-law was as honest as the day was long. She was great at giving advice and she'd know exactly what to do for the best.

She picked up her mobile and rang her number.

'Hello, darling. To what do I owe this pleasure?' Maureen said chirpily.

Maria took a deep breath. 'I need to talk to you, Maur. It's really important and I can't speak in front of Ethel. I don't want me mum to see me, so can you meet me outside The Bancroft in about an hour? I'll park up and wait in the motor.'

Maureen had known her daughter-in-law long enough to recognise how distressed she sounded. Instantly, she knew it had something to do with Tommy.

'Don't worry, darling, I'll be there.'

'Who was that?' Ethel asked nosily.

'Oh, just one of the girls from the bingo. I think she's

got some problems with her husband, wants to meet me for a quick drink,' Maureen lied.

Ethel hated having the wool pulled over her eyes. 'What girl? You don't even go to the bingo any more.'

Maureen came out with the first name she could think of. 'Maggie, Maggie Delaney. She lives in Canning Town, I don't think you know her.'

Ethel huffed and puffed. 'Of course I don't know her, she don't bleedin' exist, that's why. I know I'm old, but I'm not senile. Where you really going?'

Ignoring her, Maureen walked out of the room and rang Brenda.

'Can you do us a favour, Bren? I've gotta nip out for a bit and I was wondering if you could sit with Mum for me? I don't know how long I'll be, but I shouldn't be that long.'

Brenda agreed immediately. 'Don't worry about Ethel. Sarn's here with me, we'll both come over and get her on the Guinness. You take as long as you like.'

Maureen smiled as she ended the call. She didn't socialise as much with Brenda and Sandra these days, but they were true friends and she could always rely on them. They'd been fantastic when she'd had breast cancer. They'd insisted on accompanying her to her gruelling chemo sessions, they'd helped her with her housework and even cooked her meals for her. Diamonds they were, the pair of them, and she loved them both to bits.

Maria pulled up opposite the pub and turned off the engine. She opened her bag, took out her baseball cap and placed it on top of her head. She was well known in this area, having lived there for years, and she certainly didn't need or want to be recognised.

Waiting for Maureen to arrive felt like she was waiting

for a death sentence. She just hoped and prayed that she was doing the right thing by telling her. Disclosing your innermost secrets was never easy at the best of times and she prayed that her mother-in-law would understand.

With her eyes firmly fixed on the mirror, she saw Maureen walking towards her. She hadn't seen her for nearly a month and was shocked by how much weight she had lost. As she opened the door, Maria smiled nervously.

'Thanks for coming, Maur. Get in and we'll drive somewhere quiet.'

Maureen knew that something bad had happened. Maria's face was etched with worry and her voice sounded desperate.

As they drove along, Maria did her best to sound cheerful. 'You look ever so slim, Maur. Have you been dieting?'

Maureen shook her head. 'I've never dieted in me bleedin' life and I certainly ain't startin' at my age. Running around after Ethel twenty-four seven has probably made me lose this lot. I'm up and down like a whore's drawers trying to keep up with her needs.'

Maria drove for about ten minutes and then stopped outside a quiet-looking pub. 'I think we're both gonna need a drink, Maur. Shall we talk inside?'

Feeling apprehensive, Maureen agreed.

The pub was virtually empty, bar one or two workmen. 'Sit in that corner, Maur. What you drinking?'

'I'll have a Guinness, make it a pint,' Maureen said. She had a feeling that a crate would be more appropriate for what she was about to hear.

Maria sat down and swallowed half of her drink in one gulp. She wished now that they'd talked in the car. At least it would have been dark and Maureen wouldn't have been able to see the guilt in her face. Clearing her throat, she tore her eyes away from her mother-in-law and stared at the table.

'Years ago, before I ever got with James, I had a one-night stand with Tommy. Please don't think badly of me, Maureen. I swear it was a drunken mistake, a moment of madness.'

Maureen squeezed her hand. 'It's OK, Maria, I've always known, anyway. Did it happen the night of Susan's engagement?'

Maria looked at her in amazement. 'Yeah, but how did you know? Did Tommy tell you?'

Maureen shook her head. 'I noticed the change in atmosphere between you and him from that time onwards. Your awkwardness, his comments, it was obvious. No one else clocked it, only me. Call it mother's intuition.'

Maria carried on. 'Obviously, when I got with James, I never said anything. One night James came home and I swear he knew, so to stop him confronting me, I blurted out that I was pregnant. I wasn't lying – it was true, as I'd just found out that I was pregnant with Tara.'

Maureen smiled, 'Why are you tellin' me this now, Maria?'

Maria downed the rest of her drink and averted her eyes once more. 'Over the years Tommy has been a bastard to me, he could never let sleeping dogs lie and has many a time threatened to tell James. Anyway, a few months back, James was away on a business trip and I was in the house alone. There was a knock at the door and I was expecting some friends, so I thought they'd arrived early. To cut a long story short, it was Tommy, he was out of his nut on drink and drugs and he barged his way in. He kept rambling on about me insulting him at Susan's funeral and getting his own back. Then he, he –'

As Maria started to cry, Maureen moved seats and sat next to her. She put her arm around her shoulder. 'Ssh, now come on. None of this is your fault, Maria. What did he do to you?'

'He raped me,' Maria sobbed. 'And now I'm pregnant and I don't know who the father is.'

Maureen felt as sick as a dog as she tried to comfort her distressed daughter-in-law. What the hell had she done so wrong in raising her kids? How could anyone have raised such a fucking animal?

Maureen's first thought was for James. This would break his heart and he must never, ever find out. 'Does anyone else know, Maria? And I mean anyone? Have you told your mum?'

Maria shook her head, 'James knows there's something wrong, but I've been blaming my hormones. He's not stupid though, Maur, I'm sure he's got his suspicions. I wish I'd have come clean with him all those years ago, I should have told him about Tommy then. Keeping it a secret was a stupid idea, it's fucked my life up and now I can't say anything.'

Maureen stood up. 'You can never tell James, Maria, not now, not ever. Now, I'm gonna get us another drink and between us we'll sort this out. Everything will be all right, darling, I promise you.'

As Maureen walked back from the bar, Maria gratefully snatched the glass of wine.

'What am I gonna do about the baby? James is so excited and all I can do is pray for a miscarriage. Please don't think badly of me, but I've been secretly drinking every day while James is at work, hoping that I'll lose it.'

Maureen felt like crying herself, but what use was that? Drumming up some inner strength, she spoke firmly, but calmly.

'Maria, listen to me. Firstly you have to stop the drinking. If you don't, you might cause the baby to have disabilities and that's not the answer to anything. Now, had you and James been trying for a baby when you fell?'

Maria nodded. 'Up until Tommy attacked me, we'd been trying for months, but the hospital reckon I'm about thirteen weeks gone and that's around the same time he raped me.'

'Look, I know this is hard, but you have to think positive, Maria. These hospitals always get the dates wrong and chances are the baby belongs to James.'

'Do you really think so?' Maria asked. A glimmer of hope was vital for her.

'Definitely,' Maureen insisted.

Maria grabbed her hand. 'What am I gonna do about Tommy? When he finds out about the baby, he'll put two and two together and make mine and James's life a misery.'

Maureen slammed her fist onto the table. 'Over my dead body he will. You leave Tommy to me – I'll sort him out, I promise you. And may God be my judge, when I've done what I've got to do, he will never bother you or James, or interfere in your lives ever again.'

FORTY-THREE

After a sleepless night, Maureen made the decision to go and see Tommy first thing the following morning. Asking Johnny if he'd stay in to look after Ethel, she got washed and dressed, then ordered a cab.

'Where you off to? You never use cabs. What's goin' on?' Ethel quizzed her.

Usually, Maureen told her mother-in-law everything, but not this time. With James's happiness at stake, the fewer people who knew, the better.

'I've got an appointment at the hospital to have some tests done,' Maureen fibbed.

The fact that she actually had an appointment booked for a few weeks' time made her feel much better than usual about lying.

'Why don't you let me come with you? We can get a black cab for nothing if I come: they can swipe me card,' Ethel offered.

Maureen shook her head. 'Thanks, Mum, but I really need to do this alone.'

The journey to Tommy's seemed to take for ever and gave Maureen plenty of time to think about what she was going to say. She just hoped he was in; phoning him may have pre-warned him and she couldn't take that chance.

As the cab pulled into his turning, she asked if the driver would wait a minute. 'I'll pay you now, but will you just wait while I see if my son's at home. If not, you'll have to take me back.'

The driver grunted. Miserable bastard, Maureen thought, as she slammed the door.

Never an early riser, Tommy was still fast asleep in bed. 'Who the fuck's this?' he muttered, as the constant pressing of the bell woke him up.

Seeing it was only 9 a.m., he cautiously looked out of the window. Alfie was at his mate's and no one ever came to the house at this sorry hour.

Maureen looked up as she heard a noise. 'It's me, Tommy. Open the bloody door.'

One glance at her face told Tommy all he needed to know. She'd found out; she knew what he'd done. He chucked on a pair of shorts, ran down the stairs and let her in.

'All right, Mum? Wanna cup of tea?'

Maureen looked at him with hatred. With all her might, she pushed him towards the lounge.

'Fuck the tea. Me and you need to have a little chat, son.'

James opened his eyes to the sound of the drums being played. He picked up his mobile and rang Freddie.

'I'm sorry, mate, I never heard the alarm go off. Do you mind if we take a day off? I had a row with Maria yesterday and I got really pissed last night.'

Freddie didn't mind at all. 'That's fine by me. It'll be nice to spend a bit of time with Sarah; she barely sees me these days.'

James ended the call and put the quilt back over his head. He and Maria used to be happy – where had it all gone so wrong?

After dropping the girls off at school, Maria decided to skip the gym in favour of her husband. James hadn't gone to work and she had some serious grovelling to do. Talking to Maureen last night had made her feel much better already. It was a relief to share her burden with someone and be told that everything would be OK.

Stopping at Tesco Express, she bought a crusty loaf, bacon and eggs. Poor James, she loved him so much. Breakfast in bed was no apology for the way she'd been treating him, but it was a start. They could spend a nice day together, get things back on track. As Maureen said, the baby more than likely belonged to James and she had to think positive from now on.

Like a ferret stuck in a hole, Tommy twisted and turned, desperate to wriggle his way out of the accusation.

'Maria's an old slag, she was well up for it, Mum.'

That particular comment tipped Maureen over the edge, and she walloped him fiercely around his smarmy face. 'Don't you dare tell lies like that, you nasty no-good bastard. And so what if you slept with her years ago, it doesn't give you the right to rape her twenty years on, does it? How could you do it, Tommy, eh? How could you attack your brother's wife, of all people? What you did is the ultimate fucking betrayal.'

Tommy averted his eyes and stared at the carpet. He felt like a naughty schoolboy all over again.

'Look, Mum, I am sorry for what I've done, but you don't know the half of it. Ever since I first shagged her, she's been a right cunt to me. The gyp she's given me over the years, you wouldn't believe. She's –'

'Shut the fuck up, Tommy. I've listened to enough of your drivel to last me a lifetime and now I want you to listen to me. You have to move away from here, the sooner the better. In fact, I'll give you a deadline: next Monday. By then I expect you to be hundreds of miles away and if you're not, then I will personally make sure that the shit hits the fan.'

Tommy looked at her in amazement. She was having a giggle, right? Realising that she wasn't, he sort of fell onto the armchair, laughing.

'You're a comedian, Mum. What's got into you? Where the fuck am I meant to go?'

Maureen stared defiantly into his piss-taking eyes. 'I don't know and I don't fuckin' care. That's your problem, and you should of thought of that before you attacked that poor girl. You're a betrayer, Tommy, and I want you as far away from James and Maria as possible.'

Tommy suddenly felt angry; she always stuck up for James. Well, fuck Mummy's blue-eyed boy and fuck her. He, Tommy Hutton, being run out of town by his own mother. Who did she think she was? Violet fucking Kray?'

He stood up and flashed her his best sneer. 'Get out of my house, Mum, and don't you ever come back. As for your stupid idea, forget it. I'm goin' nowhere.'

As he none too gently pushed her towards the door, Maureen pleaded with him to change his mind.

'Tommy, I beg you to do this for me. You have to, else you're gonna get hurt.'

As Tommy gave her a final shove, she caught her foot and landed arse up on the pavement.

'Get hurt! Yeah, right, by you and who's army? Goodbye, Mum, I'll see you in another life.'

As the front door slammed, Maureen lay still on the ground. Why would he never listen to her? The stupid, stupid boy. Now she had to make a decision. Did she go ahead with plan B? Or forget the whole thing? As she pictured James's innocent face, her mind was instantly made up. She would do anything, absolutely anything, to protect her baby.

A few miles away, James was fast asleep. As the smell of good food wafted into the bedroom, he removed the quilt to see Maria smiling at him with a tray in her hand.

'What's all this?' he asked suspiciously.

Maria handed him the tray and sat down beside him. 'I just wanted to say that I'm sorry, James. I've been a right misery-guts lately and you really don't deserve it.'

James put the breakfast to one side and took her in his arms. Ever since they'd been kids, she'd had a way of making him melt.

'I love you, James, and I'm so sorry,' Maria said repeatedly.

James stroked her hair. 'Ssh, come on now. You ain't gotta keep apologising, it's not as though you're miserable all the time, is it? If anyone's to blame, it's me for getting' you up the duff in the first place,' he joked.

As Maria clung to him, she prayed that the baby was his. Please God, make James be the father.

Freddie was sitting in Pizza Express with Sarah and the kids when the call came through.

'Are you OK? What's the matter, Maureen?'

She was that upset, he could barely understand her. 'Look, we can't talk on the phone. Give us an hour and I'll come to you,' he told her.

'No,' she said immediately. 'The pub at the top of the road – you know the one I mean, don't yer? I'll meet you there. And Freddie, whatever yer do, yer mustn't tell James.'

Freddie was bemused as he ended the call. Whatever

she had to say was obviously too important to name The Bancroft or involve her son.

'We're gonna have to make a move, something's come up,' he told Sarah.

'Oh Fred, we never get the chance to spend the day together,' she whinged.

Freddie ignored her and grabbed his coat. Over the years Maureen had been like another mum to him and if anyone had upset her, he'd kill 'em.

Maria took her clothes off and climbed into bed.

'What you doing?' James joked.

It had been so long since they'd been intimate, he'd been thinking of becoming a monk. 'Are you sure you want to?' he asked her gently.

Feeling nervous, Maria nodded. Truth be known, she wasn't sure if she ever wanted to do it again, but she had to. It reminded her of falling off her bike as a kid; the quicker you got back on, the better.

She winced as he entered her. 'Are you OK?' James whispered.

Maria smiled. 'I'm absolutely fine.'

For the second time in a couple of days, Maureen felt like a secret service agent as she marched towards the pub. Spotting Freddie's car, she was relieved that he was already there. She hated hanging about on street corners; it made her feel like an old Tom. As she approached, Freddie got out of the car.

'Get back in,' she told him. 'Drive to a pub in an area where nobody knows us.'

Maureen was silent while Freddie headed towards Limehouse. Johnny was at home with Ethel, so there was no rush to get back.

'You look ill, Maur. Whatever's the matter?' Freddie asked. She looked terrible and he was extremely concerned about her.

Maureen shook her head. 'I need a couple of drinks before I can explain. We'll talk in the pub, eh?'

Freddie nodded. Not knowing what else to say, he rambled on about Sarah and the kids. Driving in silence always gave him the willies.

Pulling into a sidestreet, he stopped outside a smart-looking pub. 'This OK, Maur? It's full of City boys and far too upper class for us to know anyone,' he joked as he opened her door.

He ordered the drinks and found them a quiet table. As he sat opposite Maureen, his concern turned to shock. Not only did she look ill, but she'd also aged overnight. Gone was the plump, bubbly woman with the classic laugh; she'd now been replaced by a thin, serious lady, with pale skin and haunted eyes.

'What's goin' on, Maur?' he asked kindly.

Maureen left no stone unturned as she explained the story. She paused a couple of times, once to cough, once to wipe her eyes, but finally she got to the end.

Freddie sat in a stunned silence. Not once did he interrupt her, he couldn't have spoken if he tried. As she finished and the tears began to flow, he squeezed her hand.

'Do you want me to get Tommy sorted for you? Is that what you're trying to say?' he asked gently.

Maureen nodded. She couldn't actually say the words, because it made it all sound too real. She wondered if deep down, she was an evil woman. I mean, what type of mother asks for her son to be sorted?

'Are yer gonna do it yourself?' she whispered.

Freddie shook his head. 'He's such a cunt, I can't believe

what he's done. I've known for years about his fling with Maria – I was there the night it happened – but this is different gravy, he's gone way over the top this time. Having said that, I couldn't hurt him meself, we go back way too far.'

'Who else can you trust?' Maureen asked awkwardly.

'You leave that to me. I know exactly the right person for the job,' Freddie assured her.

His uncle Bobby had wanted to teach Tommy a lesson years ago and he was sure he'd jump at the chance of doing it now. As luck would have it, he was in England at the moment. 'He's scum: I don't trust him and he knows too much about my business,' he'd said only the other day.

Freddie smiled. 'I dunno about you, but I'm thirsty. Do yer want another pint of Guinness?'

Maureen nodded. The way she felt right now, she could easily polish off the barrel. She sat nervously while she waited for Freddie to return. There was one question that she hadn't yet asked and she didn't quite know how to.

Freddie handed her the drink and sat back down. 'As soon as I leave you, Maur, I'll set the ball rolling. You don't want these things dragging on, do yer?'

Maureen chewed on her already bitten nails. 'Will they – yer know? Will they just hurt him, or will they do him in?'

Freddie held her bony hand. 'That's entirely up to you, Maur. If you just want him roughed up and sent away, that's simple. But what you've gotta consider is, will he find out about the baby and come back? Me and Tommy were like brothers for years and I certainly don't wanna see him brown bread. But this is your call, it's entirely up to you.'

Maureen stared out of the window and looked at the clear blue sky. What a lovely day, she stupidly thought. She turned back to Freddie.

'Look, he's my son and I can't make that decision. I need you to be brave and decide what to do for me, Freddie. Please don't tell me what happens, because I don't wanna know, but whatever happens, I need to know that he will never come back to this area or interfere with the happiness of my sweet baby James. People like me and you, Fred, we call a spade a spade, so let's be honest: both Tommy and Susan turned out to be rotten to the core. James is different, he's always been my angel. Heart of gold the boy has, the complete opposite of the other two. His happiness means everything to me and I would kill for him if I had to.' She paused before carrying on. 'Between me and you, I don't think I'm long for this world. Don't say a word to James or anyone, but I think me cancer's back. I need to sort this now, 'cause if I don't, I will never rest in peace.'

Freddie felt a tear roll down his cheek as he looked into the eyes of such a wonderful woman. Genuine, kind, funny, strong – she'd been given such a rough deal in life and really didn't deserve it.

'You've always been like a second mum to me, Maureen. I want you to know that I think the world of you and I fully understand what you're doin' and why you're doin' it.'

Maureen wiped her tears away. 'You're a good boy, Freddie Adams, and I know I can trust you to make the most important decision of my life for me.'

Freddie gave her a sad smile. 'I'll sort it. I won't let you down, Maureen, I promise.'

FORTY-FOUR

Maureen's instincts about her health proved right and, after a couple of appointments, which included an MRI scan, she was told that her cancer had returned and was unfortunately at a very advanced stage.

'You have weeks, rather than months,' the doctor told her bluntly.

From the day she received the news, she decided to write down pages and pages of her life story. Why she did this she didn't know, as she certainly had no real intentions of showing anyone. As she flicked back through her memoirs, she was aware that it made extremely uncomfortable reading. Some of this was her own fault, but most of it wasn't. It was all down to the cards she'd been dealt. She knew it was time to show her hand to her family. If she didn't, the truth would die with her and she couldn't allow that to happen. She owed them honesty, if nothing else.

Something Maria had said to her had helped her to make her decision. 'I wish I'd have come clean years ago. Keeping secrets has fucked up my life and now I can't say anything,' she had said.

Maureen knew exactly how she felt, as her own secrets had inwardly ripped her apart for years. Spilling the beans was going to be the hardest thing she had ever had to do, and she prayed that her family would forgive her.

On his first visit to Kent, young Johnny Hutton was in his element. For months he had yearned to meet his dad's other family and finally his dreams had come true. His dad's wife, Candy, had been a bit cold towards him at first.

'She'll be fine once she gets to know you. It's because your mum was on drugs and that,' his dad explained to him. He could hardly tell his son the truth, that Candy didn't like him because his mum had been white.

'Mmm, that dinner was amazing. It's one of the nicest meals I've ever had,' Johnny said sincerely.

Candy smiled. She liked being praised for her cooking. Goat curry was her signature dish, an old recipe from her Jamaican grandma.

'What dinners do you eat at home?' she asked politely.

Johnny smiled. 'Some of Nan's cooking is a bit old fashioned. We have liver and bacon, rabbit stew, steak and kidney pudding, that type of stuff. Sometimes she cooks me spag bol, that's my favourite.'

Candy pulled a face. How anybody could eat offal in this day and age, she would never know.

Johnny winked at his two little half-sisters. Unlike Candy, they'd taken an instant shine to him. They couldn't take their eyes off him and all day had been following him around, like two little lap dogs.

'I'm glad you're my brother, Johnny,' said the older one, Whitney.

'I'm glad as well,' piped up Macey, the youngest.

Johnny's smile lit up the room. Whitney and Macey were adorable and he felt like the luckiest brother in the whole wide world.

*   *   *

409

Back in Stepney, Maureen was certainly not smiling. She'd just broken the news of her illness to Sandra and Brenda. All three of them were in floods of tears and no one knew what to say. Annoyed with herself for blubbering, Maureen quickly pulled herself together.

'Look, I need one of yous to do me a big favour. I have a lot of things I need to sort out and I need someone to take care of Ethel for me for a couple of days.'

'She can stay here,' Sandra said immediately. 'My Pete's goin' fishing at the weekend, so it'll be no problem. I've got a fold-down bed, she can sleep on that.'

Maureen thanked her. 'Whatever you do, don't say anything to her about the cancer. What I'm gonna do is tell the rest of the family first and I'll tell Mum last. She knows I'm ill, she's not stupid, but I don't think she knows that I'm dying.'

Brenda was distraught. She'd known Maureen for over fifty years and couldn't imagine life without her. 'I can't believe it, Maur, my life won't be the same without yer. And what's gonna happen to Ethel? You know, in the long run?'

Maureen shrugged her listless shoulders. 'I've no idea, this is what I'm trying to sort out. Apart from yous two, I've told no one yet, but this weekend, I'm gonna have all the family round, one by one. There's stuff we need to talk about, things I've never told them.'

Sandra began to sob again. 'You are so brave, Maur. I couldn't imagine telling my kids, and what about James? That poor little sod adores you, he'll be heart-broken.'

Maureen stood up and put on her jacket; she had to get away from all these tears. Strength must become her motto from now on.

'Is it OK if I bring Ethel over in a minute? I'm gonna

tell her that I've got to go into hospital for a few days to have some more tests done.'

Brenda stood up. 'Won't she think it strange? They don't normally take you in for tests on weekends.'

Maureen shook her head. 'She won't have a clue. Apart from when she had her fall, she's never had any other dealings with hospitals. I know she's had arthritis for years, but she goes to the doctor for that.'

As Maureen walked down the path, she paused and looked back. Sandra and Brenda were both standing at the front door, crying.

'Thanks for being such good friends to me,' she said sadly.

With a heavy heart, Maureen walked away.

Over in Ingatestone, James, Maria and the girls were celebrating the sale of the renovated house.

'Want another glass of champers, Nelly?'

Maria laughed. James was such a piss-taking bastard and his new pet name for her was Nelly, after the elephant. Pretending to be annoyed, Maria gently punched his arm. Giving up the gym hadn't exactly helped her weight gain. She'd intended to keep going throughout her pregnancy, but Lavinia and the girls had been such bitches to her that she'd had little option other than to cancel her membership.

'Go on, have another glass. You ain't had a drink for months and two ain't gonna hurt yer,' James said, as he waved the champagne bottle tantalisingly near her face.

'Oh, go on then, just a small one,' Maria agreed.

'Can Tara and I have some, please?' Lily asked indignantly. She hated being a child and was desperate to become an adult.

Both Maria and James burst out laughing. She was a handful, their youngest, with a capital H.

'Put a tiny splash in a glass and fill it up with lemonade,' Maria ordered her husband.

James stood up. At eight months gone, he was used to running around after Maria like a blue-arsed fly.

'Does anyone else want anything while the waiter's standing up?' he joked.

Maria giggled as he left the room. Ever since Tommy had disappeared, their relationship had improved no end. The arguments had been replaced by friendly banter and they were like loved-up teenagers once again.

Tommy's disappearance was a shock to both of them. It had happened about five months ago, Alfie had informed everybody and, by all accounts, Tommy had just vanished overnight. It was certainly one of life's mysteries and for Maria it was a godsend. Obviously, she still had worries about who the baby belonged to, but she'd sort of convinced herself that James was the father. With her tormentor finally out of her life, she could look forward to the future, rather than worry about the past.

Back in Stepney, Maureen poured herself a large brandy and crossed the first name off her list. Freddie was on his way over and should be here pretty soon. The last few months had been torture for Maureen since Tommy had disappeared. She didn't think she'd be that bothered, but she was absolutely beside herself. In the beginning, she'd been adamant that she didn't want to know the fate of her eldest, but as the months passed, the worry and disbelief over what she had done had set in. What type of an awful person was she? No decent woman would set up their own child, would they? The only excuse she had for her actions was that she knew exactly why she'd done it. Two boys she'd given birth to and it had been a straight choice between the pair of them.

Unfortunately for Tommy, James had won. Now she couldn't live with herself. Whatever the truth was, she had to know.

As the doorbell rang, she felt herself shake from head to foot.

Over the road, Ethel was chewing Sandra and Brenda's ears off. As she sipped her fourth Guinness, her voice was getting louder and louder by the second.

'I mean, I know she ain't been herself, but chucking me out of me own home, it's a fuckin' liberty. I'm nearly eighty-seven, I shouldn't have to be pushed from pillar to fuckin' post.'

Sandra sat down next to the bitter old lady. 'Don't say anything bad about Maureen; she's not well, Ethel, and I mean really not well.'

As the seriousness of their faces hit home, Ethel felt a tear roll down her cheek. Surely her cancer wasn't back – please God, no.

Freddie accepted the beer gratefully and sat down at the kitchen table. Maureen took a deep breath and poured herself another brandy.

She sat down opposite him. 'You remember me tellin' you that I thought I was ill, that me cancer might be back?'

Freddie nodded.

'Well, I was right. It's back with a vengeance and apparently I've only got weeks to live.'

Freddie couldn't look at her, he didn't want her to see him upset. 'I'm so sorry, Maur, does James know?'

Maureen shook her head. 'Not yet, I wanted to speak to you first. Look, I'm sorry to have to ask you this, Freddie, but I need to know what happened to Tommy.

Please don't lie to me. However bad it is, I have to know the truth.'

Freddie held her bony hand. 'It's OK, Maur, he is alive. After I organised things, I went to see him, told him to get out of town, fast. He knew what was coming to him, so he left that night.'

Maureen breathed a sigh of pure relief. 'Are you sure, Freddie? I desperately want the truth.'

'Honestly, Maur, he ain't been touched, I promise yer. I've got a feeling he's gone abroad, but I ain't sure. I'm just glad that I warned him as I don't think I could have lived with meself if I hadn't.'

As ill as she felt, Maureen threw herself against him like a rugby player. 'Thank you so much, Freddie, I knew I could rely on you. I haven't been able to think straight for worrying about him. Do you think he'll ever come back?'

Freddie shook his head. 'No, he knows what will happen if he does. He'll start a new life somewhere and, knowing Tommy, he'll be having a whale of a time as we speak.'

Rubbing his arm, Maureen thanked him again. 'You've always been like a son to me, Freddie, and I'm forever grateful to you. Can I ask yer for another favour?'

Choked up, Freddie tried his best to make a joke of things. 'As long as it ain't like the last one, Maur.'

Maureen smiled. She felt so much happier now; the relief was a tonic.

'I want you to take care of James for me. When I die, I need you to keep an eye on him. I've gotta tell him something that's probably gonna break his heart. I need yer to make sure he forgives me, Freddie.'

Freddie nodded. Whatever she had to tell James was obviously family business and he wasn't about to pry.

'Don't worry, Maureen, I'll take good care of him for yer, I promise.'

Miles away in Turkey, Tommy was thoroughly enjoying himself. After the initial shock of Freddie knocking on his door and telling him that uncle Bobby was about to turn him into mincemeat, life had taken a turn for the better. Mustapha had sorted him out with his new life.

'Get away fast. Go and stay with my cousin, Kazim, in Gumbet,' he insisted, giving him the address.

Gumbet was a lively little holiday resort, not too far from Bodrum. Kazim ran a bar and had given Tommy a job on the door. Sunbathing by day, then pissing it up and shagging birds by night wasn't such a bad life, after all.

Apart from Mustapha and Alfie, no one else knew where he was. His son had wanted to come with him, but Tommy had said no.

'If we both disappear, it'll look well dodgy. I need you to stay at home, act all upset. You're the only person who can cover for me.'

Alfie agreed. He loved his dad and would do anything for him.

Tommy took a sip of his beer and smiled. He'd had two bits of good news this week and he was well excited about both of them. Firstly, Mustapha should very soon walk free. The court case was next month and Emre, the guy he'd been caught with, had held his hands up to everything and insisted that Mustapha was innocent. The second bit of good news was that his son had booked a holiday to come and see him. According to everyone at home, Alfie was going away with his mates, but really he was coming to Turkey to see Tommy. He was flying to Greece first to cover his tracks, just to be on the safe side.

'All right mate? This is the life, ain't it?' said a silly, sunburnt English holidaymaker.

Tommy smiled. 'It sure is, me old china.'

In not so sunny Stepney, Maureen had had a sleepless night. For months, due to her illness, she'd slept like a baby, but last night was a no-go.

As she peered into her wardrobe, she chose her outfit with care. Just because she looked and felt ill didn't mean that she couldn't still make an effort. Today was the most important day of her life and she needed to look the part. She applied her make-up, then nervously looked at her watch. The phonecalls had been made last night and Kenny was due to arrive first.

Unable to fancy any breakfast, she made herself a cup of tea and added some brandy. Her nerves were shot to pieces. As she heard Kenny's car pull up, she felt a flutter in her stomach and scolded herself for being so stupid.

'How can you have teenager's butterflies at a time like this?' she mumbled.

Kenny was shocked as he walked into the house. He hadn't seen Maureen since he'd popped in for Sunday dinner, and to say she looked ill was an understatement. Ethel had told him on the phone that she'd been under the weather, but he hadn't expected her to look so bad.

He hugged her awkwardly. 'Are you OK, Maur? You've done some weight, girl, ain't yer?'

Maureen did not reply, but led him into the kitchen.

'Sit down, Kenny, and I'll pour us both a brandy.'

'It's too early for me, Maur,' Kenny said.

Maureen ignored him and poured the drinks anyway. Unbeknown to him, she was about to drop the biggest bombshell of his life.

She sat down and looked at the floor. She couldn't beat around the bush; she just had to spit it out.

'Kenny, I'm dying. The doctors say I've got a matter of weeks.'

Kenny gasped. 'Please, no.'

Maureen carried on. 'There's something I must tell you, Kenny, and I know you're never gonna forgive me for not telling you earlier.'

Kenny couldn't stop the tears. He hated men who cried – even took the piss out of them. 'What?' he asked, his voice shaking.

'Kenny, James is your son.'

Kenny looked at her in total disbelief. They'd only slept together once and, according to the quacks, he had a sperm count of zilch.

'He can't be, Maureen.'

She nodded. 'He is. I never slept with anyone else when he was conceived and that includes your brother.'

Kenny stood up and poured himself another drink. He couldn't look at her, there must be some mistake. He struggled to find his voice. 'If what you're saying is true, Tommy must have known that James wasn't his.'

Suddenly, he was annoyed. 'Well did he?' he shouted.

Maureen crumbled. Kenny had never yelled at her in her life. 'Oh Kenny, I'm so sorry. Tommy didn't have a clue; he was always so drunk, he didn't know what day it was. When I found out I was pregnant, I lied and told him we'd slept together. He didn't question it, he just believed me. Please don't hate me, Kenny, I've wanted to tell yer for years, but I really didn't know how to.'

Unable to stop his legs from giving way, Kenny flopped onto the chair. If he'd seen a ghost, he'd have been less shocked.

417

'Does James know?' he asked. Even his voice didn't sound like his own.

Maureen shook her head. 'I haven't told him yet. He's coming round later and I'll tell him then.'

Kenny sat in stunned silence. What else was there to say? One drunken fling all them years ago, when he'd fallen out with Wendy and Maureen had been rowing with Tommy, had led to him having a son that he'd never known about. And what a lad he was. A smart, funny, clever lad, a lad he'd always felt an inexplicable connection with. His son, his very own son.

He stood up. 'Maur, I'm glad you told me, but I need to get me head around this. Ring me later when you've spoken to James and I'll pop back then. In the meantime, I'll tell Wendy. It'll be the end of me and her. She'll never forgive me for this, I know she won't.'

As Maureen watched him walk away, she broke down. She hadn't expected him to leave so quickly. Worse still, she hadn't expected him to run straight home and tell Wendy. Now she felt like an old stray, a home-wrecker. Kenny hated her now, she sensed it, and it hurt like hell.

Obviously, she still loved him, always had and always would. He'd forever been the one spark of excitement in her otherwise dull and mundane life. She remembered their little fling as though it was yesterday; how could she forget it?

Kenny had turned up unexpectedly at a Saturday-night party at hers. He'd had a row with Wendy and everyone else had gone to bed. They'd had a real heart to heart, both their marriages were shit. Neither of them had meant for it to happen, it just had. In Maureen's eyes, it was wonderful and she'd relived that night for many years. Things had been awkward between them for ages afterwards, but they'd got through it. There was too much feeling between them for them not to.

Maureen stood up; she desperately needed another brandy. At this rate, she'd die of liver disease before the cancer came and took her. She picked up the phone. The quicker James got here and heard the truth, the better.

Across the road, Ethel was totally uncomfortable. She liked her own house, her own bed and, more than anything, her own toilet.

'I'm not stayin' 'ere one minute longer. I need a shit and I can't shit in somebody else's house. Take me home right now.'

'You've got to stay here, Maureen's gone into hospital,' Sandra lied.

Ethel got up and balanced on her frame. 'So fuckin' what? I've got me own key and I'm quite capable of looking after meself.'

There was nothing Sandra could do, bar warn Maureen that Ethel was on her way.

'She's comin' across the road now, Maur. I tried to stop her, but you know what she's like.'

Maureen was furious. James was due in an hour and she needed to speak to him alone.

As the door opened, she helped Ethel inside.

'What's goin' on, Maur? I'm not stupid, I know you're not well.'

Maureen sat her on the sofa. She'd wanted the rest of the family to be present when she told Ethel, because of her age. She couldn't tell her about Kenny being James's dad; the thought of that made her feel cheap and tarty.

She sat opposite Ethel. 'Mum, I'm dying. Me cancer's come back and there's nothin' more they can do.'

Ethel's lips began to quiver. Maureen had been the

419

daughter she'd never had, and life without her didn't bear thinking of. She started to cry.

'I don't wanna be here if you're not. What am I gonna do without you, Maur? I ain't goin' in one of them homes.'

Maureen held her frail hands; it was typical of Ethel to be more worried about herself. 'Now, don't cry, we'll sort something out. I'll make sure you don't go in a home if it's the last thing I do. I need you to do me a favour. James is coming around in a minute and I have to speak to him alone, so will yer stay at Sandra's just for today?'

'Please let me stay 'ere; I won't get in the way or butt in,' Ethel pleaded.

Maureen shook her head. 'No, Mum, I have something to tell him that's very important and I need to do it alone.'

Ethel looked deep into her eyes. 'If I ask you a question, Maur, will you promise to tell me the truth?'

'I promise,' Maureen said.

'Swear on James's and young Johnny's lives,' Ethel insisted.

Desperate to get her out of the house as quickly as possible, Maureen did as she asked. She wasn't in the mood for silly games, especially not today.

Ethel cleared her throat. 'Is Kenny James's dad?'

To say Maureen was shocked was putting it mildly. Unable to look Ethel in the eye, she fidgeted with her hands and stared at the floor.

'How did you know?'

Ethel shrugged. 'Intuition, I suppose, and the atmosphere between you and Kenny. James was always so different from Tommy and Susan, there had to be an explanation for it. I've always said, what's bred in the bone comes out in the flesh.'

Maureen began to plead her innocence, 'Please don't think I'm some hussy. It was one night, Mum, a silly

420

drunken fling, and it was the only time I was ever unfaithful to Tommy. I made a mistake, it's as simple as that.'

Ethel held her hand. 'I could never think badly of you, Maureen, and please don't call it a mistake. You have the most wonderful son and both you and Kenny should be very proud of that.'

Maureen smiled. 'I only told Kenny this morning. He was shocked, to say the least.'

Ethel hugged her. 'He'll be fine, you mark my words. I wonder if he tells Lady Penelope.'

Maureen nodded. 'He went straight home to tell her.'

Ethel had to laugh. 'Christ, that'll put the cat amongst the pigeons,' she chuckled. She stood up and balanced on her frame. 'I'll have a shit on me commode, and then I'll go back over to Sandra's. Good luck with James.'

Maureen smiled. She'd thought Ethel would throw a wobbly, but the clever old cow already knew.

'Bye, Mum,' she said. 'Kenny's coming back later. As soon as he's gone, I'll ring Sandra and you can come home.'

Ethel smiled as she walked away. Unbeknown to Maureen, she had caught her and Kenny at it that fateful night. Unable to sleep, she'd spotted that the light was still on opposite and had trotted across the road for a nightcap. But before she'd knocked, she'd seen movement through the curtains and had peeked in.

Kenny and Maureen writhing about on the floor was a sight that she'd never forgotten. At first she'd been annoyed, as they were both married, but over the years, she'd learned to see the funny side. Watching them together afterwards had been hilarious; beetroot red, they'd turn, the pair of 'em. Tommy and Wendy turned out to be the husband and wife from hell, and in Ethel's eyes deserved to be cheated on.

Just about to knock on Sandra's door, she saw a car pull up.

'Nan,' James shouted.

She waved.

'You comin' in to see me?' he asked.

'In a bit,' she shouted.

As Sandra opened the door, Ethel hobbled inside as fast as her old legs would take her. Poor James was in for a major shock and the further away she was, the better.

Back in Turkey, the weather was scorching. Drenched in sun oil, Tommy was lying flat on his back on the busy beach, reading a copy of the *Sun* newspaper. As his phone rang, he checked the number. Alfie – that was OK. He never answered numbers that he didn't recognise; in his situation, you could never be too careful.

'All right, son? What's occurring?'

As Tommy listened to what Alfie had to say, he sat bolt upright.

'Good lad, now I need you to do me a favour. Pay Nan a visit or ring her and find out exactly when it's due.'

Tommy's heart was beating at a rapid pace as he ended the call. Alfie was his eyes and ears back home, his little spy.

Maria preggers and ready to drop soon, what a twist of fate! Counting the months on his fingers, he tried to work out the dates.

He stood up and smiled. He was no mathematician, but chances were the kid was his. With a spring in his step, he headed up to the beach bar.

'You got a bottle of champagne, mate?'

The barman smiled. 'Yes I have. Very early though. What you celebrate?'

422

Tommy's grin lit up the beach. 'A baby. I've just found out that I'm gonna be a daddy again.'

The barman handed him the champagne. 'Congratulations.'

Tommy felt a million dollars as he sipped his drink. James was an ugly fucker, hence his two plain daughters. Not him though, he was the looker out of the two of them, and with Maria looking like Cheryl Cole, their kid was destined for greatness. Between them, they would create a special one.

Back in Stepney, Maureen poured two large brandies and handed one to her son.

'I really don't want one, Mum,' James said for the third time.

'Please just drink it, James. You're gonna need it, believe me.'

James sipped the foul-tasting drink and tapped his feet nervously. He knew his mum looked really ill and Maria had been banging on for months about visiting her more often.

'What's goin' on, Mum? Are you ill or something?' he asked her. It was a question he had to ask, but didn't really want the answer to.

Maureen held his hands. Telling him was harder than telling anyone else.

'My cancer's come back, James, and the doctor says that it's at an advanced stage.'

James was horrified. 'You're not gonna die, are yer?'

Maureen nodded. 'Probably, love. There's nothing more they can do for me.'

Tears streaming down his face, James took her in his arms. 'I love you so much, Mum. What am I gonna do without you, eh?'

423

Maureen held him as though he was a child again. 'Listen, James, there's something else that I have to tell you, something very important.'

He pulled away from her. 'Go on,' he whispered.

Unable to face him, Maureen turned her back and leaned against the worktop.

'My life was never easy, when yous kids were young. Your dad was never around and even when he was, you know what he was like.'

James was worried now. What was she trying to tell him? 'Go on, Mum,' he urged.

Maureen shook with nerves. 'I had an affair, James, a fling, and you were the result of that.'

Stunned, James stood up. 'What? Is this some joke? Who the fuck is my dad, then?'

Maureen turned back to face him. She was crying now, she couldn't help it; his poor confused face was enough to break her heart.

'Please don't be angry with me, but your real dad is your uncle Kenny.'

James suddenly felt claustrophobic. The walls seemed to be closing in on him and he couldn't breathe.

'James, please, come back!' Maureen yelled as he ran from the house.

Unable to think straight, James jumped in his car and sped away as though his life depended on it.

In Ingatestone, Maria was at home teaching the girls how to make a trifle, when she got the phonecall.

'Whatever's the matter, Maureen?'

Maureen was in a terrible state. 'Please come over, Maria. I need to see yer now, I have to talk to you.'

Knowing that James had gone to visit her, Maria immediately feared the worst.

'You haven't told him about you know what, have you?'

'Of course not,' Maureen sobbed. 'Just hurry, Maria, please.'

Leaving the unfinished trifle on the table, Maria ordered the girls to get their coats.

'Where are we going?' Tara asked.

'What's "you know what"?' Lily pried.

'Just shut up and get in the car!' Maria yelled. The quicker she got to Maureen, the better.

Back in Gumbet, Tommy was on his second bottle of champers when Alfie called back.

'Well?' he asked impatiently.

'Nanny didn't answer the phone, so I rang Mum. The baby's due in a few weeks' time,' Alfie said.

Tommy thanked him and ended the call. The baby's due date was perfect, a revenge gift from God. Fuck Bobby Adams: if that kid was his, he was going back home. Mustapha should be out soon, he'd know what to do, and with the Turks behind him, he'd at least have some serious back-up. If the baby was his, he wanted to be part of its life and no one, including Bobby fucking Adams, could stop him from being a father. He and Maria were about to be parents and he could scarcely believe his own luck.

Maria dropped the girls at her mum's and knocked next door. A distraught Maureen told her the full story in five minutes flat.

'What am I gonna do, Maria? Please talk to James for me. If he doesn't forgive me, I'll never be able to rest in peace.'

Maria was shocked by the whole thing. Maureen dying, Kenny being James's dad; it was like a bad dream.

'Don't worry,' she assured Maureen. 'I'll ring Freddie; he'll find him and talk to him for you. James is obviously just in shock, Maur. Once he gets his head together, he'll be fine, you'll see. If Freddie has no joy, I'll talk some sense into him meself.'

As her daughter-in-law was about to leave, Maureen called her back. 'Just to let you know, Tommy's gone away for good, as I promised. You'll never see or hear from him again, Maria.'

Maria hugged her. 'Thanks, Maur, thanks for everything.'

Freddie found James standing alone at the bar in the Horn of Plenty. 'Maria rang me; I know what's happened,' he said as he stood opposite him.

James shook his head. 'I can't believe it, it's as if my whole life has been one fucked-up lie. I don't even know who I am any more. How can me mum not have told me before, Fred?'

Freddie shrugged. 'It can't have been easy for her, James. She probably hated carrying around a secret like that. Maybe she was afraid of ripping the family apart or something.'

James took a gulp of his lager and slammed the bottle on the bar. 'Uncle Kenny, of all people. I mean, I like the geezer, but fuck me, what am I meant to do now? Go fishing with the cunt?'

Freddie smiled. Difficult situation or not, at least James had retained his sense of humour. 'I don't know how it's gonna pan out with Kenny, but one thing I do know is you have to forgive your mum. She's dying, James, and if you don't sort things out with her, you'll regret it for the rest of your life.'

Aware of the tears in his eyes, James looked away. 'Get

us another beer, Fred. Maybe I'll go and see her in the week, when I've calmed down a bit.'

Freddie got the beers in. 'Drink that and go and see her now. She's ill, you ain't got time to waste. Your mum's the bollocks, James. She's been more of an influence in my life than me own mum. Please sort things out with her today, she'll be worried sick about yer if yer don't.'

James nodded. 'All right, I'll drink this and go straight round there.'

Physically and emotionally drained, Maureen flopped onto the sofa. It was getting dark now and all of a sudden she felt very tired. She hadn't eaten properly for days and all the upset had finally taken its toll on her.

When the doorbell rang, hope helped her find the strength to leap up. Maybe James had come back to sort things out. As she opened the door, she was surprised to see Kenny. She hadn't rung him back like he'd told her to.

'All right, Maur. These are for you,' he said, handing her the biggest bouquet of flowers she'd ever seen.

She thanked him, poured them a drink and sat down opposite him.

Kenny smiled. 'I'm sorry about earlier. I didn't mean to get angry; I was in a state of shock, I think.'

Maureen shook her head. 'You've no need to be sorry, it's me that should be apologising. I should never have kept it a secret for all these years.'

He forced a smile. 'I told Wendy – she went ballistic. She's leaving me, in fact, she's packing her bags as we speak.'

Maureen felt terrible. 'I'm so sorry, Ken.'

Kenny sipped his drink. 'Don't be, we haven't got along for years and I'm sure I'll be much happier without her.'

Maureen smiled. 'You were always chalk and cheese, yous two.'

Kenny stood up; he needed a refill. 'Did you speak to James?'

Maureen nodded. 'He took it about as well as you – ran out the door, he did. Like father, like son, eh?'

Kenny sat back down opposite her. 'Things could have been so different if you'd have told me, Maur. I've always loved you, you know.'

As Maureen felt her cheeks redden, she was saved from answering by the bell. Feeling like a teenager in the first throes of love, she ran to answer the door, her earlier tiredness forgotten.

'James!' she exclaimed.

'I've had a chat with Freddie and I'm sorry for running off like that. Yer know I love yer and I wouldn't hurt yer for the world, Mum.'

Maureen hugged him. 'Kenny's in the kitchen. I'm gonna pop over the road to see your nan while yous two have a little chat.'

James looked at her in horror. 'Don't leave me. I dunno what to say to him,' he whispered.

She pushed him towards the kitchen. 'You'll be fine. I won't be long.'

Leaving them to it was the best way, the only way.

As James looked at Kenny he felt like a rabbit caught in the headlights. 'How yer doin'?' he asked awkwardly.

Kenny handed him a beer. 'I've had better days. How about you?'

James smiled at the joke, and decided to play it the same way himself. 'What happens now, then? Do you take me football, fishing or what?'

Kenny laughed. 'If you like. I'm just glad you're too old for me to have to wipe your arse.'

428

With the ice well and truly thawed, the conversation evolved.

'Are you gonna tell Wendy?' James asked.

Kenny raised his eyebrows. 'I've already had the pleasure of that. Flew at me like a tomcat, she did, and what she didn't call me. Still, I suppose she had every right. To be honest, James, we haven't been happy for years, and her leaving me is a godsend.'

'Can I ask yer something personal, Kenny?'

'Course you can.'

'Did yer love my mum?'

Kenny nodded. 'I've always loved her, James. She's such a beautiful, strong woman. If she hadn't have been with me brother, I'd have whisked her off her feet. When she met our Tommy, I was only a boy, so she wouldn't have looked at me twice.'

Relieved that he'd been created out of love, rather than some sordid fling, James was about to ask some more, but was stopped from doing so by his mum and nan returning.

'Let's go for a beer, eh? And we can have a proper chat,' he whispered to Kenny.

'Everything all right?' Maureen asked dubiously.

James hugged her. 'Everything's fine, Mum.'

Kenny smiled at her. 'If it's OK with you, I'm gonna take James out for a pint. We won't be long. We'll grab a takeaway while we're out, and we can all have a bite to eat and a chat together later.'

'Don't get any of that foreign shit, will yer?' Ethel shouted.

Maureen smiled as she ushered them towards the door. 'Get her fish or chicken and chips or something, and I'll just have a little bit of whatever you're having.'

As she watched them walk away, Maureen felt so

unbelievably proud. Her James and Kenny going out for their first ever pint as father and son. With the weight lifted off her shoulders, she did her best to tidy up the kitchen, and poured Ethel a Guinness. As she took it into the lounge, she had to smile. Ethel was fast asleep, and snoring like a miner.

Relieved to be able to sit in silence and mull over the day's events, Maureen crept back into the kitchen and made herself a brew. The day she'd dreaded so much had been sad, but yet so happy. Everyone knew that she was dying now, even Johnny, who had been told by his father. She'd prearranged that by insisting that Royston take him home and explain things gently.

'If I'm not gonna be around for him, he needs to be included and welcomed into your family,' she told him.

Johnny had rung her earlier, crying his eyes out. 'I love you so much, Nan. I wanted to drive straight home, but Dad said not to. He said you needed time on your own, as you had stuff to sort out. I'll come back now, shall I?'

Maureen had been firm with him; it was the only way that she could cope.

'Now listen to me, Johnny, I want yer to stop all them tears and look forward to your future. You've got James, Ethel, your dad, your sisters. You'll be fine: they'll look after yer and I will always be watching down on yer. Promise me that you'll be strong, 'cause if yer get all upset, then Nanny will too.'

She was glad that Royston had done the honours. Having brought Johnny up, she couldn't face telling him herself. He was still so young, bless him. Alfie, she wasn't so close to, but she still loved him. She'd rung Lucy earlier to explain the situation and Lucy had kindly offered to tell him for her.

'Have you heard from Tommy?' Lucy asked her.

'Not a word,' Maureen replied. She could tell how worried Lucy was, but she could hardly tell her the truth. Telling her son's former partner that she'd organised a heavy mob to forcefully remove him from the area wasn't the way she wanted to be remembered.

Thinking of Kenny, she felt her usual butterflies. He'd told her that he'd always loved her and that alone had made her so very happy. He'd make a wonderful dad for James and between them they'd take care of Ethel and Johnny, she was sure of that.

Dying didn't seem quite so awful now. Her body was tired, worn out and felt almost ready to go, but she needed to hang on to see James's new baby. One glance would tell her who the father was, and with that thought, she said her prayers.

'Please God, to rest in peace I need to live long enough to see my unborn grandchild. Please God, make him belong to James, and if by any chance he belongs to Tommy, please take care of my sweet baby James for me.'

Maureen went to the kitchen cupboard and took out her memoirs. She picked up a box of matches and went into the garden. She'd remembered all she had to remember, said everything that needed to be said.

As the flames took hold, Maureen smiled. Her whole life in writing, going up in smoke.

How very apt was that?

EPILOGUE

That dreaded time has come now, and I'm desperate to hang on just a little bit longer. One minute I'm conscious, the next minute I'm not, but I know where I am, I'm aware.

Everybody's here, the room is full. James, Kenny, Ethel, Johnny, Freddie, even Brenda and Sandra were here earlier.

There have been plenty of tears, but they try to hide them. I told them I didn't want tears on my deathbed and I bloody well meant it.

I wake up once more. Maria had her baby this morning, a little boy, and I'm desperate to see the child, I need to know.

'Go and find out where she is,' I urge James. My voice sounds awful. It has that rattle that sounds like a chest infection, but really means death.

As James leaves the room, I look at Kenny. He smiles at me with that beautiful smile of his.

Ethel squeezes my lifeless hand. 'I love you, Mum,' I whisper.

As she starts to cry, I shut my eyes. I need to hold on – I have to.

I wake up once more and look at Freddie. No words are needed, he knows what the look means and so do I.

Nobody else apart from Freddie knows about the phonecall, you see.

Tommy heard that I was dying and rang me up. 'I'm sorry, Mum, and I love you,' he said.

We had a little chat. 'Promise me you'll never come home,' I asked him.

He paused. 'I can't promise you that, Mum. It all depends if that baby belongs to me.'

Fearfully, I dropped the phone with shock. That was the last I heard from him; he never had the guts to call back.

As my breathing becomes more laboured, I start to worry. Please hurry, James, I say to myself.

Finally, I'm aware of the door bursting open. As James pushes Maria towards me in the wheelchair, I try to sit up. But I can't, I'm too ill, it's impossible.

James lifts the baby up so I can see him, maybe give him a little kiss.

'Mum. Meet Jack, your grandson.'

One look at the child tells me all I need to know. He has Tommy's eyes, his mouth, his nose. I gasp. How can I rest in peace now?

Tears in my eyes, I whisper my final words, 'God bless my sweet baby James.'

DISCOVER
MORE FROM
Kimberley
CHAMBERS

The Mitchells & O'Haras Trilogy

'The queen of grit . . . a thrill a minute'
Bella

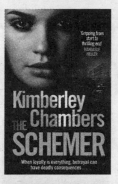

Meet the Butlers

Look out for the explosive new novel from

Kimberley CHAMBERS

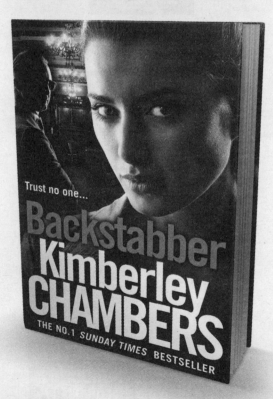

Available from 9th February 2017